BINDING ROSE

By

Ivy Fox

Binding Rose – Mafia Wars

Copyright © 2022 Ivy Fox

All rights reserved. No part of this publication may be reproduced, distributed, or transmitted in any form or by any means, including photocopying, recording, or other electronic or mechanical methods, without the prior written permission of the author, except in the case of brief quotations embodied in critical reviews and certain other noncommercial uses permitted by copyright law.

This is a work of fiction. The names, characters, places, and incidents are a product of the author's imagination or have been used fictitiously. Any resemblance to actual persons, living or dead, is entirely coincidental. The author acknowledges the copyrighted or trademarked status and trademark owners of all word marks, products, brands, TV shows, movies, music, bands, and celebrities mentioned in this work of fiction.

Cover design courtesy of Maria Spada
Editing courtesy of X-Factory Designs
Formatting courtesy of The Nutty Formatter

ISBN: 9798415475490

For more information, visit:

To Sean.
Tá mo chroí istigh ionat.

Never forget

"My Heart Is in You."

Author Note

First of all, thank you so much for purchasing Binding Rose.

This is a contemporary, dark reverse harem novel that falls within the shared world called Mafia Wars. Every book in this series is a stand-alone story written by a different author each time.

This little book baby is mine.

I would like to take this opportunity to thank the incredible writers that participated in this project with me. Rebecca Royce, CR Jane, Loxley Savage, Katie Knight, Susanne Valenti, and Caroline Peckham, words can never express how amazing it has been to work with all of you on this passion project. I'm in complete awe of your talent and professionalism. I am also blessed to have you as friends as well as colleagues. This has been an incredible ride and I look forward to working with you all in the future.

Now onto you, dear reader.

I would like to ask one small favor of you, if I may.

Reviews are life for an author. I treasure each one since they enable other readers to find my book babies. If you can spare a few minutes to write one after you've finished Binding Rose, I'd be forever grateful.

These reviews also help other readers decide if they should take the plunge in reading these types of books that have a trigger warning to them. And ladies, this book definitely does.

Since this is a dark romance, subject matters and scenes may be triggering for more sensitive readers.

If you are on the fence, please read reviews or join my readers group on Facebook – Ivy's Sassy Foxes and ask for feedback.

If you're okay with all that I've mentioned above, please proceed and get ready for the sexiest, filthiest book I've ever written.

Yep.

It's going to be that HOT!

Don't say I didn't warn you.

Much love,
Ivy

Binding Rose Playlist

Listen to full list on Spotify (search: Binding Rose)
"Jump Around" by House of Pain
"Linger" by The Cranberries
"No Sound but the Wind" by Editors
"Fine Line" by Harry Styles
"St. Patrick" by PVRIS
"No Me Ames" by Jennifer Lopez ft. Marc Anthony
"La Tortura" by Shakira ft. Alejandro Sanz
"Yonaguni" by Bad Bunny
"Fiel" by Los Legendarios
"KESI" by Camilo ft. Shawn Mendes

Binding Rose

I was sold to my enemies.

You would think that being forced into a loveless marriage to ensure an alliance would be unheard of in this day and age. And in most cases, you would be correct in that assumption.

But not for me.

A cartel princess has no vote on who she can or cannot marry —much less love.

Any decision in my life was forfeited just by being born into the most powerful Mexican cartel there is.

Still, it does sting that I'm to be hand-delivered to the Irish mob and marry into the Kelly family, who my own brother has coined to be nothing more than bloodthirsty savages.

They're animals, Rosa. Filthy, unscrupulous, vicious animals.

Those were his exact words, yet he still followed our father's orders to walk me down the aisle, making sure I didn't run from my obligation.

As if that was even an option.

All my choices were stolen away from me the minute I became another pawn to be used and abused at the hands of evil men.

Which leaves me to question…

Can a rose blossom in the dark?

Or will I have to rely on my thorns to protect me against the fate that's been bestowed upon me?

Only time will tell if I'll survive this cursed life or become another lost soul in these cruel and merciless **Mafia Wars.**

Mafia Wars Families & Territories

Boston – The Irish Mafia

The Kelly Family

Mexico City – *The Mexican Cartel*

The Hernandez Family

New York – *La Cosa Nostra* **– Italian Mafia**

The Rossi Family

Chicago – *The Outfit Syndicate* **– Italian Mafia**

The Moretti Family

London – *The Firm* **– English Mafia**

The Butcher Family

Vegas – The Bratva – Russian Mafia
The Volkov Family

Glossary

Irish/Gaelic

Máthair or Ma – mother/mom

Athair or Da – father/dad

Uncail – uncle

Mo dheartháir – my brother

Deartháir mór – Big Brother

Deirfiúr bheag – little sister

Col ceathar or ceathrair – Cousin

Seanmháthair – grandmother

Conas atá tú? – How are you?

Leanbh – child/baby

Babaí – baby

Tá mo chroí istigh ionat – "My Heart Is In You" – Irish endearment of saying I love you

Is tú mo stóirín – "You are my (little) sweetheart"
A stór – my treasure
Acting the maggot – making a fool of themselves
Dinger – a term of endearment reserved for the attractive
Acushla – darling
Damnú – fuck
Tuig – understand

Spanish

Pinche puta – fucking whore, or fucking damned or fucking fool
   Está claro – is that clear
   Sí – yes
   Por favor – please
   Mis disculpas – my apologies
   Virgen de Guadalupe – Virgin of Guadalupe/Virgin Mary
   Lo siento – I'm sorry
   Perdóname – Forgive me
   Hermano – brother
   Hermana – sister
   Novio/el prometido – fiancé
   Te lo ruego – I beg you
   Ayúdame – help me
   Cálmate – calm down
   Esposo – husband
   Jódete – screw you/fuck you

¡Vete al diablo! – go to hell

Mierda – shit

Joder. Tal vez incluso antes de eso – Fuck. Maybe even before that.

Cristo – Christ

Niño – baby

El hijo – son/baby

Pequeño – little one

Mafia Wars

Since the dawn of time, waging war on those who have wronged us has been embedded in the very fiber of mankind's true nature. The thirst for vengeance and retribution has always prevailed over turning the other cheek to one's enemies. Creating chaos and bloodshed is preferable to being subjected to vapid dialogues of peaceful negotiation.

None hold this way of life more sacred than *made men*.

Honor.
Loyalty.
Courage.
These are the codes of conduct of every mafia family.

However, the same cannot be said when dealing with their enemies.

Throughout recent decades, in the midst of civil evolution, an ancient war was being fought. From both sides of the globe, blood was spilled in the name of honor, while the brutal carnage each family bestowed upon the other was anything but noble. Soldiers, kin, and innocent lives were lost on all sides, and the inevitable extinction of the *mafioso* way of life was fast approaching.

In the most unlikely scenarios, six families came together in an undisclosed location to negotiate a peace treaty. As the leaders of the most influential crime families in the world, they recognized that a ceasefire was the only way to guarantee their endurance. Should this attempt fail, then their annihilation was all but imminent.

The treaty was effectively simple.

Each family would offer up one of their daughters as a sacrifice to their enemies. Marriage was the only way to ensure that the families wouldn't retaliate against one another. It would also guarantee that the following successor's bloodline would be forever changed, creating an alliance that would continue throughout generations to come.

Not all in attendance were happy with the arrangement.

The deep scars gained from years of plight and hatred can't be so easily healed or erased. However, even the cynical and leery knew that this pact was their best chance of survival. Although the uncertainty of the treaty's success was felt by every mob boss there, one by one, the families swore an oath that would bind them to it forever.

And as the words spilled from their lips and the scent of blood hung in the air, they made sure innocent lives would yet again be deemed collateral damage to their mafia wars—*one last time.*

Their daughters would have to pay the price of peace.

Whether they wanted to or not.

Prologue

TIERNAN

TEN YEARS ago

Fucking hurricane.

It's a bad omen that the first time the most influential mafia families in the world come face to face with each other, it's under such dire weather conditions. Who the fuck had the brilliant idea of meeting up in Bermuda during hurricane season anyway? I don't care if this island is considered to be neutral ground. Saint Brendan himself wouldn't have wanted to face such a storm.

The howling wind continues to bang furiously against the green shutters, threatening to bring the whole luxury hotel down with every ferocious pound to its walls, while the trembling windowpanes do their very best to keep from shattering completely and exposing us to the violent storm outside. How ironic that for all Mother Nature's fury, it still can't compare to the destruction made by every man sitting in this very room.

What is God's wrath compared to the devastation we can conjure up when we put our minds to it, aye?

We've been killing each other for so long, I can't recall a time when we weren't at war with one family or another. Such a thing has never happened in my lifetime, at least, that's for goddamn sure. Just because I can't remember when our feuds began doesn't mean that the memories of burnt flesh, dismembered bodies, and coffins being lowered into the ground with my friends inside them haunt me any less. Everyone here has lost more than just mere foot soldiers. We've lost friends, family, and loved ones all in the name of pride and honor.

Every boss sitting around this table knows he's responsible for all the death this blood war has provoked. The weight of that certainty, and the knowledge that if we continue on this route our way of life will undoubtedly become obsolete, forced this meeting to be unavoidable. Peace amongst the families is the only way we will be able to survive. If we insist on killing each other one by one, then soon there will be nothing worth fighting over.

My features remain carved in stone as I take in the sight in front of me. In a twisted Arthurian version of the round table, each family's boss takes his seat, ready to craft an arrangement that will ensure no more innocent blood is spilled.

Compared to the expensive suit-wearing assholes in this place, my father looks like just another tourist. In a colorful, flowery-patterned shirt that strains over his Guinness belly, *Athair* looks like your run-of-the-mill blue-collar worker on his first retirement trip to the tropics. No one would ever peg him as the boss of the Irish mafia.

Never let them see ye coming, lad.

In all the years I've been a *made man, Athair's* mantra has never led me astray. Besides, it's easier to throw out a bloody t-shirt than it is to replace a five-thousand-dollar Tom Ford suit. Even those Bratva pigs look like they spent a pretty penny on their designer clothes to be here today. I'd expect such pompous attire from the Italians, not those assholes. But I guess the occasion called for them to be on their best behavior considering where we are all meeting. It was a strategic idea from La Cosa Nostra to have planned this meeting in a hotel conference room in the Caribbean and not in some vacant warehouse where someone might get the itch to blow the competition into smithereens.

And when I say someone, I mean me.

Nothing would give me greater pleasure than seeing all these motherfuckers blow up in smoke. Can't do that with a clear conscience when innocent lives could be lost, too. But maybe I'm the only one who considered the hotel guests and staff as unacceptable liabilities. The Butcher twins haven't arrived yet, and with each passing second that The Firm's boys aren't here, my impatience morphs into dreaded uneasiness.

I'm two seconds away from getting my father far away from this place when the double doors to the room swing open–Benny and Danny Butcher finally making their grand entrance. As Benny takes his seat at the table and his twin stands tall behind him, we all notice how their clothes are covered in dried blood.

"You're late," Giovanni Moretti, the boss of the Outfit Syndicate, scolds annoyedly.

"We're here, aren't we?" Benny replies, his utter boredom

making his thick British accent even more pronounced as he slumps back into his chair. "Count your blessings, Giovanni, that we came at all."

"*Go n-ithe an cat thú is go n-ithe an diabhal an cat,*" Athair mumbles under his breath, meaning may the cat eat you, and may the devil eat the cat.

The old Irish proverb might not offend these twats, but it's my father's humorous way of telling the English fuckers to rot in hell, all while having a smile on his face.

If I had it my way, it wouldn't just be the Butcher twins I'd send off to the underworld where they belong. But then again, this whole fucking table deserves a little corner in the fiery pits of hell, considering how we make our money.

Take the Bratva, for example. Like us, they are all about guns and women, but that is as far as our similarities go. The way we conduct business could not be more different than how they go about it. We treat our whores with dignity and respect. We don't traffic them into the country against their will in shipping containers like those pigs. Our girls get a piece of the pie for their hard work, while the Russians beat and starve their girls to within an inch of their lives should they even think of asking for the same rights. Rumor has it that they like to keep their whores high as kites while their johns have their way with them, as a form of payment for their services.

Bratva scum.

But if there is one thing we Kellys hate more than treating women like garbage, it's the drugs that infest our streets. And all that supply can be traced back to one family—the Hernandez Cartel. They've made their fortune off of junkies' backs and the devastation of their families. The Mexican Cartel never once batted an eye at turning most of the U.S. into jittery zombies who would suck cock and kill their own grandmothers to get their next fix.

That's the only thing La Cosa Nostra and The Outfit have in common with us. We despise drugs. Selling, trafficking, anything related to the business we find unsavory. Not that it makes us any better than the Hernandez Cartel. We might turn up our noses on smack, but we're totally okay with smuggling enough guns around the world to start a civil war.

Then we've got The Firm.

The two English pricks, who just waltzed in looking like they went three rounds with Mike Tyson and won, are totally fine with us killing each other stateside, just as long as it doesn't interfere with their business ventures across the pond. Still, it's kind of hard for them to claim they are the most influential mafia family in Europe when the Russian mob continues to play on their turf and we, in turn, refuse to let the English bastards do any business in Ireland. The old Sicilian gangsters in La Cosa Nostra also haven't taken it lightly that London has crowned itself boss, when they are the original vanguard family that birthed the first godfather, no less.

All this animosity made it so that when word got out that Benny and Danny's father died earlier this week, no one was really surprised. Word quickly spread that Trevor Butcher died on the crapper with a bad heart, but we all know how that scenario could have been easily manipulated to disguise the true cause of his death. I know that everyone sitting around this table has their favorite suspects, but if I had to choose, my money would be on the Cosa Nostra. It was too clean a hit for it to have been anyone else.

Hell hath no fury like a Sicilian scorned.

"We all know why we have come together today," Carlo Rossi, the head of the Cosa Nostra, announces. "Every head of family sitting here has come to the realization that to preserve our way of life, sacrifices need to be made by all. We must put past grudges aside in order to guarantee our future."

At the word grudge, I feel Vadim Volkov's gaze drilling a hole into my forehead. I meet his loathsome stare head-on, knowing the old fucker is still pissed I got the drop on the son sitting at his side. I left a pretty little scar on Alexi's neck and completely fucked with his vocal cords. Every time he opens his mouth to speak, he'll have no choice but to remember how I bested him. The smug smile I offer Volkov in return only widens when I watch him white-knuckling his fists. Not that he'll do anything about it. Not here, and if this meeting goes through as planned, not ever.

"This peace treaty comes at the expense of our pride, but it's a sacrifice we all must make to ensure our survival," Rossi adds, while Vadim and I continue our little staring match.

"What are you looking at, Kelly?" The old fart snarls gruffly in my direction.

My smirk is now a full-blown taunting grin.

"Just appreciating my handiwork. It's not every day I get to see it so proudly flaunted in my face."

"Tiernan," my father reprimands under his breath.

"I'm just teasing him, *Athair*. No harm in breaking the ice with a little jab, right Volkov?"

I wink at the motherfucker to goad him and his father further.

"One of these days, the only thing I'll break is your fucking teeth, Kelly!" Alexi spits in hatred, while his father growls in fury.

"Tsk. Tsk," I taunt." That would defeat the purpose of this meeting. You ain't got a whole lot in here, do ye, big fella?" I point to my head to drive the point home.

Even from where I'm standing across the table, I can see his nails pierce the flesh of his palm, drawing out blood, resulting in me laughing in his face.

"Basta!" Don Rossi exclaims, irritated at our antics. "Niall, tell your son to keep his witty remarks to himself before his mouth gets him killed. And you, Vadim! As boss, you should know better than to be so easily rattled. Tiernan has misguided youth to excuse his behavior. You don't have that same luxury."

"*Mne nasrat', chto ty dumaesh'*. The day I listen to you, is the day hell freezes over. You know what you can do with your condescending advice, *Svoloch'*? *Za cyun v shopu*," Volkov snarls, spitting to the floor in distaste.

You don't have to be fluent in Russian to know Volkov just told Rossi to shove his advice where the sun doesn't shine.

Not a great start to this fucking peace treaty meeting.

Everyone glares at their enemies from across the table and there is no mistaking the animosity we all have for one another. There isn't a man here who wouldn't like to wring the neck of the man sitting at their side or across from them.

"We came here to ensure peace in order for us to continue on with our livelihood. That can only happen if ego and pride are set aside," Don Rossi continues with less vehemence in his tone.

"That's a tall order to make, old man," Benny chimes in.

"It's an order that will ensure you get to be as old as me. Or is life so dispensable where you come from?"

"Depends on the life." Benny shrugs, back to his bored facade.

"Are we going to sit here and do this whole song and dance of who has the biggest cock in the room, or are we going to come to an agreement where we stop killing each other?" Giovanni Moretti exclaims, frustrated. "We all know why we are here, what needs to be done. Now, are we men who want to ensure that our way of life continues, business as usual, or should we just kill each other and save ourselves from these childish tantrums?"

"As much as the idea of gutting your bellies open like fish amuses me, Moretti is right. Business must come before pleasure," Miguel Hernandez adds his two cents.

Of course, the *El Jefe* of the Hernandez Cartel has business on the brain, and it has nothing to do with saving his kins' lives. It's a well-known fact that the South American boss lives off the misery of others and doesn't care if it's one of his own that perishes in this war. All he cares about is his fat bottom line, and that his drugs continue to be spread out around the world.

I'm not ignorant to the fact that The Cartel are the richest dipshits in here. While the rest of the families have billions at their disposal, these fuckers have trillions. Enough money that they will never be able to spend it all in their lifetime. However, Miguel Hernandez's greed for more knows no limits.

That's another difference between our families. We don't want world domination, but like fuck will we roll over and concede to any man's greedy ambitions. I want their drugs out of Boston and as far away from our domain as possible. I know that will never happen unless this treaty goes through. One of our demands is that only a small percentage of their drugs enters Irish territory. I have no idea what the other requests stipulated from these assholes are, nor do I care. This is the only one that, for me, is non-negotiable, and I know *Athair* feels the same way. Especially since we know firsthand what that junk can do to a family.

"It has been a year since we started our deliberations, and the time has come to put them into action. I admit it will take some time to get used to this new reality, but resistance is futile," Carlo Rossi deadpans.

My gaze falls to the man who, in an even note, just told us to either bend the knee now or die, without looking one bit flustered at the threat he laid at our feet. The fucker is old school through and through. Like the Outfit, he is cold and pragmatic. It's served him well so far. To his discontentment, though, the only part of New York City that he hasn't been able to reign over with an iron fist is Hell's Kitchen. And that's because we rule it. I have no real beef with Rossi or his well-tailored goons, even though I highly doubt they would say the same. The Cosa Nostra think we Irish are an unruly bunch. Too unpredictable to be trusted. They like everything nice and tidy. Organized. And we Kellys have always thrived in chaos and disorder. You can't control a loose cannon, and for those who view control as a precious commodity, the unpredictability of the Kelly family sets them on edge. Still, the Cosa

Nostra has been in this game way before the word mafia was even a thing to be feared. They deserve some respect, even if just a sliver of it.

"To ensure blood will stop flowing, we need to mix the families together," he proceeds with his rant. "We must make sure we are all connected in some way, so no one thinks twice before waging war on us."

"Agreed," the heads of each family reply in sync.

"We all have daughters, and a woman's reason for being has always been to be used for alliance purposes, so it fits that they be the ones to be sacrificed here," the Cosa Nostra Don continues on.

I bite my inner cheek at that aloof comment, thinking of little Iris back home being thrown to the lions just to end our combined strife. Unfortunately, I don't see another way, either.

"Once the girls are of age, they must marry the leaders of their family, or soon to be dons and bosses. This exchange must all be done within the same time frame. We don't want to have anyone back out because they got cold feet and are no longer interested in the union. Can we agree on those terms?"

No one says anything to the contrary, establishing a silent agreement.

"Good. Now seeing as my daughter is only eight and the youngest of the girls, I propose marriage should only occur in ten years' time when she's of age."

"That's preposterous!" Miguel exclaims, looking red-faced with fury. "My daughter is of age now. How can you expect Rosa to wait to be married until she's almost thirty? People will think there is something wrong with her."

"When has public opinion ever been a concern for us?" Benny retorts smugly with an arched brow.

"This will make a mockery of my family. It will only bring shame to my daughter. At that age, who knows if she'll even be fertile enough to bear children!?!"

God, this asshole is a misogynistic pig.

Miguel Hernandez doesn't give two shits about his daughter's reputation. All he cares about is how having a twentysomething unwed daughter will look on him.

"My mother bore children well up to her fortieth birthday. I'm sure she'll be ripe enough to breed when the time comes, not to mention my father bore more bastards than you can imagine at that age," Volkov retorts with a scowl.

"Then you take her!"

"No one is calling dibs on any girl. This needs to be fair to all parties concerned. Therefore, there will be a lottery," Rossi explains patiently.

"A lottery?! What *pinche puta* solution is this? Is my Rosa supposed to be awarded like cattle to you?!"

My father, having had enough of the Hernandez' outrage, pushes his chair back and gets up to his feet. All the men in the room instantly go to their waist to grab their guns. *Athair*, unbothered by the reaction, walks unruffled to the breakfast table set at the corner of the room. My brows pull together, observing my father grabbing the large bowl of fruit and walking back to his seat. Before he sits back down, he tosses the fruit over his shoulder, and places the bowl in the center of the table. Everyone is silently observing his every move, wondering what he'll do next. *Athair* grabs a yellow pad of paper, then proceeds to rip a piece, doodling the Kelly name on it and then dropping it into the bowl.

"We all pick a name. Should the name pulled out be of our own daughter, we pick again until we have a new name."

"A little childish, but I guess it serves our purpose," Danny scoffs behind his brother.

Fucker.

"Aye, but I find simplicity always gets the job done. Why make a mountain out of a molehill, I always say."

I smirk at *Athair* teaching these Brit assholes a lesson.

"It will do," Rossi adds, throwing his name into the bowl.

One by one, each boss writes their family name on pieces of paper and throws them into the pit of despair, while looking none too happy about it.

And why would they be?

The bowl symbolizes conformity where once free will prevailed.

Yet, it's the only way to guarantee we live another day in this messed up world of ours.

Ten years.

That's all I have.

Ten years of blessed freedom until I'm chained to a woman I'll despise on mere principle alone. Worse still, she will have to bear children of my blood, making sure that every time I look at them, all I'll see is an enemy ready to take my place. I guess I'll cross that bridge when the time comes. Right now, I'm more concerned with my little sister's fate than I am my own.

Iris doesn't deserve this.

She's a free spirit, but this is going to rob her of her freedom and place her in a gilded cage of our own making. Staring at the men around me, I consider who would be the lesser evil in welcoming Iris to their home and giving her some semblance of the life she now holds so dear. Unfortunately, the stone-cold faces around the table don't give anything away, much less inspire any spark of hope.

Do they love their daughters as much as *Athair* loves Iris?

Do they love their sisters as much as I love mine?

Or do they only see them as pawns to be used in this wretched game?

I doubt any of them care one bit that these girls will be entering, without their consent even, into what most likely will be a toxic—maybe even abusive—relationship. That they will be forced to live in a hostile environment for the rest of their lives just to ensure the treaty is upheld. Just the mere idea of it makes me wish I could demand that *Athair* back out of this deal right now. Better we all die today than have Iris be subjected to such cruelty tomorrow.

I have ten years to come up with a plan to save my sister. If I can't come up with anything that will help her in the end, then at least I'll have enough time to teach Iris how to defend herself. To use her wits. Her brains and fists, if she needs to. Like my younger brother, Shay, Iris has always been fond of knives, so I make a note to gift her a sharp dagger as my wedding present. Whoever the cunt is that ends up calling her his wife will think twice about hurting her with that in her hand. Nothing keeps a man on his guard better than the suspicion that the woman lying beside him in bed can slice his throat while he's at his most vulnerable.

Once all the names are in the bowl, Giovanni Moretti stands up from his seat and picks up a discarded pen from the table. He then proceeds to use it to slice his palm, creating an ugly gash. I store that piece of information away for the future. Although he might look like any other reputable businessman that wouldn't dream of getting his hands dirty, Giovanni Moretti could kill his enemy by severing an artery in a man's neck with just a tip of a pen if he were inclined to do so. Droplets of blood drip to soak the yellow papers in the bowl as he takes turns to look every man here in the eye.

"On my blood, I swear to protect and care for the woman who will ensure the life of the Outfit. Let her sacrifice bring union to the *famiglias*."

I take his words in, dissecting their meaning.

Moretti has mostly been silent throughout today's exchange. Not that I was surprised by his demeanor in any way, since it's common knowledge that Giovanni prefers to keep his true thoughts close to his vest. He likes to observe his surroundings and catalog his foes' weaknesses just by listening to them go on and on in their rants. A trait of a great leader, if you ask me.

But the oath Moretti decided to pledge today speaks volumes of his concern. Just like *Athair* and me, he doesn't want any harm to come to his daughter either. My respect for the man increases tenfold as his blood continues to drip, and I find myself praying to the Almighty himself that if Iris needs to enter such a crime family, then let it be the Outfit.

Moretti grabs the paper and then reads it—rocks are slung to my stomach when it's not my sweet sister's name that falls from his lips.

"Valentina Rossi."

He shows us the paper and pushes the bowl to the next *made man* sitting to his side. It's no secret the Cosa Nostra and the Outfit hate each other. Picking the Rossi girl is a blow to both families.

The bowl continues to make its rounds, and when it's *Athair*'s turn to pick a name, he surprises me by grabbing my hand and pulling me next to him. My father then makes a show of slicing both our palms with the pen, clasping them together before droplets of our mixed blood fall into the wretched bowl that is to seal my sister's fate as well as my own. I hold my breath as my father utters his oath and then looks to me to repeat it, word for word. As his heir, I follow his lead and do my duty. Everyone in this room knows what my father's intention is with this one deliberate move—what it symbolizes. Even after his death, I am to uphold his oath as my own.

The men sitting at this table hear our vow and wait on bated breath to see who is chosen.

When the name Rosa Hernandez comes into view, a myriad of emotions assaults me all at once.

This is it.

This is the woman I will be shackled to.

And though I just promised not to hurt her, I hate her already.

The blow continues to make its way through my body, my heart beating a mile a minute with the realization that my future is now entangled with the cartel princess. The only thing that brings me out of my reverie is when my baby sister's name is called out.

And God help me, I've never wanted to have a gun in my hands more just to kill the Volkov fucker who just breathed Iris's name with a smirk.

The Bratva.

My baby sister is to wed the Russian pigs who view women as disposable property.

They will snuff my sister's wild spirit out.

Iris will be a pawn in their twisted games.

They won't stop until they break her.

"No," I yell out. "Choose another."

Vadim smiles sinisterly. "Now where would be the diplomacy in that?"

"You can't have her."

"I can, and I will."

"Tiernan," *Athair* mumbles softly, but unlike every man here, I hear the tremor of fear in his voice.

"I said fucking pick another one!" I slam my fists on the table.

"No. She's my son's now." His eyes gleam in triumph, while Alexi stares into blank space, not moving a muscle. "Actually, Iris will belong to all my sons. As I see it, my family needs you just as much as you all need mine. These are my terms. The Irish girl is to be made a Bratva princess to all my boys."

"Over my dead body!"

"That can be arranged."

I launch myself at him from across the table, but two pairs of hands pull me back. I look to my left to find Giovanni shaking his head, ordering me to cool it, but it's the man to my right that actually gives me pause and stops me in my tracks. Alejandro Hernandez stares me down with his dark eyes, silently commanding me to stand down. Never in my wildest imagination would I ever conceive of the idea that one day Alejandro would come to my aid and prevent me from starting a war. But in doing so, he's already making it clear to everyone here where his alliances are, considering the fact that I'm to be his family.

Fuck.

This is so fucked up.

Too fucked up for me to wrap my head around.

I shrug their hands off me, my whole body trembling with rage.

"Carlo," my father begins to protest, standing up with palms flat on the table. "This is absurd. You can't honestly allow my daughter to be shared like some common whore."

"She's a woman, isn't she? I haven't met one yet who didn't enjoy being fucked by three cocks," Vadim adds, his eyes sparkling with triumph, reveling in our misery. "Besides, it is an old Russian tradition. The most revered czars practiced such ways in the old country. It's a sign of devotion. And it's my family's way of showing just how much we will honor this treaty."

Sick fuck!

"Carlo," *Athair* repeats, his voice begging for mercy. "Don't allow this madness."

Carlo Rossi's forehead wrinkles, thinking long and hard about this turn of events. Both *Athair* and I hold our breath, waiting for his ruling.

"Gentleman, we all knew coming into this that there would be sacrifices to be made in the pursuit of peace. If the Volkov family wishes to uphold their traditions that will ensure obedience to this peace treaty, then let no man here refute their will. It is up to each family's moral code to do as they see fit."

Athair slumps back into his seat, defeat written all over his face.

I watch in horror as Vadim retrieves a switchblade from his inner pocket and orders Alexi to stand up.

"On my blood and on the blood of my legitimate heir, Alexi, we swear to protect and care for the woman who will ensure the life of the Bratva. Let her sacrifice bring union to every family here."

His demon eyes stare into his son, silently ordering him to say the same words out loud.

"On my blood, and on the blood of my brothers, we too swear to protect and care for the woman who will ensure the life of the Bratva. Let her sacrifice bring union to us all."

The words coming out seem robotic, as if he doesn't even care he just officially made sure that Iris will not only be his, but his brothers, too.

Alexi sits back down in his seat, while Vadim drinks up his victory over *Athair* and I like it's the best sweet cherry wine he's ever tasted.

"Don't worry, Kelly. My boys will take good care of her. We're family now. Isn't that the point of all this?" Volkov goads, trying to get a rise from me.

I'm not sure what pisses me off more.

Vadim's triumphant sneer or Alexi's complete indifference and disregard.

"He's right. It's done," Alejandro mutters evenly beside me, not an ounce of emotion in his tone.

"Tell me, Kelly. Do you want to go to war because of one little girl?" Vadim directs the question to my father, who is sitting down looking as stoic as ever.

"If you hurt her, I will kill you," I reply when my father refuses to acknowledge Volkov's taunts.

His haughty smirk chills my blood.

"We can call this whole thing off, if you want? We are more than prepared to continue this war if you are."

"This war ends here. You might not like it, Tiernan, but should you prevent this from happening, then all of us will make sure your last breath will be witnessed by every man here," Rossi warns. "And you, Volkov, should we hear that the girl is treated in any way less than with the respect she is entitled to as the mother of your future heirs, then the same fate will be bestowed upon you. Think long and hard, gentlemen, because this is what this treaty really means. We are now all linked. One misstep and you no longer have one or two families to war with, but all of us."

"We understand," *Athair* says somberly. "Volkov, we are honored to have you welcome our Iris into your home and family. You will not have any issues from us. I give you my solemn vow."

My father's words burn a hole through my chest.

"And you, Tiernan?" Rossi questions.

Through gritted teeth, I nod, unable to consent to my sister's macabre fate with words.

"Good. This... gentlemen," Rossi begins, planting his palms on the table as he makes eye contact with every man here, "is the beginning of a new dawn. Where we flourish and thrive in business, knowing that old vendettas are put to the side for the greater good. You have ten years to settle into this new way of life and put your demands into place. We will all honor it. This is our future now. Our survival. And if there is a man here that will put this agreement in any kind of jeopardy, then death will not only knock on his doorstep, but also greet every family member they have ever cared for."

In other words, submit or die.

My family could survive a war with two families, maybe even three. But with all five? We would all be dead within a week. And the same can be said for every family here if they also oppose it. I just hope the threat of death is enough to keep them all honorable. If not, then the previous Mafia Wars will pale in comparison to the retribution of the future.

Whatever our destiny, no one wins here today.

But to truly lose would mean our extinction.

Ten years.

That's all Iris and I have now.

Only time will tell if we'll have many more after that.

And as the outside wind continues to blow, the storm taking up new heights, I make my own vow to Saint Brendan himself, asking him to give me the strength and fortitude to strike down every man here if the fate that awaits us is filled with Kelly blood.

If my life and that of my sister is to pay the price for peace, then I pity the fool who ever tries to disrupt it.

His death will be a thing of nightmares.

I'll make sure of it.

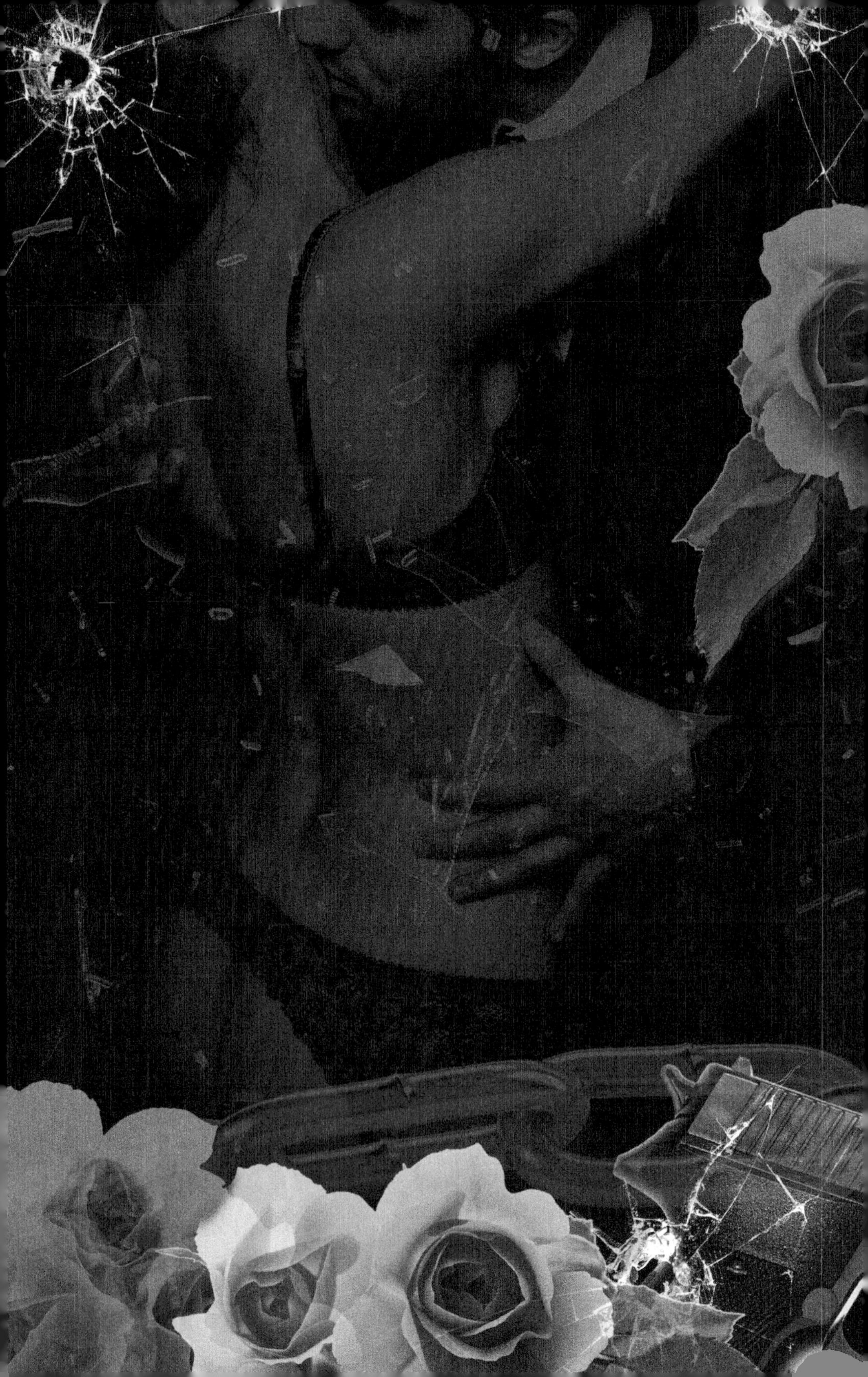

CHAPTER 1
Tiernan

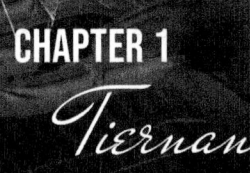

PRESENT DAY

I lean against the doorframe, my arms crossed against my chest as I stare at my baby sister packing up her luggage, filling to the very brim the carry-on and two large suitcases that are sprawled on top of her bed. Silently, I watch her store away not only her clothes, but also her most prized possessions. An ill feeling inside me whispers that those little knick-knacks won't be enough to bring Iris any type of joy, much less soothe the ache of being ripped away from everything she's ever known and into the belly of the beast.

Iris continues to sway her hips left to right to the beat of the song playing through her earphones, completely oblivious to my presence and my troubled thoughts. The whole scenario looks so horribly mundane to me. As if she's just packing her stuff to go on one of her far away exotic vacations, with the promise she will return home once she's had her fill of sangria and sandy beaches.

But nothing could be further from that delusion.

You wouldn't know it by looking at her, but today will be the beginning of a life my sister never asked for. A life where she will have to venture out all on her own without the safety net of our family name, since by the end of the week, she will no longer be a Kelly—but a Volkov.

There is a pang in my chest at that realization. I have no other choice but to bury my reluctance at that ungodly thought deep down into the confines of my soul, so I don't do the unfathomable and kidnap my sister, right here and now, and take her somewhere safe where Bratva hands can't touch her. Not that I haven't thought about doing such a thing innumerous times before. In fact, for the past ten years, I have thought of little else. Just the thought that Iris will have to fend off the three Volkov brothers every night from here on out brings bile to my throat.

"Are you going to just stand there all day, *dheartháir*? Or are you going to help a girl out and shut this bag for me?" Iris exclaims, not lifting her gaze off the stubborn bag that refuses to be zipped up.

"I didn't think you saw me standing here since you were too busy dancing up a storm." I smile tauntingly, walking over to her to lend a helping hand.

"I see everything, *dearthái mór*," she retorts smugly. "Besides, you make it too easy for me. I could feel your scowl from across any room."

"You make me sound like an old worried fart."

"If the shoe fits," she goads, playfully nudging her shoulder with mine.

"That's funny. You're funny," I reply sarcastically, pulling on one of her wild, red curls.

"Well, you better get your fill now, big brother. In a few hours, you won't have to suffer me making fun of you anymore."

Fuck.

Why did she have to say that?

I turn to my side and place my hands on her shoulders, halting her from continuing on with her task just so I can take her in one last time. Iris' emerald green eyes sparkle with mischief and so much life. It cripples my heart, wondering how long that gleam will last in the Volkov's household.

"Tiernan, I've got a plane to catch. I don't have time to stand here for you just to gawk at me," she jokes.

"Let's be serious for a moment. *Conas atá tú*? Really? The truth now, Iris. How are you feeling with all of this?"

She sighs before shrugging my hands away and going back to stuffing her suitcases.

"We've had this talk a gazillion times, big brother. I'm fine. You shouldn't worry about me."

"Teach me how not to worry about my kid sister, and I won't. You forget I used to change your diapers when you were yay high, *deirfiúr bheag*."

"Ew, gross."

She laughs, hoping her playful demeanor will lighten the mood.

But it doesn't.

All it does is remind me that the sound of her laughter will be another thing that I will miss.

"I'm serious, Iris. I will always worry. It's my job to."

"Not anymore. That will be Alexi's job now."

The mention of her soon-to-be husband irks me to no end. Instead of carving his face like I did to his neck all those years ago, I should have killed the bastard. That way Iris wouldn't have to be subjected to becoming his fucking wife.

"Besides, Shay doesn't worry, and he's my brother, too," she adds, unaware of how I just murdered her fiancé ten different ways in my mind.

"It's different. You and Shay are too close in age for him to feel the way I do."

"You mean like an obsessive, over-controlling *Athair*? Sorry to burst your bubble, *deartháir mór*, but I already have a father, and he's not one bit worried about me, just as long as this treaty goes to plan."

"That's not fair, Iris. *Athair* worries about you plenty."

"Yeah, I know." She lets out a long exhale, bowing her head so that her crimson curls can cover her face from my sight.

I pull her to face me again, the sliver of sadness so plainly swimming in her clear green meadows that it chisels away at me.

"You know that if he could, he would never willingly give you up. You're his favorite *leanbh*."

"I know that, too. Did you come in here to remind me how much you all love me, is that it?"

"Do you need reminding?" I cock a brow.

"No, I don't. So quit with the heavy talk, and help me close these damn fucking bags."

I can't help but laugh at her sass.

"You might want to temper that mouth of yours when you reach Vegas. I'm not sure how the Russians will feel about a woman who curses like a sailor."

"Tough shit. I'm a Kelly, for fuck's sake. It's in my blood, so they better get used to it."

"I'm positive that you'll make sure that they do."

With my apprehension subsided somewhat, I help her close her suitcases but leave the carry-on open.

"I have something for you."

"More pearls of wisdom?" She rolls her eyes.

"No, nothing like that. A wedding gift. Since I won't be able to be there on your big day, I thought I should give you my gift now."

Without another word, I hand her the small package I had hidden away inside my jacket pocket. She doesn't complain that it's not gift-wrapped, or that it doesn't have a pretty bow on it. That would be too girlish for Iris anyway. She's never been one to like frilly things, especially since my baby sister has always been a tomboy at heart.

When she opens the box, her eyes shine in utter awe at the push dagger I had custom-made for her inside the blue velvet casing. I made sure to request that the blade be small enough for Iris to easily hide in her palm, but lethal enough that she can slice any throat with it. And the *pièce de résistance*, the Kelly family crest embossed on the handle. If there is ever an occasion that she feels the need to use it, I want her to remember the blood that runs through her veins to embolden her resolve.

Kellys never run from a fight.

We end them.

"It's... it's beautiful," she whispers, true emotion coating each word.

"I'm glad you like it."

"I more than like it. I love it!" she exclaims with glee, wrapping her arms around my waist and placing her cheek against my chest.

I hold her tightly, inhaling her free-spirit essence and committing it to memory.

Who knows when will be the next time I even see her?

Or even be able to hold her in my arms like this?

When I hear a little sniffle, the fist that has had my heart squeezed into a pulp all morning gives another painful tug. Iris isn't the type to cry or get emotional. She's always made sure never to show such weakness, so to see her this vulnerable, she might as well have used the damn push dagger to cut into my heart and slice it into tiny pieces.

After a few seconds, she finally pulls away, her composure once again hardened steel. I lift her chin up so I can look her in the eyes once more.

"Do you remember everything I taught you?" I ask evenly.

She nods.

"Do you remember everything your teacher has taught you?"

Another nod.

"Good. Remember, Iris, you are strong. Stronger than any of

those brutes that you're about to encounter. But most importantly, you are clever. Lean into your gut. It will keep you safe."

"You should be giving the Volkovs this advice. Not me."

I grab her chin, more forcefully this time, to show her this isn't a game.

"Don't fuck around, Iris. Those assholes will eat you for breakfast if you let them."

"You forget, big brother. I have a pretty big appetite, too," she seethes, her razor-sharp gaze never wavering from mine.

"Alexi and his brothers aren't to be trifled with. They're not like us. They are animals with no code of honor to speak of. If they want to break you, they will do everything in their power to do so. Don't make it easy for them."

She snaps her face away from my grip, her emerald eyes taking on a deeper shade, one that unsettles me.

"I'm a big girl, Tiernan."

"That you are. Just don't be a stupid girl."

She snarls, her nostrils flaring in anger and resentment.

That's another thing about Iris.

She's too hot-tempered. Lord knows our parents tried their best to shake that trait out of her, but then again, she wouldn't be a Kelly if she wasn't easy to set off.

"Are you done with your little pep talk? I need to get ready for my flight."

I swipe my hand over my face, hating that this is the last interaction I will have with her—the last memory she'll have of me.

"Here, let me help," I say instead of the apology she deserves to hear.

She might as well get used to men who don't give a fuck about her feelings. If Iris is to survive in Vegas, she needs to start practicing the discipline of hiding her true emotions. Not that I'm worried she won't be able to pull it off, since acting like we don't give a fuck, when in reality our blood is boiling, is another family skill passed down through the generations. We can be hot one minute and cold the next. You never know what any of us Kellys are really thinking. We can be laughing and chugging Guinness with you one minute, only to slice you open the next. It keeps everyone on their toes. And frankly, I quite prefer it that way.

'*Always keep them guessing,*' *Athair* is fond of saying.

And that is something each one of his children have been able to do.

All but one, that is.

I shrug that thought away and pick up my baby sister's luggage.

"I'll take this downstairs so I can give you a moment alone."

"I don't need one. I'm all set."

My forehead wrinkles in disappointment that she doesn't want to say goodbye to all the memories her room holds. But it wouldn't be Iris if she didn't pull the band-aid off in one quick yank.

She trails behind me as I walk down the stairs with her luggage in hand. I drop the bags in the foyer and head to the kitchen at the back of the house, knowing that our parents are undoubtedly drinking their morning tea there, just waiting to say their goodbyes to my sister before she leaves. Iris continues to keep to her mute form as she follows me down the long corridor. Knowing she's pissed at me is eating me alive, but I also know it's the only way she will heed the warning I gave her upstairs.

Yet, her silent treatment doesn't sit well with me.

I know it's normal for siblings to fight. I've had the occasional fistfight with Shay to prove it. But Iris has always been different. Maybe it's the fact she's the only girl in a house full of unruly men, or maybe it's because she's the baby of the family. Whatever the reason, I've never liked to see her upset. And I fucking hate that I'm the reason she feels that way now.

"There's my *a stór*," our father exclaims the minute we enter the kitchen, getting up from his seat so he can hug his only daughter.

Iris's foul mood instantly vanishes as she snuggles into our father's embrace.

She would kill me if I ever said these words aloud, but Iris has always been a daddy's girl. When she was younger, we could always find her glued to his hip, and in turn, *Athair* doted on her at every opportunity.

That all changed, of course, when the treaty was put in place.

Suddenly, we all became too busy to give her our undivided attention. Especially *Athair* and I. We were too caught up in trying to make sure all the families' demands were set in place so that when the clock ran out ten years later, none of them would have reason to fall back on their promise.

And then when Patrick…

Well…

Things just grew worse for all of us after that.

I know it must have hurt Iris a great deal to be cast aside in such a fashion, to suddenly become a footnote in our grief, but she never once complained. Even right from the beginning when *Athair* sat her down and explained that her future would be sacrificed for the greater good, she didn't bat an eye and accepted her fate willingly.

Like I said.

My sister is made of the purest steel.

If she had been born a man, then maybe Athair would have named her his true heir to our family empire.

And I would have followed her lead with the most loyal of hearts.

Still, I made sure that through the years, I prepared Iris for her true destiny. I taught her how to defend herself whenever I could, and when the time came that she wanted to be educated by a professional, I made sure to step back and let her control her own life. It's the least I could have done, since I'm not sure if she'll ever have free will again to make her own decisions once she's made a Bratva bride.

"*Is tú mo stóirín. Tá mo chroí istigh ionat,*" he whispers to her, our father's blue eyes starting to glisten with unshed tears as he proclaims his love for his dearest and only daughter.

Athair reluctantly releases her from his hug, placing a tender kiss on her temple.

"I love you too, *Athair*," she croaks, her gaze falling to the floor to hide the desolation embedded in her eyes.

"That will be enough out of you two. I will not have tears in my kitchen. Shed what you will in a confessional to a priest like normal folk, and not where I cook," our *Máthair* reprimands, drying her hands on a kitchen towel as she stares them both down.

"Aye, Saoirse is right. Apologies, dear daughter, for being such an emotional old fool. I just miss ye already, child. This house will not be the same without ye."

"It sure will be quieter. My ears will finally have some peace from that racket you call music," our mother adds with a teasing tone.

Iris steps away from our father, bridging the gap between her and our mother, with her hands on her hips.

"Aye, but you won't have anyone helping you in this kitchen either. You'll miss my racket then, won't ye?"

"Maybe I will," our mother retorts, her gaze—the same bright green color as Iris'—taking a softening glow. "Not that I'll ever admit it to your face, girl. Who knows? Maybe I'll ask Tiernan's lass to help me out and take your place in the kitchen."

Iris cackles at that statement.

"Thanks for the laugh, *Máthair*. I needed it."

"I didn't realize I made a joke," our mother retorts with mirth in her tone.

"Oh dear, Saint Brigid." Iris continues to chuckle. "No way will any Hernandez spend their time peeling potatoes for you, *Ma*. I heard they have servants for everything. Even to wipe their *arses* when they go to the toilet. Fat chance Tiernan's fiancé even knows what a pot looks like."

"Geez, girl. Must ye be so vulgar? I'm sure the lass can be of use. Even if it's only to put some bloody plates on a table," our mother retorts playfully.

"The only use she has is to bear Tiernan sons. Aside from that, I would rather not lay my eyes on her if I can help it."

With that cold statement from our father, the temperature in the room declines to arctic levels, stealing any good disposition my mother and sister were trying to find under such trying circumstances. Iris' brows pinch together at the center of her forehead, obviously bothered by his callous remark.

"She is not at fault for what happened to our family. Let it go, *Athair*. Otherwise, you are just going to make things more complicated for the rest of us that are trying their best to move on."

I don't agree with Iris, but I get where she's coming from.

If each family puts blame on the women who are coming into our lives for the wrongdoings of the past, then we might as well not go through with the peace treaty since it's bound to be a disaster anyway. Unfortunately, the forgiving sentiment is easier said than done. Old grudges are hard to overcome—especially in our world. I just pray that Alexi is of the same mindset as Iris and that he doesn't hold what I've done to him in the past against my sister.

Athair doesn't respond, going back to sit in his seat at the kitchen table and refreshing his cup of tea. He stares at his mug, spinning his teaspoon round and round, trapped in his perturbed thoughts and refusing to acquiesce to my sister's way of thinking.

Not that I blame him.

These past years have not been kind to our father.

He's suffered too many losses to count, and today he's reminded that his losing streak can only truly come to an end by sacrificing yet another child. Only this time, the sacrificial lamb is his very favorite *leanbh*.

Iris anxiously looks up at me, silently urging me to be there for our father when she cannot. I offer her a clipped nod, her stiff shoulders instantly relaxing with the unvocalized promise.

"I hate to do this, but Iris really has to go. Her flight leaves in two hours," I announce.

"Plenty of time for you and your sister to have a cup of tea with us and wait for Shay and Colin to come back from wherever they went off to so early this morning," our mother interjects, walking over to her husband and placing a comforting hand on his shoulder. "I swear those two boys refuse to sleep one night in their beds, and on the night they actually do, they are up at the crack of dawn to go see God knows who. I mean, how many single lasses can Boston have to keep them so entertained?"

Iris looks puzzled at me and then turns her attention to our parents once more.

"*Máthair*, we already said our goodbyes last night at the pub. Didn't Tiernan tell you? Shay and Colin went to meet Alejandro Hernandez and his sister this morning."

My mother's eyes widen in shock. This time it's my father who covers her hand with his to keep her docile—as much as Saoirse Kelly can be when she's in a mood, anyway.

"I thought you said the Hernandez lass was only coming tomorrow, being it's her wedding day and all?"

"You forget that Alejandro will also tie the knot this week. He wanted to make sure he was here to watch his sister walk down the aisle. And seeing as we still have to work out some pending issues, he thought it best that we have time to talk shop before the festivities."

"Is that so? Hmm. Say what ye will about the Hernandez family, but at least Alejandro had the brotherly affection to make sure his sister was well taken care of."

More like he wanted to make sure I say I do or he'd kill me on the spot.

I clear my throat instead of giving her a reply, since deep down I agree with mother. I *should* be the one to take Iris to Vegas and be there for her wedding day. Nothing would have given me more pleasure than to stare Alexi and his brothers in the eye and tell them if they fuck with Iris in any way, it would be the last thing they ever do—treaty or no treaty.

Unfortunately, a few months back, Iris came to me to ask that I not escort her to Vegas, since she wanted to do this on her own and was adamant that I stay back in Boston. To my bitter chagrin, I couldn't find it in me to deny her this last request. This peace treaty has taken so much from her already, I'd give her whatever she asked of me, even if it goes against everything I stand for.

"No matter. I guess we will all have to live with the decisions you two make from here on out. I just have to hope that your father and I have given you both the skills and know-how to make good choices—even if we don't agree with them. Now, sit down and have some tea with us. Let me enjoy my daughter and son one more time under this roof. Only St. Brigid knows when we'll have this opportunity again."

Both Iris and I do as we're told, sending each other a knowing smirk as we take our respective seats. When Saoirse Kelly gets something in her head, there's no point in arguing with her. But as the seconds pass, it dawns on me how true her words are. All we have now are these fleeting moments of a life that once was. After today, our reality will never be the same.

My sister will have to face her Bratva fate on her own.

And as the boss of the Irish mafia with a cartel princess as his wife, so will I.

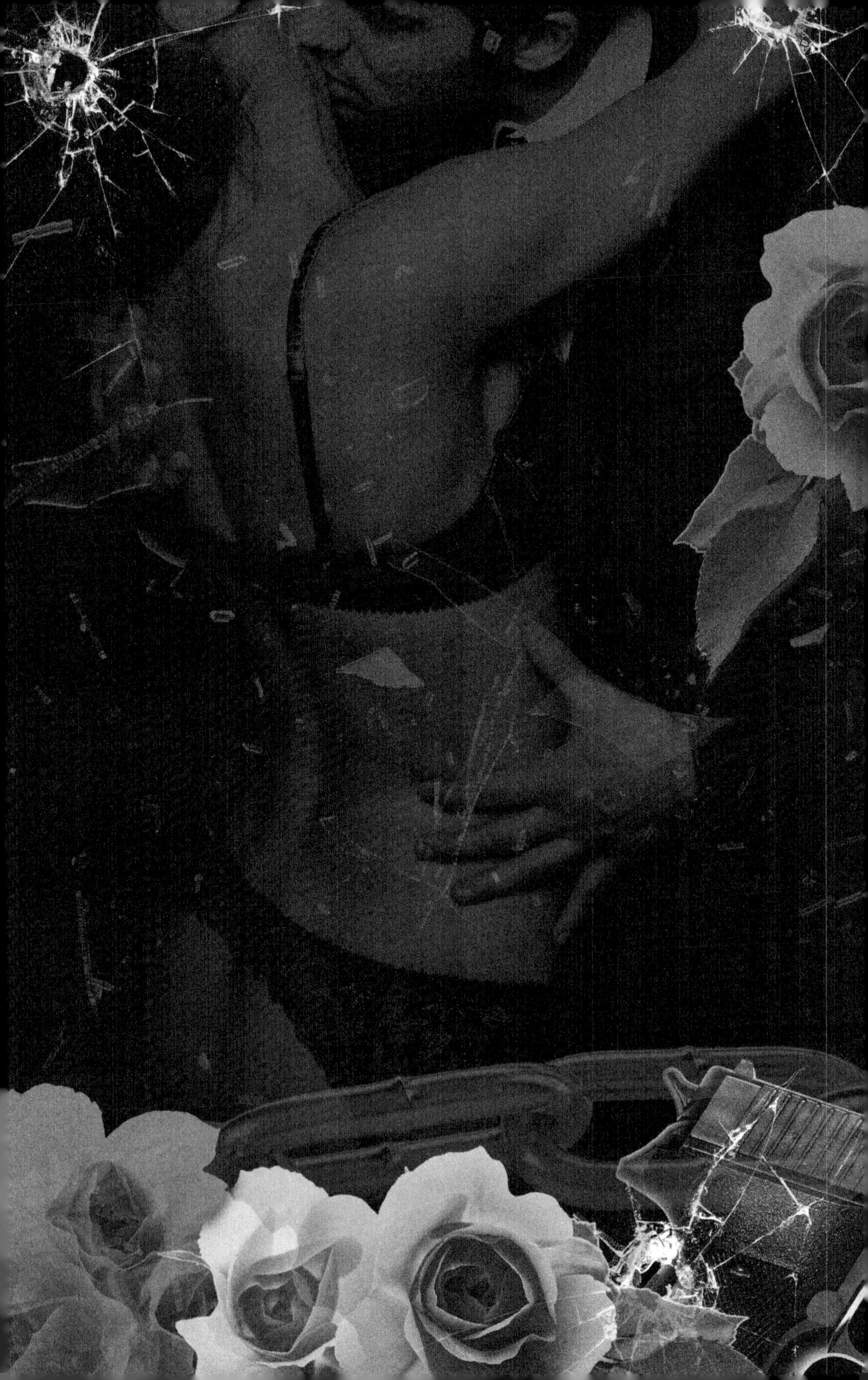

CHAPTER 2
Rosa

"WE WILL ARRIVE at Hanscom Field shortly, Mr. Hernandez. Thirty minutes to be precise. Is there anything you need before we land?" our stewardess asks, batting her eyelashes at my brother, her voice thick with insinuation.

"Another scotch on the rocks will suffice," my brother retorts, his attention focused on the screen of his laptop instead of the woman who is currently salivating at the mouth to get her hands on him.

"Right away," she says, her disappointment clear as day. She's about to turn around and fetch my brother's alcohol when he grabs her by the wrist to halt her step.

"I didn't hear you ask my sister if she wanted something. She should be your first concern."

Her face instantly pales.

"My apologies, Miss Hernandez. Can I get you anything?"

"No, I'm fine. Thank you."

When my brother finally lets her go, I don't miss how she hurriedly walks away, rubbing at her now bruised wrist.

"You didn't have to do that," I reprimand Alejandro, low enough that no one else in our private jet can hear.

"You're right. I didn't. You should have been the one to put her in her place. Not me," Alejandro scolds, never once lifting his gaze from his computer.

I bite the inside of my cheek and turn to face the window.

"Don't scowl. It's unbecoming for a woman of your stature."

It takes everything in me not to roll my eyes at him. Not that I would dare either way. Even though my face is turned away from his, my brother would sense my insubordination.

"Don't pout either."

"I wasn't. And if you could stop treating me like an insolent child, that would be greatly appreciated," I rebuke evenly, without so much as an ounce of emotion he can chastise.

"That wasn't my intention."

"Then what was?" I turn to him, my manicured brow raised high on my forehead.

He lets out an exhale and closes his laptop. That action alone should cause me to be wary, but I keep my spine straight and my regal air about me intact like I know he expects.

"I thought my intention was quite clear. You are never to let anyone disrespect you, even if unintentionally. Much less the fucking help. And you should never, *ever* give them just cause for it either. *Está claro?*"

"*Sí.*"

"Good. I'm not about to hand you over to the Irish just so they can make a fool out of you. Remember, you are still part of this family. Everything you do is a reflection of us."

"You sound like our father."

The words have barely left my lips and already I regret them.

Alejandro is nothing like our dictator of a father.

Nothing.

You'd have to be born without a heart for that to be possible. And for all my eldest brother's faults, I know a heart beats inside his chest. I know my brother's allegiance will always be with our father, but even he can't deny how cold-hearted the man is.

"*Perdóname, hermano.* That was uncalled for," I apologize, reaching out for his hand and squeezing it tightly.

Alejandro is not one to show affection or even let anyone else give it to him, but he doesn't pull away from the endearment, and for that, I am grateful.

"Do you think me cruel, Rosa?" he asks pensively.

I shake my head, hating I'm the one who planted such an idea in his mind.

"You're as cruel as you need to be, considering all that you have been through and what is expected of you. I don't hold it against you, dear brother. In fact, I have nothing but love and pride in being your sister."

His brown eyes turn a molten hue, a tinge of a sad smile on his lips.

"I haven't been there for you these past few years, and I fear that I've hindered you with my absence. Maybe I could have done more to prepare you for what's to come."

My heart swells at his words.

My brother isn't a caring man. Far from it. So, to hear such tender worry for me in his voice soothes my aching heart.

"You did your best, Alejandro. I'm ready to face my fate."

He leans in closer to me and caresses my cheek in such a way I almost find myself flinching at his touch. Not that I find it repulsive… just unexpected.

"Ah, my sweet, *Rosa*. Such a beautiful flower to be given to uncouth animals who won't know how to make her bloom. I hope they never wilt your flawless petals with their crass and brutish ways, dear sister. Such a waste of a rose like yourself to be given to such an unworthy family."

My forehead creases at his remark.

I know very little of the family I'm about to marry into. But through the years, anytime the name Kelly was uttered, I made it my mission to pay attention. Thankfully, I also had an accomplice in gathering intel. Anytime my sweet younger brother Francesco heard a new piece of gossip or news about the Kellys, he made sure to fill me in.

One of the first things he told me is that they have no sense of decorum. That they are loud, obnoxious brutes who are only happy when they are drinking and fighting. Well, that's not the exact sentence Francesco said.

"All those Boston pricks do is drink, fight, and fuck. No brains whatsoever, so don't go thinking you can have meaningful conversations with those assholes about Gauguin and Van Gogh. They are today's version of cavemen. I bet they don't even know how to use a fucking fork."

Of course, I took his opinion with a grain of salt since Francesco isn't one to talk. He, too, has an insatiable lust for life that makes him dabble in the unsavory. Not only does he enjoy his alcohol a little too much for my liking, but I have run in on him—too many times to count, unfortunately—enjoying the prettiest servants in our home, in the most embarrassing and salacious of positions. Having the image of my kid brother's head stuck in between a woman's thighs is something that I wish I could bleach out of my memory.

But then again, I guess it takes an animal to know one.

If I really want to know what I'm about to face, my best chance is to get it from the one brother who knows them best.

"Alejandro, can I ask you for a favor?"

"You may."

"Tell me about them. The Kellys, I mean. What are they really like?"

He stares at me for a spell, and after letting out a long exhale, he gives me a clipped nod.

"Very well. Who do you want to learn about first? Your betrothed, I presume?"

"Yes."

"Hmm. Tiernan Kelly is tricky to pin down. Niall, his father, stepped down as the boss of the Irish mob five years ago and gave Tiernan the keys to the kingdom when he was only twenty-five. Not many men would relinquish their hold on their empire and give it to their son at such an early age, but Tiernan was a soldier very early on and therefore ready to take over the reins from his father. I heard he got his first kill in at only fifteen years old and didn't so much as break a sweat. In his teens, I know he was hot-tempered, and he may very well still be like that today, but not when it comes to business. He's shrewd. Intelligent. Calculating. That's one thing you must know about the Kellys. They might act laid back, humble in their origins, but it's a façade. They're animals, Rosa. Filthy, unscrupulous, vicious animals. Niall Kelly and his men have put more of our brethren in the grave than any other family. And when it comes to us, their lot aren't to be messed with."

"Us? You mean the cartel?"

"Precisely. They hate our way of life. If it wasn't for this peace treaty, I have no doubt that they would have continued their crusade against our family and killed everyone we have ever cared about. Including you, dear Rosa. They would have waited until you were sound asleep, warm in your bed, feeling safe and secure, and then they would have blown the whole house up, with you in it. There wouldn't be anything left of you. We wouldn't even be able to give you a proper burial."

I swallow dryly, my pulse racing at the horrid image Alejandro planted in my head.

"Is he the only one I have to worry about?" I croak, my throat feeling dry as the Sahara.

"No. Tiernan has a brother and cousin he is tied to. They are the only two men he actually trusts and confides in. He never goes anywhere without them. Not only are they his muscle when he doesn't want to get his hands dirty, but they are also his sounding board to bounce ideas off of."

"Okay, tell me more about them. Start with the brother," I plead eagerly, needing to know as much information as I can about the Kelly clan.

"Shay Kelly is two years younger than you. Twenty-five, if I recall correctly. But don't let his youth fool you, he's just as lethal as Tiernan. He will put on an alluring smile, sweet talk you into his confidence, and then cut your throat when your back is turned. With him, you never see it coming. His kills sure didn't. He's the Irish mob's favorite assassin. And if the rumors are true, he's never missed a target."

Gulp.

"I'm afraid to ask about Colin, now." I smile, disheartened.

"You should be because compared to Colin, Shay is a pussycat. Stay away from that one if you can."

"Why?" I stammer, hating the fear that is coursing through my veins.

"He's not much for words, but I know he's the one responsible for most of the bombings to our East Coast warehouses. He's a genius at making bombs and has a weird fetish for fire and dynamite. Rumor has it, he likes to set his enemies on fire just to watch the skin peel off their bones. If you can, keep away from that sick fuck. I'd sleep easier at night if you did."

So, would I.

"Is that it? Is that all of the family?" I ask, worried that my brother is keeping the identity of another monster close to his vest.

"Aside from their younger sister, who is probably on her way to Vegas to be married off herself, there was another brother. He died a while back and never had a role in the war, so I don't know much about him. I know they have a bunch of uncles and cousins, but none that bear mentioning. Besides, who has time to list them all? They take their Catholic upbringing very seriously, so they breed like wild rabbits, popping out kids left and right. And they make sure that everyone in their family pulls their own weight if they are to have their hand in the pot. To society, the Kelly family name is synonymous with being moguls of construction and real estate and beloved philanthropists. Boston loves them. The city has put them up on a pedestal like Irish saints. They turn a blind eye to their criminal activities and reap the rewards of their generosity. So don't be surprised if you don't find many happy faces on your wedding day tomorrow."

"What do you mean?" I ask, confused.

"I mean, they would have preferred to keep their Irish blood clean and not have it polluted with ours, Rosa. That's what I mean. Haven't you been paying attention? They hate us. They spit at the mere mention of the Hernandez name."

"So, you're saying they hate me? Even if we never met before, they still hate me. Is that it?"

My brother lets out another long sigh and nods his head.

"*Sí.*"

I shake my head, wondering how my father could willingly send me to the wolves like this.

How could you, Alejandro?

Knowing what you know, why didn't you fight to keep me away?

To keep me safe from such a cruel fate?

"If all you say is true, then you might as well slit my throat now and end my misery, *hermano*. How am I expected to ensure the lineage with such a family?" I retort instead of uttering what really pains my soul.

Alejandro cups my cheeks in his palms and brings me closer to him.

"But Rosa, don't you see? That's precisely what you must do. No one expects you to be of any influence on the Kellys, but both they and Miguel will expect a grandchild. And soon."

I hear the warning in his tone well enough. If I don't bear Tiernan sons, then I'll bring shame to my family. And between the Kellys' blatant animosity towards me and my father's wrath, I don't know which one I should fear most if I don't follow through. Isn't that the whole basis for why I'm marrying this stranger, after all? To ensure the bloodlines are mixed to guarantee loyalty amongst our two families?

With all the bravery I can muster, I sit up straighter and pull back from my brother's hands, never wavering my gaze from his.

"I know what is expected of me, Alejandro. I was born a woman. I know what my role is."

My brother sits back in his chair, his expression morphing into a blank canvas, devoid of all feeling.

"We all have our crosses to bear. Gender has nothing to do with it."

When the stewardess brings him back his scotch, he drinks it all in one quick gulp.

"I'm going to freshen up before we land. I suggest you do the same."

He then gets up from his seat and goes to the back of the plane, locking himself in the private bedroom.

With my head leaned against the headrest, I ponder all the ways that my life could have been different. I still remember the night Miguel announced I was promised to the Kellys. That night, I packed everything that meant something to me into a duffle bag, with the full intention of running away from such a fate. I would have gotten away with it, too, if Francesco hadn't come to my bedroom to check up on me to see how I was handling the news of my engagement. Unfortunately for me, my baby brother took one look at the bag I was packing and knew exactly what I was about to do.

"He'll find you. No matter where you hide, he'll always find you."

"I doubt that Tiernan Kelly would mourn the loss of his bride-to-be."

"I wasn't talking about him. I was talking about our father."

That was all it took to keep me obedient.

Miguel Hernandez would scour the ends of the earth to find me. And when he did, he would beat me to within an inch of my life. But he wouldn't kill me. I'm too precious of a commodity for that. No. Once I was nicely healed, he would ship me off to Boston to make sure the treaty went through with the other families.

My death would not be my penance. But neither would my bruised body. The real punishment would be that he would kill the only person I truly ever loved—the only person my father would suspect knew about my plans of escaping all along.

He'd kill my baby brother.

He'd kill Francesco.

Francesco's life would be forfeited for my disrespect and

dishonor. Not only would my marriage still go forth, but I would have his death on my conscience. I would have to live out my days knowing that because of my decision to flee, my beloved brother paid my debt with his life. I would never be able to live with myself if that happened.

Never.

So like the submissive daughter my father expected me to be, I accepted my fate. I'd accept it all if I could spare my brothers any pain. Even Alejandro and Javier.

Too bad I was raised Catholic. At times like these, I wish I practiced another faith. If I had been born into the Hindu, Buddhist, or even Sikh beliefs, maybe I could believe that this was not the only life afforded me. I could take comfort in knowing that all I had to do was endure the next sixty-odd years, knowing that on my deathbed, I'd finally be free.

I'd finally live a life I could find joy in.

But in my faith, we only have this one life to live. After that, we can either expect our deeds to send us to St. Peter's pearly white gates or to the sulfur-smelling fiery pits of hell. I've made my peace with that, too. Either one is preferable to the purgatory I've lived so far.

With those thoughts in mind, I close my eyes and send a silent prayer to the virgin mother.

"*Virgen de Guadalupe, Te lo ruego*. Please let me do my duty with ease and grace. Let the man who I'm to marry be patient, if not kind. Let him see my struggle as his own and let him be merciful. Should he need to discipline me in any fashion, let me be brave enough to take my punishment with dignity. And most of all, let my womb bear healthy sons. If I'm to be deprived of love, let me at least know the joy of motherhood. In them, I can seek comfort when life is cruel and hard. *Por favor*, give me the poise to bring my husband pride and the good sense not to hinder whatever affection he may show me."

I whisper three Hail Marys after my solemn prayer before I'm interrupted by Alejandro's return.

"You're praying again," he reprimands. "No God above will aid you in your time of need. If anything should happen to you, then the only person you should be going to your knees for is your husband."

The crude statement makes me both cringe and, to my horror, blush.

"Yes, that's it, *hermana*. Please Tiernan in the bedroom and give him all the Irish babies he wants. Once he's had a few boys to ensure the bloodlines, then he'll tire of you and seek some other woman's bed. That is all you can hope for. Then you will live like a queen—because I'll make sure that he does—and he'll leave you alone, too preoccupied with business and mistresses to pay you any mind. From my calculations, all you'll have to endure is five years tops to be free of your shackles."

"Five years?" I ask, completely overwhelmed with everything he's saying.

Is it possible that I can have my freedom after all? One that isn't chained to the Irish mob?

"I see the idea pleases you." My brother smirks.

"I never considered it to be an option."

"Well, it is, *hermana*. Do you think you can handle five years?"

"Yes." I don't even have to think about it, blurting out the word with the biggest smile on my face.

The thought that all I have to endure is five years is like someone reducing my life sentence to a misdemeanor.

"Good. Now buckle up, we're about to land. You are finally going to meet your *novio*. And remember, Rosa, what I shared with you today. Stay clear of his brother and cousin. They have your soon-to-be husband's ear and can easily sway his affections elsewhere. Until Kelly puts a baby in you, you'll want his undivided attention. Don't let anyone get in the way of your goal. Not even Tiernan."

Suddenly the idea of meeting Tiernan Kelly doesn't scare me as it once did.

In fact, my heart is now full of something I never thought I would feel again.

Hope.

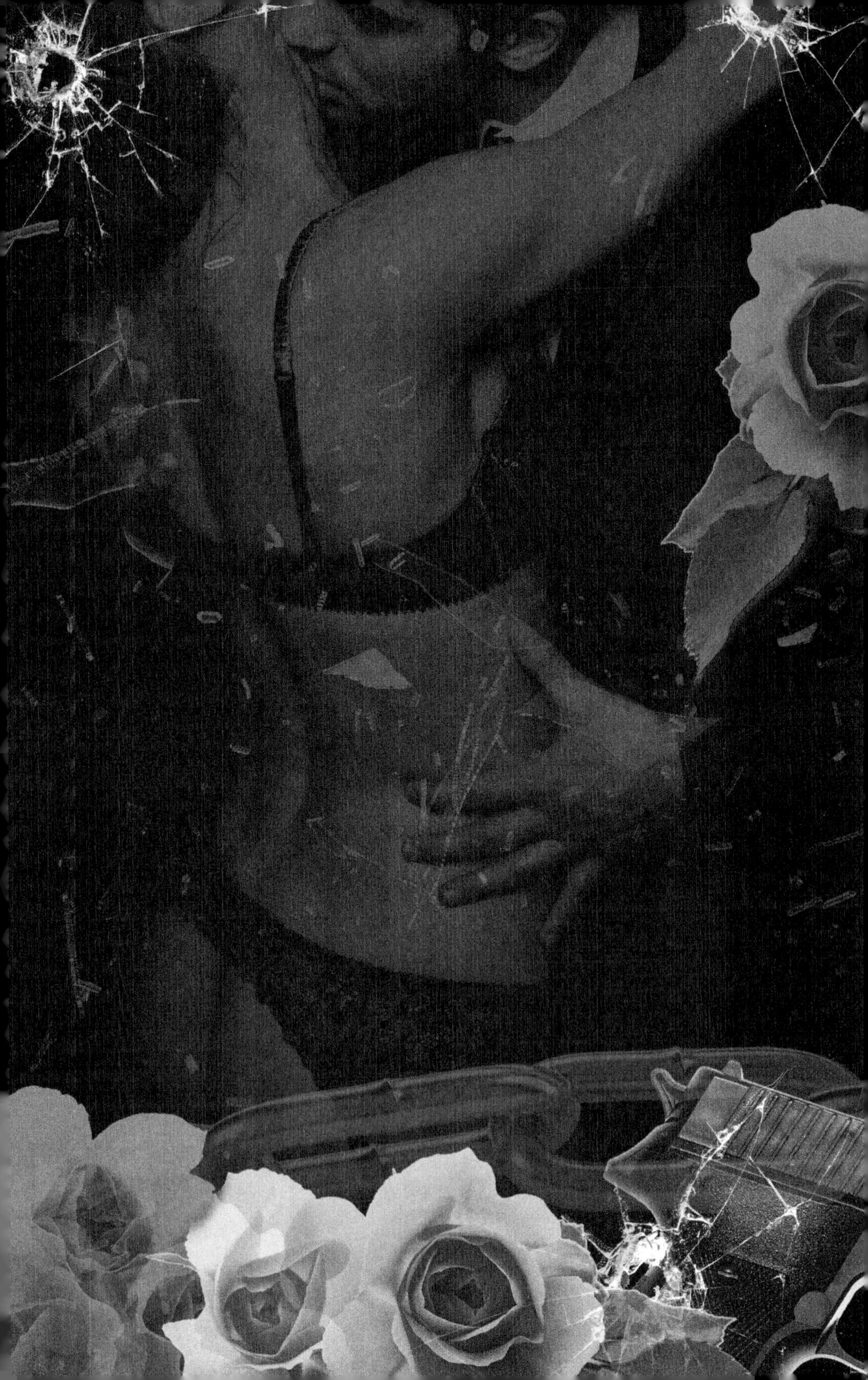

CHAPTER 3
Shay

"QUIT YOUR FUCKING MOPING, Colin. I can feel your negative energy from over here," I reprimand, shifting further away from my cousin and his bad mojo on the hood of the car.

"I don't like this. Tiernan should have been the one to be here. Not us," Colin repeats for the hundredth time this morning.

My cousin sounds like one of those one-hit wonders you hear on the radio. At first you find the tune catchy and even bop your head to the beat, but then after a while with so much damn airplay, each chord begins to grate on your nerves.

"Get over it already. He sent us to do his dirty work, and like the good little soldiers we are, that's exactly what we'll do. Think of this pickup as it being just another day on the job."

"This is different. Hernandez won't be pleased. He's going to take Tiernan's absence as disrespect."

"Fuck him if he does," I sneer at the mention of our sworn

enemy. "What would Alejandro have done in Tiernan's shoes? Pick up his fiancé from the airport, who he's never seen before I might add, or stay back home in Boston so he can properly say his goodbyes to his treasured sister? The same sister that is about to marry Bratva scum, by the way? Not necessarily Sophie's choice, now, is it, Col?"

"*You* didn't stay back," he counters sternly.

"That's because I hate fucking goodbyes," I deadpan. "Besides, if I had it my way, Iris wouldn't be going anywhere. She would stay right fucking here with her family where she belongs."

"Your father and Tiernan gave their word. There is no turning back now," Colin retorts adamantly.

"Hence why we're here. Now quit your whining and look alive. We don't want Alejandro to think we're soft."

"I still don't like it," Colin mumbles, aggravated, crossing his huge tattoo-sleeved arms across his chest.

"Yeah, what else is new? If it's not a warm wet mouth wrapped around your cock while you play with your chemistry set, there isn't much you do like," I taunt, giving him my best wolfish grin, hoping it's enough to get him out of his foul mood.

But like most days, Colin doesn't bat an eye at my light provocation. In fact, I have yet to see anything truly get under his skin. I should know, since throughout the years I've known him, I've tried my best to get a rise out of my cousin with very little success.

Athair says that's how they make them back in Ireland—brooding, big, and mean. Colin fits that to a T, alright. Born and bred in Dublin, Colin has all the traits that my father holds in the greatest esteem. *Athair's* fondness for my cousin has only grown since his folks died over a decade ago in the Mafia Wars back in the old country, requiring him to be shipped stateside to live with us. He's like a brother to me and Tiernan, albeit a taciturn one. I love the bastard, even if our personalities are like oil and water.

While Colin prefers to keep his scowl in place at every turn, solidifying his serious prickly temperament, I've always found humor to be a better bedfellow. Our way of life is somber enough to take so seriously. If you can't have a couple of laughs, then what's the point?

'Don't let your mouth write cheques your ass can't cash, Shay,' Athair is fond of warning me when he thinks I've stepped over the line with my big mouth.

It's funny really.

I remember a time where he used to say the same thing to Tiernan growing up. But that all stopped ten years ago when my older brother's fate was sealed in a twisted, almost Shakespearian-like fashion.

Iris', too.

Fuck.

Just thinking about how easily *Athair* sold her to the Bratva still sets my teeth on edge. If I had it my way, I'd rather wage war with all these fuckers than have any of us marry into their families.

But then again, I'm not the boss, nor will I ever be if I can help it.

I'll do everything in my power to make sure that Tiernan lives a good and long goddamn life if it ensures that I'll never wear the heavy crown that's currently placed on his head. Being the boss of the Irish mob comes with too many sacrifices. Too many strings being pulled in all directions, and I've never liked being anyone's puppet. It takes a level head and a cold heart to do what needs to be done, and though life has been hard on all of us, my heart still beats and refuses to be tamed.

"Looks like it's showtime," I announce, my gaze landing on the tarmac and on the private jet that is quickly traveling down it. "That must be them."

Colin nods in reply.

"Shit. I pity my fucking brother. To have to marry a Hernandez, of all people, feels like someone is stabbing a blade into my heart. I can only imagine how he must be feeling right about now."

"He's the boss. He doesn't have to feel."

I lean off the hood of the car so I can stand up straight and stare at my cousin.

"If I didn't see with my own two eyes that you bleed red just like the rest of us, Colin, I would swear you're a fucking robot. Of course, Tiernan feels. Just because he's the boss, as you put it, doesn't mean he can switch off his feelings just by snapping his fingers. We are human, you know?"

Colin refuses to acknowledge me, his focus still directed to the now landed plane behind me.

"I bet you feel shit, too, don't you, Mr. Roboto?" The corner of my lip tugs upwards. "Yeah, I bet under all that hard demeanor there is just a teddy bear dying to get out. I bet when no one is looking you're the type of guy that watches Hallmark movies with some red wine and a box of tissues."

When he growls under his breath, my head falls back in a cackle.

"You are too fucking easy to wind up, *chol ceathar*," I joke, even though my remark couldn't be further from the truth.

"Don't say shit like that in front of Alejandro," he warns.

"Please." I roll my eyes. "I know how to deal with that fucker."

"Hope that's true because he's heading this way."

I turn around to face one of our greatest enemies, ready to wind him up just as I successfully did with Colin, only to have the wind taken out of my sails. All the air in my lungs vanishes as I watch Alejandro and the infamous Rosa Hernandez walk in our direction.

Alejandro is in his usual business attire, looking like a million bucks. No shock there, since the fucker has more money to spend than most. It's the creature walking at his side that really takes my breath away. Long brown hair flows in the wind over her shoulders making way for all of us to see her perfectly-sculpted face. I've never been one to admire works of art, but Rosa's face has all the distinctions of a great masterpiece. Cupid bow lips centered low on a heart-shaped face, with high cheekbones and eyelashes that go on for days. Wearing a white full-length coat and killer heels to match, I doubt her intention was to summon images of said heels digging themselves into my back when she put them on this morning, but here we are.

Huh.

Here I was thinking my eldest brother was about to marry a girl version of Alejandro, who is one scary-looking, ugly motherfucker, when in reality Tiernan is going to walk down the aisle with the most exquisite woman I have ever set eyes on.

Suddenly my brother's fate doesn't seem too bad to me.

Some fuckers have all the luck.

"Fuck me," I finally vocalize my lascivious astonishment. "Is that Alejandro's sister? Jesus, Mary, and Joseph. Do you know if he has any more stashed away?"

I'm about to clean the drool from the corners of my mouth with my sleeve, when Colin slaps me across the back of my head.

"The fuck was that for?!" I shout.

"For eye-fucking your brother's wife, asshole."

"She's not married to him yet." I wiggle my brows, jutting my tongue out as I walk backwards in the direction of the Hernandez siblings.

Colin's scowl is deeply engrained on his face as I turn around and meet the new addition to the Kelly family, as well as her prick of a brother.

"Kelly," Alejandro utters in greeting, looking none too pleased to see me here.

"Long time no see, Hernandez," I counter with a smug smile.

"Not long enough, I'm afraid," he retorts, his gaze falling behind me and onto my undoubtedly brooding cousin.

"Aw, don't be like that. We're family now."

"Not yet we're not. Where is Tiernan?"

"Tied up on business," Colin explains, now beside me, his frown still in place.

"I see," Alejandro replies at the vague excuse.

"We have express orders to take you to him later today," Colin explains all business-like.

"Good. There is much we still need to discuss before the wedding tomorrow."

My eyes fall on the bride herself, head held unapologetically high while the grown-ups talk.

"Aren't you going to introduce us?"

Reluctantly, Alejandro nods at me before making the introductions.

"This is my sister, Rosa. Rosa, this is Shay Kelly, your soon-to-be brother-in-law and this is Colin Kelly, your fiancé's right hand."

"Actually, I'm Tiernan's right hand. Colin is his left," I joke, picking her hand up and placing a kiss on her knuckles.

Rosa pulls her hand away before my lips have had time to taste her warm olive-tone skin, but doesn't reprimand me for my forwardness.

"A man that needs two extra hands to do his business doesn't seem like much of one," Alejandro chimes in, not hiding his resentment at my brother not showing up to greet him here.

"Oh, I wouldn't say that. There is a lot more that a man can do when he has two sets of extra hands. All you need is a little imagination." I arch a suggestive brow.

"Do you always speak this way in front of women you've just met?" Alejandro scolds, displeased with my wayward tongue.

"Most of them appreciate my honesty."

"Rosa isn't like most women."

"I can tell that just by looking at her." I lick my lips, staring at the woman who is trying very hard not to fidget under my scrutinizing gaze.

"Don't look too hard, Shay. Especially when the prize has been bought and paid for already by another," Alejandro warns.

"Is that how you see your sister? As a prize?"

"She's worth more than your pockets can afford. I can tell you that much."

"I've got deep pockets."

"Not deep enough."

"You wound me." I feign hurt by placing a hand to my chest.

"Trust me, Shay. If I wanted to wound you, it wouldn't be with words," he threatens with a menacing glower.

"Enough," Colin interrupts, annoyed. "We've been out in the open for too long as it is. I say we get into the car and return to Back Bay."

"Why the rush? I doubt anyone in their right mind would use this opportunity to take us out in the middle of a Hanscom Field landing strip, of all places. Besides, isn't Rosa being here supposed to be the end of the Mafia Wars?" I mock, salaciously eyeing the woman in question, while making sure Alejandro sees me doing it.

"The wars aren't over yet," he spits out, nostrils flaring.

All the fucker needs is another little push to break that cold demeanor of his.

How fun.

"I agree with... Colin, is it?" Rosa says at last, her melodic voice doing something to my insides I didn't expect, stealing away any desire to fuck with her brother a little more just so I can hear her speak again. "We've had a long flight, and I'd like to freshen up and rest if that is at all possible."

"Follow me," Colin replies with a staunch no-nonsense tone.

Without added encouragement, she follows my cousin to the car, leaving me and Alejandro to trail behind them.

"She's very well behaved, I give you that." I smirk while staring at her pear-shaped ass.

I wish I could say it is more for her brother's benefit than it is for mine, but with each sway of the hip, I almost forget that my blatant ogling of my soon-to-be sister-in-law is only to piss Alejandro off.

"Rosa is a lady and should be treated as such," he forewarns.

"A lady, you say?" I chuckle at the word.

"Yes."

"There's no such thing."

"Maybe not in the sewer you were brought up in."

"Ouch, Alejandro. Again, is that any way to talk to family?"

"You and I both know that it's going to take more than your brother marrying my sister to make us family."

"If that's true, then why bring her here?"

"Because just like Tiernan, I'm a man of my word."

"Careful there, Alejandro. That remark could almost be misconstrued as a compliment."

He scoffs in disdain and hurries his step to get into the backseat of the car with his sister and away from me. I chuckle, pleased that I've rattled his cage a bit, and take my seat beside an impatient Colin.

"Knock it off and stop acting the maggot," Colin mutters under his breath, side-eyeing me as he drives the car away from the airport and back to Boston.

"Where's the fun in that?" I smile widely.

"Feckin' eejit," he groans low enough for the two Hernandez siblings sitting in the back not to overhear.

My smile only widens, content that not only have I irked Alejandro to no end, but I've pissed off my cousin, too. Still, the one I don't seem to be making any impression on is the tight-lipped woman in the backseat that is currently staring out the window, watching the scenery pass by.

I'm not sure what I was expecting when Tiernan ordered me to pick up his bride this morning, but this wasn't it. I've never envied my brother. Not once have I ever coveted his life in any way. While Tiernan is ruled by all the restrictions of duty, I've been allowed to live free from such chains.

But one look at Rosa has me second-guessing if Tiernan isn't the one who lucked out.

"*Cabrón*," Alejandro mutters. "The asshole will hear from me. He should have been here to greet you, not send his dogs to do it," he adds in Spanish to his sister.

"It's quite alright, brother. I'm not bothered. The less contact I have with him, the better," she retorts in the same dialect, thinking that stating her musings in her native tongue will keep her secrets safe from us.

"You'll have to have contact with him sooner or later. Successful marriages aren't exactly born from absence," her brother nags.

"Is that your hope for me? That I have a successful marriage?"

"Men like me don't hope."

I scoff loudly, interrupting their private tête-à-tête.

"Is there something you wish to say, Kelly?" Alejandro asks with a bite to his words.

"No. Just admiring your accent. *Mi acento no es tan bonito.*"

Alejandro's face grows red with fury when he realizes I must have understood his every word, but it's the little tug of amusement playing on Rosa's lips that really has me smiling.

"I'm not just a pretty face, Alejandro. *Scommetto ce l'hai piccolo.* Or if Italian isn't to your liking, maybe Russian is. *Nyet? Togda potseluy menya v zadnitsu, mudak.*"

"Are those the only languages you know?" Rosa asks curiously before her brother has a chance to talk, completely unaware I just told Alejandro he has a small dick in one language and to kiss my ass in another.

"Depends on the enemy. Pays me well to know what people are saying about us."

"I'll take that into account in the future," Alejandro spews, unimpressed.

When Colin clears his throat, his nonverbal way of telling me to knock it off, Rosa's undivided attention falls from me to my cousin in the driver's seat instead.

"Does every member in the Kelly clan have such linguistic versatility?" She directs the question at my cousin.

"Hell no. Colin barely speaks English. Isn't that right?"

"*Briseadh agus brú ar do chnámha,*" he curses me in Gaelic.

Rosa's gaze remains fixed on the rearview mirror, taking inventory of my cousin's irate demeanor.

It's only when she takes longer than considered dignified, staring at another man that isn't her fiancé, that I realize it's Colin's marred, burnt features on the left side of his face and neck that have caught her interest.

Sometimes I forget that my cousin isn't the prettiest thing to look at. Some women have too much of a frail stomach to even utter a *dia dhuit* when in his presence, while others like to add a bit of scary to their bedroom escapades and are all too eager to pull him by the hand into a dark corner just so they can jump on his face.

I wonder which end of the stick Rosa falls onto.

When she sees that I've caught her in the act, she instantly turns her face to the window once more, but not before I catch a glimpse of her crimson cheeks, almost as red as Colin's hair. I'm not sure if it's my overprotectiveness of my cousin that has me sitting up straighter in my seat and nipping our conversation in the bud, or if I don't want to add further to her embarrassment by calling her out.

Whatever the reason, all I know is that Colin was right after all.

This wasn't just your ordinary pickup.

Something tells me that after today, life as we know it will never be the same again.

CHAPTER 4
Colin

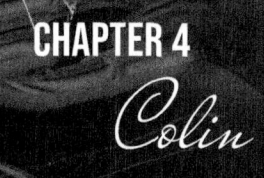

I KEEP my back flush against a pillar, vigilantly watching both entryways into the strip club. Even with my earpiece in and the men outside giving me the all-clear, I remain in my highly alert state.

Uncle Niall is keen on reminding me that I should relax more now that Tiernan is about to tie the knot, but old habits die hard. If one of our enemies decides to pull out of the treaty at the last minute, then this fucking bachelor party is the perfect opportunity to take us all out in one fell swoop.

Shay was thinking with his dick when he decided to throw his brother this fucking party on the night before his wedding. Not that it surprises me that Shay would pull this sort of stunt. What shocks the hell out of me is that Tiernan went for it.

But as my gaze lands on the Hernandez bastard in our midst and I watch him silently fume in his seat as our men enjoy a few lap dances from The Pit's finest talent, I'm inclined to think Tiernan only gave the thumbs up to this bachelor party just to get on Alejandro's last nerve.

Still, I would have preferred he'd come up with a different approach to fuck with his new brother-in-law than come to this crowded cesspool of a strip club. Anyone could easily come in undetected and hide a few well-placed bombs to blow us all to smithereens. At least that's what I would have done to my enemies if given the chance.

Thankfully, I had ample time to come to The Pit earlier and scope the place out while Tiernan and Alejandro were conducting business back at his office downtown. One can't be too careful, even if the consensus is that the Mafia Wars will be a thing of the past after tomorrow.

Wars don't usually end with wedding receptions.

At least I've never seen it happen in my lifetime.

From the second-story balcony, I continue to stand guard as I watch most of our soldiers have a grand old time throwing dollar bills onto the stage, while the strippers shake their asses at them like they are in a bad rap video. Shay is making his rounds downstairs, ensuring that everyone is enjoying themselves, while Tiernan, Alejandro, and I sit in our VIP section, watching it all go down. The music is loud and obnoxious to my ears, as the half-naked girls continue to do their job at getting as much money out of our men's pockets as they can. I guess I should be thankful that the girls handpicked to entertain us upstairs are keeping their dancing to the pole at the corner of the room, not brave enough to come to our table unless called upon.

All but one, that is.

From my peripheral, I watch one of the dancers swing her hips our way. I hold in a sardonic chuckle when she decides to plop her ass onto Alejandro's lap of all people, thinking she will win brownie points with Tiernan if she does a good job in seducing his out-of-town guest. She has barely even touched him when Alejandro pushes her away, resulting in the striper's ass hitting the grimy floor with a loud thud while the cartel prince looks down at her with a disgusted expression on his face at her audacity to come near him.

"Excuse me. I'm going outside to make a call," he utters before getting up from his seat, not even bothering to help the girl up from her knees, leaving her to crawl back to her pole as fast as she can, if she knows what's good for her.

"You want me to follow him?" I ask, feeling uneasy that one of our greatest enemies is making a quick getaway.

"The men outside have eyes on him, so no need," Tiernan retorts, nursing his whiskey, his facial features finally showing signs of his reluctance at being here.

We both stay silent, watching our surroundings, but I can tell that tonight he's uncharacteristically agitated.

And if I'm honest, so am I.

"Little odd Alejandro didn't bring his entourage with him," I state, pointing out what has been plaguing my mind since we picked him and his sister up at the airport.

"He's testing me," Tiernan explains evenly.

"By making himself vulnerable?" I counter in confusion.

"That's the thing. He shouldn't be vulnerable in Boston. By

leaving his goons back in Mexico and coming alone, he's making a statement. That this town is now as much his as it is mine."

My hands ball into fists at the remark.

"Don't let him see you look so angry, Colin. It will only amuse him," Tiernan adds before taking a sip of his drink. "Besides, he didn't do anything that I wouldn't have done if the roles were reversed. This treaty is meant to protect us all, so swallow your pride and let the asshole think whatever he wants. We know better."

"If you say so, boss."

"I do."

I square my shoulders and look straight ahead, trying my best to relax my features so I don't show how much I hate the fact we have to play host to this asshole. It's a travesty we have to endure his presence and play nice with his family in the first place.

"You know that if you wanted, you could enjoy yourself tonight. I wouldn't mind," Tiernan says, trying to get my mind off the desire to kill the Hernandez prick on the spot.

"I'd rather stand guard if it's all the same to you, boss."

"Are you sure? The Pit went all out tonight. Might as well take advantage of it and pick a girl or two to entertain yourself with."

"Don't need any entertaining, boss. I'm fine right here."

He lets out a strained chuckle under his breath.

"Shay is sure of a different mindset. I'd swear he was the one getting married tomorrow. Trying to sow as many oats as he can before the clock runs out on him."

My eyes land on my younger cousin, and I see him laughing away with some of our soldiers, drinking his fill while two dancers rub themselves up against his sides. Sometimes I envy his carefree nature. When people look at Shay, they don't see the marks of a killer. The same can't be said about me, though. One look at me, and everyone knows what kind of evil lies underneath. It's marked all over my face as a reminder.

"Shay was never one to turn down a party. I'm not as inclined."

"No. Neither am I, I'm afraid. Those days are over for me."

My forehead wrinkles at the melancholy in his voice. But then again, I wasn't the one who just shipped my baby sister on a plane to be married to Bratva pigs, so I sympathize with his turmoil.

"Iris is tougher than she looks. The Russians are no match for her," I announce, knowing that's where his mind is tonight.

"I hope you're right. I've got this bad feeling that won't go away," he says, rubbing at his chest to drive the point home.

"Maybe what you're feeling is just wedding jitters."

He turns to me with his brows arched up high to his forehead.

"Did you just make a joke, Col?" He smiles, amused.

"Humor was never my forte, boss."

"It sure sounded that way to me just now." He laughs, his broad frame relaxing a tad, his gaze falling once again downstairs where the action is.

There is a pregnant pause between us until Tiernan decides to break it with his own curiosity.

"Is it true what Shay said earlier today? That my bride is a right little dinger?"

"He shouldn't say such things to you." I scowl.

"Please. We both know that Shay could never hold his tongue.

Especially when it comes to pretty girls. I just want your impression of her to see if he's pulling my chain."

"Shay isn't lying. The lass is very beautiful."

"Beautiful, huh? Not exactly a word I'd ever think I'd hear come out of your mouth."

"Doesn't make it any less true. But she'll never fit in with us," I state poignantly.

"How so?"

"She's… well, boss, she's not like the women you usually surround yourself with."

"You mean she's not a whore. No surprise there." He scoffs, taking another pull of his drink.

"No, boss. It's more than that. She's…" I struggle to find a word that does justice to the woman I met this morning. "Sophisticated."

"As opposed to the illiterate brutes we are? Is that what you're saying?" He levels me with a stare.

"I've spoken out of turn."

"You've hardly spoken at all. Right now, all that I know of my bride is my brother's pornographic remarks of what a knockout she is and you telling me that she's a stuck-up snob."

"I didn't say that," I quickly rectify. "I don't think she looks down on us. I just think she has been… sheltered. She looks like someone who has spent most of childhood with her nose inside a book rather than being tainted by her upbringing."

"I very much doubt she isn't aware of how her father paid for such books." He scoffs again, this time with a repulsed edge to his voice.

"That's not what I meant either."

"Then what is it then? Is she a sexpot like Shay proclaimed, or is she a shy, virginal bookworm?"

"No, not that." *Fuck, why can't I find the right words?* "Not shy. Just… cautious."

"Cautious is good. I can deal with that. And she should be."

A frown crests my lips, uncomfortable with how my cousin was able to coax out of me my own impression of his future wife.

Shay wasn't bullshitting when he told Tiernan that Rosa was stunning to look at. I, for one, have never seen her equal. However, I've always known that true beauty is never skin deep. There was something in her gaze that told me she was so much more than the designer clothes she was wearing, or the immaculate hair and makeup. Like the true cartel princess that she is, I'm sure she's been used to the high-life for most of her life, but it was the elegant poised way she conducted herself in front of us that gave me pause. Rosa didn't seem fearful about meeting Shay and me, which is saying something since who knows what lies her brother fed her about us. Nothing good, that much I know.

However, what bothered me most about Rosa was that there was resolve in her spine. Almost like she was unbothered by her fate since she had forged a plan on how to see it through.

And a woman with a plan is never a good thing.

If I thought her a threat to Tiernan's life, I would have let Shay slit her throat right there and then. But I didn't get that feeling from her, though. Her whole demeanor screamed determination of a different variety, not murder, hence why she's still breathing.

When Alejandro returns, I go instantly rigid and push all notions of his sister away from my mind.

"If it's all the same to you, I'd rather go back to the hotel and check on Rosa," he announces, pretending to flick imaginary lint off his shoulder.

"Fair enough. Colin will see you get there."

"Is this your way of telling me I need a bodyguard while I'm here?" Alejandro asks, his features a blank, unreadable canvas.

"This is my way of lending you my best man to make sure you don't get lost in my town. I would expect the same care if I ever decide to visit Mexico."

This takes Alejandro aback, inflicting a crack in his stoic demeanor.

"Do you have plans to come to Mexico in the future?" he asks, his tone both incredulous as well as suspicious.

"I don't see why not? My wife's home is my home, is it not? I'm sure, from time to time, she would want to visit her brothers and see her family."

"I have to say you've surprised me, Kelly."

"And why is that?"

"Most men wouldn't like to leave their turf to enter enemy territory willingly," Alejandro connotes plainly.

"But we're no longer enemies now, right?"

"Not after tomorrow, no."

In other words, only when Rosa officially becomes a Kelly will our feud be laid to rest.

"On that, at least, we are in agreement. Colin will show you out," Tiernan dismisses, not even bothering to look Alejandro in the eye.

I start to follow the man in question back downstairs when he surprises me by halting his step and turning around to face Tiernan once more.

"She's not like us, Kelly."

"Who isn't?"

"Rosa. She may be used to this life we lead and might even be a little bit jaded by it, thinking the way we do business is the norm, but she's held on to something that we *made men* have no room for in our lives."

"And what's that?" Tiernan retorts with practiced boredom, his gaze fixed on the stage below.

"She still sees the good in people. Even when they don't deserve it."

Tiernan shifts his attention back to the cartel prince after that loaded statement.

"Are you telling me this because you think I'll steal the noble attribute away from her?"

"I know you will," Alejandro proclaims in a somber tone. "All I ask is that you ease Rosa into her misery. Let her hold on to that pure part of her heart a little while longer, if you can."

"I'm not a monster, Alejandro," Tiernan rebukes with an offended snarl.

"We're all monsters, Kelly. I'm just alerting you to the fact that my sister is used to one breed of evil. It will take her some time to get accustomed to yours."

"Goodnight, Alejandro," Tiernan brushes off his rival, obviously having had enough of his insightful advice on his sister for one night.

Alejandro gives him a clipped nod before turning his back to leave. I follow the kingpin down the stairs, keeping my eyes glued on his retreating form. I only stop when Shay shouts out my name, loud enough to be heard over the noisy rambunctious crowd of horny drunk men.

"Go on ahead. Our men are outside, so you'll be well-protected while waiting in the car."

Alejandro doesn't so much as say a word in complaint to me, eager to escape through The Pit's doors and be done with this night.

"Tiernan's got you on babysitting duty, huh?" Shay asks when he reaches me, slurring a bit of his words, proof that he's having way more fun tonight than either his brother or I are.

"I'm supposed to take him back to his hotel," is my cold response.

"Well, that sucks ass. When will you be back?"

"I won't. Tiernan will head out in a few after we leave, so I'm just going home afterwards."

I know my older cousin well enough that The Pit isn't where he wants to spend the remaining hours of his freedom. He accomplished what he set out to do with Alejandro tonight. So as soon as we leave, so will he.

"Are you sure? I've got some party favors all lined up for us." Shay tilts his head at the two dancers that are on stage currently fucking their stripper pole while their lips are glued to each other's faces.

"Take them for yourself. I'm not in the mood tonight."

"Not in the mood? You do know it's my brother who is going to be stuck with a ball and chain tomorrow, not you? Hardly a cause to become celibate all of a sudden." He snickers mockingly.

"Just because I don't want to get my dick wet tonight doesn't mean I'm entering the priesthood."

"If you say so," he taunts. "More for me."

Instead of debating with my whoremonger of a cousin any further, I leave him be and go on with the task at hand.

When I get outside, I try to hide my surprise at seeing Alejandro sitting in the front seat of the car waiting for me. His kind is known for being chauffeured around, so him sitting shotgun is not something I'd ever consider him doing. I mask my disbelief with indifference and get behind the wheel of the car, so I can drop his ass at the hotel and be done with it. I don't bother turning the radio on or instigating mindless conversation since I know he's not one for small talk. Wasting words on me would be futile in his mind.

And if his mindset is still on the discussion he had with my cousin a few minutes ago, then he knows well enough that only Tiernan can show his sister any type of leniency. I have no influence on the matter.

However, I might have misjudged the cartel prince somewhat.

I was under the impression that Alejandro was as heartless as his father, Miguel. But the way he asked for a sliver of mercy where his sister was concerned, showed me that under his rude and cold exterior lies someone that at least cares for his family, if little else. And a man who has heard more than his share of his enemies' last muttered words, that he can still hold family as sacred, can't be too bad in my book.

I doubt my uncle and cousins will be inclined to see it that way, though.

For them, the Mexican cartel will always be a sore spot.

An enemy that callously took something precious from them.

Someone that can never be replaced.

And I fear for all her beauty and good breeding, Rosa will take the brunt of their hatred.

When we get to the hotel, I breathe easy at seeing my best four soldiers alert and guarding the penthouse doors like their lives depend on it. They all refuse to make eye contact with Alejandro when he passes them by but offer me their acknowledging nods in respectful greeting.

"The limo will pick you both up tomorrow morning at ten to drive you to the church. If you need anything before then, tell one of the guards, and they will procure whatever is necessary," I tell Alejandro at the door.

"Thank you," is his short reply.

I'm about to turn around and head out when he stops me.

"Won't you come in and have a nightcap with me? There is something I'd like to discuss with you."

My brows pull together, knowing his offer to come in isn't a polite request but a command. I refuse to be ordered around by anyone that isn't Tiernan, but I won't be the reason why this wedding starts on a sour note by offending Alejandro by turning him down.

I follow him inside and watch him take off his jacket and place it neatly on the back of one of the couches in the lavish penthouse living room. I stand rigid at the entrance of the room as he walks over to the bar in the corner. I watch him fill only one tumbler with two fingers of expensive whiskey, not even bothering to keep up pretenses by offering me a glass of my own, knowing full well I wouldn't drink it if he had.

"Let's not beat around the bush. I won't insult you by trying to persuade you to be my man on the inside. I know your loyalty to Tiernan is unshakable, and it would only make me look the fool to insinuate otherwise," he starts, before taking a sip of his drink and sitting down on a nearby settee facing me. "Please, have a seat."

"I'm fine right here."

"As you wish." He lets out an unaffected breath. "Tell me, Colin. Do you think Tiernan was being sincere when he said he'd bring Rosa home from time to time?"

"Boston is her home," I tell him without missing a beat.

"As of tomorrow, that might be true, but for tonight just indulge me and answer the question."

"If Tiernan said as much, then there is no reason to think him false."

"Hmm," he mutters, running his thumb over the edge of his glass. "My sister will be pleased. I haven't been the best brother to her, so it's not as if she will miss me much. But Rosa has always had a soft spot for our brother, Francesco, and him towards her. If they both know that they will see each other soon, then maybe I can spare them a bit of their heartache."

This is the second time tonight that he has shown concern for his siblings, and I'm not sure what I should do with this information. By doing so, he's put himself in more of a vulnerable spot than when he decided to come to Boston without his men. He must know that if we were still at war, then I'd use this information to hurt him. I'd go after his brothers and sister, torture them on camera, and send him their burnt, cut-up flesh in small packages accompanied by the videotape so he could see my handiwork in HD.

His unexpected transparency is clawing at my insides, making me wonder what his endgame is.

"He's testing me," were Tiernan's words earlier tonight, and something tells me Alejandro is doing the same to me.

Alejandro continues to stare at his tumbler in deep thought, raising my hackles.

"Is that all?" I ask after a frustratingly long bout of silence.

"Just one more question," he utters. "Will you watch out for my sister as fervently as you protect Tiernan?"

My knee-jerk reaction is to blurt out no, but by the look in his dark eyes, that is exactly the answer he expects. I take a beat and think about how Tiernan would respond.

"Rosa is to be a Kelly, and we protect our own."

"Hmm," he mumbles, unsatisfied with my reply. "A Kelly she might become, but she'll always be a Hernandez here. Much like my future bride will always be a Moretti. Some scars never heal, Colin. No matter how much we want them to."

I straighten my spine and stare him in the eye.

"Unlike you, we don't take pleasure in hurting innocent people."

"Don't you?" He cocks a brow. "Can you honestly stand

there and say that no innocent lives were lost when your family sought out to avenge your parents and siblings' deaths back in Ireland? That you didn't cheer for your enemies' demise with the full knowledge that they weren't the only ones to perish? How many bear the same scars on their frail and broken bodies that you now wield so proudly on your face as the reminder of how you were able to escape death's cold grip? Do not talk to me of innocence since there is no room for such a useless word in our world."

I swallow down my rage at him bringing back those gruesome memories that I've tried my best to lay to rest over the years. When he sees the burning fury in me, Alejandro places his glass of whiskey onto a side table and stands up. He then proceeds to eat up the distance between us, staring me dead in the eye.

"This treaty we all have sworn to uphold is to ensure that no more lives will be lost, innocent or not. But I'm not naïve in thinking that everyone will yield to it. So, I'll ask you again, Colin. Will you protect my sister from any harm? Will you ensure that she is to be given the respect and protection that is fit for her role as Tiernan's wife? Think long and hard before you answer me. I'll know if you're lying."

I do as he says and think about the implications of my answer.

If I say no, then I run the risk of him sneaking Rosa off to Mexico tonight on his private jet before she has a chance of officially becoming a Kelly. Although, by doing so, the other mob families will deem him enemy number one and won't bat an eye at waging war on the cartel. Even with all the unlimited financial resources at his disposal, Alejandro will be no match for the combined forces against him, certifying his death notice before the month's end.

But would he risk it, though?

For one woman?

For his sister?

My thoughts go back to Tiernan and how he was unable to stop thinking about Iris all night. How my cousin will always be worried about his sister and that if he had the means to do so, he would have spat on this treaty if it meant he could keep Iris safe and as far away from the Bratva as possible. If Tiernan had gone to Vegas with her, wouldn't he have tried to find someone there who he could count on to safeguard his sister's wellbeing?

Suddenly I realize that the answer to Alejandro's question can only be one.

"On my life, no one will ever hurt a hair on her head. You have my word."

"Then that is all I can ask for."

CHAPTER 5
Rosa

"STOP FIDGETING," Alejandro reprimands with a scowl.

"I'm not," I murmur in annoyance, mostly because he's right.

I *am* fidgeting.

But what does my brother expect?

He's about to lead me into a church where I'll have to vow, before God and half of the city of Boston, to love and obey a man I have never laid eyes on.

As much as I didn't want it to upset me, my fiancé not even bothering to come pick me up from the airport yesterday was a slap in the face. Tiernan made time to see my brother and go over business last night but didn't see the point of meeting his bride. If this was his not-so-subtle way of sending me the message that he didn't care about me in any way, shape, or form, I heard it loud and clear.

I'm not sure if I should be disappointed, angry, or relieved that Tiernan has so little interest in who he is about to marry. But then again, he's a man. The boss of a crime family at that. Why should I expect him to act any differently in regards to who he is about to start a life with when my own father never cared about me or my brothers? I just pray I'm not about to walk down the aisle and say I do to a man that bears any likeness to my father whatsoever. I don't care if Tiernan's life revolves around the bloodshed of mob business—it's the cruelty in his own home that I'm not thrilled to experience again.

"How do I look?" I ask, putting on a brave face, hoping the classic Vera Wang wedding dress is to my brother's liking. "Not too flashy, is it?"

"It will do. Are you ready?" Alejandro asks, his cool, stern mask perfectly in place.

Feeling defeated, I offer him a curt nod and school my facial features to the same nonchalant expression he has stitched on his face. With my spine ramrod straight and my head held high, I let Alejandro lead me out of the limo and begin to walk up the stairs towards the church's wide oak doors.

Once we reach the entrance, the wedding song immediately commences, as if anxious to announce to the world that my impending doom is on the horizon. I try my best not to look at my surroundings and just stare at the large golden cross that hangs proudly behind the priest who is about to marry me off to one of my family's greatest enemies.

I go to great lengths not to look at the groom waiting for me at the altar, though. If Tiernan isn't one bit curious about me, then why should I act like I care one iota about him?

No.

Let him know that his disinterest is mutual.

It's with this thought that my brother's words from the day before come to the forefront of my mind.

All I have to do is give the Irish king an heir, and he'll discard me like yesterday's newspaper.

To most women, that bleak thought would have them running for the hills, but to a cartel princess like me, one who has already been sold and paid for, it's the only thread of hope I have to hold on to.

Bear a child and be free.

I can do that.

I *have* to do that.

It's the only way I'll be able to survive in this foreign land filled with people who hate me just on mere principle alone.

With new resolve, my hesitant steps, leading me to a fate I never asked for, become steadier. Surer. And as the wedding guests sitting in their pews gawk and whisper while I walk down the aisle, my determination only grows.

I may not like my father, but I have his blood running through my veins, which means I can be just as calculating and manipulative. Or at least in theory, I should be. I just have to find a way to tap into these unpracticed traits if I'm to endure my hellish existence with these savages.

Unsurprisingly, Alejandro's holier than thou demeanor never falters as he leads me to the altar. When we reach our mark, he pulls me to face him one last time as a Hernandez.

"Remember what I said," he whispers in my ear, before placing a tender kiss on the top of my head, over my veil.

I nod, taking his advice and words of caution to heart before turning around and stretching my hand to the man who is about to become the instrument that decides if there will be happiness or only misery in my future.

Although I refuse to look at his face, the first thing I notice about my soon-to-be husband is that his hands are huge compared to mine. The rough calluses on them tell me that he's not afraid of a hard day's work and takes matters into his own hands should the situation call for it.

How many men has he killed with those hands, I wonder?

Or, more importantly, how many of them were my brethren?

I feel the weight of his stare on me as if reading the thoughts in my head. But like a stubborn child, I continue not to look at him, turning my full attention from his hand and on to the priest so we can get this show on the road.

I was of two minds if I should have worn the traditional veil to cover my face while getting married this morning, but now, I'm thankful I have the heavy garment to shield and protect me a little while longer, since Tiernan isn't the only one who is staring me down.

Although the air inside the church is crisp and cool, a trickle of sweat slithers down my back from the heat of everyone's eyes on us, making me feel like I'm some trapped exotic fish in a bowl for everyone to admire—or in my case, scrutinize. My entire body feels itchy and hot as the Irish priest commences his spiel about holy matrimony.

Once I've gathered my wits, the priest's words become clearer to me. I shift my fixed gaze from the cross behind him and, for the first time since I've reached the altar, stare at the priest who is about to bind me to this stranger forever.

Just like with every man I've encountered in my life, his eyes hold no warmth, no sympathy for my circumstances—even when the words he's uttering are all about the sanctity of marriage, love, and family. My stomach churns with the knowledge that even this man of the cloth looks down in disdain at me. Like I'm the enemy that dared to enter his sacred domain, a serpent that should have never crawled into his holy temple and should be cast out from paradise by force if need be.

Logic tells me that I can't fault him for his blatant dislike of me.

My family has done enough damage over the years in the U.S. to warrant such contempt. But can the Kelly family say they are clean of the same sins my family has committed in the past? Don't they also have the same blood-soaked hands? I guess it's easier for this priest to ignore their crimes when his church benefits from their generosity. I doubt the Vatican is the benefactor of all the gold and jewels encrusted on the cross I've been admiring for the past half hour.

When the priest throws me another disparaging look, my eyes narrow at him through my veil, and though it is thick enough for him not to be able to see my glower, his face still pales. He then clears his throat, momentarily forgetting his next words.

Shame should accost me now that I've made a man of God tremble from just one look, but the affliction never comes. When you are born into one of the most notorious crime families like I have been, such a sentiment holds no weight.

Almost as if the priest has had enough of prolonging this ceremony, his next words chill the base of my spine and accelerate my heartbeat.

"Have you come here to enter into marriage without coercion, freely and wholeheartedly?"

"I have," Tiernan and I reply in unison, the lie feeling bitter on the tip of my tongue.

"And are you prepared, as you follow the path of marriage, to love and honor each other for as long as you both shall live?"

"I am."

Another lie.

God, please have mercy on my soul.

"Are you prepared to accept children lovingly from God and to bring them up according to the laws of Christ and his Church?"

"I am," I'm quick to reply, knowing that bearing children is the only light at the end of this dark tunnel.

However, in my haste to respond, it takes me a few seconds to realize that the groom has yet to open his mouth. This time it's Tiernan who is on the receiving end of the priest's scornful frown.

"Are you prepared to accept children lovingly from God and to bring them up according to the laws of Christ and his Church?" the priest irksomely repeats, directing the question solely at Tiernan.

"I am," he finally concedes.

Sensing that the groom isn't as keen to be here as his steadfast demeanor might have misled us to believe, the priest dives right into the vows, before the Irish mobster's cold feet start another Mafia War in front of the parishioners in attendance.

"Do you, Tiernan Francis Kelly, take Rosa Maria Hernandez, to be your lawfully wedded wife? Do you promise to be true to her in good times and in bad, in sickness and in health? And will you love and honor her for all the days of your life?"

You can hear a pin drop in the church, everyone holding their breath, thinking the mighty mob boss will back out at the last moment.

But I know he won't.

Even if he's reluctant to marry me, his honor in keeping his father's vow to the other families prevents him from turning back now.

"I do." Unlike his rough hand, his voice comes out smooth like expensive velvet.

"And do you, Rosa Maria Hernandez, take Tiernan Francis Kelly, to be your lawfully wedded husband? Do you promise to be true to him in good times and in bad, in sickness and in health? And will you love, honor, and obey him for all the days of your life?"

"I do," I reply, grateful that my voice is just as strong as Tiernan's was.

"Do you have the rings?" the priest asks, his full attention on the man standing beside me.

Tiernan retrieves a simple gold band from his pocket and pulls my clammy hand in his, before the priest instructs him to say the words that will forever bind us to one another.

"Rosa, receive this ring as a sign of my love and fidelity, in the name of the Father, and of the Son, and of the Holy Spirit."

I swallow dryly when it's my turn to reciprocate the vow.

"Tiernan, receive this ring as a sign of my love and fidelity, in the name of the Father, and of the Son, and of the Holy Spirit."

It takes everything in me not to stare at my wedding ring and curse the damn thing.

"To make your relationship work will take love," the priest commences, knowing full well his words of love will fall on deaf ears. "This is the core of your marriage and why you are here. It will take trust to know that in your hearts, you truly want what is best for each other. It will take dedication to stay open to one another and to learn and grow together. It will take faith to go forward together, without knowing exactly what the future brings. And it will take commitment to hold true to the journey you both have pledged here today."

I'm not sure if I should laugh or weep at the beautifully spoken sentiment, so instead, I just stand there and count down the seconds until this charade is officially over.

"My dear friends, let us turn to the Lord and pray that he will bless this couple that has united in holy matrimony today. Father, you have made the union of husband and wife so holy as it symbolizes the marriage of two humans through Christ to God. Look with love upon this couple and fill them both with love for each other, both honoring and respecting each other, and always seeing their love as a gift to be treasured. May the commitment which they are making be sacred, not only for today, but for the rest of their lives. We ask this blessing for them in the name of the Father, the Son, and the Holy Spirit," the priest ends his futile rant by making the sign of the cross on us both. "By the power vested in me by God and the Holy Mother Church, I pronounce you wife and husband. Those who God has joined together, let no man put asunder. You may now kiss the bride."

On a somber sigh, I turn to face my newly-wed husband so that he can lift my veil and kiss me to seal this twisted pact with the devil in God's house. However, I'm at a loss when he takes longer to do it. I'm about to turn around to look at my brother for directions, when Tiernan stops me from moving an inch by grabbing hold of my hands in his. My heart does the unthinkable and flips of its own accord at the tenderness of his grip. I lick my dry lips and patiently wait while he lets go of my hands in favor of pulling back my veil. And as my veil lifts higher, so does my vision of him become clearer.

And what a vision it is.

The man is exquisite.

His hands now look tiny compared to the larger-than-life persona that stands before me. In all black, from top to bottom, he looks like Hades himself. Unfortunately for me, this Greek tragedy won't allow me to return home come springtime. I'm to be his captive all year round.

My surprise at how handsome he is must amuse him because there is a little tug on his lips, a smirk at my stunned state. And what a pair of lips this man has. Full and perfectly drawn, like two soft pillows you would like nothing more than to lie your head on. With a strong, masculine square jaw and defined cheekbones, he has all the traits of a living, breathing Irish god. As my gaze continues to travel up his face, my chest tightens when I finally get a good look at his eyes. An unfamiliar warmth begins to trickle down my spine as I become mesmerized by them. One blue eye and one green eye stare back at me with the same unrestrained curiosity, making my cheeks flush crimson.

My lips part to say something, anything that will give me back the upper hand, but it all dissipates when Tiernan's hand softly cups my left cheek and brings my lips to touch his. Without my consent, my lids close shut and I marvel how a man who has been groomed to take lives can breathe life into me with such soft, demanding lips. It's only when my hand finds purchase on his chest to steady the unstable ground at my feet that Tiernan's mouth pulls away from mine, leaving me oddly destitute and wanting.

I'm brought back to reality when loud cheers and applause break out, reminding me that the first time I ever set eyes on my husband—the first time he kissed me—was witnessed by a large audience of strangers.

I swallow my embarrassment down and take a step back to gather my composure. Tiernan offers me his arm, the little smug smile on his lips no longer visible; in its place is a no-nonsense expression. I take his lead and link my arm through his, making sure my own facial features have turned to stone. As we take our first steps as husband and wife, I can't shake the ominous feeling that this man will be my ruin in more ways than one.

My lips still burn from his kiss, and I wonder if the people standing at their pews can see the imprint he left on them.

Inwardly, I curse my inexperience when it comes to the opposite sex. If I had spent my youth kissing a bunch of frogs, then when the Irish king laid a kiss on my lips, it wouldn't have left such an impression on me.

Unfortunately, not many men were brave enough to kiss a

cartel princess already promised to the Irish mob boss. I can count on one hand how many times I've kissed someone. I'm sure my husband hasn't suffered the same affliction.

Husband.

The word lies heavy on my tongue.

More like a jailer.

Imprisoned to a life so far from the reality I've experienced.

My new home is cold and grey compared to the warmth Mexico provided. Even the air feels different here. Arctic. Much like the man leading me out of the church, I presume.

The limo I arrived in waits at the curb, and like the gentleman he's not, Tiernan makes no move to open the door for me, but waits for the chauffeur to do it for him. My cheeks blaze in resentment as our wedding party witnesses the subtle insult, resulting in little snickers of amusement at my expense.

"*Gracias,*" I thank the driver, keeping my wide smile front and center as he ushers and helps me into the backseat.

The minute I'm inside, my smile drops. I turn my head towards the window, not wanting to see the faces of our guests, much less the man I just married. The car door slams a few seconds later, resulting in Tiernan's looming presence eating up the oxygen in the small confines. I shift closer to the window as he gives a little knock on the partition, his way of telling the driver to head to our reception.

I count the beats of my heart, willing it to slow down, and quell my unexpected rising temper. Compared to my brothers, I've never really been known to have a foul temper to speak of. Rationally, I shouldn't even be mad at Tiernan for the minor snub. Maybe the real reason I'm aggravated is that in the few minutes I've known him, he has been able to stir up unfamiliar feelings in me that I'm not too comfortable with.

Resentment.

Anger.

Curiosity.

And dare I say it… even lust.

When the car starts, I push all those idiotic notions away and keep my gaze on the passing cold buildings on the sidewalk. Grey. Lifeless. Unbecoming. My gut twists, yearning to see some warmth in the architecture passing by.

'It's an omen,' my subconscious whispers, and to my chagrin, I agree.

This city will offer me nothing but cold winds and dull, empty days.

Can a flower bloom under such dire conditions?

How will I be able to give this man an heir when he won't even open a simple car door for me seconds after I had pledged to obey, love, and honor him?

I shake that thought away.

No matter the striking resemblance, Tiernan is not the ruler of the Underworld. Or at least not a mythical version of it. He's not Hades—even if I do share some similarities with Persephone's plight.

He's a man.

Made of flesh and bone.

With worldly desires and basic urges.

I'm his now. To do with whatever he pleases. He'll take me, willingly or not.

Can a woman get pregnant on her wedding night, I wonder? Will one time be enough to solidify our union? Or will I have to spend my honeymoon on my back as he ruts his seed into me?

How long do most honeymoons last, anyway?

A week?

Two maybe?

Surely not more than that.

My head is still working out the math when I feel a little tug on my dress. My gaze lands on Tiernan's thumb and finger that are currently rubbing a small patch of my flowing skirt in between them.

"You wore white."

It's not a question. More like an accusation.

I nod, my throat suddenly too dry to utter a word.

"I wasn't expecting white," he utters under his breath.

My forehead wrinkles in confusion.

"Don't most brides wear white on their wedding day?" I ask after a long, insufferable pause.

"Most brides, yes. But you're not most brides, are you, Rosa?"

Heat fills my cheeks at the sound of my name coming from his lips. My name on his tongue sounds obscene to my ears. X-rated and salacious even.

"I'm sorry to disappoint you. I couldn't find a blood-red dress that would do the occasion justice," I reply with a bite to my tone, not wanting him to pick up on the dirty images the sound of his voice saying my name conjured up.

He lets go of the dress and swiftly captures my chin in his ruthless grasp, his gaze, filled with such hate, holds all the oxygen in my lungs captive.

"Black. That's the color I was waiting for. It would have been less of a lie than the white you chose." He lets go of my chin and then turns his head away from me to stare out his passenger window. "Lie to me again and I'll make sure that black is all you know from here on out."

The threat lies heavy in the air as I take in his black ensemble with fresh new eyes.

I came dressed for a wedding.

Tiernan came dressed for a funeral.

CHAPTER 6
Rosa

"CAN'T you stay just a little longer?" I blurt out and then inwardly cringe at the sound of panic in my voice.

And by the way Alejandro's brows immediately pull together in discontentment, he heard it too.

"Unfortunately, I've stayed longer than I should have. You forget I have my own wedding to attend to when I arrive back home," he explains, making my teeth pull at my bottom lip at the somber reminder.

Somewhere out there is another girl in the same predicament I find myself in, anxious and afraid of what her future holds, alongside a man who, for her entire life, was dubbed to be her greatest foe. My selfishness in wanting my brother to stay for the entirety of my wedding reception suddenly dissipates, knowing that he too must make the same sacrifice as I have in the name of peace.

Although, I don't need to nitpick much to know that our

circumstances are far from being the same. Nothing is really going to change in my brother's life, aside from the fact that he will now be tied down to a total stranger. Unlike me, Alejandro will still be able to live in the same house we grew up in. He will be able to enjoy Javier and Francesco's company every day if he so wishes. He will walk down the familiar halls of our home or wander around in our garden, feeling the warm Mexican sun on his face. And at night, my brother will be able to sleep in his own bed, the only difference when he opens his eyes in the morning, will be the enemy lying asleep beside him.

The six daughters of the notorious crime families that came up with the treaty cannot boast the same, as we will be forever changed. Ripped from the bosom of our families, our homes, and everything we've ever known–all of us will be shipped out and delivered to live in cities we had been cautioned since birth never to enter. We will be expected to converse and live out our days with total strangers, and warm the beds of men that at one point would have rather wrapped their hands around our throats and extinguished the light from our eyes.

Even when men in our world are subjected to some form of sacrifice, it's never as cruel or harsh as what a woman faces.

"I'm sad I won't be there to see you get married, *hermano*," I say at last with a tender smile. "I wish you all the happiness in the world. Who knows? Maybe one day I'll be able to meet her."

"That might be sooner than you think."

"What do you mean?"

"I don't want to get your hopes up, but your husband insinuated to me last night that he might not be averse to visiting Mexico should you wish to see your family."

"He did?" My eyes widen in astonishment, searching the large crowded reception hall for the man in question and not finding him amongst the many guests. "Do you believe him?" I ask hopefully.

"Men like us are born liars, Rosa, but there are some things we still hold sacred. When we give our word, then that is as binding as the wedding ring on your finger," he states evenly, eyeing my wedding band that feels like a noose tightening around my neck every time I look at it.

"Then I guess I have something to look forward to," I offer him another small smile, praying he doesn't see how truly miserable I am. "Go, *hermano*. I don't want my future sister-in-law to be cross with me because you showed up late to your wedding."

My brother's expression remains as stoic as ever, but by the way his jaw ticks, I know that he's reluctant to leave me here alone with the Kellys.

"Five years, sweet sister. They fly by faster than you think."

My throat tightens with the tears of sorrow that threaten to drown me, but like the well-groomed cartel princess that I am, I flash him a comforting smile, hoping that it will dim his anxiety at abandoning me here in this vipers' nest.

"Safe travels, brother. Please tell everyone back home I'm thinking of them."

He nods, grabbing my hands to give them a tender squeeze, knowing full well that if he hugged me right now, I'd break into a thousand pieces.

After I watch him leave, I go back to my seat at the large table at the head of the room, shrugging off the curious stares that follow my every move. I should get accustomed to them since I'm sure they will be my companions for the duration of my marriage, or at least until the shine of the novelty wears off.

But as the hours pass and the alcohol flows, the Kelly's guests begin to show their true colors where I'm concerned. I squirm in my seat as the men throw out lewd remarks about my impending wedding night, while they cheer for their king's good health and sexual prowess. A king who hasn't said more than two words to me aside from the threat he uttered in the limo on the way here.

He called me a liar.

We haven't even had a full conversation with one another, and already I've displeased him.

Not that the incident has dulled his sudden celebratory mood any. In the limo he acted as if our wedding was a mournful occasion, yet the minute we stepped into the reception hall, his disposition did a complete one-eighty. I've sat on the sidelines and watched Tiernan dance with every pretty girl here and drink from every cup handed to him. Since he's made no attempt to include me in the festivities, I'm not naïve enough to think his gregarious nature has anything to do with being thrilled at our union. It almost looks like this wedding reception is more of an excuse to have one last hurrah with his men, than it is to commemorate the vows we took earlier today.

Not wanting to stare at my husband having a merry time of it, I take in his guests to see if there are any sympathetic faces to my plight. Anyone that can become a friend in this land filled with foes.

My gaze first lands on the less than obvious choice, my in-laws —Niall and Saoirse Kelly.

"Welcome to the family, Rosa," was the only statement that Saoirse had said to me when Alejandro introduced us earlier. She said it in a way that didn't hold any animosity in it, but not much affection in it either. My father-in-law, on the other hand, stood rigidly still beside her, making no attempts to look at me whatsoever.

Of course, I didn't expect them to welcome me into the fold with open arms, so I wasn't offended by their lukewarm greeting. But as the day unfolded into night, I got a feeling that me marrying their first-born son wasn't exactly on the top of the list of concerns for them, either.

On one of my many trips to the lady's room to get some much-needed solitude, my suspicions were confirmed when I overheard some women gossip about how the Kelly's youngest daughter, Iris, was probably marrying one of the Volkov brothers in Vegas as they spoke.

A shudder went down my spine at the frightening thought.

Up until that point, I never truly considered that marrying into the Kelly family was preferable in comparison to some other families—the Bratva being one of them. The Irish mob might be the unruly savages that my brother claimed them to be, but rumor has it that even Satan himself is afraid of the Volkovs, and has made sure that they remain unscathed just so he could buy himself some time before they enter his infernal domain and wreak havoc in hell.

It's no wonder that my in-laws can't crack a smile tonight.

Unlike my father, it's obviously apparent their thoughts are solely on the daughter they can no longer protect.

Unable to see so much restrained suffering, my gaze continues to scan the ample room, finding another person who looks just as unhappy to be here as I am.

Colin Kelly.

Alejandro was adamant that I stay away from him, and if he hadn't forewarned me the man was as dangerous as they come, then one quick glance his way would have done the trick. Surprisingly enough, the reason behind me wanting to maintain a wide berth from the man, has nothing to do with the burn marks that crest the left side of his face. Those are simply scars of war, and Colin cannot be held accountable for the evil of other men. It was the emptiness in his green eyes that told me I need to be careful whenever I find myself in his presence in the future. Maybe it's a childish notion, but I've always believed that the eyes were the window to a person's soul. And in Colin's case, his told me that he doesn't have one.

Soulless.

Lifeless.

Unmerciful.

For a man's soul to be that damaged, he must have endured too many horrors to count, ultimately making him unleash nightmares of his own. I wouldn't be surprised if loud, tormented screams and tear-stricken pleas of mercy were like lullabies to him. The marks that have been branded on his skin are just a cautionary tale of what he must have done in order to ensure his survival. Men like him might not have been born evil, but they sure have been molded into becoming it.

Afraid that somehow Colin can sense the horrid images of him I'm conjuring in my mind, I shift my attention away and continue on with my perusal until someone catches me in the act. My throat tightens when Shay Kelly's curious eyes meet mine from across the room.

Unlike Colin, Shay doesn't seem to hold one facial flaw or have any scars that are visible to the naked eye. I've never considered myself to be a shallow person nor based my regard for a person purely on looks, but even I have to admit that Shay's handsome features are too pronounced to ignore.

With shoulder-length light brown hair and a trimmed beard, paired with stunning clear blue eyes, he reminds me of Leonardo da Vinci's infamous painting of The Last Supper, whose replica adorns one of my own childhood home's walls. While his brother has an uncanny resemblance to the god of the underworld, Shay is his complete opposite, looking like the Irish version of Jesus Christ himself. But unlike the son of God, Shay wields his handsome looks like a sword, sure to capture the hearts of women all along the Massachusetts coast. While I've watched Tiernan limit himself only to dancing with the prettiest female guests here tonight, I've seen Shay do much more than just dance. He's kissed at least five different women in a span of an hour from what I could tell. Lord knows what else he's done where no one could see.

When my manwhore of a brother-in-law begins to walk in my direction, I curse at myself for not having been more discreet with my perusal. The crowd parts for him like the red sea, and all too soon he reaches my table. With a smug smile on his lips, Shay pulls out an empty chair beside me, twirls it around, and straddles it. He crosses his arms over the top rail of the chair, placing his chin on his wrist while staring at my side profile with no inhibitions whatsoever. When I refuse to look his way, he snickers in amusement.

"Not having fun?" he asks, his tone filled with mirth.

"Am I supposed to?"

"Don't see why not? No one will judge you for having a good time on your wedding day."

"Then hopefully no one will judge me if I don't, either."

Even from my peripheral, I can see the gleam of mischief in his eyes. I tilt my neck left to right, frustrated with the tension building up in it and my shoulders with the way he's staring at me. I almost let out a relieved breath when his gaze falls away from my face and onto the untouched flute of champagne on the table.

"Don't like champagne?"

"Never acquired much of a taste for it."

"So, you're sober like a judge, huh?"

I nod.

"Shit. No wonder you're bored." He laughs. "Want a sip of mine?" he asks, holding out his beer bottle for me.

"I would rather stick with water. Thank you."

"Water won't make any of these pricks any more interesting, petal. Come on. Just one sip."

"No, thank you."

"Fuck. Are you always this polite?" He chuckles again in blatant mockery of me, making my lips pinch into a fine line.

"Fine," he relents when he sees I don't find his light teasing amusing. "You don't want to drink, then I won't force you."

It takes everything in me to bite back the thank you that wants to come out on reflex alone.

"But it will be a shame if you don't have a little fun on your wedding day. Everyone else is having a grand ol' time. Don't see why you shouldn't."

It's true.

Everyone is having a good time, while I sit here all alone, watching life pass me by.

"If getting stinking drunk is off the menu, then what would you like to do?"

"What do you mean?" I ask, confused, turning my head to face him at last.

The beaming triumphant smile that crests his lips should have me on high alert, but surprisingly, it doesn't. I can see how Shay is able to snare his prey so easily. His smile alone is disarming.

"There must be something we can do to remedy the shitty time you've been having tonight. I mean, do you really want to look back on your wedding day and only remember how bored you were?"

"This is a transaction. Not exactly a cause for celebration."

"You're right," he replies somewhat regretfully, as if only now remembering the circumstances that brought me to Boston in the first place. *"Perdóname."*

I shrug off his apology.

"It is what it is. I've made peace with it," I lie, turning my attention back to the party in front of me.

"Hmm," he mumbles unconvinced. "Even so, you'll only get married once. Which means this is all you've got, petal. Might as well make the most of it."

I'm not sure what troubles me more. Shay wanting to salvage my night by imposing his glass half-full mentality on me, or his insistence on calling me petal. I'm about to chastise him for the ludicrous nickname and remind him of acceptable decorum, when I let out an unladylike shriek the minute Shay grabs the chair beneath me and turns it towards him.

"Nuh huh," he reprimands, shaking his head while his hands grip the sides of my chair, his body leaning too close for comfort to mine. "Let's imagine this is a happy occasion. That you have just married your prince charming and that everyone you love is here."

I open my mouth to lecture him on the absurdity of his statement, but close it shut and widen my eyes when he has the audacity of pressing one lone finger to my lips.

"Just do it, Rosa. Come on. Name one thing you always imagined yourself doing on your wedding day. Just one thing and then I'll leave you alone. Promise."

"I don't need your pity," I rebuke coldly, leaning as far away from him as I can.

"Good, because you don't have it. Now answer my question. All little girls fantasize about their wedding day. So don't tell me there isn't one thing you envisioned yourself doing today. I'm not buying it."

All the humor in his expression has been stripped away, leaving only a man resolute in his mission. My nose crinkles and my shoulders slump as I turn my head away from him and watch the cheerful crowd laugh and dance the night away.

"I... um... I would have liked to dance at my wedding. At least once."

I don't have to look at Shay to see that his victorious smile has returned.

"That's it? Just one dance?"

I nod shyly, hating that I've let him see such silly vulnerability in me.

"Then if that's what you want, that's what you'll get," he states, but before he's able to stand from his chair, I hold onto his wrist to stop him.

When his gaze zones in on my fingers on his skin, I quickly remember myself and pull them away. I swallow the lump in my throat as he waits for me to explain why I stopped him.

"Why are you being so nice to me?"

"I'm a nice guy. Just ask anyone," he jokes lightheartedly.

"That's not what I've heard."

"Your brother's opinion of me doesn't count."

To me, his is the only opinion that ever has.

"I'm being serious, Shay. Why do you even care? I'm no one to you."

He takes a bit to think about it, his happy-go-lucky expression turning serious once again.

"You want the truth?"

"*Sí.*"

"Because I need to believe that someone in Vegas is showing my kid sister the same kindness right now."

The rough chain of steel that had been tightening its hold around my heart since I stepped foot on U.S. soil suddenly gives way and loosens. My own self-pity goggles lift from my eyes, and for the first time tonight, when I turn my attention to the Kelly family feasting amongst the joyful crowd, I see pain hidden behind their smiles.

I watch my husband camouflage his sadness over his absent sister by surrounding himself with his men and drinking the night away. I notice how Colin stands guard on the side, vigilantly watching his fearless leader, making sure no outside threat can harm him while he drowns his sorrows.

I remember how Niall Kelly refused to look at me. How his wife, Saoirse, was only able to say a couple of words to me, since my presence must be a painful reminder of the daughter they lost to the treaty.

And last but not least, sits Shay in front of me, who throughout the whole night has been trying to keep his hands and mind busy and away from his sister's fate by seeking warmth in any woman's arms.

The Kellys may be savage beasts like my brother had forewarned, but even an animal is capable of feeling the pains of love and loss. It's Shay's raw honesty that has me conceding to his wishes.

"One dance," I say at last.

His wide smile is immediate.

"One dance," he agrees. "Just give me two seconds," he says before rushing off to the DJ on the other side of the room.

I try not to fidget in my seat while I wait for his return.

But when he does, I can't help how my heart flutters in my chest when he offers me his hand.

"May I have this dance?"

"How can I say no to such a request?"

Virgen de Guadalupe, ayúdame.

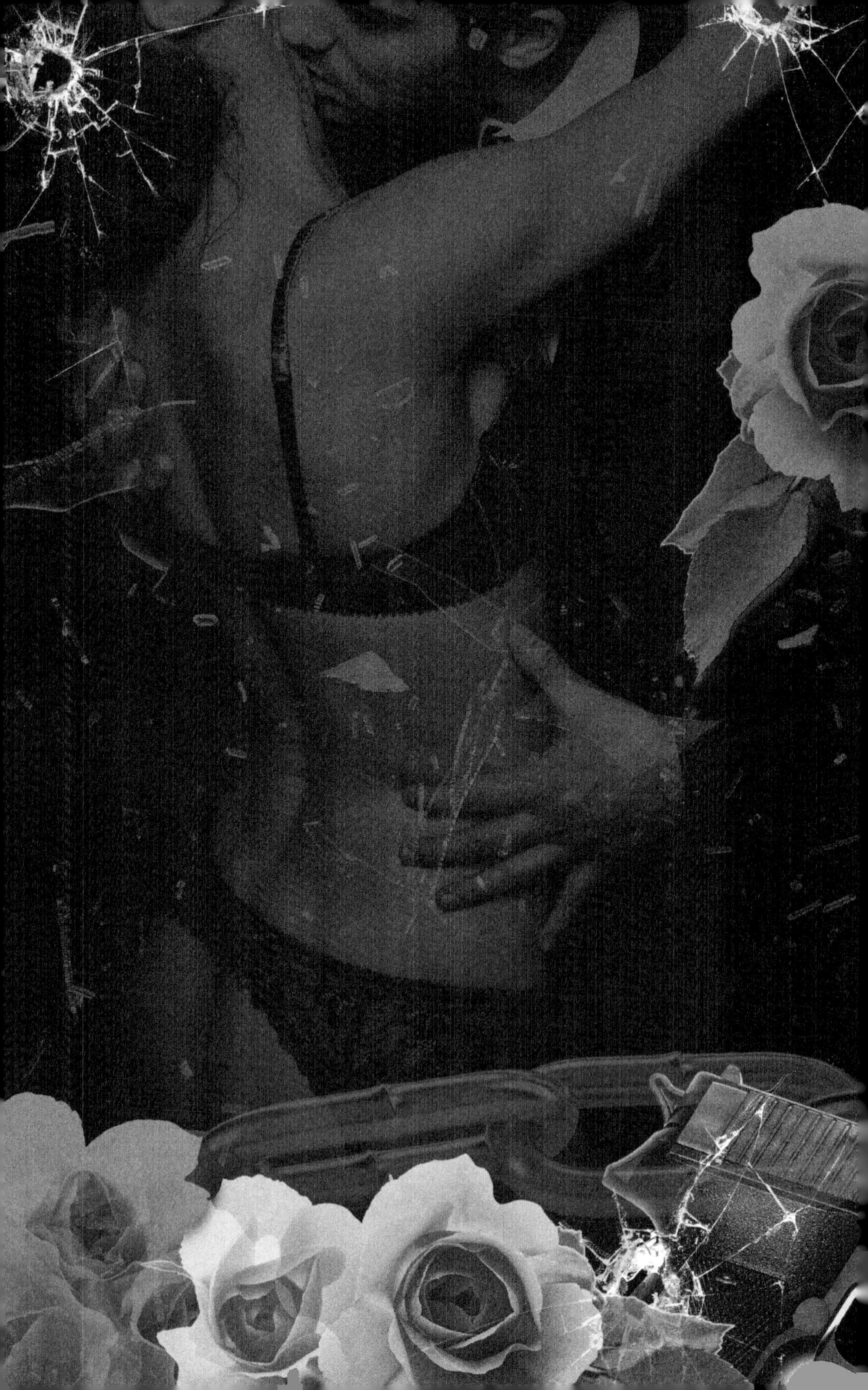

CHAPTER 7
Tiernan

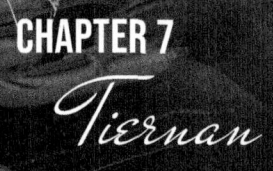

"SHAY HAS SURE GONE and done it now," I hear one of my men say behind me.

"Can't see a pretty lass and not put his hands on her. Shame," another one utters critically.

"Boss, I think your brother is trying to sneak off with your prize." A few others cackle unashamedly.

I turn around to see what all my men are snickering about, only to find my wife, hand in hand with my brother, as he leads her to the dance floor. The music suddenly stops when their feet touch the vinyl, making everyone that was dancing disperse to the side, leaving the floor empty for my new bride to have her first dance with my brother, no less.

Custom says that I should have the honor, but apparently Shay doesn't agree.

When Colin sees the unlikely pair and figures out what's about to happen, his green eyes turn a shade darker. Instantly, he breaks from the rigid stance he's held all night, with the goal of pulling Shay by his hair, if need be, far away from my bride. Before my cousin has time to fly past me in a disgruntled rage, I shake my head, keeping him from taking another step.

"Leave him be," I order, taking another sip of my whiskey, hating that the liquid hasn't made much of a dent in my sobriety tonight.

"I don't like it," Colin mutters beside me.

"You don't like most of Shay's shenanigans. So why should this be any different?" I take another pull.

"Boss—"

"I said leave it," I repeat more harshly.

This time Colin doesn't protest, crossing his arms over his chest disapprovingly.

It's not that I don't understand why my cousin is pissed at my baby brother's latest show of insubordination. It's just that I don't care. Shay has always danced to the beat of his own drum, and thinking that I can control him in any way, shape, or form is setting me up for failure. I've always given Shay free rein to do as he pleases, knowing that ultimately his loyalty starts and ends with me. If I learned anything from the great leaders of the past, it's that family can either make you stronger, or it can be the chink in the chain that finally destroys you. Many a mafia boss have been overthrown and killed by their own kin—brothers, cousins and uncles who got weary of taking orders and decided that they could do a better job of being in charge of the family business. Shay has never given me any reason to think he wants my seat at the head of the table, but I'm not foolish enough to give him one, either.

If dancing with Rosa is how he'll get his kicks tonight, I say let him have at it.

I won't berate him in front of all our family and guests and start the rumor mill going that my new wife has barely been here a day and is already causing a rift between us.

I do, however, wonder what her motives are, though.

She doesn't look the type to be easily seduced by a pretty face.

And she also doesn't look dumb enough to try and purposely embarrass me in front of my men.

Which leaves me to think this is her manipulative way of paying me back.

Either because she's still licking her wounds at my lack of presence before our wedding, or because I was less than welcoming on our drive to the reception hall. Whatever the reason, if she thought that accepting Shay's offer to dance would somehow upset me or put me in my place, she has another thing coming.

When they are both at the very center of the dancefloor, Shay nods over to the DJ and a Spanish ballad begins to play through the speakers. Rosa's eyes lift up to my brother in unspoken gratitude, to which he smiles back almost dotingly. He then places a respectful hand carefully on her lower back, while the other clasps her hand. They start to waltz around the dancefloor, seemingly uncaring that every pair of eyes in this room are on them, and like everyone else, I study their interaction down to a T.

Shay is just being Shay, putting on a show, but Rosa looks stiff as a board while my brother leads her in the dance. When her gaze constantly lowers, unwilling to meet anyone's eyes, it's blatantly apparent that she's uncomfortable with the attention they are getting. When she looks at her feet for the third time in as many minutes, my brother takes his hand off her back and tilts her chin up to look at him.

"Just keep your eyes on me," I watch him mouth to her.

The gesture is supposed to be comforting, Shay's way of putting my bride at ease, but from the outside looking in, it looks intimate.

Almost as if he cares.

Hmm.

Maybe Colin wasn't so off-base after all.

Maybe I should put a stop to this.

Although, I can't blame my brother for wanting to use any excuse in the book to touch my wife.

The fates must have had a hell of a laugh at my expense when my father picked Rosa's name out of the dreadful fruit bowl ten years ago. The fact that she is a Hernandez was my first cause for concern, but when she stepped into the Holy Cross Cathedral earlier today, I knew in that instant she was going to be more trouble than she was worth.

I'm not a man that is known for getting caught off guard in regards to anything.

I'm always prepared for any and all eventualities.

But I have to admit, even I wasn't expecting *her*.

Not that there was any way I could have prepared myself either.

A few months after that horrid day in Bermuda, I succumbed to my curiosity and looked Rosa up online. I just wanted a glimpse of her, nothing more. Just a face to put to the name. However, her father, Miguel, had been careful and ensured that not one picture of his daughter could be found, leaving her existence limited to just a name online. And as the years passed and our deadline to marry approached, my curiosity about my future wife waned.

Somewhere along the way, I had made the decision that's exactly how Rosa Hernandez would remain.

Just a name.

First online.

Now a scribbled signature on a wedding certificate and nothing more.

I had no intention of giving Rosa more importance than that. I'd give her my protection, set her up in some lavish brownstone in Beacon Hill, and forget she existed after that.

But then I lifted that fucking veil.

I wasn't expecting her to be so fucking breathtaking.

Large brown doe eyes looked up at me, and suddenly every intention I had went out the window. I'm still not sure what I'm going to do with her, but keeping her secluded and away from my sight doesn't seem as appealing to me as it once did.

Beautiful.

That's the word Colin used to describe her.

I should have known that my cousin's limited vocabulary could never do her justice.

My wife is so much more than that small word.

She's devastating.

An exotic flower plucked from her homeland and gifted to me

on a silver platter to do whatever I want with. I could pluck out her petals, one by one. I could cut out her thorns and leave her defenseless. I could crush her in the palm of my hand if I so wished. Or I can nurture her and stand back to watch her blossom.

Such a frail thing to be put in my ungodly hands.

But as I watch her cheeks tinge a pretty shade of red, and her cupid-bow lips part for breath while her gaze remains fixed on my brother's, the sudden need to remind her that I'm the one who is the master of her fate violently springs free from my chest.

When the song finishes, both Shay and Rosa stare into each other's eyes, as if they are sharing a private little secret that no one should be made privy to. Annoyed with the cozy display, I step onto the dancefloor and walk over to them. Shay instantly lets go of her hand, his usual carefree expression nowhere in sight, while the wedding guests wait on bated breath to see what I'll do.

"I'll take it from here, brother," I state evenly.

"Are you sure? I don't mind giving her another twirl?" He smirks at me, his innuendo clear as day.

"You've warmed her up enough. It's time to let the adults have their turn."

Shay runs his tongue over his teeth before directing his attention back to my nervous bride. He lifts her hand and places a tender kiss along her knuckles.

"Now you have something to look back on," he says playfully.

"Thank you," she responds with genuine sincerity in her tone, making my usual cocky brother timidly smile back at her.

"Go," I order, my patience starting to wear thin.

"Yeah, yeah. I heard you the first time. Can't have any fun

around here."

"I'm sure there are plenty of women here that you can have your supposed fun with that aren't my wife."

"But none of them as lovely."

He offers her a little bow and a flirtatious wink before leaving us alone in the middle of the dancefloor. I give the DJ a tilt of the head, and he puts on an old traditional Irish ballad. Rosa stands a good distance away, waiting for my next move.

"Come here."

She blinks twice as if English is a foreign language to her.

"I won't ask again."

"It didn't seem like you asked the first time. It sounded more like an order."

"Are you so keen to break your marriage vows to me so soon? If I recall, you did promise to obey me, did you not?"

The flash of hatred that crosses her chestnut gaze loosens the knot in my chest I didn't realize was even there. Reluctantly, she bridges the gap between us but insists on leaving a few safe inches. Tired of her resistance, I snake my arm around her waist and pull her to me so fast her chest hits mine. She sucks in a startled breath, but doesn't utter a word in retaliation at my manhandling her.

Like a rag doll needing instruction, I take both of her hands and place them around my neck while mine settle around her slender waist. Her cheeks are flaming red at how our bodies are pressed together, but her brown eyes continue to hold the same contempt as before.

We begin to sway back and forth in sync with the melody playing around us. Unlike with Shay, she isn't as bashful in making eye contact with me. In fact, her piercing, menacing glower, intent on showing me she's not one bit happy to be dancing with me, almost coaxes a smile out of me.

Almost.

When she absentmindedly diverts her attention away from me and onto the crowd watching us for a split second, I tighten my hold on her to remind her that I'm the only one that matters here. Her narrowed gaze rises to meet mine in displeasure.

"If your intention is to kill me in front of all your guests, then I'm sure there are more creative ways of doing it than smothering me to death," she finally says through the fakest-ass smile I've ever seen on a woman.

"As much as the thought has crossed my mind, I have no intentions of killing you."

"Why do I feel there is a *yet* left out of that statement?"

"You weren't this vocal when my brother was dancing with you," I rebuke, instead of giving her an answer.

"He wasn't trying to suffocate me."

"No. He was trying to fuck you."

This time I do smile when her gorgeous eyes widen and her jaw falls to the floor in utter astonishment.

"Hmm. You're what? Twenty-seven? Twenty-eight? Given your age, I was under the assumption that I had gotten the more mature girl in the pack. I didn't think you'd embarrass so easily. Or be this naïve."

"You didn't embarrass me. And I'm not naïve," she bites back through gritted teeth. "Your brother didn't... I mean he wasn't trying to... to seduce me like you said."

"Oh, no? Then what was he trying to do?"

"He was just trying to be nice. A trait I see isn't common in the Kelly family."

"Nice, you say? My brother has never been nice a day in his life. You've known him for a hot minute. I've known him his entire life. Who between us knows him and his true intentions better, I wonder?"

"Maybe you're not as in tune with your brother as you think."

"Believe me, *acushla*, I'm well aware of the thoughts running through my horny brother's mind, as I am of most of my men here. Next time you feel the need to get groped, be more subtle and do it where lingering eyes can't see you."

Her nose crinkles in disgust.

"Thank you for taking a perfectly innocent and kind moment and twisting it into something indecent and ugly. I won't forget it."

"You're welcome."

On impulse, she turns her eyes away from mine, but then remembers herself and keeps them exactly where they should always be—on me.

For the remainder of the song, we don't say another word to each other, but that doesn't mean there isn't a silent battle of wills being fought between us. Like her namesake, this rose came with sharp-edged thorns, and she isn't shy in using them to cut a man down if the need arises.

Unfortunately for her, no prick or cut she can inflict will ever cause me an ounce of pain. And if she's not careful, she'll learn the true meaning of the word agony soon enough.

But the night is still young.

Who knows?

Maybe I'll give her just a little taste.

My cock hardens at the idea, and for the first time in a decade, I'm eager to perform my husbandly duties.

"We're spending our wedding night back at the hotel?" Rosa asks, unable to hide her displeasure when I instruct our limo driver to take us to the Liberty Hotel where she stayed last night.

"Is the room not to your liking?" I cock a brow, wondering if her disapproval of where we are to start our so-called honeymoon has anything to do with her somehow learning that the place used to be a prison in its heyday before it was converted to the luxurious five-star hotel that it is now.

Some might have thought my choice of having my bride lay her head there her first night in Boston distasteful. Maybe even sadistically macabre.

I thought it was fitting.

If I'm to fulfill this imprisonment, then I might as well start it off in a place that holds some form of symbolism to it.

"No. It's fine," she mumbles, turning her head away from me, so I can't read the disappointment on her face.

If this marriage wasn't a sham, then maybe I wouldn't be so reluctant to take her back to my place tonight. But as circumstances stand, just the idea of having a Hernandez walking around my sanctuary, touching my things, or running the risk of her sweet floral perfume floating all throughout my apartment nauseates me.

I'm going to need some time to get used to married life, and I'd rather do that in neutral territory before I invite the enemy into my home.

Still...

Rosa has been able to accomplish the impossible tonight. Her presence alone served as a great distraction, keeping my mind, even if only at times, away from the hell my sister must be experiencing back in Vegas. But just as the realization dawns on me that I haven't thought about Iris once since I danced with my wife, a tidal wave of guilt hits me straight in the chest like one of my construction company's cement trucks, accompanied by the worst nightmare my fiendish mind can conjure up. My hands ball into fists with the image of three Bratva bastards charging at my sister, her only means of defense the simple dagger I gave her as a wedding present.

The horrid thought has me so tense that it takes me a second to register delicate fingers covering my balled-up fist on the leather seat beside me. My nostrils flare as I snap my head over to Rosa, whose gentle gaze is fixed on our hands.

"They won't hurt her," she whispers, running her thumb over my scarred knuckles, eyeing the movement ever so carefully, like I'm some wild animal that will bite her hand off at any given moment. "They can't. The treaty prevents them from doing so."

I quickly pull my hand away from hers, burned by her tender touch as well as repulsed by her naivety.

"Is that what you think?" I growl, disgusted.

"It's what I know," she states plainly, clasping her hands together on her lap.

"And what exactly do you know, pray tell?"

Her forehead wrinkles at the venom in my voice, but either bravery or mere stupidity prevents her from not answering my loaded question.

"I know that if your sister is harmed in any way while she's under Volkov's care, that the families will retaliate against them. The Bratva gave their word to protect her on penalty of death. I don't see them breaking such an oath for mere sport."

I grab her chin, uncaring of how my fingers dig into her soft flesh or how they are bound to leave their mark.

"The word of monsters means nothing," I spit out.

"That's not true," she counters steadfastly, her gaze never wavering from mine. "Many would call you a monster, yet no one would dare question your word. Not even my brother. If Alejandro thought my safety would be in question in any way, then he would have killed you before I stepped one foot on U.S. soil."

The menacing low laugh that rips through my throat pales her olive-toned cheeks.

"If you believe that, then you're an even bigger fool than your brother. There are many ways to make someone's life a living hell and still leave a person physically intact, so as to not to warrant the wrath of the families. Do not speak of things you do not know. It only makes you sound ignorant."

She pulls her chin from my grasp, tilting her head away from me and towards the passenger's side window.

"Men like you think they hold a monopoly on suffering and pain. Just because you are experts in doling out misery doesn't mean you know one thing about true anguish. Proclaiming that you do only makes *you* sound ignorant."

I stare at the back of her head, suddenly wanting to pull her silky brown hair and crane her neck back to look at me. It's so fucking long that I'd have no problem in spinning it twice around my wrist.

"And what does a cartel princess know of suffering?" I sneer in contempt.

"Who I am has nothing to do with it. Everyone hurts. Some people just hide it better than others."

"Hmph," I grunt, turning my attention away from her.

She talks of pain like it's her secret confidante and lifelong companion, but I'm not fooled. What could she possibly know of true suffering, when all her life she's been sheltered and spoiled, living the life of grandeur and decadence at the expense of innocent lives? Her family feeds off lost souls and reaps the profit of their demise. She doesn't know the first thing about misery, and her professing that she does only serves to make me hate her more.

"Can I ask you a question?" she finally asks after a long, heavy pause.

"I don't see how I can stop you."

"When did your sister leave?"

My brows pull together, wondering where she is going with this.

"Yesterday morning. Around the time you got into Boston."

"I see. And why didn't you go with her? Why didn't you accompany her to Vegas like Alejandro accompanied me here?"

"Not that it's any of your business, but Iris asked me not to," I grumble, annoyed with her interrogation. "Unlike you, my sister didn't want a babysitter when being hand-delivered to the devil. Iris wanted to face hell alone. On her own terms."

"Do you always do what people ask of you?" she continues on, unphased by my dig or the vivid picture I just painted for her.

"No. Only for the ones that matter to me."

"So, you gave her your word?"

"Yes." I grind my teeth.

"I see."

"And what exactly do you see?" I tilt my head towards her again, finding her back is still facing me, her gaze fixed on the passing scenery.

"That you're a good brother."

"Hmph."

"And that even when it goes against your very nature, you keep your word when given. Just like Alejandro said you would."

When she looks over her shoulder back at me with a gleam of triumph in her eyes, my jaw ticks. By conning me into confessing that my word is my bond, she is now assured that her life is safe in my hands, despite what I think of her and her family.

"You're clever. I'll give you that," I relent with a frown.

"Is that a compliment?"

"Take it however you want to. I don't care."

"Then I'll take it as a compliment. It's better for my ego that my husband thinks I'm clever and not a naïve, ignorant fool," she says with a thin smile, throwing my own words back against me.

"You have a good memory."

"I'm sure everyone does when they've been offended." She

shrugs nonchalantly.

"Is your confidence so frail that you need to keep track of every insult someone throws at you?"

"No. My self-worth cannot be damaged by simple words alone. However, most brides do care what their husbands think about them. Why should I be any different?"

"Trust me, Rosa. My perception of you should be the least of your concerns."

Instead of the fear I was sure that remark would coax out of her, all I see is sadness clouding her big brown eyes. Her somber demeanor rubs me the wrong way. Irritates me even. I would much rather deal with her when she is trying to cut me down a peg. Her bravery, no matter how idiotic, is preferable to melancholy.

I can even deal with hatred.

Sadness, however, strikes too much of a nerve inside me.

By the time we reach Beacon Hill, I'm wired as all hell as well as painstakingly exhausted by today's events.

Who knew that getting married to my sworn enemy was such a strenuous affair?

I shrug off the other hotel guests' stares as Rosa and I walk side by side through the large luxurious foyer and head towards the elevator. I've lived all my life in Boston's public eye, so I've become accustomed to the attention of strangers. However, it strikes me that the curious glances being sent our way aren't directed at me. Not that I'm surprised. The real showstopper is Rosa in that fucking wedding dress. I make a note—after tonight, I'm either going to burn the thing or never let it into my sight again.

As much as I hate to admit it, the image of her entering the cathedral in that goddamn dress will forever be branded into my memory. Even with a fucking veil covering her face, it took my very breath away. Like the woman herself, the dress was elegant yet provocatively bold, making sure that I was the envy of every man there, wishing they could fill my shoes on that godforsaken altar.

Hmm.

Now that I think about it, maybe it was a good thing Rosa kept her face hidden from me to start with. I'm not sure how I would have reacted if I had a full view of all of her at once.

I was expecting a frightened lamb to be led to her slaughter.

But what I got was a queen ready to sit on her throne.

It pissed me off as much as it intrigued me.

When we arrive at our floor, my men are already there guarding the penthouse suite. Seeing them there reminds me that I'll have to find someone permanent to guard my wife. Someone I can trust. I didn't think the position would be a hard one to fill, but now that I've laid eyes on Rosa, I'm not so sure. I mentally scroll through a list of names of men I would feel comfortable enough leaving Rosa alone with and in their care and come up empty-handed. Even the married ones will have a hard time not lusting over my exotically beautiful wife. And though I have no intention of keeping my own marriage vows, I will not be made a cuckold either. A woman like her will need her bed warm at all times to be content, and like hell will I let one of my soldiers fill the empty spot I've made.

I haven't been married a full day, and already this woman is making my life difficult.

Fuck.

I push through the double doors of the penthouse and rush towards the bar in the corner of the living room, needing a drink to cool my temper. I find a bottle of a fifty-year-old single malt and fill my tumbler halfway with it, drinking it all in one go. I don't have to look at her to feel Rosa's judging gaze on me as I refill my glass.

"Want one?" I ask, taking another shot.

"No, thank you. I don't drink."

"You're a Kelly now. Kellys drink."

"Not me," she rebukes evenly, with the same dignified grace she's fought tooth and nail to hold on to all day.

The urge to see her superior mien crack, to run a hammer to it and obliterate it until all that's left is tiny shards of glass that I can easily crush with the sole of my shoe, is overwhelming.

I fill the glass again and walk the distance over to her as she tries not to fidget under my cold scrutiny.

"Drink," I order, forcefully grabbing her hand and clutching our combined fingers around the base of the glass.

"No."

"I said drink." I tighten my grip on her hand.

If looks could kill, then I'd be ten feet under.

Her glower burns bright with a hostility I know all too well.

"And I said no."

I stare into her eyes, watching her watch me put the glass to my lips with our entwined hands and taking another swig of my whiskey. I then grab the nape of her neck and harshly crash my lips onto hers, the shocked gasp she lets out granting me enough access between her lips to pour the bitter liquid into her mouth and down her throat. I don't let up until I've made sure she swallows all of it to the very last drop.

When my cock hardens at the idea of forcing my newly-wedded wife to do the same with my cum, I immediately let go of my hold on her, making Rosa stumble back on her unsteady legs.

"We Kellys drink. Get used to it," I warn with an unforgiving sneer.

As I continue to stare into the pure animosity that is swimming in her eyes, it bothers me how my cock decides to swell even further the minute I encounter small flecks of gold around her irises.

Not wanting her to see the effect she's had on my traitorous dick, I turn my back to her and walk, yet again, to the bar in the corner for another refill. When I raise my glass to my lips this time, my tense muscles instantly relax at finding myself alone in the room.

Fuck.

How long is this excruciating day going to last?

I just want it to be over and done with already.

One thing I've taken out of today is that if I was a smart man, I would do everything in my power to limit our time together. Go back to my original plan to set my bride up in a swanky apartment or house fit for her stature and just forget her very existence.

That's what my logical mind is screaming for me to do.

But there are other parts of me that aren't so easily convinced.

My cock being one of them.

Not that I have ever let him make my decisions for me in the past. I've never been one to romanticize my interactions with women. Up to this point, the only use I've had for any female has either been in counting the profits they made me professionally or the few hours I've spent balls deep inside them just to get the edge off after a hard day's work. Fucking for me has always been about the release, not companionship. I'm usually out the door before they've even come down from the earth-shattering orgasm I've given them.

I don't have to know the inner workings of my wife's mind to know that Rosa is the kind of woman that yearns to be intellectually stimulated. She's definitely not the kind that wants to be ass fucked from behind while she's spread out on all fours on top of my bed.

My cock twitches in my pants, daring me to put that theory to the test.

Like that will ever fucking happen.

Still, I can't deny that she intrigues me. Both physically and mentally.

The way she braved facing me head-on, head held high, not only irritates me, but it also brought forth this insistent need to break her bravado in any way I could. The sudden urge to see her cheeks turn pink in both shyness and embarrassment, and leave her breathlessly tongue-tied is too seductive for words.

Much like the way she looked when she was dancing with Shay earlier tonight.

I crack my neck to the side, releasing the tension there as I recall how she looked into my brother's eyes with complete and utter trust embedded in them.

Not that I can fault her ingenuity on that front.

Shay has always had an uncanny knack when it came to dealing with the fairer sex. His silver tongue could coax a faithful married woman of twenty years into an orgy just as easily as it could soothe a little girl's tears from shedding after falling off her bike. My brother could smooth talk a nun to her knees, have her deep throat him in a church confessional, and then have her thank God Almighty for the privilege. I should know since I'm the one who had to write a big fat check to Bishop O'Sullivan when Shay was caught fucking Sister Riley with her own crucifix when he was barely eighteen years old.

I'll have to have a word with him in regards to Rosa.

He'll see her as a challenge, even if he should only see her as a reminder of the pain her family has caused us.

Whenever we reminisce on the past, *Athair* sometimes likes to remind me that there was a point in my life that I used to be just as carefree and reckless as Shay is today.

Feels like a lifetime ago, though.

A life that no longer exists thanks to the Hernandezes.

I empty the remaining contents of my glass at the thought, letting the burn trail down my throat. I've drunk more than my fill tonight, yet all I got was a small buzz for my troubles. Not strong enough to dull the senses or the hectic thoughts ruminating around my head, unfortunately.

A quick glance at my Cartier watch tells me it's close to midnight, and a good hour has passed since Rosa retreated to the bedroom. I need to wash the day off my skin and try to grab a few hours of sleep if I can. I'm not sure how much I'll be able to get with Iris always on my mind, but I'll be no use to anyone tomorrow if I don't at least try.

Hopefully by now, Rosa is fast asleep in bed and won't hear me going into the ensuite to grab a quick shower. I take off my suit jacket and throw it over an armchair before heading towards the bedroom. But to my chagrin, when I enter the room, the infuriating woman is still in her wedding dress staring at her reflection via a standing black framed mirror, as if she knows its only purpose is to torment me.

Pissed that I'll have to go without my shower since she's still awake, I grab a pillow off the bed and start heading back to the living room.

"What are you doing?" she asks, turning around to face me.

"What does it look like?"

"Aren't you going to sleep in here? With me?"

"Do you want me to?" I counter with a dry tone.

"You are my husband now. Don't husbands share the same bed with their wives?" she retorts instead of answering my question.

"Not all husbands. I know many couples who sleep in separate beds and are perfectly content."

She chews on her bottom lip in deep thought, unaware that the nervous gesture provokes salacious thoughts of my own teeth piercing through the same soft flesh.

"That may be true," she begins somewhat hesitantly, "but I doubt they started off that way. Especially on their wedding night."

"I'll ask you again. Would you prefer that I stay?"

Her chin tilts upwards as if remembering herself and who she is dealing with.

"Whether you stay or don't is completely up to you. I would, however, prefer that you didn't insinuate I have any vote on the matter," she bites back. "We both know I don't."

There is that spirit again.

Alejandro should have taught his sister that if she insisted on poking at a caged animal, sooner or later, not even the bars keeping it hostage would protect her.

Instead of entertaining this conversation any further, I pick up a discarded blanket on a nearby settee and start to head out of the room.

"Wait," she half-whispers, half-yells.

"Yes?" I turn around.

"I'm not going to beg you to stay, if that's your intention. In all honesty, I'm extremely tired and look forward to a good night's rest."

"Then you shall have it," I mutter, starting to walk back out.

"But," she adds forcefully, stopping me again from getting out of the room. "If I'm to do that, I'll need some help getting out of this dress. I won't grab a wink of sleep tonight with it on."

"Are you asking me for help?" I ask suspiciously, thinking that somehow this is some sort of trap.

She turns her back to me and points at the ties holding up her white corset that are impossible for her to reach on her own.

"I've been trying to untie this dress for the past hour with no luck. If you can't do it for me, then you'll leave me no choice, and I'll have to ask one of your guards outside to help me out instead."

"Careful," I warn, pointing a threatening finger her way. "I'm not one for ill-humored jokes or manipulation."

I'd sooner grab my knife and cut her out of the damn dress than have any one of my men lay a finger on it.

"It's not one or the other. It's mere desperation. Will you help me or not?" she exclaims, perching her hands on her hips.

Seeing that she's being sincere in her exasperation, I throw the blanket and pillow back on top of the bed and begin to bridge the gap between us. She turns to face the mirror once more, squaring her shoulders to look impassive as I draw nearer to her, but I know it's all for show.

She's nervous.

Agitated.

But then again, it's expected since most brides usually are on their wedding night. Especially when they are about to let their husband see them naked for the first time. A rite of passage that I think Rosa would have preferred to have skipped altogether.

Sensing her unease with the whole situation, I harshly pull at the garment with more force than needed, making her gasp in surprise. Since I'm a good few inches taller than her, I have a perfect view of the swell of her breasts, her chest slowly heaving up and down as she tries to control her shallow breathing.

"Do I make you nervous, Rosa?"

When she doesn't answer me, I give one of the ties another tight pull, making her gasp out again.

"I believe that's a yes." I smirk.

"Any woman would be nervous around a total stranger taking her clothes off," she counters once she's gained control of herself.

"I see you haven't had many one-night stands, otherwise you wouldn't say that," I goad.

She raises her head upwards to catch my eyes with hers, searing contempt plastered to her face.

"You know I haven't. And insinuating that you have is not only cruel but distasteful."

"Would you have rather I stayed celibate for the ten years I had to wait to marry you?"

"Why not? I was forced to," she deadpans, those golden flecks like tiny daggers to my chest.

I'm not sure if it's her confession of not having been touched by another man in the last decade that has me spiraling, but before I know what I'm doing, my eyes land on her mouth. Soft lips tantalize me, the bottom one fuller than its counterpart, begging to be tugged, sucked, and pulled. When she sees my tongue lick my suddenly parched lips, her breathing picks up, drawing my attention away from her luscious mouth back to the fullness of her breasts.

"There is no need for you to be nervous with me," I say, my voice rough and telling. "I'm not a stranger. I'm your husband."

"Right now, they are one and the same," she replies despondently, lowering her gaze from me and onto the mirror in front of us.

"If that's the case, then why were you disappointed at the fact that I would rather sleep on the couch than share a bed with you?"

"Who says I'm disappointed?"

"Are you saying you aren't?"

"Disappointment was my father telling me at seventeen that I was to marry a man I've never met. A sworn enemy at that. Disappointment was me being sent out to live in a country where I have no family or friends to speak of. You wishing not to sleep in my bed on our wedding night pales in comparison. In fact, I'm sure it's the only blessed reprieve I'll get for what undoubtedly will be a life filled with more disappointments."

Fuck does she know how to push a man's buttons!

I tug the ties of her corset again, this time forcing her back to be flush against my chest. I do my best not to focus on how her body perfectly molds itself to mine in all the right places, or how easy it would be for me to lift up her flowing skirt and sink deep inside her. I'd make sure to erase the word 'disappointment' from her vocabulary, one thrust at a time.

Instead, I lower my mouth to her ear, her skin instantly breaking out in goosebumps with just my warm breath tickling her long neck.

"If this is your way of enticing me into your bed, then someone should have taught you the art of seduction."

"Seduction?" She breathes out the word in such a way it feels like a gentle stroke to my cock. "You've won your prize, fair and square, Tiernan. Why seduce someone if the world views them as already yours?"

Fuck.

I swallow the groan that wants to come out at the sound of my name on her lips.

"Is that what you are, Rosa?" I ask as my fingers run circles on her bare shoulder. "Mine?"

As I anticipated, she refuses to give me an answer, but she

doesn't have to. My wife's body betrays her when she's unable to hide the shiver that runs down her spine.

"To do with as I please?" I add hoarsely as my hand travels up from her shoulder onto the pulse point on her neck, feeling her heart rate speed up under my fingertips.

"Is that how you saw this playing out tonight? That I would take you just because some piece of paper said you were mine?"

"If I'm not yours, then whose am I? Not mine, that's for sure. I've never been mine."

The melancholy that resurfaces in her voice stops me cold in my tracks.

I take a step back, and immediately she lets out a relieved breath.

"One thing you should know about me if we are to get along is that I don't believe in ownership. I prefer my women to come to me willingly. I know that doesn't mean much considering the situation we find ourselves in, but I will not take something that isn't freely given. Hence why I am going to sleep on the couch. So, breathe easy, Rosa. Your virtue is safe."

I watch her forehead crease in confusion but don't say anything more on the matter. With nimble fingers, I start taking the rest of the ties out of her corset. When I pull the ribbon out of its last loop, her dress falls to her feet in an instant, making my breath catch in my throat, and I curse the fates that delivered her to my door. If I knew that underneath the dress would be virginal white lingerie that leaves very little to the imagination, then I would have forced her to sleep in the damn thing.

Gorgeous sun-kissed skin glistens along every groove and

valley of her body, only serving to stretch my restraint to its fullest extent.

No one could ever mistake Rosa for a delicate flower.

She's all woman.

Long legs that lead up to thick thighs and a mouthwatering pear-shaped ass, paired with a slender waist that is perfect for large hands to grab on to.

However, when she turns around and I see those ample breasts being covered up by lace, as well as her crossed arms, I frown.

"Thank you for helping me," she struggles to say under my watchful eye.

"If you want to thank me, then I suggest you put some clothes back on. And quickly."

"Why the rush? I thought you said my virtue was safe with you?"

"It is. But that doesn't mean I'm a saint. Unless, of course, you've changed your mind and want to get fucked tonight?"

Her cheeks flame red at my crudeness, making her lean down and pick up her dress to cover her front with it. Unfortunately for her—and I'm starting to suspect for me as well—when she bends down, she unwittingly gives me a better view of the double D's she's been trying to shield from my wandering eyes. She swiftly picks up a small discarded bag sitting on the floor next to the bed and hurriedly races to the bathroom, closing the door shut behind her.

It's only when I hear her turn the lock that I exhale.

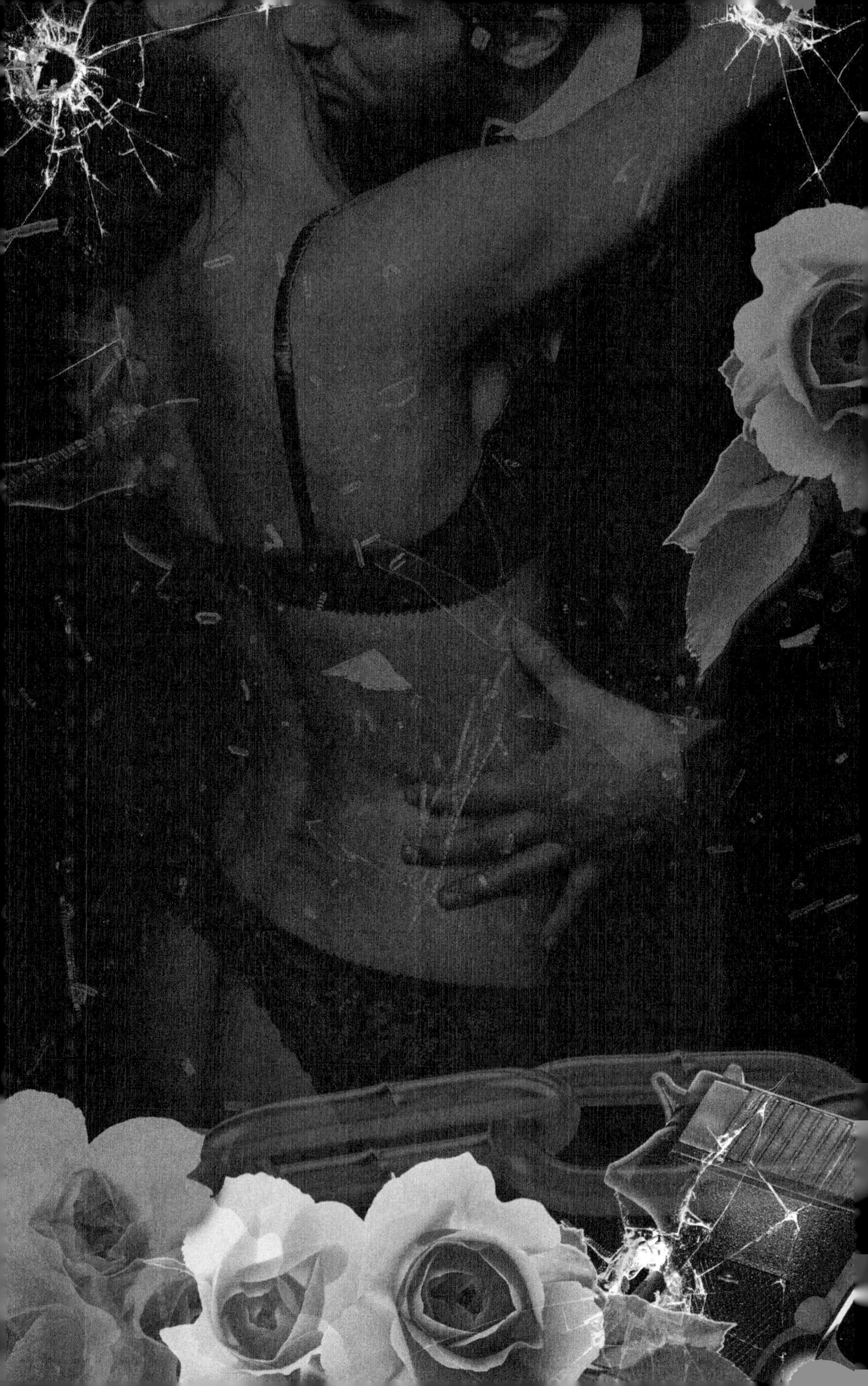

CHAPTER 8
Rosa

I SHUT my eyes and lean against the bathroom door, placing my hand over my chest, praying that the pressure is enough to get my beating heart under control. Its thunderous pulse is so loud I wouldn't be surprised if Tiernan could hear it clear as day in the next room.

Virgen.

It's only my first night with this man, and already I feel like I'm way out of my depth.

His presence alone is intimidating enough, guaranteed to suck all the oxygen out of a room, ultimately making it hard to breathe. But what's even more unnerving is when he directs that intrusive gaze of his and focuses all its attention on me. Summoning air into my lungs takes a back seat in priority when such eyes are hell-bent on picking away at the scabs on my soul.

One green.

One blue.

They would be beautiful if their intense stare didn't make me feel like they were slowly peeling away every layer within me, pulverizing every wall I've ever built to keep me safe. I've never met anyone who could strip someone bare with just one look. And frankly, I don't care for it.

It's as both terrifyingly frightening as it is exhilaratingly seductive.

"*Cálmate,*" I whisper to myself when my heart refuses to settle.

Tiernan is just a man.

Made of flesh and bone.

Not a god ruling over the underworld, even if his subjects proclaim him as such.

"Just a man," I repeat to myself as my heart slowly simmers down to its normal rhythm.

Once I've made sure I've collected myself, I dutifully hang my wedding gown on the door's hanger and turn the shower on. Before I step in, I slide off the rest of my clothes and frown when I see a wet mark right at the center of my panties. As much as I should loathe my husband, it's plainly obvious he affects me in other ways, too.

More carnal, sinful ways.

The evidence of my reaction to his hands on my body when he was helping me out of my dress currently stares back at me, mocking me for being so weak.

I wish I could call Francesco and ask for his advice. He would know how to handle this situation of desiring someone while still maintaining the upper hand. I fear with Tiernan he'll always be the one to hold all the cards in this twisted union of ours. Most *made men* do in marriages, so why should mine be any different?

I get into the shower and let the warm water hit my skin, wishing it could wash away all my doubts and fears as easily as it can cleanse me of the day's sweat and grime.

My thoughts are still on my *esposo* as I spill the fragrant hotel soap into my hands and begin to wash myself with it. I scrub the small patch of skin on my neck, shoulders, and back, making sure I cover every inch that Tiernan had defiled with his caress. To my utter annoyance, my lower belly warms at the memory, making the inside of my thighs slick with heat.

When I left Mexico to marry into the Kelly family, I expected many things, but not this. Not once did it ever occur to me that I could somehow become physically aroused by a man I barely know.

Maybe it's a good thing that I'm physically attracted to my husband.

Maybe it will make it easier to compartmentalize when he finally decides to take what is now legally his.

I've heard Francesco say a million times that sex doesn't have to involve feelings for it to be good. You don't even have to like the person you're fucking to have a good time. In fact, it's an added bonus if all you feel is blinding hatred for each other. Makes the fucking that much better.

His words, not mine.

Unfortunately for me, Francesco's experience in that department is all I have to go on. Neither Alejandro nor Javier would dare talk so openly on the subject of sex with me, which leaves my baby brother's sexual exploits as my only point of reference. Bringing up such a topic to an outsider, or God forbid my parents, would only gain me ridicule, as well as Miguel's punishing temper.

My hand presses down on my chest again, only this time it's not to slow my racing heartbeat, but to try and fill the gaping hole from missing my dearest brother. I wish he was here with me right now. Even if Francesco couldn't help me maneuver this new life of mine, he would have been able to brighten up my days with his smile and coax out one of my own.

I doubt I'll be smiling anytime soon.

Worst of all, I fear that without me home in Mexico, Francesco might try to fill the void I've left behind by losing himself at the bottom of a bottle or any other of his many vices.

Just as the worrisome thought passes through my mind, another quickly replaces it.

This one is even more troubling.

'Drink.' Tiernan had ordered, and when I refused to budge, he took my mouth hostage with his and poured the sharp sour liquid inside it.

I can still recall how the alcohol burned its way down my throat, but it was Tiernan's lips and tongue that really left their scorching mark on me, heating every nerve ending and making my pulse race. Everything about the small exchange held a heady electric quality to it, inflaming me from within and leaving me rooted to my spot to burn.

Like his first kiss back at the church, his second left me just as wanting. I have no doubt that Tiernan has an arsenal of weapons at his disposal to eviscerate his enemies. However, I'm hesitant to believe he's unaware that his kiss is also one of them.

Dangerous and downright lethal to any woman's sanity.

But apparently my mental stability is of no concern to my husband.

Only my virtue.

He said it was safe.

I'm not sure it is, though.

Not if he insists on kissing me like that whenever the whim hits him.

I push all thoughts of my husband away and finish washing up. By now, he's probably in the living room, either finishing his whiskey bottle until it's completely empty or blissfully asleep on a chaise lounge, dreaming up different and creative ways to unsettle me. Although Alejandro's advice was for me to get pregnant as fast as possible, knowing that I can postpone sleeping with my husband for one more night is the answer to a prayer I didn't even know I had made.

Before meeting Tiernan, I would have blamed my reluctance to sleep with him on us being lifelong enemies. Our families spending decades trying to kill each other doesn't exactly lay the best foundation to elicit trust in the bedroom or even outside of it.

However, I'm very aware that my hesitation is now purely because of the man himself and the unfamiliar emotions he's been drawing out of me. Maybe it's my inexperience that beckons caution, but the small voice inside my head whispers that no amount of prudence will ever prepare me for Tiernan when he decides to take me.

And take me he will.

It's all a question of time.

Virtue be damned.

Once I've rinsed the shampoo out of my hair and the liquid soap from my skin, I get out of the shower and dry myself off. Feeling too exhausted to blow dry my hair, I dry it with a towel and run a brush through it so as not to let it entangle throughout the night. I then open my bag to get some pajamas and cringe when I see a provocative almost see-through teddy one of my father's servants purchased for me to wear on my wedding night. In his mind, pleasing a husband in bed is a wifely duty, right up there with keeping a home spotless. A chore that needs to be done, no matter how unappealing.

I push the lingerie back into the bag, making sure it's out of my sight, and decide to sleep in the hotel's guest robe instead. I would rather sleep in the nude than put that horrid thing on me tonight. I'm at my wit's end with how much I've given of myself today as it is. After brushing my teeth and rubbing some coconut lotion on my legs, I'm ready to call it a night and be done with this day.

Of course, the saints don't seem to agree with me that I've paid my full penance already

Their displeasure is made obvious when my gaze lands on my husband and verifies that he's still in the room. While I was locked away in the bathroom, Tiernan decided to walk over to the floor-to-ceiling window and open its blinds completely so that he could admire the view of his city.

From where I'm standing, it's just another expanse of skyscrapers, with little depth and even less soul.

"You're still here," I say so that he knows he's no longer alone in the room.

"I am," he replies with a tight-lipped smile I can see from the window's reflection.

"It's late," I state the obvious, hoping he takes the hint and leaves.

But when he doesn't move a muscle to get out, my hackles start to rise.

"Tiernan—" I start to protest, but when he turns around to face me, all my objections to him being here die a quick death on the tip of my tongue.

My hands fasten on to my robe's waist belt, clutching at it to have something to do with my hands while my husband just stares in my direction. I swallow the boulder-sized lump in my throat as he walks over to the bed and sits on its edge, his impressive muscular back turned away from me.

"Come here."

Unlike earlier when I refused to drink his whiskey, I heed to the sternness in his voice and do as he commands. I'm not keen on finding out what he would do if I refused him again. At least not tonight. On feather-light feet, I slowly walk over to him, bracing myself for whatever he has in mind. I stop just a few inches away from him.

"Closer."

With my back ramrod straight, I take another step his way.

"Closer," he repeats, the chill of his tone only increasing my nervous state.

Not that I let him see it.

I tilt my chin up and walk to him until his knees graze my legs.

When Tiernan's gaze remains fastened on my waist, I realize that my hands are strangling my belt's knot. I quickly lower my arms to my sides and straighten my spine. This earns me a smile.

"I think we can do better than that," he taunts, widening his legs before pulling my belt in one hard tug until I'm standing in between his legs.

"Why are you still here, Tiernan?" I ask, not wanting to stretch out this little game of cat and mouse. "I'm tired, and I would very much like to go to sleep now."

"Hmm," he hums, the illicit sound bringing with it a dark undercurrent of desire I don't want to feel or focus too much on. "You'll get your sleep," he adds. "But first, it's time I'm paid my due."

I'm so perplexed by what he could possibly mean by that vague remark that on reflex my jaw slightly falls open. But just as quickly as it does, it also shuts back into place when Tiernan's hands begin to slowly rake up my legs from behind until they reach the back of my thighs. My teeth hurt from the force of keeping them shut, but the discomfort is preferable to the mortification I'd feel if he heard the wanton sigh that his touch provoked.

As my husband continues to rub his calloused palms up and down my thighs, fanning the flames I desperately want to extinguish, he tilts his head up until his intense gaze collides with mine.

"Tell me, Rosa, what exactly were you thinking when you decided to dance with my brother earlier tonight?"

What?

My astonishment must be clearly stitched on my face because he lets out a sardonic exhale when I don't respond quick enough.

"Did you forget already?" he asks, almost sounding bored, as if his hands rubbing on my feverish skin had no effect on him whatsoever.

"I don't understand the question," I respond, thankful my voice comes out sounding just as detached as his.

"Then let me simplify it for you. The first dance of the bride should always be given to her groom. It's his right as her lawfully-wedded husband, and you stole that privilege from me by offering it to my brother. You don't strike me as a woman who easily breaks tradition. Especially for a man you haven't said more than two words to. Therefore, there must have been a reason you accepted Shay's offer to dance. Naturally, I'm curious." His domineering gaze sparks with a gleam of said curiosity.

I bite down on my bottom lip to keep the truth of my actions from spilling out of me. Not that my brother-in-law has earned any such fierce loyalty from me with one little dance. But then again, neither has my husband, for that matter. The only thing that stops me from confessing why I chose to dance with Shay is that I take no comfort in being cruel for cruelty's sake. I've seen how the Kellys suffered in silence today at the absence of their daughter and sister, and I, for one, will not use her memory to justify my actions nor use it to stab at the open wound they all share.

If there is one Kelly that deserves my loyalty, then it's her.

Since she and I are the same.

Two women sacrificed in the name of peace.

Two women now at the hands of their enemies.

"Well, Rosa? Will you not satisfy my curiosity? Was your reasoning for dancing with my brother based on pure boredom, or was it intentionally done to hurt me?"

"Can a man like you even get hurt?"

He shakes his head with a haughty, thin grin, his piercing eyes glued to mine, his fingers digging into my skin.

"No. Only the image I wish to uphold can."

"So, it wasn't the impropriety of dancing with another man that wasn't my husband that offended you, but that others saw me do it?"

"I think we both know the answer to that question."

I'm not sure I do, but it's hard to decipher his remark when his fingers are so dangerously close to the wetness building in between my legs. My heart kicks back up when his hands pull away from my thighs, preferring to lean back onto the bed and place them on his lap. I try not to notice the way his square shoulders strain under his black shirt or the fact that his defined six-pack threatens to rip his buttons out.

The man is majestic, I'll give him that.

"Do you know what I've learned since becoming boss of the Irish syndicate?" he starts, pretending to check his cufflinks. "It's that when someone begins to toe the fine line of my patience, sooner or later they'll pass a point of no return and regret every choice they've made that got them there."

"It doesn't bode well for our marriage if one innocent dance tests your patience in such a way."

"No, it does not," he states pointblank, the severity in his tone making me grasp for balance. "But I am a fair man. You'll learn that about me soon enough. There is so much I have to teach you."

Right now, I don't want to learn anything from this man.

Something tells me being his student is a recipe for disaster.

For my heart as well as my soul.

"If you want to discuss the merits of fairness, then I'm sure it can wait until tomorrow, can it not?"

He shakes his head.

"I'm not a big believer of procrastination. Why leave a lesson left untaught for tomorrow when you can do it so diligently today?"

"And what exactly is this lesson you are so eager to teach me?"

"That the wedding band on your finger doesn't protect you as much as you think it does."

My jaw slacks open again.

"You can't hurt me," I state with all the confidence I have.

"No." He shakes his head again, wagging his finger at me. "The treaty stipulated that I can't *kill* you. No one ever said a thing about hurting you."

He's lying.

He must be.

Alejandro swore to me that every family member made a blood vow to protect and care for the daughters that were sold into bondage for the sake of ending the Mafia Wars. He wouldn't have lied to me.

Would he?

"You're lying," I rebuke, looking down at his relaxed

demeanor on the bed and feeling utterly unnerved by how at ease he is.

"Am I? I might be. It's possible. *Made men* aren't known for being trustworthy. But there is one truth that not even you will be able to discard so easily. You vowed today to honor and obey me before God and all his witnesses. Which means that if I feel you have broken those vows in any way, then I'm within my right to punish you for it."

My eyes widen at the threat gleaming in his distractingly exquisite eyes.

"Take off your robe."

"No," I'm quick to reply, my heart rattling double time in my chest.

My apprehension multiplies at the devilish smile that tugs at the corner of his upper lip. The sinister grin tells me that my refusal to do as he says was the exact response he was hoping for.

At lightning speed, he lifts off the bed and pulls me onto his lap, my chest hitting the edge of the mattress in such a way that the only thing preventing me from falling is his large palm pressed down on my lower back.

"If this is your idea of rational behavior, then I shudder to think when you're being completely obtuse?!" I bite back through gritted teeth.

"Such big words," he mocks. "So elegant. So fucking sophisticated. Let's see how well-spoken you are after a few hard slaps on that rear of yours, aye?"

I don't know what has me more frightened—that my husband

of a few hours is about to spank me, or the fact that his accent just became that much thicker and more arresting.

When Tiernan lifts my robe over my head, I'm thankful it covers most of my face and how the debasement has my cheeks flushing a deep red.

"Do you always come to bed naked?" he asks, using that same husky tone in his voice that puts me on edge.

I don't answer him.

If I'm going to end my wedding night being punished like an errant child, then I'm going to act like one and stubbornly keep my words to myself.

The cold air on my heated skin isn't enough to cool my temper or my imagination. Suddenly I wish I could see his face so I can at least try and tell what he's thinking.

Tiernan takes his sweet-ass time just appreciating my bare bottom. Undoubtedly, he's doing it on purpose just to agitate me more.

"I see this isn't the first time you've found yourself over someone's lap," he utters faintly, while his thumb lightly traces over the bite marks my father's belt buckle left on my lower back, ass, and upper thighs. "Miguel's handiwork, I presume?" he adds, but I don't make a sound, not wanting to confirm his perceptive deduction either way. "I've never liked your father. Now I hate him even more," he whispers softly, making sure to brush with the pads of his fingers every scar that he can find.

But it's the ones lying dormant inside my soul—the ones that will forever remain out of anyone's reach—that yearn for the same delicate attention.

I push the weak thought away and bury my head into the mattress, biting into the duvet cover to keep myself from begging him to continue on with his soft caresses. He begins to slowly massage each ass cheek, running his hand back and forth, squeezing the sensitive flesh every so often in between every gentle stroke.

But I'm not fooled. This is just the eye of the storm that is coming.

It dawns on me that while Shay needed to believe that someone was being kind to Iris, Tiernan wants to make sure that his sister will not be the only soul that suffers tonight.

"This will hurt much worse if you don't relax."

"Isn't that the point? For it to hurt? For you to punish me?" I snap back, cursing myself for breaking my vow of silence so quickly.

"Who says you can't find pleasure in pain?"

"Right," I scold. "If that's the case, then remind me the next time you do or say something I don't like to lay you over my lap."

CRACK!

The sound of his palm connecting with my butt cheek sounds scarier than the pain he inflicted. In fact, compared to my father's heavy hand, Tiernan's is quite tame. If his intention was to scare me into obedience through the threat of pain, he'll have to do much better than that.

"Do you always speak your mind like that? So freely?"

I wrinkle my brow in confusion.

I wasn't aware that I had been up until he said it. I've tried to maintain a cold barrier between us, but I guess being face down and ass up, waiting to be spanked, opens up old resentments that prohibit me from keeping my mouth shut.

"If me speaking my mind offends you, then maybe you should double how many slaps you intend to give me."

"Maybe I will."

"Maybe I don't care."

"Hmm. I think you do."

God, I wish he didn't hum like that. It makes other parts of my body tingle. Parts that have no right doing so.

With one hand, he restarts his soothing massage on the butt cheek that I'm sure has his five large fingers imprinted on it, while his other begins to sneak up my inner thigh.

"What... what..." I stammer, aghast, when he's mere inches away from the apex of my thighs. "What... are you doing?"

"Proving you wrong."

I suck in a breath when warm fingers begin to sink into my folds. I start to thrash on his lap, needing him to pull his hand away from my core before he finds proof of how much he affects me.

"Shh, *acushla*. Be still. This is going to end quicker than you think. Trust me."

Trust?

Can that word even exist between us?

Especially with the circumstances we find ourselves in?

Highly unlikely.

Unfortunately, no matter how much I try to pull myself off him, the strenuous endeavor ends up being pointless. Tiernan is just too strong to loosen his grip on me. The robe has also slipped enough off my head that I now can see my nemesis's face with utter clarity. And to my chagrin, this also means he has a perfect view of mine.

"Please… don't," I rasp out, not wanting his fingers on me like this.

Especially when they are starting to make me feel too good for words.

"Fuck," he groans, staring right at me with that penetrating gaze of his. "That's it, *acushla*. Beg."

Refusing to give him what he wants, I bite my inner cheek so hard that blood begins to pool in my mouth. The snicker he lets out when I turn my head away from him has me clutching the duvet in my fists.

"So stubborn, aren't you? Don't fret, Rosa. I know many ways to eradicate that awful trait in you. Just give me time."

"*¡Vete al diablo!*" I think to myself, my bravery confined only to my inner thoughts now.

He continues to rub his fingers up and down my slit until they are fully soaked with my juices.

Francesco was right.

Hate is a great aphrodisiac.

Mierda!

It's only when his hands travel higher and his thumb finds my throbbing clit that I squirm. I do everything in my power to swallow down the moan lodged inside my throat, unwilling to give Tiernan the satisfaction of ever hearing it. He's already taking enough pleasure with my body's natural response to him as it is. Like hell I'll give him more to gloat about.

"Pleasure and pain are more alike than you think. You would

never know the difference of either one if you've never experienced both," he muses, while his deft fingers play with my sensitive nub to the point that I'm almost panting.

SLAP!

Virgen!

"Hmm. I can tell you're starting to understand," he cajoles, with a mocking tone.

But I'm suddenly too far gone to care since he's replaced his thumb on my clit with two fingers, moving them in slow, deliberate circles. His other hand kneads my ass cheek in tandem with each stroke of the clit, guaranteeing I lose my mind, one stroke at a time. After that, it doesn't take much more to have my body madly trembling on top of him. The pleased groan that escapes him both irritates me as well as kindles the fire threatening to burn me alive.

SLAP!

Oh, dear God!

I'm so close.

So damn close.

All it will take is either a few more seconds of his knowledgeable fingers playing with my clit or another hard slap to my ass cheek for me to grab the orgasm that's within arm's reach. The need to cum starts blurring my vision and has me actively searching for Tiernan's hand to do its worst.

But the instant he feels my body aching for his touch, he brutally pushes me off his lap, making me fall to the floor on hands and knees like a cat breaking its fall. It takes me a minute to recover from the shock of hitting the ground so brutishly like that.

I can't say the same thing about my denied orgasm, though. It's going to take me much longer to recover from that.

"Hmm," he hums, staring at the wet mark on his knee. "You've ruined a perfectly good pair of pants, wife. Next time, I'll make you lick them clean with your tongue."

My cheeks burn from embarrassment as he gets up from the bed and walks towards the bathroom as if nothing happened between us just now.

I'm still on my knees, listening to the sound of falling water from his shower, when the stark truth of Tiernan's intentions hits me like a slap to the face—his reasoning for tonight's so-called punishment, and I fear for our marriage, as well.

My husband doesn't want my humility.

He wants my humiliation.

CHAPTER 9
Colin

"TO ANSWER YOUR QUESTION, no. I did not sleep with her," Tiernan confesses, tired of Shay's constant badgering since the moment we came through the door.

"Are you fucking serious? It's been almost a week?!"

"Your point being?" Tiernan arches a brow.

"My point is that you're a fucking killjoy, brother. Goddamn it!" Shay curses, reaching into his jacket, pulling out a wad of cash and handing it over to me.

I don't say a thing as I pocket my cousin's money.

"You bet on me sleeping with my wife on our honeymoon?" Tiernan asks, his amused brow lifting even higher on his forehead.

"Sue me. I thought it was a sure thing," Shay accuses, slumping into a chair across from Tiernan's desk.

"And I'm sure Colin told you there is no such thing." Tiernan smirks, his attention falling back to his computer screen.

179

"He did. I just didn't believe him. I mean, come on. I'd do your wife in a heartbeat—Hernandez or not."

Tiernan's humor disappears at his brother's lewd remark right at the same time I slap Shay across the head. It's better that I put my cousin in his place before his brother decides to.

"Fucker! What did I do now?" Shay asks, aggravated, rubbing the back of his head while simultaneously staring daggers at me over his shoulder.

"It's not what you did but what you said," Tiernan intervenes on my behalf. "My wife isn't like the women you take to your bed. You can't say whatever pops into that head of yours whenever you feel like it."

"Hello?! It's just us here. No one is around. I know how to behave in mixed company."

"Since when?" I add with a scoff.

"Fuck you, Col. I can behave. I just choose not to," Shay sulks, crossing his arms over his chest in his tantrum.

"Hmph," I mumble, unconvinced.

"So, if you haven't been banging your wife twenty-four-seven like a normal red-blooded man would on his honeymoon, just exactly what have you been up to this past week?"

"What do you think? I've been working." Tiernan points to his computer screen to drive the point home.

"Sometimes I wonder if *Máthair* didn't drop you on your head when you were a baby," Shay reprimands, shaking his head in disappointment.

"Funny. I sometimes wonder the same thing about you." Tiernan grins.

"Hardy har har." Shay rolls his eyes, gaining a low chuckle from his older brother. "So where is your Spanish flower anyway? Since she's not sore in bed, sleeping off the good fuck you were too much of a pussy to give her, what has your new wife been up to?"

"Why do you care?" Tiernan asks indifferently as he examines whatever spreadsheet is in front of him. "What Rosa does or doesn't do with her time shouldn't be any concern of yours."

I know from experience that when my cousin uses that dry apathetic tone of his, he's anything but.

And so does Shay.

"Do I hear a smidge of defensiveness in your tone, *dheartháir*?" Shay counters, not hiding his teasing grin from Tiernan.

Tiernan redirects his cold gaze from his laptop towards his brother.

"I suggest you see a specialist since you're obviously hearing things. If you must know, I left Rosa back at the hotel. Does that satisfy your curiosity, *dheartháir*?" he adds the last part mockingly.

"Why is she still at the hotel? I would have thought you'd have moved her into your apartment at The Avalon by now," Shay retorts in confusion. "Did you leave her there to pack or something? I don't remember her bringing a lot of shit with her when we picked her up at the airport."

"Why would she be packing?" Tiernan asks, muting out most of his brother's ramblings.

"Huh, I don't know, asshole. Maybe because she knows she

can't stay at the hotel forever. It has been a week, after all. I would have understood you keeping her there if you were having hot dirty hotel sex, but since it's obvious you've become a fucking eunuch all of a sudden, I don't see the point of keeping Rosa locked away in a hotel room."

Tiernan doesn't so much as flinch at his brother's provocation. Not that it's the first time Tiernan hasn't reacted when his brother provoked him. Shay is the only man breathing that can talk trash to the boss like that. If anyone else dared to do so, Tiernan would have cut out their tongue before they even uttered a word.

"The Liberty Hotel has all the amenities a woman like Rosa needs. She's fine exactly where she is."

"Jesus, Mary, and Joseph! You cannot leave her caged in that hotel forever, Tiernan. Sooner or later, you'll have to take your wife home."

"Then I choose later. Now... is there any more sound advice you wish to give me, brother, or can I get back to work?"

The heavy stilted silence between them as they stare each other down is so thick, you'd need a chainsaw to cut through it.

"It wasn't her fault, Tiernan. You have got to get over it. You can't punish her for something that wasn't in her control. She had nothing to do with Patrick—"

"Enough!" Tiernan shouts, slamming his fist on the desk, silencing his brother once and for all. "I've got shit to do, Shay. Actual fucking work that needs my full attention. My wife does not. Since I'm sure you have more pressing things to do than waste your time trying to piss me off, I suggest you get right to it and do them before I lose my patience."

"Whatever you say, *boss*," Shay replies sarcastically as he gets up from his seat. "I have to go to the harbor to check on the shipment that arrived last night and do inventory anyway. When you're in a better mood, give me a fucking call. If I'm up to it, who knows? I might even answer it."

When Shay starts to retreat from the office, I'm right at his heel.

"Not you, Colin. My brother can take care of the shipment himself. Alone."

"Fucker," Shay mumbles under his breath, since taking inventory of a gun shipment that size is usually a two-man job.

I half expect him to give Tiernan more shit, but Shay surprises me when he doesn't object and leaves the office without saying another word. I close the door behind him and stand in the center of the room, waiting for Tiernan to give me my orders.

"Have a seat, Col."

I do as I'm told and take the seat in front of his desk that Shay just vacated.

"I have a job for you," Tiernan says, not beating around the bush.

"What is it, boss?"

He clasps his hands under his chin and stares at me.

"What I have in mind might not be to your liking. You can refuse to do it if you so wish. I don't want you to feel obligated to say yes just because I asked."

"What do you need, boss?" I repeat, unfazed.

"It's about Rosa."

His somber tone, more than his wife's name, takes me a bit off guard.

"I need someone that can watch over her. Just until I can find someone else to do the job. Someone I can trust."

"You want me to babysit your wife?"

He chuckles sardonically.

"You're spending way too much time with Shay, *ceathrair*. You can scarcely call it babysitting since my wife is hardly a child. But I do need someone I can trust unequivocally to protect her when I'm not around. And I don't anticipate being around her much, hence, why I need you."

I don't ask him why he doesn't want to spend time with his wife. I'm more concerned as to why he feels she needs to have her own personal bodyguard.

As if reading my thoughts, Tiernan leans back in his chair, his palms laid flat on his desk.

"This treaty *Athair* forged with the other families is still too fragile a thing. Like a newborn, it needs a village to ensure its survival. Someone might have a hard time letting the war go, and killing my wife, while she's under our care, would make it extremely hard to keep the peace."

"You think someone wants to hurt Rosa?"

"Not her, but us. Or even her brother, Alejandro. I might be wrong, but it's a risk I can't take."

"What about the men that are protecting her now?"

"They're good and fine standing outside a door. Not so much when it comes to accompanying her out in the real world."

"Fair enough. McCarthy and Walsh have experience in doing

that type of service. They used to be Iris' bodyguards when she was a young lass. I'm sure they will be up for the job."

"McCarthy is a bastard that can't keep his dick in his pants, known for stepping out on his wife whenever a pretty face is involved. Walsh, on the other hand, is pushing fifty, has a bad knee, and rumor has it he's become a raging alcoholic in his old age. Neither one is a good candidate to keep my wife safe."

"What about Murphy?"

Tiernan shakes his head.

"Too young."

"O'Brien?"

Another shake.

"Too old."

"Hmm. What about Ryan? He's a good lad. Competent. Trustworthy." *And gay.*

But I decide to leave that part out, even if my gut tells me that Ryan's sexual preferences might make him the perfect fit in Tiernan's eyes.

"Too soft," he rebukes evenly.

"How so?" I question, confused, since the lad is over six-foot-four in height and weighs well above two hundred and forty pounds of pure hard steel. There is nothing soft about him.

"Rosa's strong and bullheaded. She needs someone who won't be a pushover. Someone who isn't afraid to tell her no. Ryan is used to dealing with foul-mouthed brutes, not delicate flowers. He wouldn't know how to handle Rosa, and she would use that to her advantage. I wouldn't even give him a week before she had him wrapped around her finger."

"You think she could redirect his loyalty that easily?"

"My wife can be very convincing. She's used to getting her own way. Ryan wouldn't stand a chance. Let's leave it at that." He smirks, almost sounding proud of his new bride.

"Is that why you think I'm the only one suitable for the job?"

"Yes. I can't think of anyone else up for the task. Can you?"

When I don't answer him, he pulls his chair forward, extends his arms on his desk, and clasps his hands together.

"The men you chose to guard the penthouse can stay. But Shay is right. Rosa will soon tire of spending every waking moment in that hotel room, no matter how luxurious it is. I need you to accompany her at all times whenever she goes out. When she retreats back to the hotel, you can let your men take it from there."

I don't have to think too hard on my answer since Tiernan's request falls in line with the one Alejandro had forced on me. When I told Tiernan about the conversation I had with his brother-in-law before his wedding day, he didn't seem one bit surprised, nor did he share Alejandro's worries about his bride's safety.

But something must have happened between then and now for the boss to change his tune. Tiernan might not have slept with her, but it took less than a week living with Rosa to change his mind and make him care about her welfare. It will be a cold day in hell before my loyalty could shift towards the cartel prince, but I gave him my word where his sister's safety is concerned, and now I will do the same for Tiernan. Although it took the boss this long to see the writing on the wall, I've known since the beginning that Rosa would need to be protected.

It's because of Rosa and the other sacrificial families' daughters that there was a ceasefire in the Mafia Wars, after all.

But peace is a tenuous brittle thing.

It only takes one person's malicious actions to light the fuse on this dynamite keg of a treaty and blow up ten years of arduous, peaceful negotiations. And what better way to do it than to eradicate the very thing that was sacrificed in the name of peace.

With that thought in mind, I get up from my seat and start to head out the door.

"Should I take that as a yes?" Tiernan utters behind me, a tinge of mirth to his voice.

"I'll keep her safe. You have my word," I concede and leave him to his business.

I pass the busy open office space and head towards the elevator as fast as my feet can take me. Tiernan might feel at home here in this large skyscraper—making sure that the Kelly's clean, reputable construction business casts a large enough shadow to hide his criminal empire—but I, for one, hate it here. I have never liked being cooped up between four walls, especially this high up, where the exits only lead to stairwells that would take a good fifteen minutes to get down to the ground floor. But that's not the only reason why I don't like coming here. I prefer the grime and dirt of the streets over the sweet smell of fancy lattes and pastries in a boardroom. Give me busted-up knuckles, some cracked ribs, and sweat pouring down my brow after a heist any day of the week. Hustling on the streets compared to claustrophobic cubicles, boring computer screens with open Word documents filled with endless jargon, or the backstabbing that happens between colleagues just to get a leg up in the business world, just feels like it's a more honest way to make a buck.

I leave that ugly monotonous part of the business to the boss.

Tiernan is a chameleon in that regard.

He can hold meetings in a boardroom just as easily as he can conjure fear in a dark back alley.

I'm not as versatile.

When I finally step out of the Kelly's main headquarters, I rush to get into my car and drive over to The Liberty Hotel, intent on getting down to business. When I arrive at the floor of Tiernan and Rosa's hotel suite, I turn to Darren, one of the higher-ranked soldiers standing guard, and ask him to fill me in on all of Rosa's coming and goings.

"Not much to tell. Since she's arrived, she hasn't left the suite. Not once. Unless you count the time she left to get married. Other than that, she's stayed put," Darren explains with a shrug.

She's been in Boston for five days now, and all she's seen is the inside of a fancy prison cell. Maybe Shay is right. Maybe Tiernan is taking this a bit too far.

"Fair enough. I'll ask Mrs. Kelly what her plans are for today and the rest of the week. That way we can arrange a schedule between myself and your guards."

Darren offers his agreement to my plan then stands to the side so I open the double doors to the penthouse suite and formally introduce myself as part of Rosa's security entourage.

The instant my eyes land on her though, I freeze to my spot and lose my train of thought.

Rosa is sitting on the floor, hugging her knees so that they are pressed against her chest, while she watches over the Boston skyline. She doesn't have to turn my way for me to tell that she's been crying. Uncomfortable with witnessing such a private moment, I clear my throat to make her aware that she's no longer alone in the room. She wipes whatever tears remain and puts on a smile before she turns to face me. Instead of saying hello, or some other bullshit people say in greeting, she tilts her head to the side and just stares at me. When a few minutes pass, and neither of us say anything, I take a few more steps into the room, pretending to take in the surroundings instead of looking straight at her.

"It's Colin, isn't it?" she asks, her voice soft and delicate.

I nod, taking another step closer to her.

"We've met before. You came to pick me up at the airport."

Another nod. Another step.

"You were at my wedding, too."

Nod. Step.

"You're my husband's cousin."

"I am."

"Ah. And you talk, too. I was starting to believe you didn't have the capacity." There is a teasing quality to her voice, but unlike Shay teasing it's not meant to offend, only just to be friendly.

She relaxes her head onto her shoulder, angled just so, her brown eyes looking straight into my green ones. My brows pull together in confusion when she makes no attempt to lower her gaze and gawk at my scars. They are usually the first thing people see when they look at me. But Rosa is perfectly content just staring into my eyes. It's unnerving, to say the least.

"Why are you here, Colin? Not looking for my husband since I'm sure you know his whereabouts better than I do." She laughs sullenly, the sad melodic tune only serving to unnerve me further.

"The boss has requested that I be your bodyguard for the time being," I explain.

"Bodyguard? Aren't the prison guards with AK47s standing outside my room enough to keep me safe in my cell? Or is my husband fearful that one night he might come home and find that I've flung myself out the window? If that's the case, remind him that these windows are all made from bulletproof glass. It will take more than a chair to break any of them." She knocks on the glass to drive her point home.

"Are you suicidal?" I question hurriedly, worried that her mind went there.

"No, Colin. Sadness and homesickness have not yet made me that desperate. Ask me again in a month's time. Maybe my answer will be different."

My Adam's apple bobs away as apprehension sinks its ugly claws into my chest, sure to leave its mark.

"I've made you uncomfortable." She sighs. "I'm sorry. I guess you just caught me at a bad time."

When I don't say anything in return, her chestnut gaze sparkles with curiosity.

"You're not much for words, are you, Colin?"

I shake my head.

"Then maybe my husband got something right after all. If I'm to have a bodyguard, I'd much rather it be someone who didn't need to fill the silence with useless chatter. It would be awfully tiresome if I had to spend my days making small talk, when I'm perfectly content having deep, meaningful conversations with my conscience."

She throws me a meek smile, and I hate how my chest suddenly tightens.

"So, *bodyguard*, what exactly are you here to do? Watch me do nothing? If that's the case, then I can tell you right now that you'll be begging Tiernan for another job in no time."

"What would *you* like to do?" I ask, my soft voice sounding odd to my ears.

She cracks a smile. The first genuine one I've seen so far on her lips since I've known her.

"What can I do confined to this cell?"

"We could leave."

"Leave?" she repeats suspiciously.

I nod.

"And go where?"

"Wherever you want."

"Mexico."

I squint my eyes at her with a frown.

"Sorry. I couldn't help myself." She lets out a halfhearted laugh. "Even if I knew where I wanted to go, I couldn't tell you. I've never been to Boston."

I take that in and think about where a woman of her caliber would feel at home. It takes me less than ten seconds to realize I haven't the faintest clue.

"What kind of shit... I mean... things, did you like to do back home?"

"I liked spending time with my brother."

"Alejandro?" I question, surprised, since Alejandro doesn't exactly give off the "family man" vibe. He might care for his sister's safety, but I don't see him willingly wanting to spend time with her.

"No. Not Alejandro. I meant Francesco, my youngest brother," she explains with true deep longing in her voice. "He had a knack for keeping me busy since he was always up to no good." She laughs again.

Between her sad sighs and her genuine giggles, I don't know which one I'm having a harder time dealing with.

"What did you do when you weren't babysitting the brat?" I mumble.

"I like art. I loved going into Mexico City and visiting the historic museum they have there and seeing whatever new exhibit was in town. Does that help?"

I eat the remaining distance between us until my body eclipses hers in my shadow and I stretch out my hand. She blinks twice before she understands and places her hand in mine. I lift her up from the floor in one fell swoop.

"Let's ditch this place."

When her eyes begin to water with happiness, my throat starts to clog. Before I can stop her, Rosa launches her arms around me, her cheek pressed against my chest.

"Thank you, Colin. Thank you."

I let her hold on to me longer than I should, but when she seems to have composed herself enough, my hands go behind my back and unlatch her grip on me.

"Let's go."

Her smile is a mile wide as she grabs her bag and walks side by side with me out of her hotel room for the first time in days. I take her to the Boston Museum of Fine Arts and we spend the whole day there. For a girl who said she didn't mind the silence, she sure talked her head off, describing how every painting and artifact made her feel. After we have lunch at a nearby restaurant, we decide to go back and see another exhibit, one where the artist preferred to paint portraits. After all we've seen today, these are my least favorite.

"You don't like it," Rosa says after we've stared at one particular painting.

It's of a girl wearing only one pearl earring. She either lost the other earring sometime during her sitting, or the painter was just too lazy to add its counterpart.

"Why don't you like it?" Rosa insists when I don't give her an answer.

"It's a painting." I shrug, not understanding what more there is to it.

"Yes, I'm aware it's a painting." She laughs. "But I can tell you don't like it. I'm just curious as to why that is."

I offer her another noncommittal shrug.

"Okay. Then at least tell me how it makes you feel?"

My forehead scrunches at the question, but this time I answer her.

"Nothing."

"Nothing?" She questions back. "You have no reaction to it whatsoever?" She places her hands on her hips, looking none too convinced. "I know that can't be since you've been looking at it like it's personally offended you. So, tell me, what is the first word that pops into your head when you look at it? One word."

"It's a lie."

"How so?"

I fumble with my words, trying to come up with the best way to explain myself so she'll understand.

"You see that one?" I point to an artsy painting of a lone river with a bunch of trees and bushes around it.

"The Monet?"

"Yeah. Whatever. That one right there reminds me of cold Irish mornings. Or when Da and I would go fishing at the crack of dawn to a nearby lake we had close to our home. It's serene. Simple. Honest," I admit, giving the painting another glance and calculating how easy it would be to steal it and gift it to my Uncle Niall, who is always homesick for Ireland.

"But this one…" I begin to explain looking at the eyesore in front of us, "doesn't say shit to me. My guess is the girl either lost the damn earring after fucking the artist, or that he was in too much of a hurry to get her clothes off to even bother painting the other one on her ear. Every time I look at it, all I see is some asshole painter wanting to get into a young girl's panties by making her look ten times more beautiful than she really is. It's shallow and uninspiring."

Rosa lets out a giggle, causing a couple standing close by to give her a side eye. She covers her mouth with her hand to muffle her laughter while I throw the pricks my best menacing glower. They take the hint and quickly leave.

"Colin Kelly," she whispers, my name sounding like delicate porcelain coming out of her mouth. "I think there is an art aficionado in you after all."

I scrunch my nose at that.

She snakes her arm through mine and pulls me into the next room where more nature paintings—Monet's I think she called them—hang on the walls.

"I was starting to doubt Tiernan would give me a wedding present, but now I see he chose his timing perfectly. You, Colin Kelly, are the best gift I could have ever hoped for. This might just be the beginning of a wonderful friendship. And I could use a friend more than you know."

I don't say anything to the contrary or risk bursting her happy bubble.

No one has ever been excited about calling me their friend.

And if I'm honest, the only ones I have are my cousins.

For the rest of the day, we tour the museum and make plans to visit the Institute of Contemporary Art next week. When I leave her back at the hotel, Rosa doesn't look half as desolate as when I found her.

She looks happy.

Or as happy as she can be under her current living conditions.

As I step into the elevator, my phone vibrates in my pocket, Tiernan's name flashing on the screen.

"How was it?" he asks when I answer the phone.

"Fine."

If he was Shay, my one-word answer would have pissed him off.

But Tiernan takes it at face value.

"Good. That's all I need to know," he says, ready to end his check-in on today's outing, but when he doesn't, I know he can sense my hesitation on the line. "Unless there is something else you want to add?"

"Shay is right," I grunt, thankful the asshole isn't here to hear me say it.

"That must have been as difficult to say as it was for me to hear," Tiernan jokes halfheartedly. "And just exactly what is my pain in the ass brother right about?"

"Take her home, Tiernan. Or I will."

CHAPTER 10
Rosa

TIERNAN CURLS his hands into fists only to unclench them open a second later. I've been transfixed by the nervous tick for most of our car ride to Back Bay. To say I was surprised when he came home early tonight and told me to pack up my things because we were checking out would be the understatement of the year. I was starting to believe that The Liberty Hotel was going to be my permanent home throughout my entire stay in Boston. It was only when I began to pack my things into my suitcase that I remembered that Boston is my home now. Not just a place I am visiting.

But I guess today has been a day full of surprises.

I wasn't expecting Colin Kelly to show up on my doorstep either this morning. Much less spend the day with him at the Boston Museum of Fine Arts. All in all, this was probably the best day I've had since I left home. Alejandro had made it a point to warn me off Colin, almost hinting at the fact he was far more dangerous than my husband and brother-in-law, Shay, combined. But after spending a full day in his company, I don't see it. Colin was intellectually precise in his musings, even if he couldn't appropriately articulate with them. He was thoughtful, kind, and at times even made me laugh with his spot-on commentary. For the first time in God knows how long, I forgot the treaty, my homesickness, and for that matter, even my husband.

I'm just worried that Tiernan might spoil my budding new friendship with his cousin somehow. That he'll see this small speck of happiness inside me and decide to crush it with his bare hands before I get used to the feeling. It's not like he's given me any proof to the contrary, that he wants me to be happy. In fact, Tiernan Kelly has gone to great lengths to ensure that I'm not.

My first week being married to him has been less than pleasant. Since our wedding night, he has barely said two words to me. Coming home at all hours of the night, smelling like whiskey, cigarettes, and cheap perfume. I think I even saw glitter on the lapel of his collared shirt once, evidence that he was at some strip club before he decided to come back to the hotel suite.

Not that I would demand justifications to his face. In fact, I made sure to always be in bed when he came home. I would fake being asleep and watch him from under my eyelashes, going into the bathroom to take his usual nightly shower before he retreated into the living room to sleep on the couch.

One thing I've learned about my husband is that the man is a creature of habit. He likes things to remain a certain way, in their proper spot, and to deviate from that just sets his teeth on edge.

Hence my surprise when he told me he was taking me to his

home in Back Bay. I'm positive that his abrupt decision to take me home is the reason why he can't stop balling his fists every five seconds.

It's the lights from the SUV trailing behind us with our security detail that grab my attention away from Tiernan's nervous tic and onto the man himself.

"Will I need so many bodyguards if I'm living at your place?"

"Why?" he retorts, using that same cold tone of his that I've begun to detest.

"I would think Colin would suffice. I don't see the need of having four men guard me when one can do the job."

If I expected him to explain why he sent Colin to be my personal bodyguard this morning, then I'm bitterly disappointed when he refuses to answer me.

"I doubt anyone would dare ambush me in the great Tiernan Kelly's private home," I try again, hoping my hit to his ego will incite a reaction from him.

"Are you saying that when you lived in Mexico, your father didn't have guards with machine guns guarding his property?" he says, acknowledging my presence for the first time since we got into his town car.

"He did."

"Then why should I be lenient when guarding mine?" He cocks a brow.

I bite back my tongue at the gleam of loathing in his distractingly beautiful eyes.

Property.

That is what I am to him.

Just another prized possession to do with as he wishes.

Resentment in his choice of words has me turning my attention to the passenger window and pretending he's not even in the same car with me.

"Tomorrow we are having lunch at my parents' home. I expect you to be ready at noon for us to leave," he decides to break the deafening silence between us after a few minutes.

"Tomorrow?" I ask, snapping my head his way.

"Yes."

"But tomorrow is Sunday."

"I'm well aware what day it is. What of it?"

"I'm used to going to church on Sundays," I protest, making him turn slightly towards me, staring at me like I've grown a second head. "I'd very much like to go. Will that be a problem for you?"

"No. I can take you if that's what you want."

"Thank you. I appreciate it."

He turns his attention towards the window, his fist flexing and relaxing yet again.

"Tell me, am I to expect my blushing bride to always be this overly devout?" he asks after a spell, still glaring at the passing scenery.

"Is going to church regularly a real indicator of anyone's faith? If I'm not mistaken, most *made men* have no qualms committing the most horrendous crimes and murders Monday through Saturday and still find the time to go to church every Sunday morning. I don't think attending mass holds any weight on whether I am a devout Catholic or not."

"I'm not interested in other people. I asked you the question," he says, this time looking me dead in the eye.

"I don't consider myself to be a religious zealot if that's what you're asking."

"But you still want to go to church?"

"I do."

"Why?"

"Why?" I parrot, aghast.

"Yes, why?"

I take a moment to consider his question since it's clear he's not going to drop the subject otherwise.

"It comforts me."

"Comforts you?"

"Are you going to repeat everything I say? Yes, it comforts me. I've been going to church since I was a child. I see nothing wrong with the ritual."

"So, you go out of habit?"

God, this man is infuriating.

"I go because it makes me feel good."

He takes my explanation and chews it on it for all but ten seconds.

"There are many things a woman can do on her knees that can make her feel good that don't involve prayer."

I hate how my cheeks flame at the innuendo. And I hate him even more for planting the idea in my head.

"I wouldn't know," I bite back.

He smirks.

"Maybe one day I'll teach you."

"One lesson taught by you is enough for me. Thank you very much."

"Maybe not for me," he cajoles, his gaze falling from my eyes and landing on my lips.

We're so consumed with our banter that it takes us a minute to realize the car has stopped.

"We're here," Tiernan announces, opening his car door, looking right as rain while I'm a complete hot mess from the way he was devouring my lips with just one look.

I don't wait for him to open my car door for me since I've learned that such gentlemanly behavior is beneath him. I get out of the car and follow him towards the front door of the large building —the words Avalon Exeter in bold silver letters right above the main doors.

"Good evening Mr. Kelly. Mrs. Kelly," the doorman on call announces as we pass through the large reception area.

My forehead instantly creases at the unfamiliar greeting. I'm not alarmed at the fact this man knows who I am since there was a picture of Tiernan and me on our wedding day spotlighted right on the front page of every Boston newspaper there is.

I do, however, think that it will take me two lifetimes to get used to being called a Kelly.

"Good evening, Jermaine. Please ensure that my wife's luggage is brought up in a few minutes. My men will help you carry them upstairs."

"Of course. Is there anything else that you might need?"

"Yes. Can you tell me if Elsa has been to the apartment today?"

"She has, sir."

"Good. Then that is all."

Jermaine gives him a pleasant nod but doesn't spare me a second look.

When we get to the elevator, I watch Tiernan insert a key to gain access to the top floor.

"Who is Elsa?" I ask curiously, since the name doesn't sound Irish to me.

Latvian, Polish, maybe even German, but definitely not Irish.

"My housekeeper and cook. I told her to have everything in order and a meal ready for us when we arrived."

"Oh." I bite my lip.

"Who did you think she was?"

"I don't know. A friend. A colleague. A mistress even. I don't know that much about you to make an informed guess on who you let into your apartment."

"Aside from Elsa, no one else," he rebukes dryly, making it painstakingly clear that he wished things would stay that way.

I really don't understand him.

If bringing me home is this much of an inconvenience to him, then why do it?

Unless, of course, this is his olive branch. His subtle way of wanting to give this marriage an actual shot. If that's the case, then I will milk this opportunity for all it's worth.

When the elevator doors swing open, we step right into a living room with bare floor-to-ceiling windows all around, giving way to the city's lights beyond them. My shoulders slump as I take in his sanctuary. The apartment is extravagantly cold and practical. Just like Tiernan. The colors of the interior design never stray from the basic white, black and grey—a bachelor pad if I ever saw one.

"There is the kitchen." He points to the open-space kitchenette filled with the latest gadgets that I'm sure only Elsa ever uses. "This, of course, is the living room."

"It's nice."

It's not.

It's completely soulless.

And I fear that trait fits Tiernan's personality down to a T.

"Let me show you to your room," he says, walking to the back of the apartment in long, fluid strides.

I have to quicken my step just to keep up with him.

"Wait? My room?" I ask when his hand is already clutching at a door handle.

Instead of gifting me a response, he opens the door so I can take a peek inside.

Another room with little color and even less imagination.

"Across from you is my home office, and at the end of the hall, my bedroom. I'm going to take a shower, and then there is some work I still have to do tonight. Help yourself to whatever Elsa has cooked us for dinner. I already ate." And with that explanation he leaves me to it, strutting towards his bedroom, leaving my mouth agape while staring at his backside until he slams his door shut.

Great.

I was stupid to think we were making progress by him moving me into his home. It seems he just switched one prison cell for another.

I slam my bedroom door loud enough for him to hear and fall on my mattress, wondering how my life got this way.

After an hour or so has passed, my stomach begins to grumble, demanding that I venture out of my room in search of food. When I crack my door open, I can hear Tiernan in his office, talking on the phone at the same time he clanks on his keyboard. I slip out and head towards the living room and kitchen. The yellow post-it left on the counter by Elsa tells me I can find a pot roast in the oven. I slice myself a few cuts and add the vegetables to my plate, heating it up in the top-of-the-line microwave. After it dings, I take the plate out and plop onto a nearby stool and begin to eat my dinner.

Alone.

Again.

I should be thankful that my husband doesn't want to spend any time with me. Wasn't that why Alejandro had suggested I get pregnant as soon as possible? So I can have a life away from my betrothed? But this doesn't feel like living. It just feels like I'm letting the days pass me by without any joy to speak of. This isn't a life.

No.

Alejandro's plan is a good one.

If I have a child, an heir to the Kelly dynasty, then I'll finally be able to have a life worth mentioning. Tiernan might not want to be around me—for which I am truly thankful since the man gets on my every last nerve— but he will no longer see me as a nuisance if I just bear him a son. Right now, it's plain to see he doesn't know what to do with me. He doesn't want to be married to me, that much is clear, but he doesn't know more than that, either. He's grasping at straws on how to deal with the awkward situation we find ourselves in. As I see it, two lives are being put on hold for the sake of the treaty. His and mine. We are both stuck on an eternal pause button, and neither one of us knows how to press play and just get on with our lives.

With a child, or maybe even more than one, both of us will have some kind of neutral ground to work with. I'll gain his respect as the mother of his children, and he will leave me to do with my days as I see fit, only conversing with me in regards to his heirs.

He will no longer feel burdened with the shackles of the treaty and will feel free to live his life parallel to mine. Most *made men* have girlfriends on the side. Some even have homes for their mistresses and share their beds on the daily, leaving only the weekends occupied with their real family. It's not the fairytale marriage most girls dream about having, but it's a marriage I can live with.

Who knows?

If I please him enough, Tiernan may even be open to the idea of me having paramours of my own.

Although, as I ponder the idea, it doesn't seem very likely.

After I've had my dinner, I tidy up the kitchen and then take my luggage that his men left beside the elevator doors back to my room. Instead of unpacking, I decide to go back into the living room and spend the rest of my evening watching TV. I scroll through the channels to find something worth watching, but nothing really grabs my attention. I leave it on some show about rich wives and how they go about their spoiled days. I've never been a fan of reality television, but their train-wreck drama is preferable to wallowing in thoughts of my own. I'm not sure how long I watched the show for, but somewhere between one blonde slapping another housewife on the show across the face and another making a drunken fool of herself in some swanky restaurant, I must have dozed off. When my lids flutter open, I see that the television has been turned off and that someone has placed a fleece blanket on top of me as I slept.

No. Not someone.

My husband.

Since he's the only other person in this apartment with me.

Still a little bit groggy, I get up from the couch and walk back to my room. As I walk down the hall, I realize that Tiernan is no longer in his office. A quick glance at the grandfather clock inside his office tells me that it's not even midnight yet. Either my husband's busy week has finally taken its toll on him, or he's avoiding me in his room.

How am I ever going to get pregnant if the only way I can get my husband to touch me is when I've somehow pissed him off, so he feels the need to spank me?

If I'm to get what I want, true freedom, then I have to take my future into my own hands and do something about it. With a new resolve, I go into my room and take a quick shower. Once I'm finished, I go in search of the bag that holds my honeymoon lingerie. I pull it over my head and quickly check myself in the mirror to see how it looks.

I feel bite-size chunks of my pride being ripped out of me as I pull down my panties so that all I have on is the embarrassing sheer teddy. I throw a quick prayer up to *Virgen de Guadalupe* and beg her to give me the courage I need to see this plan through.

I take a deep breath, leave my room, and walk down the hall towards the bedroom where my husband is holed up. I let out a relieved exhale when I turn his door's knob and find it unlocked. I step inside the dark room, my heart beating a mile a minute that I'll get caught, or worse—get thrown out on my ass before I'm able to accomplish my mission.

Even through the blanket of night, the full moon casts enough light that I can see Tiernan's silhouette lying under the covers on the left side of the bed. I walk to the other side and slide in next to him, letting out another sigh of relief when he doesn't stir awake.

Although now that I'm lying beside him, him being asleep isn't exactly part of the plan. I was supposed to seduce him, not just lie here looking up at the ceiling, not knowing what to do next.

Mierda.

What now?

"Your thoughts are as loud as your feet," Tiernan suddenly says, making my heart flip of its own accord.

"You're awake," I croak out.

"Hard not to be with all your racket," he mumbles, still half asleep as he turns around to face me. "What do you want, Rosa? What was so goddamn important that you felt the need to sneak into my bed in the middle of the night?"

"Teach me," my response is immediate.

"Come again?" he asks, sounding more alert than he was a second ago.

"I asked you to teach me."

The room is shrouded in darkness, yet I can still see how his blue eye turns a shade darker than his green one.

"And what lesson do you want to learn tonight?"

My stomach flutters at the sound of his voice going an octave lower.

"What you said in the car. How can a woman have pleasure while on her knees? I want to know."

"Do you really?"

"Yes," I whisper hoarsely.

"Very well. Turn on the light."

"Is that really necessary?" I grip the bedsheet for dear life.

"If I'm going to teach you to suck cock, then I'm going to see you do it."

God.

Does he always have to be so crude?

And why the hell does his dirty mouth always bring such salacious imagery to my mind?

When I don't budge, he turns over to his bedside table and switches the light on.

"There. Much better."

For him, maybe.

Not for me.

When I planned how this was going to go, I envisioned my actions would be concealed by darkness. I could have mustered enough courage to do what had to be done in the shadows. Not out in the open like this.

"Having second thoughts?" he asks smugly, not hiding how my embarrassment amuses him.

When he snatches the covers out of my death grip, my mortification multiplies tenfold with the loud shriek I let out.

"If you were on the fence about your tutoring, you shouldn't have worn that." He points at my teddy.

I'm about to fly out of his bed when Tiernan stops me by wrapping his arms around my waist and holding me hostage.

"Let go," I seethe through gritted teeth.

"Tsk. Tsk." He shakes his head behind me. "Haven't you ever watched the Discovery Channel? You can't taunt a lion by flaunting such a delicious treat in his face and not expect him to take a bite out of it."

"I said let go. I've changed my mind."

A shudder runs along my spine as Tiernan leans in closer to my ear, his sweet breath on my skin making my insides melt.

"Next time you decide to sneak into my bedroom and slide into my bed, be prepared to get fucked. Otherwise, get out." He pushes me away with such force, it's a miracle I don't fall to the floor. On shaky knees, I get up off the bed and start making my exit. Tiernan doesn't so much as let out a snicker as he watches me retreat with my tail tucked between my legs.

Virgen.

Am I this much of a coward?

Even when my own happiness is at stake?

My fingers grip the door knob, but my feet refuse to budge.

When I turn around, Tiernan is sprawled on his bed in nothing but boxers, his arms resting behind his head. There is a large Gaelic crest tattooed to his left muscled pec. Other than that, I can't see any other tattoos on his firm, muscular body. And to my shame, my greedy eyes are taking in each flawless patch of skin just to make sure I don't miss one hidden away somewhere.

"I thought you were leaving?" he asks dryly, pulling my attention back to his face.

"I changed my mind."

"I didn't know you were so fickle. I'll make sure to add it to your long list of flaws."

"You're making a list? I don't think you're the most qualified person to do that. You don't know the first thing about me."

"It's a figure of speech. And I know enough."

"No, you don't. We've hardly spent any quality time together as husband and wife for you to say that."

"Does the time I left my handprint on your ass count?"

"No, it doesn't."

"Are you sure?" He cocks a brow. "Because in that outfit, that's the only quality time together as husband and wife I'm interested in right now."

And to drive the point home, he removes one hand from beneath his head and hides it underneath his Armani briefs. I swallow dryly as I watch him stroke his cock, up and down, ever so slowly.

"Since you've changed your mind, does that mean you still want to learn?" His smooth velvety voice makes my lower belly coil in desire.

I nod, licking my suddenly chapped lips.

"Good. Come here."

I take a step towards the bed, his eyes fixed on me while he strokes his cock in his hand.

"Get on your knees on the bed."

My pulse quickens with every order, threatening my heart to explode inside my chest at any given moment, but still, I do as he commands and place my knees on the edge of his bed.

"Good girl."

"Don't patronize me," I try to snap back, but my words hold very little heat behind them.

"You don't like to be called a good girl?" he teases.

"I'm twenty-seven years old. I haven't been a girl for quite some time."

"True. But how many twenty-seven-year-olds do you know that still have their hymen intact? Your virginity doesn't help your argument, now does it?"

The frown that springs forth on my face is immediate.

As if it's my fault I held on to my virginity for this long.

Like he didn't have a hand in my forced celibacy when he swore to uphold the treaty.

It was because of him, and men like him, that I spent most of my adult life unable to have friends, much less a boyfriend who was brave enough to touch me. Since the ripe old age of seventeen, everyone knew I was engaged to the notorious Tiernan Kelly, and because of it, my father made sure that any man with a working penis, who even dared to be within arm's reach of me, needed to hold the last name Hernandez. I don't know about Tiernan's sexual past, but I doubt any of his lovers included family members. And if I was to lose my virginity before my wedding day, then that was the pool of men I had at my disposal. Having sex with a cousin, even if twice removed, felt too much like incest for me. I preferred being a virgin to the alternative.

"Just spare me the good girl commentary."

"Does this mean I shouldn't expect you to call me Daddy either?" he taunts with a low chuckle.

The man is having fun at my expense while blatantly jerking off in front of me.

God, he's infuriating.

I would tell him as much if I wasn't so fascinated by how his cock just seems to grow larger and thicker with each stroke.

"Come closer," he commands when he sees how transfixed I am by what he's doing.

I inch closer to him, until my knees hit his bare feet.

"Closer. Put your knees on either side of me," he instructs, his voice once again sinfully throaty.

Again, I do as he says, until my ass is seated on his knees. He pulls his hand out of his boxers and returns it to behind his head.

"Take it out."

"And by it, you mean—" I point to his bulging shaft.

"My cock, Rosa. Or is there a more sophisticated way to say cock where you come from?"

"Dick," I mumble more as an insult to him than the name I'm comfortable with to describe his privates.

"Dick will do." He chuckles. "Just quit stalling and take it out."

I bite my bottom lip, my gaze falling from his face back to his member. Tiernan lets out a groan, his cock bobbing under the thin black material of his bedsheet.

"How did it do that? You didn't even touch it," I ask curiously, honestly amazed that a body part could have a mind of its own and move whenever it felt like it.

He lets out another low chuckle, and it's the first time I register that he looks relaxed. He doesn't have that permanent scowl on his face that he persists on keeping anytime he's with me. He looks boyish somehow. If I squint my eyes just a little bit, he almost looks like his brother, Shay.

Carefree and playful.

"What's so funny?" I ask, not as nervous as I was a minute ago.

"You. You're the one that's funny."

"Because I don't know how a man's anatomy works?"

"Because you are a grown-ass woman, yet you are acting like a child at Christmas, looking at my cock like it's a toy she desperately wants to play with but doesn't know how."

His statement isn't too far from the truth, I'll give him that.

"Are you going to tell me or not? How can it bob like that all on its own?"

"You want to see how?"

I nod.

"Bite your lip again," he orders.

My forehead creases in puzzlement, but I do as he says and bite my lip.

This time instead of him groaning, he mutters the word fuck just as his cock bobs again.

"See? Magic," he teases, melting further into his mattress.

"Does that happen every time a woman bites her lower lip around you?"

He shakes his head.

"It's a pesky little habit that only started since you came into my life."

I don't know why that provokes butterflies to flap their wings and fly frantically in my stomach, but it does. With the warmth his words bring me, I bite my lip again as I pull his boxers down enough to free his cock. My ass falls back on his legs as I stare at the monstrosity lying in between them.

"I... I was not expecting that."

"No? What were you expecting? A candy cane?" He plays it off, adding to his previous metaphor.

"Who's being funny now?" I joke, slapping his thigh. His large muscular mouthwatering thigh.

Gulp.

"Now, what do I do next?" I ask almost breathlessly.

"Touch it," he instructs, his tone dark and delicious.

Not wanting to spend too much time pondering the pros and cons of what I'm about to do, I fling into action and run a finger up the length of the bulging vein on the side of his cock.

"It's smooth. Almost like velvet," I say absentmindedly, in complete and utter awe.

"It will taste even smoother down your throat. Trust me."

A delicious shudder runs down my spine at his words as I keep stroking his cock, up and down his length, loving how it bobs up, searching for my touch. Once I'm confident that I know what I'm doing, I wrap my hand around the crown and stroke it to its base.

"You're a natural," he grunts.

I look up at him through half-mast eyes and see that he's

propped himself up, using his elbows to keep him up so he can have a better view of what I'm doing.

"What now? Tell me what to do."

The genuine smile that crests his lips makes me preen with pride that I've pleased him somehow.

"Use your tongue and lick it. When you feel brave enough, put me inside your mouth."

The way he tapped into the fact that I'm summoning all my bravery to do any of this makes the whole exchange less frightening to me somehow. It also shows me that there is a hidden side to Tiernan that can be caring. Even affectionate. I much prefer this side of him to the one who has no regard for me whatsoever. Needing to keep him like this, docile and sweet, I make a note to try and please him with my tongue in any way I can.

Slowly, with my eyes locked on his, I lower my body until his cock is inches away from my face. My eyelids only close when my tongue twirls around his crown, tasting his salty essence and breathing into my lungs his very male musky scent. There is also a hint of citrus that drifts off his warm skin.

And Tiernan is definitely warm.

The man is a furnace, burning away and scorching my tongue.

A total contradiction to the arctic chill he's thrown at me for the past week.

I try not to focus on that thought and instead put all my attention into licking his cock clean. But as I do it, the most confusing and unexpected thing happens. My core begins to constrict with every lick and languid stroke of the tongue. The apex between my inner thighs becomes slick with wetness, and I feel it pouring down my legs and onto his. If he feels it, he doesn't say anything, content in me performing the task at hand. The sudden need to have more of him is overwhelming, and before I know what I'm doing, my mouth latches onto his length and pulls him into my mouth as far as I can take him.

"Jesus, fuck," Tiernan groans loudly, his fingers going straight to my hair. "Give a man a fucking warning, *acushla*."

I don't ask him if I'm doing it wrong, since I can taste on the tip of my tongue that I'm not. The salty sweetness burst onto my tastebuds, urging me on. The way his fingers dig into my hair, forcing me to swallow him up and down, only increases the hollowness between my legs. I feel bereft as well as powerful.

He was right.

This is a much better way to enjoy being on my knees.

"Relax your throat, *acushla*."

I do as he says and try to relax my throat, although I'm not really sure how someone can do that. Tiernan uses my hair, like one would use reins on a prized stallion to race to the finish line, and guides me to swallow more of him. His hard shaft dominates me completely as it fills my mouth, until it's touching my tonsils. Tears start streaming from the corners of my eyes, but he doesn't let up, and I wouldn't want him to, either. I try to relax my jaw, my hands finding purchase on his hips, so that I can take in more of him.

"Fuck. Just like that," he praises, making me work ten times harder to hear him say those words again.

Unashamedly I begin to rub myself on his legs, desperate for the friction, as he plunges in and out of my mouth. I'm wet and needy and so turned on I think I'm about to combust into flames. But just as I'm getting into the rhythm that will ensure we both cum like this, I'm suddenly pulled off my prize and flung onto the bed.

"What... What... did I do something wrong?" I ask, saddened that he pulled me away from his cock.

But as I stare into Tiernan's eyes, his blue one the color of a sea storm, my insides quiver in anticipation. He licks his lips, his gaze falling from my face, to my chest, and then quickly back to my face again.

"My turn."

CHAPTER 11
Tiernan

ROSA'S beautiful brown eyes hide behind two fine heavy slits as she purposely bites into her fat bottom lip, knowing full well what it does to me.

"I wasn't done yet," she utters, her voice so fucking needy, it's a miracle my cock isn't ten inches deep inside her yet.

"That's not how this game works. I'll tell you when you're done."

"So that's it? School's out?" she taunts, throwing my game back on my lap.

Like fuck it is.

But instead of saying those words, I just shake my head and get down to what I really need to know.

"Are you on the pill?"

"Why would I be on the pill?" she counters back in confusion.

"Doesn't matter."

It does since I'd like nothing more than to cum inside her sweet dripping cunt, but I guess cumming on her tits is a good runner-up.

Or her mouth.

Her flat, taut stomach.

Her ass.

The options are limitless.

My gaze trails over her body, making my mouth water, unsure where to start off first, much less finish. There is so much of her. So much skin. So much smoothness. So much soft.

Just… so much.

"Tiernan," she breathes out, her hand gently caressing my cheek, pulling my attention away from her temptress body and back to her lovely face.

I hate how her just saying my name stirs something inside me.

Something possessive.

Something dark and far too fucking alluring.

But it's the way she strokes her thumb over my stubbled cheek that really does me in.

"I told you that if you came to my room dressed like this, then you wouldn't leave it until I've fucked your silhouette into my mattress. Those were my terms, and you decided to stay anyway. But you're in luck. I'm feeling merciful tonight. I'll let you leave if you've changed your mind again. I know how indecisive you can be."

Instead of the scowl I expected to gain from her, all I get is another soft caress to my cheek, creating another spasm in my chest.

"I'm fine right here," she whispers. "I want to learn. Teach me."

Fuck me.

But how can I say no to that?

Especially when her pussy is soaking my bedsheets, needily rubbing against my aching cock.

While keeping my gaze fixed on hers, my hands begin to crawl down the sides of her body until they go to the hem of her flimsy see-through lingerie at its center.

"Don't say that I didn't give you an out." I smirk, tugging gently at the material. "Once I've ripped this off you, there is no turning back."

"I don't want you to. This is what I want."

"And what exactly is that?" I ask, giving the teddy another tug and making her breasts jiggle. "What do you want?"

She struggles forming her next words, but then lets out a soft exhale when she realizes she's going to have to say them out loud if she wants me to start with her lesson.

"I want you to make love to me," she confesses at last.

I don't even try to hide my chuckle from her.

"Oh, *acushla*. If lovemaking is what you are looking for, then you sneaked into the wrong bedroom."

Her brows pull together.

"Are you saying that you're not going to have sex with me tonight?"

"Aye. Sex, yes. I'm perfectly capable of fucking you every which way 'til Sunday. Figuratively and literally. Making love, as you put it, is not within my many capabilities."

She mauls her lower lip, as if considering her options, making precum drip down the head of my cock.

"Very well. Then do that."

"Do what?"

Her cheeks bloom a pretty shade of pink when she realizes the words I yearn to hear.

"Fuck me then."

Damnú.

Fuck.

"Oh, I intend to, *acushla*. Thoroughly. Roughly. And repeatedly."

Her breath catches in her throat as I rip the garment in half with one hard tug. My eyes wander up over her naked body, seeing her light brown nipples perk up at attention under my scrutinizing gaze. I lean my head down and pluck one between my teeth, giving it a good bite, making her back arch up from underneath me. I suck on it until she is a quivering mess of nerves, panting for breath, and on the verge of cumming just from me sucking on her pebbled bud. I only let go of her nipple to show its counterpart the same abusive treatment.

"Tiernan," she croaks, her fingers latching on to my hair, weaving in between my locks and tugging on them to keep her tethered.

I release her nipple from my mouth with a loud pop and stare at her.

"Did I tell you that you could touch me?"

She shakes her head.

"Then put your arms above your head if you don't want me to

spank that fat ass of yours for misbehaving. You do what I say, when I say it. Is that understood?"

She gives me a small nod, holding her arms up and resting them on the pillow, nervously biting her bottom lip as she goes about it.

Fucking temptress.

"Enough of that," I mumble, pissed. "From this point on, I'm the only one who gets to do that."

And before she has time to ask me to explain, my mouth crushes onto hers, until my teeth have a good grip on her lower lip. I suck, tug, and bite at it, until I'm sure my teeth marks are permanently imprinted on her soft flesh. If she dares disobey me and decides to chew on her lip again without my say so, I want her to feel the half-crescent moons my teeth have left on it.

"Argh!" she wails, as I lick the seam of her lip where I drew a little blood.

I plunge my tongue into her mouth and grab her by her wrists, so she doesn't move from her spot. She wiggles and thrashes under me as I take all the air from her lungs and suck it into mine. When her legs widen and wrap around my waist so she can rub her bare pussy on my cock, I don't punish her for it. Instead, I just deepen our kiss until there isn't one thought in her mind besides needing my cock inside her.

Unfortunately, the kiss backfires on me, leaving me just as consumed with desire as she so obviously is, and when she wiggles just enough to have my crown firmly at her entrance, all my plans to torture her some more fly out the window.

I pull away from her lips, breathing hard and heavy like I've just run a fucking marathon instead of only giving my wife one simple, sinful kiss.

Rosa's eyes are wide in alarm as my dick decides to inch inside her all on its own.

"Wait! Wait," she bellows, her chest heaving up and down.

I've never been one for taking orders, but I do as she says and wait for her to catch her breath.

"Is it going to hurt?" she asks, her shy blush clawing at my control.

"Yes."

I don't see the need to beat around the bush or lie to her.

Most virgins cry bloody murder their first time. When I was a kid and hungry for pussy, I didn't care who I was balls deep inside of, but it only took taking the virginity of a few Catholic girls that went to my high school to know that popping cherries wasn't my kink. I quickly changed tactics and started fucking the teachers instead, leaving the inexperienced schoolgirls for some other asshole who could console them afterwards.

"How much?" she asks.

"On a scale of what?"

"I don't know. On a scale of one to ten, I guess."

"Eleven."

"That's reassuring," she mumbles, her teeth instinctively going to her lip but then stopping halfway, thinking better of it.

Good girl.

"I'll tell you what. Since I'm in such a benevolent mood, I can give you a choice. I can either go inch by inch until you're used to my size, or I can rip off the band-aid in one go. Your choice."

Again, she thinks hard on her decision before giving me an answer, like it's some quiz she doesn't want to fail. I wouldn't mind her hesitation so much if her cunt clenching around my cock didn't physically pain me.

"Rosa," I mutter through gritted teeth in warning.

"Rip it off," she blurts out.

"Are you sure?" The words stumble out of me before I have time to stop them.

Immediately I reprimand myself for the stupid-ass question.

Why the fuck should I care?

But instead of taking her first answer to heart and just fucking her raw in one go, I actually wait for her reply.

"I am." She nods assuredly. "I only have one condition."

To this, I arch a brow.

"You are hardly in a position to negotiate, *acushla*." I grin, looking down to where my dick is connected to her pussy.

"I know. But I'm still asking."

"Fine. I'll indulge you, this once. What do you want?"

"I want to touch you."

I frown.

"That isn't part of the deal."

"Again, I know. But I'm scared now. I just want to be able to hold on to something. Just to keep my bearings. *Please*."

The vulnerable way she's looking at me in this very moment strikes too much of a chord inside me. Up until now, Rosa has tried to mask such vulnerability from my eyes. For her to expose herself like this and let me have a full view of her fear is the reason why I concede to her wishes.

Or maybe I'm just getting soft in my old age.

I blame the latter.

"Fine."

The relief that instantly blooms on her face makes her features look almost innocent. Trusting. It's an aphrodisiac that I didn't know could have such an effect on me. But as my cock swells painfully to its full extent, I can't deny how looking at such trust in her eyes is tipping me over to the edge and making me want to fuck her even more.

Ever so carefully, she brings her arms down and places her delicate hands on my taut forearms. Her touch alone burns my already feverish skin, making me wish I hadn't been so clouded by lust and just declined her request to touch me.

But it was that damn trust in her eyes that spurred me to offer some leniency.

"Do you trust me?" I ask, needing her to verbalize what I can see so clearly in her eyes.

"Yes."

"You shouldn't."

"I know."

I run my tongue over my front teeth, my pulse racing in my veins, prompting me to just fuck her already and be done with it. But it's her goddamn fear of the unknown that has me hesitating. Instead of doing what every cell in my body demands and breaking her seal with one hard thrust, my hand trails down in between us and begins to play with her clit.

"What are you—"

"Shh, *acushla*. This will make it all the better. Trust me."

Her tongue peeks out from between her parted lips as she lets out a sigh when my ministrations begin to have their desired effect. I lean down to her ear, nibbling on her lobe, as my fingers draw small circles on her sensitive nub.

"You're fucking drenched, wife. I can smell you from here. How much does that greedy pussy want to get fucked?"

She starts to moan with every dirty word that falls out of my mouth, her nails sinking into my skin in tandem with my fingers quickening their pace.

"Such a perfect little slut. I bet you fooled everyone back in Mexico with your holier-than-thou air you like to flaunt so much, but you don't fool me. You're just another stupid cock-drunk whore who is only content when her cunt is filled to the hilt."

Her eyes widen in utter outrage at my words, acting like she's never been this insulted in her entire life, but the way her canal opens up for me, so that my cock can bury itself a little deeper inside her, tells me that my virgin bride likes every foul-mouthed word I throw at her.

"That's it, *acushla*. Act like you're not so fucking turned on right now that all it would take is your cunt swallowing my cock to have you seeing stars. You like me calling you my dirty little slut. You like it when I treat you like the insolent whore you are. Because that way you can justify in your head why your pussy is begging to be fucked by your greatest enemy."

When her dripping cunt begins to clench around my dick, a tell-tale sign that she's about to cum, I slap her pussy down hard, gaining another shocked glare from my pretty little innocent wife.

"You cum when I say you cum," I grunt before biting her neck, making sure to leave my mark for every motherfucker out there to see who this fragile flower belongs to now.

"Argh!" she wails uncontrollably when I begin to play with her clit again.

This time I'm not gentle with my touch. I spit into my hand and use the saliva as lubricant to toy with her bundle of nerves. This only makes her pant out harder, shout incoherently, provoking the smug smirk on my face at witnessing how responsive she is to my touch. As if unimpressed with my cocky grin, her nails scratch at my forearms, making me hiss when I see she's drawn blood.

"You've made me bleed, wife. Not many people can say they've had the honor. But I guess it's only fair. Since I'm about to make you bleed all over my cock."

"*Virgen!*" she yells in Spanish, while I'm coaxing out her first orgasm of the night.

"Not for long," I grunt into her ear. "Cum, *acushla*. Cum on your husband's dick like you want to."

And just as her orgasm hits her, I thrust deep into her core, breaking her hymen and stealing the last remains of innocence she has been holding on to for long enough. Her loud wail of ecstasy merges with the hint of pain I've just inflicted on her. My lids close, and my breathing becomes shallow, as I try hard not to cum inside of her from just one thrust. A hard thing to accomplish since her cunt strangles my cock, intent on milking it dry.

She's so fucking warm.

So tight and inviting that it takes inhuman effort on my part not to pound into her and cum.

"Tiernan," she says softly, looking into my eyes with both tears of joy and misery. "Don't stop. I can take it."

Fuck.

"Such a greedy little slut. I've already stolen your prized possession, and still you want more."

Instead of rising to my provocation, she lifts up her head a little until her teeth scrape over my stubble, her tongue following suit.

"It didn't hurt as bad as I thought it would," she whispers, placing chaste kisses on my neck, jaw, and cheek. "I can take it now. The worst is over, right?"

I stare into her eyes with a menacing grin on my lips.

"The worst hasn't even started, *acushla*."

And with those words, I pluck her hands off my shoulders and pin her down by the wrists like I wanted to. I bite hard into her neck again and start to repeatedly thrust into her, making sure she won't be able to walk straight in the morning.

"Oh God!" she begins to yell in my ear, making me let go of her wrists so that one of my hands can cover her mouth.

My cock plunges into her pussy in unmerciful strokes, her eyes rolling to the back of her head with each thrust.

"Look at you," I hoarsely mumble in her ear. "You just lost your virginity, and already your pussy is stretched and begging for a beating. Is this what you wanted, wife? To be used like a fucking ragdoll for your husband to get off on?"

Her muffled cries are too muddled by my hand for me to understand what she's saying. The only thing I make out is that she's no longer speaking in English. Since I'm not fluent in Spanish, she could be speaking in tongues for all I know.

When I'm close to my own tipping point, I remove my hand from her mouth and kiss her, swallowing up all her loud moans. She tastes like the sweetest sin, her core constricting around my length, spurring blind spots to begin to blur my vision. The minute her eyes become two large saucers, surprised she's cumming again, I bite down on her lip, just so I can fuck the orgasm out of her. Once I've made sure she's ridden her high to its conclusion, I then quickly pull out and jerk my cock in my hand until spurts of my cum cover her stomach. Sitting back on my heels, I stare at my handiwork and frown.

Not wearing a condom was stupid.

But then again, she caught me by surprise.

Next time I'll be better prepared.

When I feel her eyes on her belly, staring at my release, my frown disappears.

I rub my cum into her skin and then lift two fingers to her lips.

"Open your mouth," I order.

Her eyelashes bat a mile a minute, but she obeys and parts that gorgeous mouth of hers open for me.

"Suck."

She doesn't put up a fight, which is a testament to how good a fuck I gave her. The small amount of time I've spent with my wife has taught me she lives to fight with me.

Her tongue wiggles around my fingers, licking them clean, her gaze once again going half-mast.

For a woman who has never had sex in her life, she sure as fuck knows how to play with a man's heartstrings. If I had a heart, that is, then I'm sure I would have gotten on my knees to give her whatever she wanted, just to have her suck my cock as well as she is sucking my digits. My shaft instantly hardens with the idea, telling me it's done waiting for the second round of tonight's big event.

"Does that taste good?"

Under hooded eyes, she nods, her cheeks turning pink in embarrassment now that the full haze of lust has lifted somewhat.

"Good. Get accustomed to it. Because my cum will now be your breakfast, lunch, and dinner until I say otherwise."

Her flushed cheeks only increase in color when I pop my fingers from her mouth.

I get off the bed and put my arms under her limp body to lift her up.

"Where are we going?" she asks, startled, wrapping her arms around my neck, afraid I might drop her.

"I'm going to give you a bath to get you nice and clean, wife. But don't you worry. You won't remain that way for long. Or do you want to end tonight's lesson here?" I arch a brow.

She shakes her head and then cradles it into the crook of my neck.

"I told you I want to learn," she whispers, making the hairs on the back of my neck stand on end at how fucking trusting she's being right now.

I could do whatever I wanted to her at this very moment, and she'd let me.

It's as much a turn-on as it is aggravating.

But instead of revealing my thoughts to her, all I do is tip her chin up with my knuckles and stare into her warm earthy-brown gaze.

"Be careful what you wish for. Some lessons you can't take back once you've learned them."

"I'm not afraid."

"You should be."

※

The next morning, I wake up with strands of hair in my mouth. I brush them away, my eyes landing on the woman lying beside me, blissfully asleep, using my chest as a pillow.

I replay in my head all the things I did to her body last night, my cock hardening at reclaiming my wife again this morning.

"Good morning," she coos, her voice dripping like molasses.

"Hmm."

She raises her head and places her chin on my pec to look at me. I brush away the errant locks that keep straying to her face and gently tug them behind her ear.

"I must have fallen asleep after the second shower we took," she says shyly.

To my cock's bitter disappointment, she did.

After I had my way with her against the bathroom vanity after our bath, and put her on her knees so I could cum on her breasts, I had no alternative but to give her a shower. Of course, I didn't waste the opportunity and fucked her from behind, but that last fuck took its toll on her, and before I had her wrapped up in a towel, she was already half asleep in my arms.

"Did you sleep well last night?" she asks, tracing the Kelly family crest tattoo I have on my chest with the pad of her finger.

"One thing you have to learn about me is that I don't do small talk in the morning. I don't do small talk, period."

"Then what do you do in the morning?" she asks innocently, as if last night's sex-fest didn't give her any clues.

I gently run my knuckles up and down her bare back until her skin breaks out in goosebumps.

"It all depends," I reply.

"On what?"

"On whether or not I have a beautiful woman lying naked beside me in bed."

"You think I'm beautiful?" she preens, as if no one has ever uttered those words to her before.

Instead of stroking her nonexistent ego, I ask her a more pressing question. One that me and my cock are both far more interested in.

"How sore are you?"

Like clockwork her cheeks blush crimson.

"I'm okay."

"That's not what I asked."

"A little sore."

My frown is instant.

"Why?" she asks curiously, pulling her finger away from my tattoo in favor of running it over my frowning lips.

I slap her finger away with more force than was needed and grip her wrist in my hand.

Her eyes widen in alarm, her whole body going tense at my knee-jerk reaction.

To soften the blow, I pull her wrist to my lips and press a tender kiss on its inside. This makes her melt into my body, as if the silent apology is enough for her.

"I didn't mean to scare you," I tell her in earnest.

"You don't."

I arch my brow calling bullshit on that statement.

"Okay, you do. But just not now. Not after well… you know."

"You mean after we fucked?"

"Yeah. After that." She blushes again, and I think a part of me is becoming a full-fledged junkie when it comes to her shy smiles and flushed cheeks.

It's fucking addicting.

So much so that I want all of them just for me. Not wanting to think too hard on why that is or run the risk of getting angry so early in the morning, I turn her over to lie on her back until my body is looming on top of hers.

"How sore are you?" I repeat.

"On a scale of one to ten?" she teases.

"Aye."

"Eleven."

"That bad, huh? Shame. I was hoping to school you some more before we went to church this morning."

"You're coming with me?" she asks, surprised.

"Do you not want me to?" Her bewilderment chafes at my resolve to escort her.

"No. I do. Thank you," she replies with such sincere gratitude that for a moment I'm at a loss for words.

"Don't thank me yet," I groan once I've recollected myself. "And if you really want to thank me, then I can think of better ways to do it."

"Such as?"

I smirk at the way she tries hard not to bite her lip as she gazes into my eyes. Using my knee to push her thighs apart, I crawl down her body until her delectable pussy is a hair's breadth away from my mouth.

"Let me show you."

"You mean, teach me," she taunts, twirling a lock of my hair with her finger.

I slap her pussy, eliciting a loud shriek from her.

"Lesson number one. Never interrupt me when I'm about to have my breakfast. Now open your legs and put them on my shoulders. I'm a sloppy eater."

The sound of her giggle dies the minute my tongue laps at her slit.

The woman is too fucking sweet, inside and out. I'm pretty sure I'll become a diabetic in no time with her around.

"Look at me," I order between licks.

"Okay," she mumbles breathlessly.

"Don't you dare fucking cum until I say so. Understood?"

She nods shyly, only amping up my determination to eat her out like no man has ever gone down on a woman before.

And like the good girl she is, she only cums when I order her to.

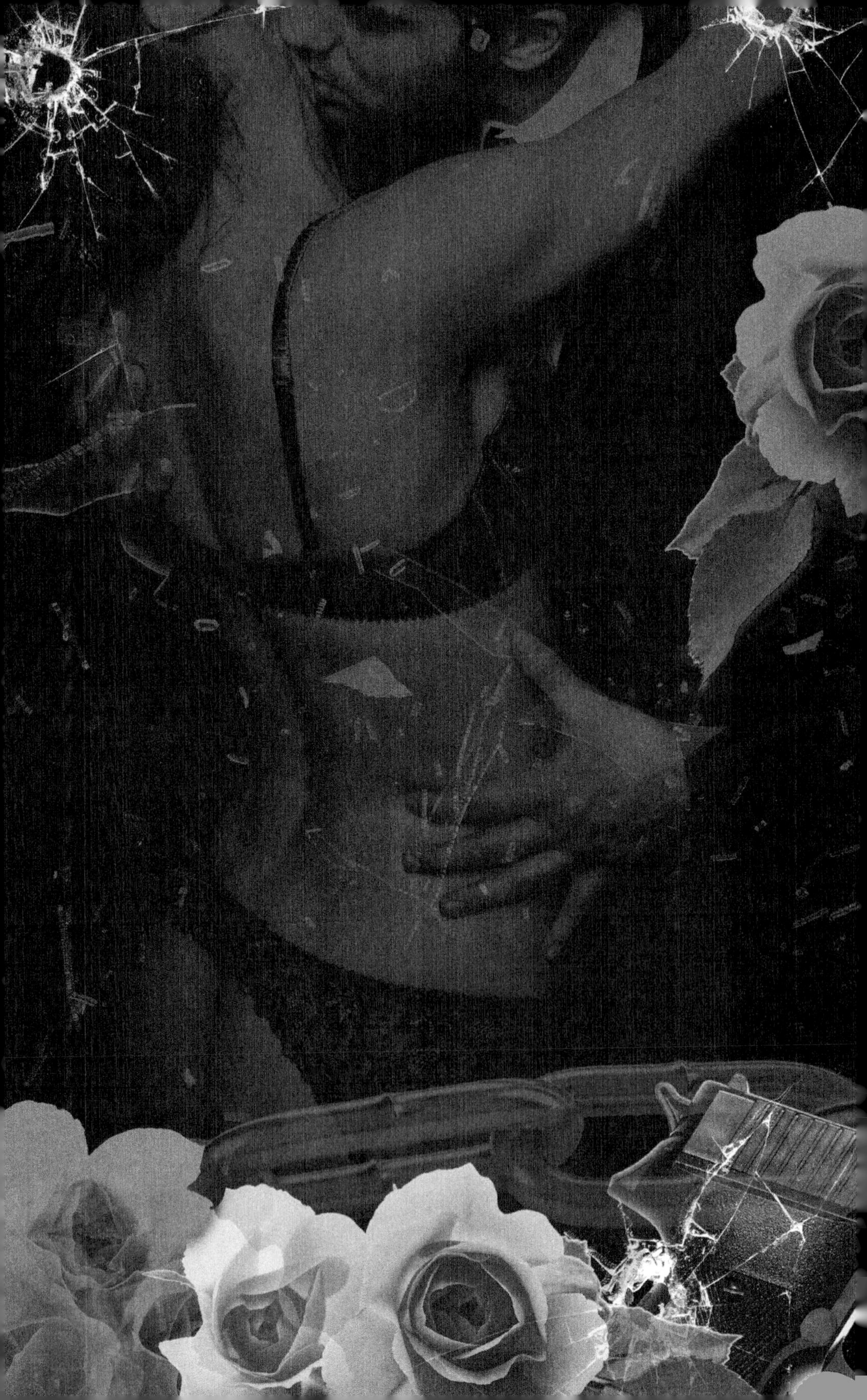

CHAPTER 12
Rosa

"I DON'T CARE what anyone says. If you're able to bring my rotten son to holy mass, then how bad a lass can ye be?" Saoirse Kelly announces so loudly at the entrance of the Holy Cross Cathedral, it's a wonder that everyone already seated inside the church didn't hear her.

"Enough of that, Saoirse. You're scaring off the wee lass," her husband, Niall, intervenes on my behalf, again avoiding looking at me much like he did on my wedding day. "Come with me, woman, before all of Boston hears ye," he adds, pulling her away by the hand.

"Now, you just hold your horses, Niall. I'm curious at how Rosa got our stubborn son through the church's doors without him kicking up a fuss. I can't remember the last time he voluntarily came to hear Father Doyle's sermon."

"Stop busting his chops, *Máthair*. Tiernan was just here a week ago. Or did you forget he got married in this church?" Shay counters, his expression full of mirth.

I have to admit, when I asked to attend mass, I wasn't thinking that the whole Kelly clan would attend, too. Aside from Colin, my immediate new family is all congregated here. If my mother-in-law wasn't so shocked to see Tiernan here with me, I would have assumed this was a weekly ritual for all the Kellys.

"I know what I said, Shay. I said willingly, didn't I?" Saoirse mumbles to her son, suddenly making me feel uncomfortable with my decision to come here.

'Willingly,' she said.

As if making it clear that I wasn't the only one forced into this marriage.

"How about we stop the idle chit-chat and get to our pews?" Tiernan announces, sensing my unease.

"Aye, I agree," Niall chimes in, successfully pulling his wife away and walking her down the church aisle to their seats.

Tiernan places his hand at the hollow of my back to urge me to follow his parents along. My face must be ten shades of red when his hand slips a little bit lower until he grabs a full ass cheek before I'm able to take a seat.

It's official.

He really is the devil.

Hades at his worst.

Tempting God's wrath right in his home of all places.

The man really has no shame.

Why I presumed he had any after all the things he did and said to me last night and again this morning is beyond me. Memories of what I let him do to me with his fingers, mouth, and cock have me fidgeting in my seat.

Virgen.

And the debasing things he said to me.

Slut.

Whore.

I have never in my life had any man speak to me that way.

My father would have had them hung and flung off the highest bridge by the ankles for everyone to know that talking to his chaste daughter in such a manner would be their death sentence.

It was degrading and demeaning.

And to my shame, I got off on it.

It was like I was another person. One who could do the most perverse things because he gave me carte blanche to do them. I never imagined sex could be like that. Francesco never once told me about this type of foreplay. I mean, I did catch some dirty talk on the few occasions I caught him red-handed with a woman, but nothing like this. I feel like I should bathe myself, head to toe, in holy water just to purify my soul. Because there is no question that my husband is determined to drag me to hell with him—one way or the other.

When I'm able to push all those carnal thoughts from my head, afraid that Christ will free himself from his cross just to spite me, I realize I'm smushed right in between the Kelly brothers. I only realize this now because Shay is manspreading his legs so wide, his knee is inappropriately rubbing against my bare leg every two seconds. I'm about to say something to him when he beats me to the punch, shifting in his seat just to try and grab his brother's attention.

"Psst."

"Psst."

"Psst," Shay whispers, placing his arm a little too close for comfort behind me and resting it on top of the pew rail.

"What?" Tiernan mumbles.

"Surprised to see you here, that's all, brother. Come to confess your sins, have ye?" Shay taunts, leaning his head a bit back so he can face his brother.

Tiernan doesn't so much as move, looking straight ahead.

"Aw, you still pissed at me?"

"As I recall, you're the child who threw a tantrum yesterday."

Shay shrugs.

"What can I say? I don't like losing. Especially hard-earned cash."

"You've never hard-earned anything a day in your life, brother," Tiernan is quick to rebuke, a trace of a smile beginning to tug at his upper lip.

"Even so, I hate parting with five Gs like that. To Colin no less."

"Didn't Sister Riley teach you that gambling is a sin?"

"She taught me plenty, but not that." Shay chuckles.

"Hmm," Tiernan hums, and as he does it, my imagination goes back to his bedroom this morning and how he hummed against my wet slit, telling me how sweet I tasted. The memory is so potent, I can't stop the shudder that runs down my body because of it.

To my utter mortification, both Kelly brothers see my involuntary reaction.

"I bet if I made a bet today, I wouldn't lose, would I, *dheartháir?*" Shay's eyes unashamedly skate over my body, completely uncaring that his brother is sitting right beside me. "Yep. Your wife looks properly fucked. Good on ye," he whispers low enough for only his brother to hear, but not low enough that I don't catch every word of his taunt.

It's a miracle that my eyes don't pop out of my head in both shock and embarrassment. It's only when Tiernan's hand goes to my thigh and gives it a squeeze that I realize Father Doyle is about to begin his sermon.

Shay hides his chuckle by feigning a cough, but then leans his lips into my ear.

"Can't say that I blame him. If I was in his shoes, I'd make sure to have deflowered you right after you said I do on that altar there. *Joder. Tal vez incluso antes de eso.*"

I swallow dryly before snapping my head to his side to offer him my most displeased glower. But to my amazement, Shay is looking straight ahead, seemingly enraptured by the sermon taking place. He's acting like he didn't just say he would have screwed me before I ever made it up the aisle if he had been in Tiernan's position. He's so committed to the façade that it almost makes me question my sanity and wonder if what just happened was all in my head.

I know what I heard.

He did say those things to me.

Didn't he?

It's only when Shay lets out a little chuckle that I know I'm not losing my mind. I almost elbow the big jerk in his stomach, but as Tiernan's grip on my thigh tightens, I'm forced to ignore his mischievous brother and pay attention to the service instead.

After a few minutes have passed, I start to relax and feel more at ease here.

I wasn't lying when I told Tiernan that going to church gave me comfort. Ever since I was a little girl, I liked dressing up in my Sunday finest and listening to the word of God. Even when the sermon talked about how hell would be full of sinners, and I knew that sooner or later that meant my entire family would feel its hellish flames, it still gave me a small sense of comfort that justice would prevail in the end.

That every evil thing my father did, he would pay for it with his soul.

Especially when he would beat my ass raw with his belt for my insolence, it comforted me knowing there was a deity out there that would make sure he paid his due in the end. Of course, those were the thoughts of a child. As I grew into womanhood, it pained me when I understood that, like my father, demons would also feast on the flesh of my brothers for all the things they would end up doing as *made men*. Every day, I would get on my knees and pray every Hail Mary I could in the hopes it would save their souls from such an ending—Francesco most of all.

Just as I'm thinking this, it suddenly dawns on me that, as Tiernan's wife, I should probably pray a few rosaries for his soul, too.

But can any prayer save the devil from returning to his rightful home?

Doubtful.

I'm still in my head, debating all these things, when I feel the weight of a pair of scrutinizing eyes land directly on me. Father Doyle begins to talk about Salome and how she enticed her mother's husband, Herod, by dancing seductively for him, just so she and her mother, Herodias, could ask for the head of John the Baptist.

"Take cautions when dealing with these jezebels, for they will entice you with their silver tongue and sinful body to commit the worst crimes known to men. Be true to God, and cast such temptation out of your green pastures, for if it lingers, it will do no less than burn all your hard labors down to ash."

The way he stares at me as he says it has me shuddering for a whole different reason.

I feel Tiernan's body go instantly stiff, his grip on my thigh leaving a mark.

"Fucking hypocrite," Shay utters through gritted teeth and then spits on the floor like it's a sidewalk and not the Lord's holy church.

But for the life of me, I can't find it in myself to reprimand him for his outburst or the blasphemous action. Mostly because I believe the priest's sermon had but one audience today. And that was me and my husband.

"He doesn't like me," I mumble under my breath over to Tiernan.

"Fuck him. You're a Kelly now. He doesn't have to like you. He just has to fear you," Shay responds on his brother's behalf.

I look at Shay, his kind blue eyes making me feel like I at least have one person here that doesn't hate me. He's a brazen flirt, but there is no malice behind his actions. I then turn to Tiernan, hoping to see that same empathy in his eyes, and frown when I find none. Tiernan lets go of his hold on me, his expression a blank canvas that I'm unable to read or decipher.

It surprises me that I suddenly feel cold now that he's no longer touching me. Even when all he has to offer is pain and humiliation, it's preferable to his cold shoulder.

For the rest of the service, I feel like all eyes are on us. As if the priest put a target on my back for everyone to stare and gawk at. I feel people's attention on me even more when Father Doyle breaks the body of Christ for all of us to take communion, and only Niall and Saoirse stand up from their pew to take it. When we get up from our seats in unison to say the Lord's Prayer, calling an end to mass, I'm ready to leave this church and never come back again. There are plenty of churches in Boston. I'm sure I can find one where no one knows who I am and won't hate me just because of who my family is.

Kelly or Hernandez.

"Well, that was... interesting," Saoirse says when we leave the church.

"It was a crock of shit, Ma," Shay blurts out, sending daggers to Father Doyle, who is currently blessing everyone to have a good week at the church's gates.

"Aye, boy, don't go cursing on the Lord's holy day," his mother reprimands as she tries to tame her red locks from blowing all over her face in the cold Massachusetts wind.

"Yeah, whatever. I'll see you all back at the house. Are you coming for Sunday lunch?" Shay launches the question at his brother.

"Aye. Rosa and I will drive right behind you."

We say our goodbyes and then walk over to our car that's parked at the curb. This time, Tiernan surprises me by opening the car door for me.

"Get in," he orders, and I quickly do as he says, not wanting to make a spectacle of myself by fighting with my husband right where the priest can still see us.

Once we're both in the car, he tells our driver to take the long way round to Beacon Hill instead of following Shay and his parents in their car as he suggested he would a few minutes ago. When Tiernan's hands start trailing under my skirt, I understand why the sudden need for a detour.

"Still sore?" he whispers in my ear before giving my earlobe a good tug with his teeth.

"Yes," I breathe out, but that doesn't stop him from pushing my panties to the side and running a finger down my slit.

I can't even pretend I don't like his touch since my traitorous body's reaction to him confirms that I do.

A lot.

"I haven't even touched you and you're already wet."

I moan when his deft fingers begin to play with my clit.

"I guess you bring it out of me," I pant.

"I can see that. I'm having a similar problem."

My gaze falls to his crotch and finds a large bulge straining his pants.

"Put it in your hand," he orders just as he plunges two of his fingers inside me.

"*Virgen!*"

"Not anymore. I took care of that last night," he goads, nipping at my neck and chin and then capturing my lips in his.

I let out a wanton moan because this man's kiss is sin incarnate.

"*Acushla*," he whispers. "I gave you an order. Defy me and I'll have to put you across my knee."

"What does that mean? *Acushla*?" I ask between moans, trying my best to unbuckle his pants and take his dick out before he follows through on his threat.

"It means curious whore," he grunts when I finally pull down his boxers low enough to get his cock free from under its confinement.

"No, it doesn't." I grin when his cock hardens in my hand.

"Enough talking, wife. Your mouth should be put to better use right about now."

His dirty words spur me on, giving me the courage I need to bend down and take him in my mouth.

"Fuck," he hisses when my tongue swipes over his crown.

While one hand teases my center, his other hand goes to the back of my head, pushing me down until all of him is fully seated inside my throat. It's hard to take air into my lungs as he fucks my mouth like his life depends on it. I try to breathe through my nose and relax my throat more like he taught me. This must please him since his hard grasp on my hair loosens, letting me suck him at my own steady pace.

"Such a pretty little slut. My fucking driver can smell your juices on my fingers as you blow me."

I still for just a second, thinking that maybe his chauffeur can in fact smell me, but Tiernan pushes my head down with more force this time, making sure I don't get sidetracked.

"That's it, wife. Suck me off. Let me cum down your throat as you get off fucking my fingers."

Cristo.

The words that come out of this man.

And what does it say about me that every time he says something lewd and deviously delicious like that, I only want him more?

In less than twenty-four hours, this man has corrupted me, body and soul.

Not an hour ago, I was considering praying for him, to keep him out of the sulfur-infested pits of hell, but maybe I should have been more concerned for my own soul's salvation.

When he inserts another finger, I let out a hiss of discomfort, my walls still too raw from his monstrous cock defiling my innocence last night. He senses it immediately and pulls his extra finger away, making me puff out an exhale on his cock.

"Fuck," he grunts, drawing circles on my clit. "You're in so much fucking pain, and yet you're disappointed you can't do more than only ride my two fingers. Don't worry, wife. Two fingers is all I need."

And as if to drive the point home, he scissors his digits inside my core until it's hard to concentrate on my mouth's current task.

Tiernan doesn't let up, fucking me with one hand while the

other plays with my hair.

"All you want is to get fucked. Isn't that right, *acushla*?"

I nod, spit and saliva running down the corners of my mouth.

"Do you still have your wedding dress?"

It takes me a good long minute to nod in answer to that out-of-left-field question.

"Good. I want to fuck you with it on one day. Have you look angelically sweet on your knees as you beg for my cock. I'm going to make sure to cum all over this gorgeous face of yours and then use your wedding dress to clean you off."

The image he planted in my head is enough to tip me over the ledge, and before I know it, I'm cumming hard, my pussy clenching around his fingers, wishing it was his cock inside me.

"Fuck. Such a good girl," he praises and I don't have the heart or energy to reprimand him for his word choice.

"Look at me," he orders, and even though it's uncomfortable, I crane my neck as far back as it can go without taking his cock out of my mouth.

"You're going to swallow my cum down to the last drop, aren't you, *acushla*?"

I nod.

"You're going to use that wicked tongue of yours and make sure my cock is nice and clean afterwards, aren't you, my dirty little slut?"

Another nod.

"That's my beautiful wife. Always so ready for my cum. Drink it all, *acushla*. It's yours."

He pounds into my mouth without mercy, provoking tears to

stream down my cheeks. I can feel his dick swell painfully inside my throat before ropes of cum glide right down it. As promised, I drink it all up, and then clean his cock with my tongue until there isn't a drop left.

He pulls me up by my hair, and crashes his mouth to mine, making me even needier than I was a second ago. His kiss is a battle. A war that I want no part in winning. I let him have all of me, and when he's made sure that I've waved the white flag in surrender, he breaks our kiss.

He stares into my eyes as I stare in amazement into his.

His blue one, always darker than his green.

"Fuck John the Baptist," he grunts, and gently cleans my tears away like I'm his most prized possession.

And for all intents and purposes, that is exactly what I am.

His to use and abuse.

But while that thought used to unsettle me, now all it does is arouse me.

🍀

We are all seated around the dining room table, eating a large roast accompanied by colcannon and paired with a shamrock salad, when Colin walks into the room.

"Col, my boy. I was starting to worry that you weren't going to make it to Sunday lunch," Niall greets affectionately.

"My apologies, *Uncail*," he says, walking to the head of the table where his uncle is seated, looking both perplexed at me being here as well as troubled by it. "I got you a present."

"A present? For me? But my birthday isn't until March, lad. You shouldn't have gone to the trouble," Niall explains at the same time Colin hands him a long plastic black tube.

Everyone remains silent as Niall gets up to his feet and uncaps the container. He tips it over and spreads out its content onto the table. My first impression of it is that it looks to be some sort of poster. No. The piece of paper looks older than that. Like it's a treasured heirloom of some kind, passed down from generations.

"Col… You shouldn't have," Niall says as he stares at his gift in awe. "Damn thing looks like you cut out a piece of my childhood, lad. Thank you. I'll hang it up in my office so I can spend my days surrounded by a little bit of Ireland."

My father-in-law picks the fragile sheet up by each side and shows us Colin's thoughtful gift. My nails sink into my palms when I realize what he's showing us.

It's the Monet.

The same one we saw yesterday at the Museum of Fine Arts.

He went back and stole it.

I can't believe him!

"What do you think, Saoirse? Doesn't it look like Ireland?"

"It's actually a portrait of the Seine near Giverny. That's in France, not Ireland," I explain bitterly, taking a sip of my wine before I say something I may regret. Like how Colin is a dirty, rotten thief.

But when Niall throws an ugly glare my way, I already regret my outburst. He sits back in his seat, not sparing me another look, and starts conversing with his sons in Gaelic so that I'm left completely out of the loop.

Wonderful.

The man hates me, and it shows.

I should have kept my mouth shut. This man is never going to welcome me into his family if I continue to piss him off. Although, I think my very presence here already does that. When looking at him, Niall Kelly looks like your everyday grandpa, sans grandchildren, that is. He's got a belly to him, two rosy cheeks, and is quick to laugh and smile.

That is, until I'm in the room.

Since we arrived at the Kelly residence, he's made it a point not to be in the same room as me if he can help it. I'm sure if my mother-in-law agreed that he could eat lunch in the kitchen alone, he'd jump at the chance just to not have to suffer my presence.

I don't get it.

Alejandro had told me that Niall Kelly had been adamant to do his blood vow with Tiernan, to watch out for me and protect me at all costs. To show me the respect the wife of his first-born son and heir to the Irish mob should receive. But I guess Alejandro should have read the fine print on that deal. Nowhere in it did it say Niall or any of his kin had to like me.

The only ones in this family that have shown me an ounce of kindness throughout this whole meal have been Saoirse and Shay. While my mother-in-law's attempts to bring me into the conversation seemed honestly genuine, I think Shay only talked to me because he knew it would upset his older brother. He would purposely leer and wink at me, and when that didn't work, he would shamelessly flirt with me in my mother tongue just to see if he could get a rise from Tiernan. I don't know if I should be upset or relieved Tiernan never took the bait. Or maybe my husband isn't as fluent as his brother is in Spanish. Maybe the reason why he hasn't flipped this table over and put Shay in his place is because he doesn't understand a word of all the things Shay has said so far at the dinner table.

"I have never been more jealous than I am right now of a damn fork."

"Some fuckers have all the luck."

"Are you sure you don't have a sister back home? A cousin, maybe? Never mind. I never did like runners-up. I'm a first prize kind of guy."

"I bet you would look lovely handcuffed to a bedpost."

"Being king sometimes has its perks."

He's been like this all throughout lunch.

If my husband had a clue, I'm sure he'd disapprove.

At least, I think it would upset Tiernan, but with him, I never know where his head is at.

Once Colin has carefully placed the one-of-a-kind painting back in its container, he walks over to my side of the table and has the nerve to sit beside me.

Great.

Another Kelly for me to be angry with.

"How could you?" I chastise under my breath, making sure no one hears my reprimand.

"I told you I liked it," he mumbles with a shrug as if that justifies stealing a painting from a museum.

"Yes, you did. So do many other people who are now going to be very disappointed that they'll never see its like again."

Another noncommittal shrug.

"Don't you have any remorse for what you've deprived the art world of? Any whatsoever?"

"No." He shakes his head.

"Hmph! Well then, I'll make a note in the future to keep an eye on things you like, now that I know you aren't averse to stealing them away from their rightful owners' hands."

"Count your blessings that isn't true," he mutters.

"Oh, no?" I raise my brows at him, truly upset with what he's done.

"Aye. I don't steal everything I take a fancy to," he protests, then mutters low enough that he thinks I can't hear him. "But you're sure making it hard not to."

My forehead wrinkles in confusion at the weird remark, but I decide to just ignore him for the rest of our meal so he can feel the full weight of my disapproval of what he's done. That painting should have stayed in a museum where art lovers all over the world could visit it and enjoy. Now it will be hung up in an old Irish boss's office where no one will have access to it.

It's more than a crime.

It's downright heartbreaking.

I'm so consumed by my anger that I carelessly tip my wine glass all over myself.

Mierda!

"Oh, lass, don't fret. I'm sure my Iris must have something that can fit you while I put your dress in the wash," my mother-in-law says, getting out of her seat and urging me to do the same.

"Oh no, it's fine. I don't want to trouble you."

"Never you mind. Family exists for that very reason. To be trouble." She smiles widely, and my heart warms that at least *she* doesn't hate me. Or if she does, she sure has me fooled. "Come now, girl. Let me take you upstairs so ye can change into some clean clothes."

I offer her a genuine smile of my own and get up to follow her upstairs. I don't even look at Tiernan, not wanting to see his face as I've just made a complete fool of myself the first time he brought me to his parents' house. I'm usually not this clumsy, but because of the unsettling nerves at knowing Niall hates me, Shay's blatant flirtation, or Colin having stolen that priceless piece of art, I'm a complete hot mess today.

"I'm not giving off a good first impression, am I?"

"Hush, girl. There is no need for such ceremony with me. With any of my boys, either."

"Your husband might disagree with you."

"Don't pay Niall any mind. He just has to get used to you, that's all."

"Used to me? How can he do that when he leaves the room anytime I enter it?"

Saoirse smiles sadly at me, giving my shoulder a light squeeze.

"The Mafia Wars were hard on all fronts, Rosa. Unlike my boys, my Niall lived through most of it. It will take him some time to see you as I see you."

"And how do you see me?"

"I see you like the daughter I just sent away. A poor girl whose future was stolen from her in the name of a ceasefire. It's not your fault who your Da or brothers are, as much as it isn't Iris'. No. You girls are paying a hefty price, and I won't make your life harder by blaming you for what you had no fault in."

"Thank you," I croak, unshed tears starting to blur my vision.

"No need for those either," she says, wiping away at the tears that are relentless enough to fall. "Life goes on, lass. It all depends on what kind of life you want for yourself. Do you understand?"

"I think so, yes."

"Good. Now go on inside. This is my Iris' bedroom. I'm sure you'll be able to find something that fits. If not, then I'm sure my Shay might have something you can borrow. A hoodie, at least."

"Thank you," I repeat, and I feel like I will say thank you to this woman many more times in the years to come.

I walk into my sister-in-law's room and immediately I can tell that I am nothing like the girl that was sent away to Vegas to suffer under the Bratva's ruling thumb. There are nunchucks, throwing stars, and a display of various knives and daggers all around the room. I don't think Saoirse has come here since her daughter's departure since there are clothes all over the floor and an empty cup from a coffee shop on the bedside table.

I walk over to her closet and see that her clothes are also much more adventurous than what I would wear. I try to find a top that would fit me, but unless I want to show the men downstairs a good portion of my cleavage or navel, then my best bet is to go over to Shay's room and hope he has a hoodie I can borrow.

I walk back to the hall and start to open the bedroom door right across from Iris's bedroom, hoping that one is Shay's.

But before I'm even able to crack the door open, a dark shadow looming in the hallway prevents me from doing so.

"What are you doing?" Tiernan asks, his hands balled into fists at his sides.

"I was looking—"

"You were snooping," he accuses before I have time to explain.

"No, I wasn't. I was looking for a hoodie. I thought this might be Shay's room. Or Colin's."

He scoffs.

"Let's go. We're leaving."

"Already? But we haven't even finished lunch. Your mother said she made your favorite dessert."

"I've lost my appetite. Move, Rosa. Now."

I've never seen him this incensed. Fear above all has me moving my feet and rushing downstairs. I'm about to pop in the living room just to thank Saoirse for the lovely meal, when Tiernan grabs my upper arm and drags me out of his parents' home.

"You're hurting me," I tell him, trying to break free from his unyielding grip.

He loosens his hold but doesn't let go. He shoves me into the backseat of his car and tells the driver to head back to The Avalon. The whole drive home I don't dare say a word. I thought I had seen the worst of Tiernan, but that was a lie. He's capable of so much more. In fact, all this time, he was probably using kid gloves with me, only showing me enough of the brutish beast that dwells inside him.

They're animals, Rosa. Filthy, unscrupulous, vicious animals.

That had been Alejandro's warning to me, and now I see how foolish it was not to pay it more heed.

He's going to punish me.

And by the way his nostrils flare, and his one blue eye is so dark it's almost pitch black, I doubt he'll use his hands.

But why?

I did nothing wrong.

His father completely dismissed me.

His brother tried to make a pass at me.

And his cousin stole a priceless work of art that I introduced him to.

In no way, during the entire two hours we were there, did I do anything that even compared to his kin's behavior.

So why am I the one that is about to get punished?

By the time we walk into the apartment, I'm no longer afraid of what's to come.

I'm angry.

I'm beyond angry.

I'm enraged.

We're halfway down the corridor when I halt my steps, even though he continues in the direction of his room.

"I don't understand what I did. What could I have possibly done for you to be this angry with me?"

He doesn't even have the decency to reply while opening his bedroom door.

"So that's it?" I throw my arms in the air. "So, this is the part where you tell me I have to be taught another lesson?"

He turns around, eyeing me up and down with such hatred in his eyes, my heart shrivels to the size of a penny inside my chest.

"Class is no longer in session. School is officially out for you."

And with those words, he slams his door in my face.

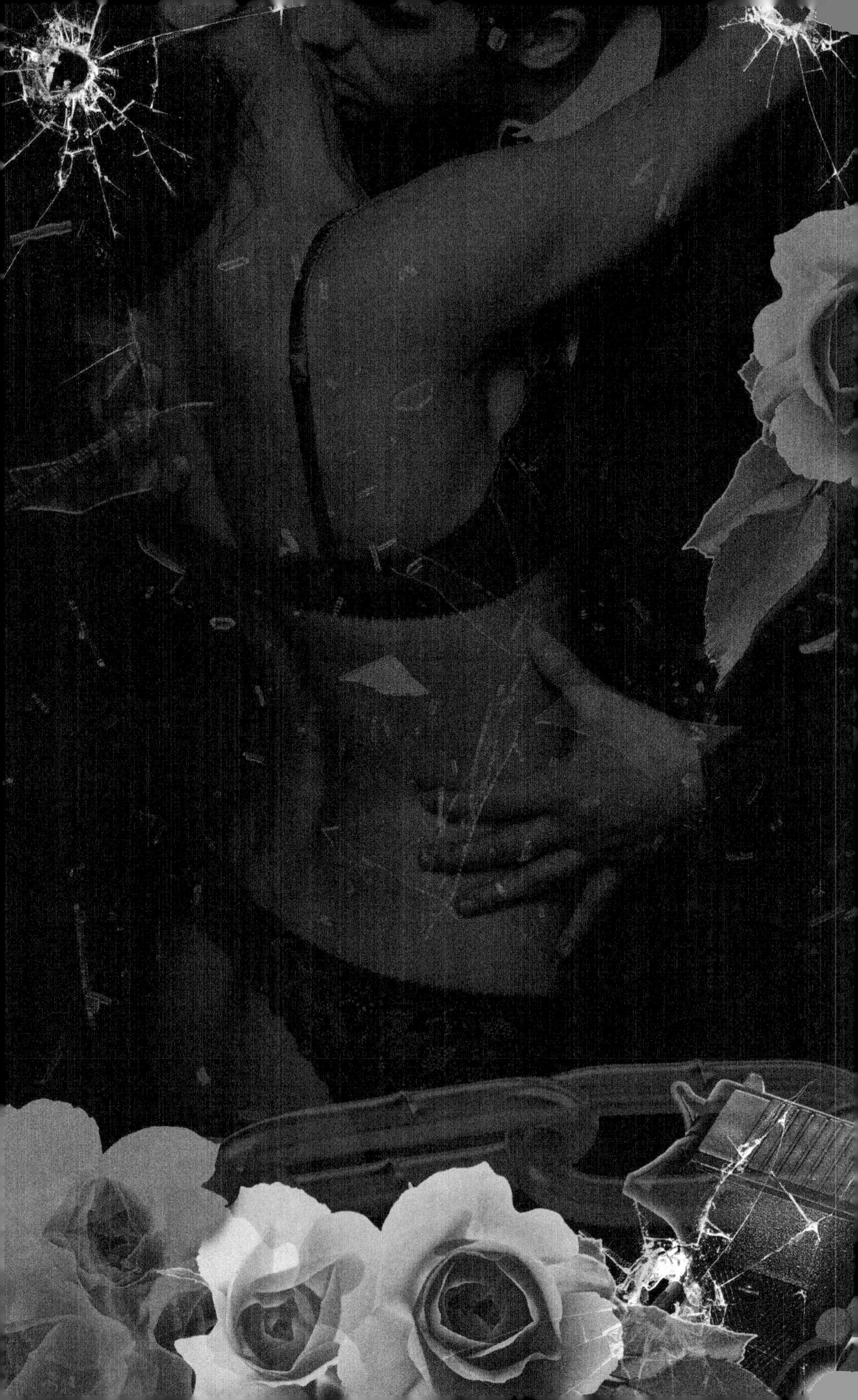

CHAPTER 13
Rosa

THE NEXT DAY when I wake up, I find Colin sitting on a stool next to the kitchen island and Shay sprawled out on the sofa, his legs crossed at his ankles on top of the coffee table, hands behind his head.

"Morning, petal. You're stuck with us today."

"Where's Tiernan?" I ask since he wasn't in his room.

To my bitter resentment, I checked to see if he was still avoiding me, locked away inside it. But when I woke up, his bedroom door was left wide open, his not-so-subtle way of notifying me of his absence. I stayed up most of the night waiting for him to step out of his room just so we could talk.

I mean, he had to leave sooner or later.

Either to eat or work. But he never left.

Apparently, I must have missed him when I finally dozed off in the early hours of the morning, exhausted after a long night of thinking of what I could have possibly done to make him so upset.

"So, are either one of you going to answer me? Where is Tiernan?"

"Where you'd expect a workaholic like him to be. He's probably back at the office. Someone has to rule the world. Might as well leave that pesky task to the grown-ups." Shay smiles, but it doesn't reach his eyes.

Something is off.

"Why are you here, Shay? Colin is perfectly capable of watching over me all on his own," I state somberly, walking over to the kitchen to grab some coffee. "Not that you're my favorite person right now." I throw a frown at Colin. "I still haven't forgiven you for what you did."

Colin at least has the good sense to bow his head in shame.

I guess not all of the Kelly men are arrogant know-it-alls.

I wish my husband was one of them.

"Big guy does okay with being a watchdog and all, but he's not so hot at house hunting," Shay jokes, jumping off the sofa and strolling over to the kitchen. He picks up a red apple from the fruit bowl, rubs it against his shirt, and takes a big chunk out of it.

"House hunting? I thought you lived with your parents? Are you moving?"

"Not exactly," he says, throwing a quick glance over at Colin thinking I'm too coffee-deprived to catch it.

"What aren't you telling me?" As he chews on his apple a little longer than necessary, I know nothing he'll say next will be any good. "Shay?" When he still refuses to speak, I look at Colin for answers.

"The house is for you," Colin explains evenly, without having me ask him outright.

"For me? Why? Does Tiernan no longer like this apartment?"

"My brother likes it just fine. He just thinks you'd be more comfortable in a larger home in Beacon Hill. Maybe closer to my folks."

"Oh."

That makes sense. If we're going to give this marriage a shot and have children someday, it would be nice to have their grandparents living nearby.

"Okay. Let me just grab a quick breakfast, jump in the shower, and we can be on our way."

Shay looks at Colin in astonishment and then back to me.

"So, you're cool with this?"

"Why wouldn't I be?" I shrug, grabbing some tortilla chips and eggs to make *huevos rancheros.* "A larger home makes perfect sense to me. Especially if we're going to start a family. This whole apartment doesn't exactly scream baby-friendly."

"Oh fuck, beautiful. You are fucking breaking my heart over here," Shay states looking pained.

"I don't understand."

Shay walks around the island and places his hands over my shoulders, giving them a little squeeze.

"We're going shopping for a house for you. Not for you and my brother. And it's sure as shit not for you, my brother, and all the nonexistent babies you think you'll have with him."

"What?" I croak. "I don't understand. What are you saying?"

"I'm saying my brother has done his duty. And now he's going to put you back in his toy chest because he's done playing with you."

Done playing with me?

Playing with me?!

"Where is he? Where is Tiernan right now?!" I seethe at Shay, but when his eyes widen, shocked that I've yelled, I turn to the one man in this kitchen who always seems to have his wits about him.

"Colin? Where is my husband at this very minute?"

"He's at the gym." He doesn't even hesitate.

"Thank you. I'll be ready in five minutes."

"Hey, hold up. Hold up," Shay tries to calm me down, firmly grabbing my shoulders this time. "Just exactly what do you think you are going to do when you see him? What do you think you'll possibly gain by confronting my brother like a banshee off the rails?"

I think on that question for a moment, take it in, and really dissect it.

The answer comes to me just as easily as the sun rises every morning.

"Freedom."

Shay steps back, puzzled by my response, and I use his bewilderment to my advantage, bypassing him and running to my room in a dash.

"Five minutes, Colin. Then I want you to take me to my husband. He has a lot of explaining to do."

And by God, I'll make him pay if it's the last thing I do.

Not a half-hour later, we arrive at an old gym that looks to be on its last leg. I would have assumed Tiernan would prefer to use the personal gym provided to him back at The Avalon, but apparently, he likes to get his sweat on in a gym that looks days away from being called a demolition site. With Colin and Shay at my heel, I strut with purpose through the gym's doors, ignoring all the catcalls and whistles I get just for being the only woman here.

Men are pigs.

No way around it.

My eyes scan the seedy gym until they land on the man I came looking for. In black shorts and nothing else, Tiernan is inside a boxing ring, throwing punches at a guy twice his size. If I had any doubts that my husband had more arrogance than good sense, then this little show he's putting on is my answer. Every swing his opponent makes is a direct hit to his chest. I cringe inwardly at the loud sound of each punch, thinking for sure he'll have more than a few busted ribs before the fight ends. It's only when his boxing opponent sees me standing by the ropes, that the man halts his jabs and gives my husband a little reprieve from getting his ass kicked.

"Give me two seconds to finish him off, baby. Then you can finish me off in the locker room."

Like I said.

Men are pigs.

But before I have the opportunity to tell him where to shove it, Tiernan's gaze lands on me, and he realizes who the ill-formed pick-up line was intended for. It all happens so fast after that. Tiernan swings his arm back and sucker punches his opponent so hard under his jaw that the over two-hundred-something pound behemoth falls flat on the mat, knocked out and probably in need of medical assistance. Tiernan doesn't even flinch at the comatose body lying at his feet, using his teeth to tug his boxing gloves off, staring daggers in my direction.

"What is she doing here, Shay?" he accuses with a repugnant tone.

"Hey, I tried to stop her. Col was the one who narced where you were," Shay explains, lifting his hands in the air as if absolving himself of any crime committed in bringing me here.

Tiernan slants his eyes at Colin.

"Your defiance lately is starting to piss me off, Col."

Colin doesn't reply, but I can tell he doesn't like being the target of Tiernan's rage.

"Get her out of here. Now," he orders, like his command is duty-bound to be upheld.

I look around and realize that the whole gymnasium has gone eerily quiet. If I don't do something now, then someone will drag me out of here before I've said my piece.

"No!" I exclaim, getting inside the ring with him. "You are going to hear me out, even if it has to be in front of all your lackeys." I point to all the men that are drawing closer to the ring to get a better view.

Tiernan snarls, throwing his boxing gloves to the mat.

"Rosa," he grinds my name through his teeth, chopping it into tiny bits, as if he could swallow me up just as easily. "I won't repeat myself. Go back to the apartment with Shay and Colin if you know what's good for you."

"Enough!" I yell, having reached my wit's end.

My unladylike outburst startles him, and there is a part of me that takes pleasure in the fact that I've shocked him.

"You are my husband. It might not have been of my choice or doing, but the fact remains the same. We vowed in front of God and family that we are now one. I promised to obey and be faithful to you until death do us part. But in that vow, I expect the same form of loyalty. You have obligations that you must comply with."

"Obligations? You make it sound like this is some form of business arrangement?" He scoffs.

"And isn't it? Was I not sold to your family to keep mobsters like you in business? Is my wedding ring not proof of such a transaction?"

His nostrils flare as I point to my ring finger.

"My family isn't in the business of selling women," he spits out.

"Really?" I laugh maniacally. "If that were true, I'd be back home in Mexico with my brothers. No matter how you want to paint our circumstances, this is exactly what it is. I was sold to you for the price of peace. And that peace can only prevail by the combining of your blood with mine."

"What the fuck are you talking about, Rosa? Stop with the fancy wordplay and just speak your mind already."

I fist my hands at my sides, hating that this man would make me spell it out for him and humiliate myself even more than I already have.

"How am I supposed to bear an heir if my husband refuses to live in the same house as me? To even touch me?"

His stare goes dark and he eats up the distance between us in such a way that my heart literally jumps to my throat. I don't dare move, not wanting him to think I'm weak or that he intimidates me.

But he does.

I see the boss of the family when he places his hands around my neck and slams me against one of the boxing ring's ropes.

"Is this temper tantrum just your way of saying you want to get fucked again, Rosa?"

His crude words whispered in my ear should offend me, but instead, they make the lower part of my belly twist in anticipation. "Is that all this is? Are you so cock-hungry that you've decided to come to my gym and make a show of yourself in front of my men? Is that what you want? For me to fuck the insolence out of you, once and for all?"

"I want you to fulfill your oath to me and my family."

"I don't remember fucking your brains out being in the terms and conditions of the agreement," he taunts, just adding to my humiliation.

"No. But if there is any other scenario you can come up with where I can bear a child of your blood, then I'm all for it."

His features change from mocking to downright lethal. This must be the face his enemies see up close when he's about to cut them down and steal their life away.

Tiernan leans in even closer to me until his sweaty chest rubs against mine, coaxing a trace of a shiver to run rampant within my body, making it impossible for me to stand still. His breath kisses my skin, my heart running a mile a minute at how close he is. But while his body is running hot, his gaze is as cold as the Antarctic.

His eyes look like a thunderstorm, ready to electrocute me where I stand.

He doesn't say a word, but in this very moment, he doesn't have to.

He hates me.

Hates everything about me.

And my heart withers up inside and dies, mourning the life I could have had with a husband who actually cared for me. I don't cower and lower my gaze, although I'm sure he sees the sadness written in it. But to look away would mean defeat. Let him read how miserable I am. Let him choke on my misery just as I have since I set foot in Boston. I have felt like a stranger and an enemy from day one. His dark glower only serves to confirm what I've known all along.

I'll never make a home here.

I'll never find a sliver of happiness or joy.

This is my plight, and I'll never be able to outrun it. If I was ever to slip away and return to the brothers I love so dearly, it would only mean that they would have to go to war with these savages. I can't have their blood on my hands. But I sure as hell can threaten to have Tiernan Kelly's.

By suggesting that he is somehow in breach of the treaty, he knows that his life would be forfeited if the other families were to find out about it. It might be the most despicable lie I've ever inferred, but it's the only card I have to play in this twisted game of ours.

"Is that your only complaint, wife?" he whispers the last word with acidic bitterness.

I let out an exhale and square my shoulders, making myself look more confident than I really am.

"I had no hand in my fate, but I am woman enough to face it head-on. Hate me if you must, but don't despise me for following to the letter of the sacrifice that was forced upon me. This marriage might not be the one I dreamed about when I was a little girl, but it's the one that will ensure that thousands of lives will be spared. Are you so proud in your arrogance that you would risk the lives of so many just to get rid of me? Because I'm not. I will not be responsible for death knocking on my family's door and restarting the Mafia Wars just because your hatred of me prevented you from fulfilling your duty."

After my long rant, his eyes take on a different hue to them. He twirls a loose strand of my hair around his finger, making my breath catch in my throat when he gives it a gentle tug.

"Always so selfless. So pure. So self-righteous. If that's what you want me to be, then I guess I can be that, too."

I lower my eyes because I know he can't.

Men like him are born and bred to not show mercy. Selflessness to them is a sign of weakness. Only brute force and ruthlessness have any part in our world. I know that much.

"You don't believe me, do you?" he asks, taking a small step back and allowing air to fill my lungs.

"I don't know you well enough to say either way."

"Oh, you know me. I think you've known men like me for most of your life. And you have managed to learn how to bend them to do your will, haven't you, *acushla*?"

"Can a man bend to a woman?" I arch a brow. "I've never seen it done before."

He runs the pad of his thumb over my full lower lip, and again I feel an ache in my lower belly.

"Depends on the woman."

"What a fierce creature she must be then to hold such power over a man."

"Yes. Beautiful, too."

My throat dries as his eyes soften, but all too soon does this one moment of vulnerability vanish into thin air, bringing forth the Irish king yet again.

"Meet me at my office at three. No later. And alone."

The sudden change in topic alarms me.

"Why?" I stammer nervously for the first time since we started this fight.

His upper lip curls.

"Do you think I'm asking you to come into the city because I want to kill you?"

"You've been adamant that I stay locked away since I got here. Only leaving me to go out once with Colin as my personal shadow. So, excuse me if you asking me to come into the city unattended doesn't raise my alarm bells."

"I will not kill you, Rosa. Not today anyway."

My shoulders stiffen, and my heart stops.

Which means he's thought about it.

Killing me, I mean.

Not that the thought hasn't passed my own mind. It would be easy enough to get rid of me. I'm not a fighter. All I have are my brains and foolish bravery. There are so many ways someone could get rid of an unwanted spouse without getting a divorce. He could hire an outside assassin and say that I was a casualty of an unnamed rival trying to take him out. He could throw me into an institution for the mentally ill, saying I lost my mind somehow, or he could lock me away in a grand house and forget my very existence. All three are preferable to divorce in our world.

Ironic how I'm fighting tooth and nail for the last when he was about to offer me just that.

"I expect you there at three, sharp. Don't be late."

And with that order still hanging in the air, he leaves me standing all alone in a boxing ring with about thirty male pitying gazes on me.

At a quarter to three, I arrive at the public square right in front of one of the largest skyscrapers in this city.

Kelly Enterprises.

That's what the world thinks my husband does. Build gigantic skyscrapers.

The Kelly name in Boston is synonymous with being real estate moguls. They build monstrosities like these and sell them for a pretty penny. Sure, they also have their hands in other pockets, such as tech, media, publishing, and other avenues, but real estate was where they made a name for themselves.

A clean name bought with dirty money.

Not that I can throw rocks on their glass roof when my own family's source of income is less than exemplary.

Wearing a vintage white Gucci dress and Jimmy Choo high heel boots, I walk into the building like I own the place, even if, in part, there is a bit of truth to that statement now that I'm married to Tiernan. Knowing I have any ownership of such a cold thing is demoralizing, to say the least.

For me, this soulless building is just a reflection of the soulless man who actually has a personal interest invested in it. However, I'm sure that one of the reasons behind him spending so much time in his high castle is because it just gives him another way to look down on everyone else.

A few minutes later I arrive on his floor, and tell his pretty receptionist at the front desk that I'm here to see my husband. She quickly jumps out of her seat and leads me to a private boardroom, nervously offering me a variety of fancy lattes or coffees on the way there. It seems working for Tiernan isn't a walk in the park either by the way she's trying her very best to accommodate my every need in hopes that my husband will get wind of how affable she was.

I graciously decline and thank her for her help.

She gives me a grateful smile, and I wait for her to leave before I enter the room. Inside, my husband is seated at the head of a large cherrywood table, his brother Shay seated at his right, and Colin to his left.

If I naturally presumed that Tiernan's invitation for me to meet him at his office was so that we could privately discuss the state of our so-called marriage, I can now see how wrong my assumptions were.

"Come on in and grab a seat. We don't bite," Shay jokes, always with his trademark cocky grin plastered on his face and a mischievous gleam to his light blue eyes.

I offer him a stern grin and take the seat opposite the three men at the other side of the table, making sure I'm seated right across from my husband.

"Thank you for coming," Tiernan greets, looking sharp and devilishly handsome in his black five-thousand-dollar Tom Ford suit.

"Thank you for inviting me," I return the fake pleasantries. "However, if I knew I was going to be in here for an actual business meeting, I would have dressed the part."

"What you have on is good enough. Isn't that right, Tiernan?" Shay taunts, smacking his lips and not making any excuses for his leering gaze on me.

"Why am I here?" I ask pointblank, instead of rising to Shay's attempts to unsettle his older brother.

Tiernan taps his fingers on the edge of the table, just taking me in, as if he hasn't quite decided yet why he summoned me here this afternoon.

"Well?" I repeat, unable to hide my annoyance, only to gain a tug of amusement on his upper lip.

"Stop being a dick and just tell her already," Shay huffs out, sounding bored. "On second thought, why don't you start by explaining why you forced Colin and me to be here, too? I mean, it's obvious you two need some serious marriage counseling, but I hate to break it to you, *dearthair*, me and the big guy over there aren't exactly the touchy-feely kind you can count on to kumbaya your issues away. Either just fuck it out amongst yourselves until you can bear the sight of one another without going all nuclear like you did at the gym this morning, or get a real professional to help you with your issues. Leave Col and me out of it."

"Sit your ass down," Tiernan orders when Shay begins to rise from his seat.

Shay curses under his breath but does as he's told.

No wonder my husband is so bossy.

Even his kin follow his every command.

"It has come to my attention that I am not fulfilling my required duties of the treaty," Tiernan begins to explain.

"That's a load of shit," Shay counters, pissed. "You married Rosa just like they ordered you to. What more do those old farts want?"

"No. It's not the families that have reminded me of the small print of the contract, but my dear wife here."

Shay snaps his neck my way, accusation and disappointment in his eyes.

"I don't understand," Colin interjects with less venom to his tone.

"For the agreement to be truly fulfilled, Rosa must continue the Kelly lineage. That way, our families will, in fact, be forever bound."

I shift in my seat but keep my schooled features intact.

"Having been so eloquently reminded of my shortcomings this morning, I have asked you all in here today to make a request."

"And what request is that?" Shay asks apprehensively.

"I need you both to carry that burden for me. Father the next Kelly heir."

I gasp, getting out of my seat so fast the chair falls over.

"What?! You cannot be serious!"

"Sit down, wife. The walls are thin, and I don't particularly want anyone to listen to this conversation. What is said here, dies here. Is that understood?"

Both Shay and Colin nod, but I'm not so easily subdued.

"What you're proposing is absurd."

"Is it?" He smirks. "If I recall, I was there the day the treaty was forged. Not you. Nowhere was it specifically said that to guarantee our mixed bloodline that I had to be the one to do it. Only that you must."

I frown.

"You will get a Kelly heir, Rosa. Just not mine."

I let that piece of information fester in my mind.

What is he saying?

That he would rather whore me out than touch me again?

"Before you start with your rebuttals, I want you to listen very closely. This is the only way to ensure you get what you want."

I let that sink in.

Is he telling me that he can't have children?

Cristo.

Shame hits me like a tidal wave at how I treated him earlier. Maybe that's why he was reluctant to sleep with me at first. I mean what would be the point? Sex with a person you have been chained to unwillingly probably didn't seem very appealing to him from the start. The only other reason to have sex is to have kids. And here he is, telling me he can't.

Or am I being naïve right now?

The night that we had sex, Tiernan made sure never to cum inside of me. He even asked me if I was on the pill. A man who is physically incapable of having children wouldn't be concerned if their partner was using that form of contraception or not.

No.

He *can* have children.

He just chooses not to.

At least, not with me.

"Fine," Shay mutters, running his fingers through his Jesus-like long hair. "I don't necessarily like being blackmailed and backed into a corner," he starts off, throwing another disappointed glare my way for insinuating I would go to the other families and tell on his brother. "But like hell if I'll let our family be the cause of breaking the treaty on a technicality. Just tell us which clinic you're working with, and I'll make sure Colin and I fill as many cups as we can to put a baby in your wife."

He makes it sound like some kind of joke, and I guess to him, it is.

But not to me.

"We are not using a clinic." Tiernan shakes his head, getting confused looks all around the boardroom table.

"So, how do you expect us to knock up your wife?"

"Can you please not be so crude?" I interrupt, feeling embarrassed enough with this situation as it is.

"Sorry, petal. But Tiernan needs to be clear in his demands. You sure the fuck were with yours."

I'm sorry, I want to tell him.

Explain to him that I didn't see another way.

That I would never purposely put the lives of thousands of people in danger just on a whim.

But instead, I pick the chair I knocked down up off the floor and sit right back on it, waiting to hear what Tiernan's concocted as a solution to our problem.

"Boss?" Colin calls out when Tiernan takes too long to reply.

I swallow the lump lodged in my throat as my husband, my enemy, my one-time lover, stares me down with such sadistic malice in his eyes that the room begins to spin. I grasp on to the edge of the table to keep steady and face the consequences of my actions.

"Rosa will get her heir the old-fashion way."

Gulp.

Both Colin and Shay are stunned into silence as Tiernan gets up from his seat and plants his palms flat on the table.

"You're a woman of tradition, are you not, wife? Why run the risk of going to a clinic and having others find out about this new arrangement of ours, when to ensure your pregnancy, all you need is a bed and a man willing to plant his seed in you? I wash my hands of such a privilege and want no part of it, but as you can see, wife, you're in luck. You have two Kelly men right here up for the challenge."

This is a test.

He's testing me.

He came up with this sordid plan thinking I'd balk at it and immediately refuse.

The only thing he didn't account for when he came up with this scheme was how desperate I am to finally live a life of my own.

I get up from my seat and mimic his form down to the planted palms on the table.

"Are you sure there is no other way?"

Money isn't an object for a man like Tiernan Kelly. He could buy a fertility clinic if he wanted and buy the silence of everyone working there. But that would defeat the purpose of putting me in my place and reminding me who holds the key to my future and happiness in the palm of his hands.

"Very sure." He smirks in victory.

"Well then," I start evenly, my severe gaze never wavering from his. "If this is the only way you see to uphold the treaty, then I have conditions."

"We're negotiating now?" He arches an amused eyebrow.

"A man like you should be accustomed to such things by now."

"True. Negotiate away, wife. You have the floor."

"Every night, you will come home at a decent hour and have dinner with me. I'm tired of eating my meals alone. But the minute you walk through the doors, I'll also want you to leave the day's work outside."

It takes everything in me to keep my composure in place when Tiernan fights not to roll his eyes at the pitiful excuse of a negotiation attempt.

"I can accommodate that request. But only until you give birth. After that, I see no need for such pleasantries."

"Fine," I concede.

"May I include a clause of my own now?"

"By all means. The floor is all yours," I reply sarcastically.

This time the smirk that rises to his lips doesn't hold any malevolence to it, only odd amusement.

"I asked Shay to accompany you today to find a house that is to your liking. If you are to mother the next Kelly generation then it's all the more important that both you and the child live in an accommodating setting."

"Child? As in one?" I interrupt before he picks up from where he left off.

"Are you planning on wanting more?" His brows pull together in suspicion.

"I think to guarantee a Kelly successor, it would be prudent to have more than one, yes."

His fingers begin to tap on the table as he seems to genuinely consider my statement.

Tap.

Tap.

Tap.

"Very well," he relents. "Once your first child turns two-years-old, then we can revisit this proposition and see if you are still interested in having more. Childbearing and motherhood aren't for everyone. You might find that having just one child is enough of a challenge and change your mind. You and I both know how fickle you can be."

"Fair enough," I reply stoically, proud that my cheeks didn't burn a flaming red with the memory he just conjured up of the night I lost my virginity to him.

"How many children were you thinking?" he questions dryly, once he sees his little dig at me didn't get the desired effect he expected.

"Three," I state evenly, looking directly at the three men sitting in front of me.

Tiernan's jaw ticks, giving my own smile of triumph free rein having gotten a reaction from him.

"What else?"

"I think it's your turn to make demands, husband," I coo, batting my eyelashes at him.

"As long as you are no longer living under my roof when all of this is done, I have all that I want."

I smile sweetly, hiding the hurt his cold words have caused.

"Very well. Then my next demand is that I don't want the transaction to happen at the apartment. I want it to be on neutral ground. For all parties involved."

"I can consent to that. There are a few apartments at The Avalon I rent out. One of them is currently vacant, so you can use it for your *gatherings*. Anything else you need to add, or are you content with your negotiations?"

"I only have one more thing that I want. Then I'll sign anything you put in front of me."

"Now, wife, there is no need for contracts. That's not the world we live in. My word is my bond. That should suffice," he adds with a sardonic grin.

"It does."

"Good. Then what is this last demand you want?"

I look at an ashen-faced Shay and then towards an even more stunned Colin, only to land my final stare on the man who is determined to pull all our strings.

"Whenever Shay, Colin, and I fuck, you'll have to be in the room to watch."

I'm not sure if it's the shock of hearing me say the word fuck that got to him, or my request that he be in the room when I have sex with his cousin or brother that did. The proof of how I just pricked the Irish king and made him bleed is all in the way his hands immediately balled into fists.

And with the knowledge that I tipped the crown off his head, I pick up my purse and begin to strut to the door. With my hand on the door knob, I turn my head over my shoulder and give my husband some parting advice.

"Those are my terms, husband. Fail to meet them, and I'll tell the families how this treaty is null and void. You have until midnight to give me your answer. Tick tock, Tiernan. Tick tock."

CHAPTER 14
Shay

I WAIT IMPATIENTLY for Rosa to leave the room before I tear my brother a new one.

"You cannot be fucking serious, Tiernan?! The fuck are you thinking?"

My brother ignores me completely, walking over to the floor-to-ceiling window to stare at our city.

"Tiernan?! Did you hear what I just said? This is fucking insane. Even for you," I shout, but all I get is my brother's silence and his back facing towards me.

I turn to my sullen cousin, whose head is bowed, thinking about God knows what.

"Why didn't you say anything, Col? You agree with me, right? This is some twisted-up shit. I mean, can you honestly sit there and tell me you're okay with fucking Tiernan's wife?"

His head snaps my way, rage like I've never seen before marring his features.

"Don't talk about her that way. She deserves our respect."

"Oh yeah, asshole? Then tell me, how are we showing her any fucking respect by tag-teaming her like some whore from The Pit?!"

When he begins to growl like some kind of feral animal, I know I've struck a nerve.

Fuck it. In for a penny, in for a pound and all that.

"What? You thought Tiernan wants us to wine and dine Rosa before we take turns fucking all her orifices?"

Colin stands up from his seat, ready to launch at me and make me swallow every last word I just uttered—even if he has to break my teeth to do it.

"You think you scare me, fucker?" I laugh, pulling out my favorite blade and toying with the handle over my knuckles. "I'd have your heart carved out of your chest before you even laid one finger on me."

"Enough," Tiernan calls out behind me, his tone sounding more annoyed with my shit than he is with the fucked-up deal he just struck with his wife.

"Fuck you, *dhearthái*r. I'll say when it's enough. And right now, you couldn't shut me up, even if you wanted to. This is one fucked-up scenario you put us in. Rosa, too."

"Tell me, Shay. Did my wife look in any way bothered by the proposition I made her?"

"She didn't jump for joy if that's what you're getting at."

"But she didn't say no either. You heard her when she agreed to my terms. She even negotiated ones of her own. If you honestly have a problem with any of this, then I'm sure Colin can go at it alone."

"If that was true, then why bring us both here today? Why not just pick one of us and spare the other ever knowing about this shit?"

"Maybe I wanted to increase her chances of getting pregnant."

"The fuck you did," I snort bitterly. "You wanted to shock her. Have her rethink your so-called solution of not wanting to father a child. You thought that by offering me and Colin up as substitute baby-makers, she would concede and not go through it. Your foolproof plan bit you in the ass, brother. And now you're screwed. Or in this case, your wife is."

"Are you in or out, Shay? That's all I want to know."

"Of course, I'm in. Someone needs to be there to make sure Rosa is okay. Or better yet, to pick up the pieces of the shell of a woman you are going to turn her into when this shit blows up in her face."

I run my fingers through my hair, tugging at the strands, frustrated that I can't find the right words to say to talk some sense into my headstrong brother.

"I'm not saying she didn't fuck up when she threatened to expose you to the families. She did, okay? That shit isn't kosher. But come on, brother. She's just a frightened, lonely girl, not our actual enemy. She might act like she's onboard with this shit now, but believe me, it's her pride talking. She doesn't want to be seen like a fucking piece of property or a doormat, and this is her way of standing up to you."

"I don't care what her reasons might have been. It's done."

I stare at my brother and wonder where the guy who used to wear the same old t-shirts and ripped up jeans for days on end, the one who always had a warm smile and a joke on the tip of his tongue, went off to.

Oh, that's right.

He's dead.

Died a painful death when my father handed him the keys to the kingdom five years ago.

Now all that is left is this cold, calculating, heartless corpse that parades in a fucking suit he wouldn't have been caught dead in a decade ago.

No.

The brother I looked up to all my life started to fade away the day my other brother decided to take his own life.

"I always admired you for being fair, Tiernan. The way you lead the men and demand their loyalty is admirable. But I never knew you could be this fucking cruel." I get up from my seat and start walking out the door, fucking done with this meeting.

"Be at The Avalon tomorrow at noon. I'll tell Rosa this starts tomorrow," my brother orders, using his business-as-usual tone with me.

"Fuck you, Tiernan. I hope one day she will forgive you because I never will."

I storm out of the boardroom and head towards the elevators, Colin right at my heel, just as he always is. When the doors close, I face my taciturn cousin and shove him right in his chest.

"Thanks for the support in there, dipshit. This is wrong, and you know it. You could have at least backed me up in there."

"The Boss had his mind made up long before we entered the room."

"Jesus, Mary, and Joseph! Can you quit being a robot for one goddamn second and think about the repercussions of this shit?" I yell in his face. "She's a scared girl. She doesn't have anyone here to hold her hand. And now my brother wants to send her off to be fed to the lions."

"We're not animals," he counters.

"You sure?! Then what do you call fucking the same woman while her husband watches? Pretty fucking savage to me."

"We've shared women before."

"Whores! We've shared easy pussy before, not a woman like Rosa."

Jesus. The world is utterly fucked if I'm the voice of reason.

When did life get so fucked-up?

Oh, I know.

When fucking *made men* decided the only way they would ever put their guns down would be if they offered up their daughters as sacrifices instead.

Fuck.

"We can't do this," I mumble in defeat.

"We can, and we will. It was an order."

"Fuck my brother's orders."

Colin growls.

"And stop with that shit, too. Stop growling at everything I say."

"When you stop being an ass, I will."

"Funny, motherfucker."

This time I'm the one who growls.

Great.

I'm losing my damn mind.

I run my fingers through my hair again just as the elevator doors ding open. I should step out and go about my day, trying to forget what tomorrow is going to bring me. But I don't move an inch. And neither does Colin.

"Tell me why you're onboard with this hare-brained scheme?"

"I've upset them."

"Who?"

He scowls at me.

"Okay, how then?" I fling my arms into the air, realizing he means Tiernan and Rosa.

"Rosa is upset with me for stealing that wretched painting I gave your Da. And the boss… well because I gave him an ultimatum the other day."

"What kind of ultimatum?" I ask, honestly interested in his response since Colin has never once defied Tiernan in anything.

"She was lonely. Sad back at the hotel," he mumbles, shifting his weight from one foot to the other.

"And?"

"And I told him to take her home. And if he didn't… then I would."

"No shit," I blurt out, impressed.

"Shit," he mumbles in frustration. "Now he thinks my loyalty has been compromised. I can't have that."

"Hasn't it?" I wiggle my brows at him.

"No," he deadpans, stepping out of the elevator. "And I'll prove it by doing what he's asked of us. And so will you."

"Right. Because that's exactly how someone sane would show their loyalty. Fuck his wife while he watches you do it." I scoff, trailing behind him and kicking the air at my feet.

Colin hurries his steps and only slows down when we pass through the main entrance's doors to our building.

"Fuck this. I'll go to *Athair* and tell him what Tiernan intends to do. If word got out and the other families learned about this, then I'm sure the treaty would be in jeopardy. *Athair* won't want that, and he'll talk Tiernan off this ledge he got us all on."

Colin suddenly stops at the center of the public square outside our office building and turns to face me.

"No, he won't."

"Like hell, he won't. *Athair* vowed on his life that no harm would come to Hernandez's daughter. Having a threesome with men that aren't her husband falls into that category, don't you think?"

"You forgot about Iris," he says cold-faced, sending an icy chill down my bones. "At this very minute she is fighting off three Volkovs. Three. And none of the families give a damn."

"That's different," I seethe at the reminder.

"No, it's not. The only difference is that Rosa accepted Tiernan's terms of sharing her bed with us. Iris had no say in the matter."

My hand instinctively goes to my dagger, as if the Bratva scum is right here in front of me.

"The least we can do is make this as painless as possible. Stop being selfish, Shay. And be a fucking man for once. She deserves that much from us."

And with those words, he leaves me to stew in the middle of the square, right as St. Brandon opens up the floodgates, and lets the rain fall down on my body, washing my temper away.

She deserves that much from us.

And by she, Colin means both women who have sacrificed more than we ever will in our entire lives.

※

The following day, neither Tiernan nor Colin were surprised that I showed up at The Avalon at noon on the dot.

My brother takes his seat on the settee in the corner of the room, the perfect spot that would ensure he wouldn't miss a single moment of this twisted affair.

For the first time in my life, I'm grasping at straws as to what Tiernan's endgame is. Does he want to show Rosa that she can't blackmail him into submission? Is this his way of holding some kind of dominance over his pretty bride? If so, there were a million other ways he could do it that wouldn't have involved me or Colin.

Or is this some perverse game he's playing to humiliate his wife?

To cause her just an ounce of the torment her family had put us through without laying his hands on her?

Whatever his goal, I'm not sure I'm a hundred percent onboard with his chosen theatrics.

Colin remains leaning against the bedroom door, almost like he's waiting for his boss to give him the go-ahead to leave. But as I stare at my brother, I don't see an ounce of hesitation in his eyes.

No one is leaving here until the deed is done.

When the bathroom door creaks open, my heart stops in my chest, and all thoughts of making a quick escape vanish from my mind.

Damnú.

Rosa really is the most beautiful woman I have ever seen.

In a white spaghetti-string nightgown that falls almost to her bare feet, she walks into the room, chin held high. She looks as if she's about to bravely face a firing squad and wants to meet her maker with him knowing she never once flinched when facing sure death.

"Well, wife? You have us here. May I remind you this is your show? You give out the orders."

But just as my brother looks resolved in seeing this through, so does Rosa.

She walks over to the bed, not sparing her husband another look as she directs her attention to me and Colin.

"Can you come closer?" she asks, her voice a soft caress.

"You'll have to be more precise than that. Which one do you want?" Tiernan states, sounding bored.

Fucker.

Even with all the nerves of steel she's trying to demonstrate she has, it's obvious she's nervous.

Fuck.

I'm nervous.

Tiernan's mockery of her won't lessen her nerves, nor will it ease the heavy air that hangs thick in the room.

Without her having to say anything, I take a step in her direction, relief and gratitude instantly transforming her facial features.

This is fucking bullshit.

My brother should just swallow his fucking pride and put a baby in her already.

Hmm.

Maybe all he needs is a little push in the right direction.

I doubt he really wants Colin and I to fuck his wife in front of him. He's never been one to share. He's always looking down on Colin and me when gossip reaches his ears that we sandwiched another girl between us.

But all the women Col and I took to our bed were either paid whores or girls with insatiable appetites that enjoyed having both holes filled. Hey, I've never been one to slut shame. I'm all for a woman's right to sexual empowerment. Especially when I get to be part of the action.

This is different, though.

This isn't some naughty fantasy that Rosa wants fulfilled.

This isn't just sex for fun's sake.

She wants to start a family.

You don't have to spend too much time with her to see that maternal streak in her. She'll make a great mother—Hernandez or not. Tiernan fucking lucked out when he got her name in the raffle. The bloody idiot is just too stubborn and proud to see it.

If he doesn't wise up soon, then he will never be happy in his marriage.

And as much as I would like nothing more than to sink my dick into this woman's sweet pussy, she's still his wife. Not mine.

I guess the fucker just needs some reminding.

How lucky for him he has a brother who isn't shy about putting him in his place from time to time.

"What do you need me to do, petal?" I cajole, putting all my charm into my voice.

Her long lashes flutter up, her eyes filled with fear.

"Tell me what you need, and I'll help you."

"I'm... I'm not sure what to do," she mutters softly, low enough that only I can hear the insecurity in her voice.

The girl has at least two years on me, and still, she is as untouched as a virgin.

"Colin," I call out loud enough for him to hear me from across the room. "Come here."

I don't have to turn around to know my cousin will follow my order. His steps are silent over the plush cream carpet in the room, but when he surfaces behind this frightened rose, I breathe easy that he's in this with me.

Rosa's eyes are on her husband, as I gently pull on one silk string of her nightgown and push it down her shoulder. Colin mimics my action and pulls down the other string, making the nightgown drop fully to the floor and pool at our feet. I stare at her toes grasping at the carpet to tether her to the ground, as she stands naked between men that a week ago were just strangers. Her chest heaves up and down, drawing my attention to the swell of her breasts.

And what perfect breasts they are.

I've gotten so accustomed to fake tits that when I see real God-given ones, large enough to fit in the palm of my hand, my cock instantly goes hard.

Shit.

I want her.

I really fucking want her right now.

Shit!

"Fuck this," I say when I'm close to losing my goddamn mind and following through on Tiernan's plan after all.

I'm about to turn away to leave when Tiernan calls out my name, halting my step.

"Move another inch, Shay, and brother or not, I will chain you up in one of our cellars and leave you there for a full month without you seeing the light of day. Same goes for you, Colin."

"If that's what you want, then go for it. I couldn't give a rat's ass."

I'm about to head out the door when Rosa grabs my wrist, stopping me in my tracks.

My forehead creases at the mere desperation on her face.

"Please, Shay. Stay."

It's the fucking please that gets me in the end.

And then it hits me.

Like an epiphany that was staring me right in the face all along, I begin to understand why she wants this so badly. Her life with us Kellys will never be a happy one. She will always be seen as the enemy. She will live the rest of her years here being hated for something she has no control over. Rosa wanting to get pregnant has nothing to do with being fearful of breaking a treaty or wanting to stand up to her husband.

She wants someone she can love.

Someone that will love her unconditionally.

A child will never see her as Hernandez scum, but as the mother who will keep it safe and loved.

This is not sex.

This is her already in love with a child that does not yet exist.

Because in the end, it's the only way she will ever experience real love.

I bridge the gap between us and snake my hand through her long brown hair to palm her cheek.

"Okay, Rosa. For you, I'll do this."

The look of gratitude she gives me cracks my heart further down the middle.

Ever so slowly, I lower my head, my soft eyes always on her, as I kiss her bare shoulder. Colin follows suit and mimics my action on her shoulder's twin, his hands falling to her hips to keep her steady and in place.

I know Colin well enough that Tiernan's order is law to him. He won't back down unless specifically told to do so. But if the conversation we had yesterday is any clue, then my cousin has his own agenda in regards to this Spanish rose.

Her breaths become shallower as my tongue trails its way to the crook of her neck, in tandem with Colin placing open-mouthed kisses to her shoulder blades and back.

She tastes like exotic wild fruit, making my mouth water for more. The need to taste her lips and see if they are just as sweet festers in my mind. Unfortunately, I doubt my brother would take too kindly to that intimate act.

On second thought...

Fuck him.

Rosa gasps when I hold the nape of her neck so that I can capture her lips in mine. Her eyes widen for a millisecond and then slide shut, relishing the tender kiss. I'm usually not this delicate with a woman, but if there is anyone that deserves some sweetness in her world, it is this gorgeous, fierce creature standing in front of me.

My teeth nip at the seam of her lips, silently requesting entrance. When she parts her lips to intake air or to offer her approval, I use it to my advantage and plunge my tongue into her mouth. Another small gasp leaves her and I eat it up, determined to hear her moan with just one kiss. The minute she does, I pull away so my fucking brother can hear it loud and clear from his seat.

Rosa blinks twice as if completely taken aback by how much she took pleasure in kissing me. I lick my lips and gently tug at her hair so that she has no choice but to crane her head to the side for my cousin to have his turn.

Colin doesn't hesitate and captures her lips in his, his tongue forcefully breaking the seal, making sure to take her very breath away. I feel her nails clutch my shirt as Colin eats up all her pleas and makes her body sing and crave for more. When he eases up, his eyes are a molten hue of desire. I've seen their green shade burn like that plenty of times to know he wants the woman he has in his arms as much as I do.

I lean into her ear, goosebumps spreading all along her olive-toned skin.

"We are going to make you feel so good, petal. Don't be scared. Trust us. We know what we're doing."

"I believe you." She sighs, her rosy cheeks making her even more endearing in my eyes.

I throw her a cocky smile before entwining her fingers with mine and leading her closer to the bed. She throws a quick nervous glance over to her husband, but I nudge her chin with my hand to look only at me.

"Fuck him. Let him watch. You're ours now."

Rosa bites down on her plush lower lip and lets me lead her onto the bed until she is on her knees, naked as the day she was born right smack in the middle of the mattress. Colin walks to the other side of the bed, discarding his clothes, while I quickly do the same. Her eyes widen when she sees the effect she has on us both.

I stroke my bare cock, taking a knee on the bed and inching closer to her.

"I know you're used to smaller dicks, but trust me, Colin and I will fit just fine."

I chuckle when I hear my brother groan in irritation with the dig I made about his dick. I'm sure by now she knows I'm talking out of my ass, since all the Kelly men are well-endowed. I'm not stupid enough to think Tiernan has never taken his wife to bed for her not to know his dick is just as big as his ego. I also bet all the money I have in the bank that she came to him untouched, and her innocence was just too much of a temptation for him to refuse.

I don't care if he did have her first.

We have her now.

And that's all that matters.

"Lay on your back, petal," I instruct softly, running the back of my hand against her cheek.

The way she instantly melts into my touch has me all sorts of fucked-up. This woman is so deprived of love that the smallest kindness makes her light up from the inside out. Not one to wait around, Colin runs his tongue up her neck and then jaw, while his hands on her hips urge her to lay back on the bed like I asked.

"What… what are you going to do now?" she stammers when two pairs of eyes stare down at her from either side of her naked body.

"Colin here is going to make sure you are nice and wet for us. While his mouth is fully occupied, I've got a few tricks I want to try out with mine." I wink.

She offers us both a shy smile, but before she lets us enjoy her body, she places her palms on each of our cheeks.

Colin's brows pull together as he stares down at her, while I grab her wrist to place a kiss to her open palm.

"Thank you," she says to us both.

"*Damnú*," Colin grunts out, her sincere gratitude starting to do a number on his heart as well as his dick.

"Just lie back and enjoy, petal. And don't be afraid to be loud. Let's show that husband of yours what the fucker is missing."

Without further provocation, Colin quickly settles himself in between her thighs, wraps her legs around his bulging shoulders, and goes right to it.

"Argh!" she shouts, arching her back so high up off the bed, I have to place my hand on her flat stomach to hold her down.

"Guess you got Colin more worked up than I thought," I tease. "But now that he's had a taste, it's only fair that I get mine, too."

I bow my head in between her breasts and pluck one nipple into my mouth, moaning the minute I do.

Fuck, but the woman is sweet.

The sweetest nectar I've ever come across.

I tease her nipple with my teeth and then use my tongue to trace over the sting they've left. I palm her other breast in my hand, needling its bud with my thumb and index finger, until her perked nipple is so hard it could cut a diamond in half. I take a peek under my lashes to see her face and witness that her lids are shut tight, her lips parted wide open in utter ecstasy. Sweat covers her temple, trickling down her face to her neck, and in between the cleft of her breasts. I lick it up with my tongue and then switch my attention to focus on her other phenomenal breast.

"Argh!" she shouts out again, only this time there is a hint of pain to her wail.

Afraid that I've hurt her somehow, I look up and see that she isn't staring at me, but at Colin. My gaze follows hers over to my cousin to find the fucker eating her out with gusto but fucking her entrance with most of his fingers.

I slap him on the head to stop him at once and make him look up at me.

Of course, the fucker has the nerve to growl.

"Get her wet enough to take only one of us at a time, Col. She's not ready to take us both. Not yet, anyway."

"She's soaked. She can handle it."

I roll my eyes.

That's the thing about my dear ol' cousin. When he sees something he likes, he has this incessant need to possess every nook and cranny there is of them. But no matter what the horny asshole says, I highly doubt Rosa can handle us both in one go today. Like her namesake, she needs a lot of nurturing and warmth before she can truly blossom.

"All in due time." I scowl, putting on my 'don't fuck with me' face so he gets the picture not to fight me on this.

Disgruntled, he pulls his digits away from her drenched pussy, solely to lavish her clit with his tongue's attention. Her body instantly relaxes, and all too soon Colin has her thrashing on the bed, seconds away from cumming on his mouth. This time I don't tell my fiendish cousin to let up and allow him to get our girl across the finish line first.

And when she cums, Saint Brigid herself could have never conceived of a better aphrodisiac to make a baby.

"Now," Colin growls like a wild beast drunk with lust.

I don't even have the will to tell him not yet, to want to prolong this. Not when she makes that O face that is begging to get fucked. Colin hurriedly lies on his side, grabbing Rosa's hips to pull her ass to his crotch, while she faces me.

Her hooded gaze tells me she's in too much of a daze to know what's going on anymore.

I lean in and kiss her lips, knowing that I'm pissing Colin off with the delay.

"Petal, look at me."

Her heavy lids look like they weigh a ton, but thankfully she's lucid enough to follow my command.

"Do you really want this?"

Colin's grip on her hips tightens as he throws me a disparaging glower over her shoulder. But I ignore him since I'm determined for her to give us her full consent before we do this.

"Petal?"

She licks her lips and stares at mine, offering me a small nod.

"Use your words, baby. I need you to say it."

Again, I'm shocked at how gentle I'm being with her. I don't want to cause her pain. Something tells me she's had enough of it in her life, and I will not add on to the pile of misery she's already suffered through.

"I want this, Shay," she whispers to me, batting those long fucking eyelashes that were made to make men like me stupid.

She then tilts her head over her shoulder, a wild-eye Colin staring back at her.

"I want you, too, Colin. Please."

That's all he needs to plunge inside her.

"Oh my God!" she wails, her eyes rolling to the back of her head.

I grab her face to look my way again and kiss her gently and sweetly while Colin fucks her to within an inch of her life. I feel her heart pound against mine, the smell of her juices filling the air around us and making me punch-drunk with lust, desperate to have my turn.

"You're so fucking perfect, petal," I praise, as my own shaft painfully starts leaking precum all over her stomach. "Look how well you're taking Colin's cock in you. So damn perfect, baby."

Her half-mast gaze stares up at me in utter adoration, and I swear in this very moment, she chips a piece of my heart and steals it away to latch it onto hers.

When I catch a glimpse of Colin's face screwed up in pain, I know he's seconds away from tossing his load. She hasn't cum a second time yet, and with my cousin being balls deep inside her, ready to burst at any second, I know she'll need a little extra stimulation to get her there. I sneak my hand in between us and give her clit a few strokes, and sure enough, she shatters into a million pieces. As her orgasm rips her in half, Colin cums inside her with two vigorous thrusts and then pulls out, leaving the door wide open for me to take my rightful turn.

"Jesus! Fuck!" I shout when I fill her to the hilt.

Nothing could have ever prepared me for how good Rosa's pussy would feel on my dick.

It's a miracle Colin lasted as long as he did because, in less than ten minutes flat, I'm cumming like a horny pre-teen who just learned how to jerk off. My cock is still fully inside her as she milks me dry, panting out my name like it's God's answer to all her prayers. My head falls to her shoulder, feeling like someone just whacked me across the chest with a baseball bat.

The fuck just happened?

Sex has never once had me questioning all my beliefs, not that I have many, but magical fucking pussies are definitely not on the list. I hear Colin's heavy breathing in sync with mine, telling me that he knows exactly what I'm feeling right now.

We are so fucked.

Because I doubt that even after we get Rosa knocked up, neither one of us will want to stop fucking her.

Once you have a taste of heaven, it's hard letting go of it.

And as if Tiernan has a direct line to my thoughts, I hear him scoff from his seat.

"That was quite the performance," he says dryly. "I think that's enough for today. You can show yourselves out while I have a word with *my wife*."

I don't miss how he adds just a bit of emphasis on the words —*my wife.*

I've never once wanted anything my brother had.

Not the seat on the throne of the Irish mob.

Not the loyalty and respect of his men.

Not even the constant praise he receives from our father.

There was never anything that would ever entice me into stepping into his shoes.

Until now.

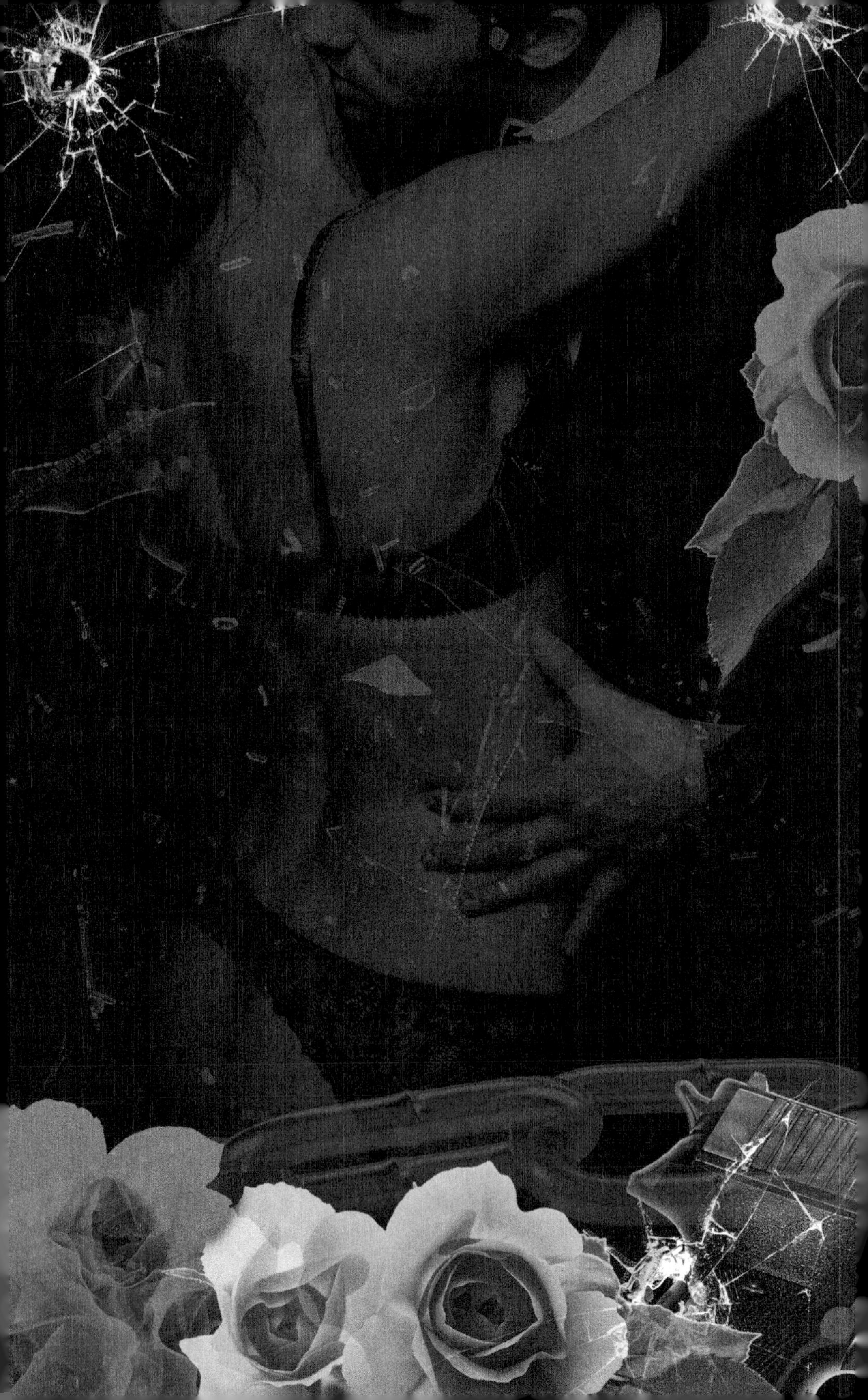

CHAPTER 15
Rosa

TIERNAN WAITS until he hears the front door of the apartment close behind Shay and Colin before he gets out of his seat and walks over to the dresser where I left my handbag. I pull the sheets up to cover my naked flesh, although modesty went out the window the minute I agreed to go through with having sex with two men that weren't my husband.

I watch in silence as he flips my bag upside down and disposes of all of its contents on top of the dresser. He picks up a tube of my lipstick and then walks over to the same chair he had been sitting in while he watched his own flesh and blood take turns fucking me.

Although can I really say what transpired between us was just sex?

I swear there was a connection that was made between me, Shay, and Colin.

Maybe it was all in my head, but I felt something twist and turn inside me with every gentle kiss they gave me.

Or maybe—and this feels like a more realistic reason—I'm just not the type of woman who can have sex just for the sake of having it without feelings being involved.

I might have just romanticized the whole event, and what I felt when Shay and Colin touched me was just one-sided.

Right now, my world has been tipped on its axis, and I'm not sure which way is up or down. All I know is that when I slept with Tiernan, it was raw, unadulterated passion. Maybe hatred spurred that sentiment on, making our moments of intimacy that much more intense.

With Shay and Colin, however, I felt the opposite. I felt delicate. Precious—even loved.

I felt like I could breathe.

With Tiernan, I didn't feel like I could even touch him without being reprimanded for it.

Shay begged for my touch.

His blue eyes burned at the way my hand ran down his chest.

And as for Colin?

His ardent caresses made me feel like he had never been in the possession of something so precious.

It reminded me of the way he would stare at a landscape painting he liked and want to submerge himself in it. Get lost in something beautiful since his world is anything but.

I liked the power they both let me have.

To wield it against them.

The way they fell apart just by being with me.

It's not at all what I expected.

A part of me even screamed for me to put a stop to this before I even walked into the room. Only my pride and stubbornness prevented me from backpedaling and calling the whole thing off.

I made a deal with the devil, and if my soul was the price I had to pay to get what I wanted, then so be it.

"Come here," Tiernan commands once he's made himself comfortable in his spot.

I hesitate just for a second but think better of it when he flexes his fists. As much as I didn't want to look at my husband as his men had their way with me, every so often, my gaze was drawn to his. All throughout the scene, Tiernan's expression remained completely stoic, as if he was just watching an old rerun of a television show and not his wife having sex with two men at the same time.

The only telltale sign I was able to see that he was affected by what was happening in front of him was the way his hands would ball into fists and then release open every few seconds.

"I won't ask again," he says when I've taken longer to execute his command.

I begin to get up off the bed, clinging to the bedsheet for protection, when he shakes his head and stops me cold in my tracks.

"Tsk tsk," he taunts. "I want you to come to me naked like you are now. Crawl your way over to me, wife. And do it fast. My patience is wearing thin as it is."

My chest, neck, and cheeks burst into flames at his order, but like the stubborn fool that I am, I let go of the sheet and slide out of the bed, just to go onto my hands and knees, crawling my way over to him. The sardonic smile that crests his lips has my lower belly fluttering.

When did I become such a masochist?

Or was it his sadism that brought it out of me?

I try not to think too much on the answers to those questions and inch closer to him until my knees land close to the tips of his Italian loafers.

"Sit," he commands, like I'm a bitch in heat who needs to be ordered around.

I sit back on my haunches and hold my head up high so he can see that no matter how he treats me, how belittling his words are, I'll always have my pride.

He leans into me, his face within a hair's breadth of mine.

"Tell me, wife," he begins, his knuckles caressing my cheek, while his other hand uncaps my lipstick and twists it open. "Was that all you envisioned? Did it live up to your high expectations?"

I don't answer him. I don't dare utter a word. Instead, I remain perfectly still as he keeps stroking the back of his hand on my cheek.

"You've surprised me," he confesses, and to this, my forehead creases, breaking the schooled features I was trying so hard to keep intact. "I can count on one hand how many people have surprised me in my lifetime. I never expected one of them to be you."

He pulls back just an inch, his gaze falling to my chest. I don't have to look down to see that my nipples are pointing at attention in his direction. My body, unlike my mind, finds Tiernan's gaze on it one of the most exhilarating things it has ever experienced. I continue to look straight into his peculiar eyes as he uses my lipstick to write something just above my breasts. When he's done branding me with my own lipstick, he throws the tube on the floor, leans back into his seat, and admires his handiwork.

I don't give him the satisfaction of looking down.

"I'm curious. Did you like my brother's cock inside you?"

Yes.

"My cousin's?"

Yes.

"I want the truth. I think after all of this, I'm entitled to it after all."

"Does it matter if I liked it or not, as long as the end goal is met?" I utter with steel in my voice.

"Right. How could I forget? You want a baby. I never would have assumed you had baby fever when I met you."

"I don't."

"But you still want one?"

"Yes."

"Why?" he asks sternly, as if the mere idea of a woman wanting a child pisses him off.

"Because it's expected of me," I lie. "To ensure the treaty is upheld."

He shakes his head with a scowl.

"I said the truth, wife."

"My truth is irrelevant and not included in the bargain we made yesterday in your boardroom. If you wanted it, you should have asked for it. Now I'm not in the mood to re-negotiate terms when I'm perfectly content with the ones we've already agreed on."

He tilts his head to the side and carefully scans my face until there isn't an inch of it he isn't familiar with.

"I didn't want this," he mutters through clenched teeth.

"You didn't want me, either. I guess it's true what they say, you can't always get what you want."

He leans forward, gripping my chin in his hand, his fingers digging into my flesh.

"Why should I want you? What could you possibly have that a million other women don't?"

I snap my chin away from his grip, my daunting gaze piercing his chest like the dagger I wish I could plunge into the hollow hole that should hold a heart.

"If that's true, then why do you look rattled?" I bite back.

"I'm not."

"No? Then why do you feel the need to embarrass me at every opportunity?"

"Because pretty things shouldn't exist in my world. Their only use is to be broken."

I throw him my best glower while staring him dead in the eye.

"I was broken long before you ever put your hands on me. Don't think your abuse will make a dent or cause a crack."

At this, he smiles, genuinely pleased with my answer.

He taps on his knee, his silent command for me to sit on it.

Or maybe it's just his nonverbal way of telling me he's about to spank my ass raw.

"I'm not going to hurt you. Not physically, at least. Sit," he relents when he realizes why I'm hesitant to move.

I get off the floor and sit on his lap, his hand pulling my legs to lie on top of his. Without missing a beat, he then grabs my chin and stares into my eyes. We stay like that for an infernal moment, and to my shame, my core begins to soak his pants with just his eyes on me.

"You came."

It's not a question but a mere spoken fact.

"You never said I couldn't."

"That's true." He grins, almost sounding pleased that I took advantage of the missed technicality. "It's fine. I don't care if you cum or not. I don't even care if you fully enjoy being sandwiched between Shay and Col. All I care is that you know one solemn truth."

"Which is?" I whisper softly when his hand begins to trace up my inner thigh.

"That just because I let you fuck them doesn't mean you should forget who you belong to. You're mine, Rosa. And don't you forget it."

"I thought you didn't believe in ownership?" I throw the words he said on our wedding night back in his face.

He smirks.

"I didn't."

"What changed your mind?"

"You."

And before I have time to process his admission, he crashes his mouth on mine.

His hand falls from my chin and onto my throat as his tongue wrestles for dominance with mine. As always, I let him own my mouth with his sinful kiss and let the wave of desire run through me. His fingers meet my wet slit and play with my sensitive nub until I'm panting into his mouth.

"Fuck," he moans, his bulging cock pressed up against my ass cheeks. "Look at what you do to me."

The accusation falls flat on the floor with the way he plunges into my hot core with his digits, determined to make me cum on his hand. If I have any effect on this man, then it pales in comparison to the one he has on me. He plays my body like a fiddle, and in turn, it shows him how greedy it always is to sing the song he alone wants to hear. His kiss is as deadly as his deft fingers, and before I know what's happening, my body spasms on his lap as I wail out my climax for him to swallow down.

He pushes me to the floor, my euphoria breaking the fall, as I watch him unzip his pants and stroke his cock in my face.

"Put it in your mouth, *acushla*. Feel what you do to me just from one fucking kiss."

I don't hesitate and go to my knees to suck on his cock. His hand goes back to my throat, squeezing it to the point that my airway is constricted by both the force of his grip on my windpipe and his cock pounding away down it.

"Play with your pussy, wife. Show me just what a little whore I'm married to."

I do as he says, opening my thighs wide enough so that my hand can slip in between them and play with myself. My sensitive core drips on my fingers as I continue to suck at my husband's cock like my life depends on it. Tiernan wraps my hair around his wrist, while his other hand continues adding pressure to my throat. The stimulation coming from all sides is just too much, and being deprived of air only seems to heighten my other senses.

"Are you fucking yourself good and proper now, wife? Are you imagining that your fingers are my tongue lapping at your cunt, cleaning the cum your lovers left inside of you?"

Virgen.

"Is that what you want? To be fucked by all of us at the same time? To have all your holes filled and still beg for more?"

I can't.

I can't.

I can't breathe.

I'm not sure if it's Tiernan's filthy imagination or his cock ramming down my throat as his hand constricts my airflow completely, but somehow, against all odds, I cum, almost blacking out as my body is ripped in two.

Tiernan follows right behind me, loosening his hold on me just enough for me to swallow his essence. And after he's made sure there isn't a drop left, he lets me go with brutish force. I fall back on my hands and knees, frantically trying to gasp air into my lungs and calm my rapid heartbeat.

Through my peripheral vision, I watch my husband slide his cock back into his pants, fix his cufflinks, and stand up straight, like what just happened between us was the most mundane thing he's ever experienced. He picks up his suit jacket and puts it on, bypassing me on the floor and heading towards the door.

"As per our agreement, I'll be home for dinner around eight."

And without further word, he turns his back and leaves, while I'm still battling for air and some sort of composure to come to me.

On shaky knees, I use the armchair he was sitting in to pull myself up. I walk over to the bathroom, hoping that a long shower will relax all my abused limbs, when I catch my reflection in the mirror.

In large red letters, the word SLUT is written on my chest.

The parting gift my husband left me after he made sure he had corrupted my soul.

I spend the rest of the day back in Tiernan's apartment, sleeping off all the ways my body had been used and abused in the apartment just a few floors below this one. Thankfully, I wake up a couple of hours before I have to go to the kitchen and prepare a meal for the dinner date with my husband.

After all he's done to me, I should poison him and be done with it.

But just as the murderous thought enters my head, I banish it away.

Even though he's cold and ruthless, I couldn't imagine a world where he didn't exist. Maybe I'm being naïve, or just downright stupid, but Tiernan brings out something in me that I never knew was there. A flame that burns so bright, that I fear one day I'll be consumed by it and turn to ash.

Logic tells me I shouldn't feel this way. That even Icarus perished by trying to fly too close to the sun. But logic and sense had no hand in the deal I made with him either, so I fear I'm no longer capable of rational thought when it pertains to my husband.

After I've made sure the *birria de chivo* is up to par, I put on a sleek white sleeveless dress and put my hair up to accentuate my long neck. I know it's not exactly proper attire to be wearing for dinner at home, but I doubt I'll ever use it on an actual dinner date to a fancy restaurant. Tiernan is perfectly content to keep me under lock and key.

After finding some matches to set-up the candlelight dinner I've prepared, I stand back and admire my handiwork, fully knowing Tiernan will disapprove of the romantic setting.

Let him.

This is more for me than it is for him.

I wasn't lying when I said I was tired of eating my meals alone. Back home, even when everyone was running around busy with their lives, we always made it a point to have at least one meal together. I miss that familial comradery more than I want to be wooed by my husband.

If I'm honest, the only reason why I even went to such an effort to make this dinner extra romantic was because I knew it would piss Tiernan off. And getting under his skin has become something of an addiction to me. I feed off it just as much as my humiliation seems to satiate Tiernan's hunger.

I'm at my seat, one long leg crossed over the other, when the elevator doors open at eight on the dot.

Say what you will about my husband, but the man sure is a sucker for being punctual.

"Hi."

Tiernan's gaze takes a second to travel up my Louboutin heels, ankles, up my calves and thighs, before they even reach my eyes.

"Hmm," he mumbles, frustrated, and inwardly I clap myself on the back for a job well done.

"Bad day?" I arch a brow.

"Getting worse by the second," he grumbles, taking off his suit jacket and flinging it to the couch.

"That's too bad." I fake a smile. "Aren't you going to ask about my day?"

"I already know how your day went," he replies while loosening his tie.

"So, you do. Still, it's only nice to be asked anyway."

"I don't do nice, wife. I thought you would know that about me already."

"You're right, I do. I just thought you might surprise me. Only fair since I've managed to surprise you today."

The malicious smirk he throws at me has me clapping with glee inside my chest.

It's official.

The man has turned me into a lunatic with no common sense and less self-preservation.

He takes his seat across from me and pours wine into his glass. I don't even put up a fight when he fills my glass, too.

Kellys drink, after all.

And as he constantly likes to keep reminding me, I am a Kelly now.

"So, what did Elsa cook for us tonight?"

"Not Elsa. Me. I cooked. I told her from now on she didn't have to bother herself with that part of the job and could just focus on housework."

"And what do I tell her when you're no longer here to cook my meals, wife?" Tiernan says, reminding me that my time here has a countdown.

"Not my problem."

To my chagrin, the small chuckle that leaves him warms me up.

"So, what am I about to eat?"

"*Birria de Chivo*. I hope you like it."

"Do you really?" Another chuckle. "And just what is *Birria de Chivo*?"

"Goat stew," I singsong.

He pales for just a split second and then laughs. A true loud and proud laugh that I would never expect a man like him capable of. It almost makes him look softer somehow.

"Well, I guess it's only fair you give me goat to eat. I would have assumed you would rather see me starve than ever feed me, wife."

"Everyone deserves to be fed. I'm not that heartless, husband."

"No. You're not," he whispers under his breath, staring right at me.

I have to look away and bow my head towards my plate when I catch his green eye softening while his blue shines bright. When I take a forkful of the delicious stew into my mouth, Tiernan takes that as his cue to start eating.

When a few long minutes pass and neither one of us attempts to say anything, I decide to break the silence by asking a few questions that have been on my mind lately.

"Not that I'm complaining, but this apartment needs a woman's touch to make it more inviting. Didn't any of your previous girlfriends ever offer to decorate it for you?"

Tiernan almost chokes on his stew, grabbing his glass so the wine can help it go down smoother.

"Is this really an appropriate conversation to have over dinner?"

"Why not? You've never given me an inkling that you care too much about propriety anyway. I don't see the harm in wanting to know how many women have come to your apartment before me."

"I thought your interest was purely on its décor, not how many women I've fucked here."

Of course, leave it to Tiernan to leave me tongue-tied just by the way he uses the word fuck.

"I was trying to ease into it. Forgive me if I'm not as blunt as you."

"You're forgiven." He chuckles, entertained.

"Well, are you going to tell me, or are you determined to leave me in suspense?"

"I think I'll go with the latter." He whips out that devilish grin of his before taking another sip of his wine.

When I glare at him, it only seems to amuse him further.

"Fine. I can honestly say I have never brought a woman home. I wasn't even sure I'd ever bring you here, and I'm married to you."

"What changed your mind?"

His humor disappears.

"Next question, *acushla*."

Sensing that I struck a nerve, I don't pester him into giving me an answer.

"How many girlfriends did you have before marrying me then?"

"None."

"Not one?" I ask incredulously.

"No."

"You have never had any relationships with any of your sexual partners whatsoever?"

"That's what I said."

When I absentmindedly bite my lip to take that tidbit of information in, he groans and turns his attention back to his plate. I immediately pull my teeth off my lip before his willingness to answer my questions vanishes.

"Have you slept with many women?"

"Yes."

Well, that was a stupid question.

Of course, he has.

The way he holds court in the bedroom is enough proof of his experience.

Ask him what you really want to know, Rosa.

"Let me rephrase. Have you slept with anyone more than once?"

"A few."

"How many is a few?"

"Two, maybe three."

"You don't remember?"

"I have more important things to occupy my mind with than remembering such things."

He's right.

A man like him probably doesn't even remember a woman's name after he's had her, much less the number of times he took her to his bed.

"For how long? How many days did those relationships last?"

"If you can call banging a woman's head into a headboard while I fucked them from behind a relationship, then I would say no more than a couple of days. A week tops."

"Figures. That would explain why you got tired of me after only a day," I mumble, distracted by the imagery he planted in my head.

"Hmm."

I maul my lip while tapping my fingers onto the table.

"Stop punishing your bottom lip and just ask what you really want to ask, wife," he orders, his eyes not lifting once off his plate.

Instead of wondering how he knew I was chewing on my lip, I ask the burning question that has been slowly driving me up the wall.

"Have you slept with anyone else since we've been married?"

"No."

With this question he has the decency to look me in the eye.

"I don't believe you."

"I don't care either way."

We grow silent as we continue on with our staring contest, waiting until one of us breaks.

Neither one of us does.

"I saw glitter on your shirt that first week back at The Liberty Hotel. You came in smelling like cheap perfume, too."

"Did you really?" he asks, engrossed in my small confession. "I thought you were asleep?"

"I wasn't."

"You waited up for me?"

"Yes."

"Why?"

I shrug, preferring to feign nonchalance than to tell him the truth.

If I admit to him that I was slowly going out of my mind wondering when he would touch me again, or that I couldn't get our wedding night out of my head, and that him spanking my ass like that until I came had been the most lurid and fascinating thing I had ever experienced, I'd never live it down.

Nope.

Not happening.

Fabricated nonchalance it is.

Tiernan's gaze on me never falters as he leans back in his chair and crosses his arms over his chest.

"Before you came to Boston, I hadn't touched a woman in over a year. The stress of the treaty and sending Iris off to be married to the Bratva killed my sex drive."

"It didn't seem dead to me the other night."

"Things change." He smirks. "But there you have it, wife. I haven't slept with anyone that wasn't you, and for the foreseeable future, I don't intend to, either."

"Because you're too busy for such things." I snort, irked at the 'foreseeable future' remark he just had to include in his rant.

"No. Because if I want to get off, I have a beautiful wife waiting for me at home, ready and willing to assist me."

"You sure think highly of yourself."

"I only speak the truth, wife. If I wanted you this very minute, I could have you. Tell me I'm wrong."

"I hate you," I seethe when the mere sound of his velvety voice calling me wife has my lower belly aching with need, wanting him to put his theory to the test.

"No, you don't, wife. But you will."

He then gets up from his seat and walks over to me. My forehead wrinkles when he gently picks my chin up so I have no choice but to crane my head back and look him in the eye.

"Thank you for dinner, *acushla*. I will now anxiously look forward to them in the future."

He bends down and places such a sweet and gentle kiss to my lips, that I'm left both confused and utterly bereft when he pulls away.

"Goodnight, Rosa." He smiles softly, running the pad of his thumb over my lower lip.

"Goodnight, husband," I breathe out on a sigh and then watch the infuriating man retreat to his office, leaving me with even more questions than I had answers.

CHAPTER 16
Shay

WHEN ROSA WALKS into the living room in white flannel pajamas that mostly cover her from head to toe, I'm not only disappointed but oddly fascinated.

"Shay?" She rubs the sleep out of her eyes as she draws closer.

I can't blame the poor thing for being tired after the number Colin and I did on her body yesterday.

"Morning, petal."

"Morning." She yawns, walking over to the kitchen to grab some coffee.

"Don't I get a kiss good morning?"

She crosses her eyes at me but blushes all the same.

"It's too early for your teasing," she says between yawns.

I wasn't teasing.

She could be wearing a potato sack over her head and I'd still want to kiss her stupid first thing in the morning.

But saying such things will only get her and me in trouble.

For all I know, Tiernan has his apartment bugged just to make sure no one touches his prized possession when he's not around.

Fucker.

After she's filled a mug full of her daily dose of caffeine, she walks over to the couch and sits right beside me.

"Where's Colin? Isn't he supposed to be babysitting me today?"

"Nope," I pop the p at the end. "I got you all to myself for the day." I nudge her shoulder playfully with mine.

"Isn't there an off switch with you?" she mumbles in between sips and then melts into the cushion, a sign of how tired she really is.

If she only gave me the chance, I could perk her right up with my tongue. I quickly shake that thought away before I do something stupid and place her on my lap so I can show just how.

On second thought…

"Hey!" she squeals, almost spilling her coffee all over us as I plant her ass on me. "What do you think you are doing?"

"Just wanted to check something out. Give me a minute."

She's stiff as a board, holding on to her mug for dear life, as I run my fingers through her hair and nuzzle my nose into the crook of her neck.

"Shay?" she stammers, unsure of what to do.

"Ten more seconds," I whisper in her ear, before planting a gentle kiss behind it.

My cock swells in excitement when a light shiver runs down her spine after the kiss.

But before I'm able to get comfortable and really test the waters of her restraint, the apartment elevator dings open, Darren walking through it like a man on a mission.

I knew it.

"Yes?" I ask with a blasé tone while making a point to gently brush Rosa's long hair off her shoulder so I can pop my chin on it.

Darren clears his throat and pretends to look everywhere around the apartment but directly at us.

"Boss wants to talk to you," he mutters, handing me his cell phone, trying hard as fuck not to look at his Boss' wife on my lap.

"He couldn't have reached out to my phone instead of yours?" I cock a smug grin.

"He knew you were… busy."

Of course, he did.

I discreetly scan the living room, trying to find the camera he must have hidden away somewhere. When I find the minuscule blinking red light just above the television set, I throw my dear old brother a wave, before planting my hand on Rosa's thigh and giving it a squeeze.

"Having fun?" Tiernan asks on the other end of the line, his voice as dry as the Sahara.

"Not as much fun as I could be having. If you call off your dogs and turn off all your little gadgets, then I'm sure I'll have plenty of fun. Oh. That's right, I forgot. You like to watch."

"Funny," he says, but no one is laughing. "Didn't I give you a job to do this morning?"

"You did." I grin.

"Then I suggest you do it."

"I'm in no rush," I taunt, running a finger up and down Rosa's thigh, while using my other arm to hold her still by the waist.

The line goes silent for a minute before my brother's cold hard voice returns.

"Remember when you were little, and I let you play with my toys?"

"I do."

"Those days are long gone."

I roll my eyes at his lackluster and uninspired remark.

"Be careful, *dheartháir*. You can look, but you can't touch. Not without my say so. If you do, then you force me to take something from you."

"I don't have anything worth having. You're the one who has it all, remember?" I shrug, unbothered.

"I can think of a few things you'd miss. It would be awfully hard to use those blades you love so much when you don't have hands. Touch my wife without my consent again, and I'll make sure you'll never touch anything ever again. *Tuig*?"

And with that threat dangling on the line, he hangs up.

Prick.

"Sorry, petal. Playtime is over," I mumble, shifting her lovely ass off my semi so it's firmly planted safely on the couch.

Rosa doesn't miss a beat and rushes to the kitchen, putting as much distance between us as she can. Since she was basically glued to my body, I'm sure she heard everything my killjoy of a brother had said on the phone.

"Here," I grumble, throwing the phone back to Darren.

He catches it in one go, throws me a disappointed glower, and leaves.

When the elevator doors ding shut, Rosa comes out of her spot, her gaze scouring the room.

"He can see us, can't he?" she asks sullenly.

"Yep." I point to the hidden camera right in front of me. "That's just one of them. I'm sure he has more eyes on you everywhere around the apartment."

"On me?" she questions, surprised.

I turn over on the couch to stare at her.

"Who do you think he has the cameras for?"

"I don't know. To see if anyone got into his place without him knowing. A burglar, perhaps."

I chuckle.

"Trust me, petal. Before you came along, Tiernan didn't have anything valuable enough to him in this whole damn place that anyone would even want to steal. Now he does. I bet he only got these little gadgets when he made up his mind to bring you here."

Her forehead wrinkles as if doubting my words.

"You don't believe me?"

She shakes her head.

"Why not?"

"Because that would imply that he cares. Tiernan doesn't."

"I wouldn't be too sure about that," I mumble, disheartened, taking all of her in. "It's hard not to care about you, petal. Trust me."

I'm trying really hard not to, and it's becoming fucking impossible.

"That's sweet of you to say, Shay. But I know my worth in my husband's eyes."

I don't know what troubles me more—the fact she thinks a killer like me is sweet or the way Tiernan is chipping away at her heart.

I can see it as clear as day in her big brown eyes.

She wants him to care.

Needs him to.

And why that is unsettles me more than I want it to.

"Enough of the downer talk about my brother," I say, hoping the smile on my face fools her. "We have a lot of shit to do today and we're burning daylight as it is. Have your breakfast, and then get dressed so we can leave this joint."

"Where are we going?" she asks, a tinge of excitement in her voice now that she knows she has the green light to leave the apartment.

Again, I'm reminded how my brother is a total dick and has not been treating his new bride right.

"You and I are going shopping."

"Shopping?" She laughs as if it's the most absurd thing she could be doing with her time.

"We have to find you a house for you and all your babies, remember? Chop, chop, petal. Let's go find you a real home to live in."

And just like that, her smile is a mile wide, making the organ in my chest flip of its own accord.

Shit.

I'm so far gone it's not even funny anymore.

♣

The real estate agent's eyes light up when Rosa and I get out of my Aston Martin and start walking up to the gate of the home she's going to show us this morning. I guess if I was in her shoes, I would be, too. I mean, just from the outside of the estate, I can tell this home has a large price tag on it. A cool thirty million at least. Which means her commission for the sale will make her year, if not her decade.

"Wow," Rosa mutters below her breath. "This place is… just… wow."

"Can I pick 'em, or can I pick 'em?" I tease with a wink.

"You found this house?" she asks with genuine surprise.

"Hey, just because I live with my parents doesn't mean I don't like to dream about other places to live."

"I didn't think *made men* dreamed about anything aside from slaughtering their enemies."

"What can I say? I'm an enigma."

"Yes, I'm starting to see that." She smiles at me, making my insides turn to goo.

Shit.

When did I get so pussy-whipped?

The next thing you know, I'll end up like one of those teenage girls who spend their days flipping through their diary, writing fanfiction about Shawn Mendes or some other teenage heartthrob.

I swear this woman's smiles are making me stupid.

"Too bad Colin couldn't come with us today. I think he would really enjoy this front garden."

I don't touch that remark with a ten-foot pole.

Colin is going to need some time to get his head on right.

If I thought fucking Rosa only once was doing my head in, then Colin was currently having an even harder time compartmentalizing the need he has to fulfill his duty to his Boss and the way he wants to steal this Spanish rose right out from under him.

I've never seen the big guy so out of it.

But then again, it must be overwhelming for the tinman to suddenly be burdened with a heart and feelings and shit.

I sure as hell am having a tough go of it.

"Mr. and Mrs. Kelly, I presume? My name is Morgan Tracy, and I'm about to show you your brand new home," the real estate agent beams self-assuredly.

I take her confusing me with my brother as a cue from God himself to play a little trick on her while also using it as an excuse to touch Rosa and not get slapped for it. I wrap my arms around Rosa's waist from behind, making her stiffen in my embrace while I shower the agent with my best cocky grin.

"Now, just hold up there, Morgan. My wife and I have many more houses to see today. You don't expect us to fall in love with the first one we go to, do you?"

Her head falls back in laughter.

"How about we take a tour, and then you can tell me if you don't love it? I will have to warn you, though. I have more clients lined up today to have the same tour. This home has only been on the market for less than a week and is in high demand. I wouldn't be surprised if I got a few offers before the day's end."

"I'm not worried. In fact, play your cards right, and you might just get an offer from us higher than the asking price. I'm sure that the number I'm thinking would blow the competition out of the water. If my wife says this is the home she wants, then this is the home she gets. Money is no object."

"A man who knows what he wants. Your wife is one lucky lady," Morgan coos, her hungry eyes scanning me from top to bottom with a newfound appreciation now that she knows how deep my pockets are.

"Yes, I am," Rosa chimes in, throwing daggers at the agent, not one bit impressed this woman is brazenly flirting with her fake husband.

I tilt Rosa's chin to the side and gently caress her face.

"As am I," I whisper, placing a small kiss to the tip of her nose.

Her gaze turns soft, and her body begins to melt into my embrace, almost as if she's forgotten that this is just a game and that I'm not really her husband.

If only I were.

I would treat her like the fucking queen she is.

Not a whore to be passed around between my men.

When the real estate agent clears her throat, it's enough to break the little spell Rosa and I were momentarily under.

"How about I show you around then?"

Rosa pulls away from my embrace and offers the woman a thin smile.

"Yes. Please."

"Very well, let's go in."

For the next half hour, Morgan shows us around the large estate, talking about original crown molding and marble kitchen counters that came all the way from Italy. I zone her out for most of her babble and focus on the siren that gracefully walks around each room, completely spellbound by the home. The way her body moves and glides around every room makes me feel like I'm watching a beautiful dance taking place right in front of my eyes. And when we go upstairs so Morgan can show us the nursery, that's when Rosa really swoons and shines.

"This home is perfect to raise a family. A large one at that," Tracy adds when she sees how in love with the room Rosa is. "Are you expecting?"

"I'm not sure yet. But hopefully I will be soon," Rosa explains, still eyeing the room like it's some fairytale wonderland she just stepped inside.

"How about I leave you and your husband for a few minutes so you can fully appreciate the room? Maybe even talk about making that offer we discussed earlier?" Morgan adds shamelessly.

After the infuriating woman leaves us alone, I stare at my brother's wife, wondering if my suspicions about her wanting a baby so bad are on the mark.

"Can I ask you a question?"

She hums absentmindedly, enthralled with her surroundings as if picturing in her mind where she would put the crib or bassinet. I bet she even has the color scheme down to a T.

"Why do you want a baby so bad? I mean, is this degradation Tiernan is putting you through really worth it?"

She chews on my question and then breathes out a yes.

"Why?"

"You want the truth?"

I nod.

"At first I thought a baby would be the ticket to my freedom. That maybe by having a child, I would gain Tiernan's respect. That he would allow me to live in a home like this one to raise his children and let me have a life of my own without too much of his interference or presence."

She sighs.

"But I was lying to myself, Shay. I now know the real reason why I want a baby so much. I need love in my life. Unconditional and pure," she explains, looking straight at me, ensuring she kills me with the sadness mixed with hope in her eyes.

"When I left my home to move here, I knew all that was waiting for me was a life full of hatred and resentment. I can't live like that, Shay. I need to love something, someone, and be loved in return. Having a baby from my body, from my blood, will ensure that at least I'll have one pure thing in my life. Someone I can be totally devoted to, and who, in turn, will love me back with all their heart. The closest I've ever come to that type of love was the affection I felt for my baby brother, Francesco."

"If you think a baby is the answer to your loneliness, you're wrong."

"Not to my loneliness. But to my aching heart. My baby will be a vessel to receive all the love I have to give. And I have so much of it inside me, Shay. So much. It's almost stifling how much of it I have dwelling inside my chest, begging to be set free."

"I can see that."

She lowers her gaze from mine, embarrassed by her confession. As if it's completely mortifying to admit she needs love in her marriage to a man who has spent most of his with blood pouring down his hands—if it was even possible a man like me could relate to or even fathom such a need.

But I understand perfectly.

Until her, I might not have known the first thing about love, but the more time I spend with her, the more I begin to have a sense of the feeling. And it's not just because I want to play with her body until she screams out my name. It's also because the small insights she's given me into her heart threaten the sanity of my own.

I eat up the small distance between us, pick up her chin with my knuckles, and stare into her eyes.

"You can love me, petal," I hear myself say, shocked that I mean every word.

Her eyelashes flutter a mile a minute, not knowing what to say. But before she has time to say anything, I press my lips against hers in the chastest kiss I can muster.

"You can love me. And if you want, I can love you right back."

Her gaze remains on me as her shallow breathing kisses my cheeks.

We just stand there, staring at one another, unsure of what to say next.

When the persistent agent returns, I almost let out an exhale of gratitude, thankful she wants this sale so badly. Bad enough that she would disturb what undoubtedly looked like a very intimate moment between man and wife.

"Shall I show you the back gardens now, or would you prefer to see the large entertaining area up on the roof?"

"The roof will be fine." Rosa doesn't say anything more than that and follows the agent out of the room, leaving me to stew in my own fucking torment.

Another hour passes before we are saying our goodbyes to Morgan, telling her to expect a phone call from us soon. I'm almost disappointed that Rosa loved the house so much. If she hadn't, then I would still have an excuse to see her every day. I doubt Tiernan will let me get close to her again alone. Not after the little stunt I pulled this morning.

Sometimes I'm my own worst enemy.

"Shay! Rosa!" I hear a familiar voice call out to us.

My smile is immediate when I see my Ma push a sullen Darren out of her way so she can walk over to us. I chuckle when I see he's still pissed that I ordered him to stay back in his SUV with his other goons while Rosa and I went inside.

"I was coming from the market when I saw your car parked out front. Had to see what my wicked lad was up to."

My mother laughs, wrapping her arms around me and pulling me by the hem of my t-shirt so I can bend down and let her kiss my cheek.

"And I see whatever mischief you got going on, you decided to recruit your brother's wife, too." She smiles, patting Rosa's cheeks lovingly.

While Tiernan has always been glued to *Athair's* hip since he was a toddler, I've always been more of a momma's boy myself. Sure, I can crack a joke at the spin of a hat like my Da and have everyone busting a gut, but it's when I flip the switch and leave them in stitches with my knife that people truly see the resemblance between us and say that I'm more like my father than most of his other sons. True as that may be, I've always had a softer spot for my *Máthair*.

Saoirse Kelly doesn't have one mean bone in her. She'd take in any stray, feed it and give it a home, even if everyone around her told her that the damn thing would end up using its sharp fangs to bite her for her troubles. I guess I've always been a sucker for women with soft hearts and kind eyes. It sure would explain my inconvenient feelings for my brother's wife.

"So? Are you going to tell me what you two are doing here, or do I have to guess?"

"Shay and I were just house hunting, Mrs. Kelly. Tiernan has offered to buy me a home as a wedding present," Rosa lies with a straight face.

But then again, I can't fault her for not wanting to tell my Ma the truth about how Tiernan negotiated the home to be included in their dysfunctional and fucked-up arrangement.

"Now, lass, what did I tell you about being so formal with me? Call me Saoirse. Or better yet, call me Ma or *Máthair* since you're my daughter now."

See?

Biggest heart this side of Boston you'll ever encounter.

My mother looks at the house behind us and gives Rosa a genuine smile.

"I think my Tiernan might be a little sweet on ye if he's gonna buy you that huge mansion of a house. Probably has some ideas on how to fill up all those empty rooms, too. You'll be walking around barefoot and pregnant in no time, by the looks of it. Can't say I'm too upset about being a *seanmháthair* soon, either. I sure do miss the smell of a baby's head and nibbling on their chubby legs. It's when they grow up that they become a real nuisance." Ma tilts her head over at me.

"Hardy har har." I laugh.

Rosa doesn't say a word, too tongue-tied to pull one out of her mouth with how my Ma is going on and on about babies.

"Are you going to see some more next, or do you have time for an early lunch? I'm making my famous Irish stew."

"I could eat. What about you, petal? In the mood for some home cooking?"

Rosa doesn't even have enough time to nod her consent before my Ma laces her arms through hers and pulls her in the direction of our house just two blocks away.

An hour later, Ma has Rosa crouched over the sink, peeling potatoes, while she goes on and on about how much of a hassle her children were growing up. Rosa laughs at all of Ma's witty anecdotes while I lean back in my chair, hands behind my head, watching the two women bond in utter awe.

It's only when I laugh a little too loudly at a certain memory my Ma is reminiscing about, how Tiernan used to let Iris piggyback ride him, while she yelled for him to go faster and make horse noises just because *Athair* refused to buy her a pony for her fourth birthday, that both women stop what they're doing and look over their shoulder at me.

"Aye, ye think that's funny, do ye? How about you get off that *arse* of yours and start working for your supper? Set the table at least, lad. Don't you know that idle hands are the devil's workshop? Get moving, Shay, before I get my wooden spoon and show Rosa here how I got you to do your chores."

I jump out of my seat and wrap my arms around my Ma's waist, kissing the side of her cheek repeatedly until she is puffing for air with how much she's giggling.

"Joke's on you, Ma. I always wore more than one set of boxers just in case that wooden spoon ever got out of its drawer."

"Get off me, lad." Ma continues to giggle, slapping my hands away.

"Aye. I was going to run upstairs and get a quick shower before lunch anyway. You know what they say, cleanliness is next to godliness." I wink, walking backwards to the door to make my great escape.

"You see that, lass? That's the face of the cheeky devil I was telling ye about. Only knows scriptures when it suits him. He would sweet-talk Saint Brigid herself if he thought he could get away with it."

"I can see that," Rosa mumbles, her brown eyes turning the same molten hue they did yesterday when her pussy was strangling my cock.

Great.

Not only do I need a shower, now I'll have to beat my cock into submission, too.

Who am I kidding?

My excuse for taking a shower before lunch was so I could jerk one off anyway. Just knowing she's so close that I can almost taste her is doing a number on my restraint.

I make a mad dash upstairs, lock myself in my room, and sure enough, five minutes later I'm cumming in my hand with the fantasy of Rosa's soft lips around my dick. After that, my shower loses all its appeal, and I hurry just to wash the evidence of my weak will off my body, dress up, and hurry downstairs.

I'm just about to close the door to my bedroom when I feel Rosa's presence in the hallway.

"Hey, petal. What are you doing up here?"

"Your mother told me to fetch you. She wants you to get some red wine from the cellar. Is that your room?" she asks, pointing to where I just left.

"It is. Want me to give you a tour?" I wiggle my eyebrows suggestively.

"I thought it was that one," she dismisses my poor attempt at getting her alone and points to the bedroom door everyone in this family avoids even looking at.

"That's Patrick's," I mumble, shoving my hands in my jean's pockets.

"Patrick," she repeats the name, rolling it on her tongue like it's some secret she should avoid saying out loud.

She's not that far off.

"Your mom was just talking about him after you left."

Of course, she was.

Leave it to Ma to only talk about her dead son when neither of her children or *Athair* can hear her do it.

Rosa takes a step closer to his bedroom door but doesn't make any move to open it. It's almost as if she knows that inside all that exists is pain and misery. I bridge the gap between us until I'm standing at her side.

"And what exactly did my mother tell you about him?"

"For one, she said he wasn't nearly as adventurous as the rest of you. She said he preferred books to climbing trees and riding bikes."

I let out a sullen sigh.

"Aye, that he did. You would have liked him. He had a kind heart like Ma, too—like you do."

She turns her head my way, sadness coloring those gorgeous eyes that have seen their own share of suffering.

"But Patrick was too sensitive to survive the kind of life we lead. Too frail. He felt other people's pain like he was the one who had been wounded."

"An empath," she whispers the word like it's a curse, and in our world, it is. "He's dead, isn't he?"

I nod, my shoulders instantly slumping.

"Did I... I mean, did we... I mean," she struggles to say. "Did my family have anything to do with his death?"

"Oh, petal," I whisper lovingly, cradling her cheek with my palm. "Best leave ghosts where they belong and can't do you any harm, aye? Life is for the living. It shouldn't be wasted on the dead. They are at peace now. Can we say the same?"

Her eyes lower from mine, suddenly unable to look me in the eye.

"Shay... about what you said earlier... back in the nursery..."

I shake my head to silence her protest.

"I meant every word, petal. You don't need a baby to love. I can love you." *Because as unexpected as it is, I think I already do.* "You just have to let me. It's your choice."

"Tiernan could kill you if he knew you were talking to me like this," she warns, and I hear the flicker of fear in her voice.

"Let him try."

Just let the fucker try.

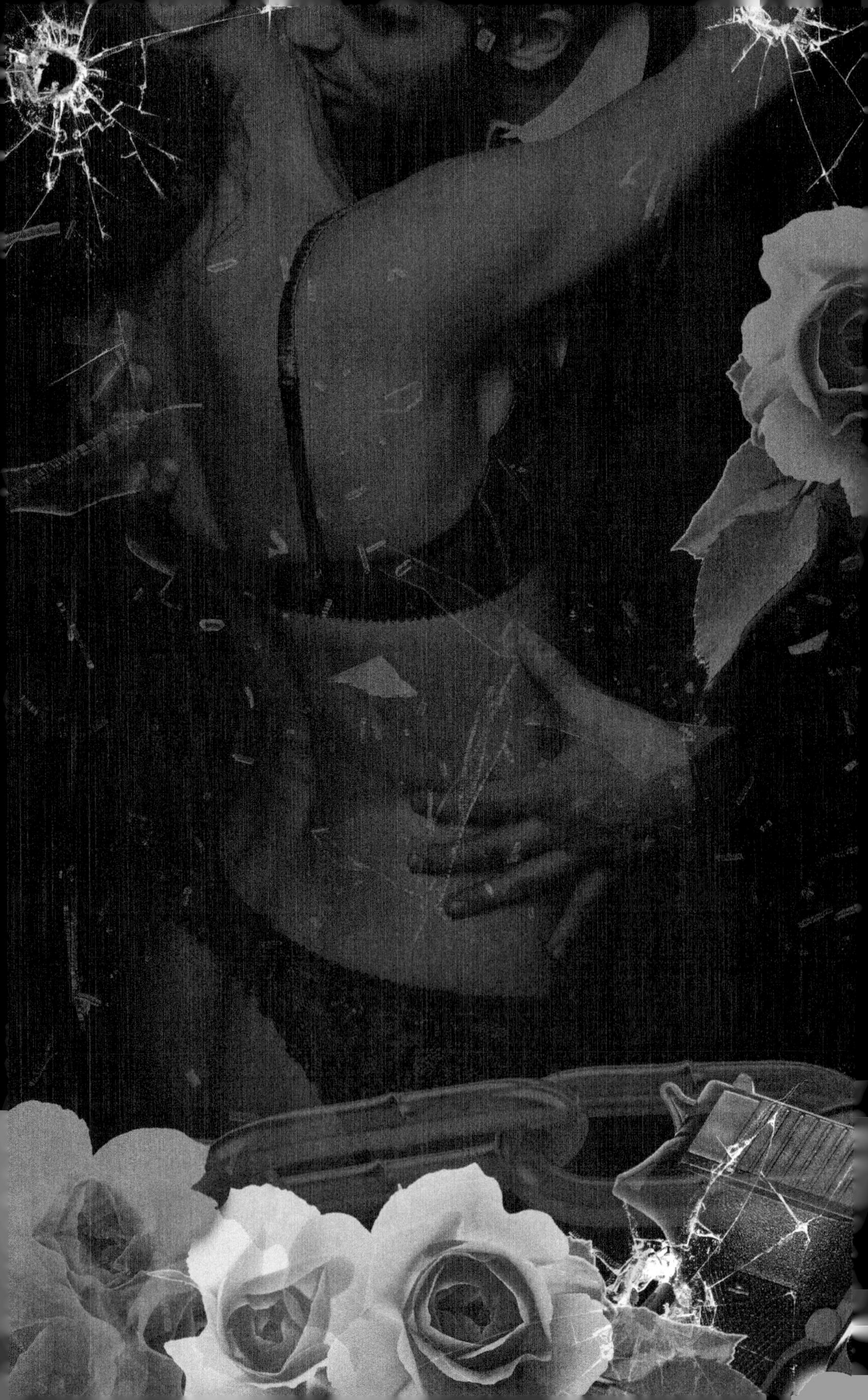

CHAPTER 17
Colin

"I WAS STARTING to think I scared you away," Rosa muses, trying to garner a reaction from me as we walk through the Isabella Stewart Gardner Museum.

I've had it on my list of places I wanted to take her to, but after our obligatory conjugal visits these last few weeks, I haven't been in the right frame of mind to take her anywhere. Thankfully, our noon encounters in apartment 9B back at The Avalon also ensure that most of Rosa's energy is fully depleted, forcing her to stay indoors for the rest of the day, leaving Darren and his crew to watch over her.

"Well, Colin? Did I scare you off?" she asks again just as we stop in front of one particular painting depicting a full moon on a snowy winter's day.

"Nothing scares me," I lie, pretending to be focused on the

artist's handiwork instead of looking at the woman standing by my side.

"Is that true?" she questions curiously, craning her head back to stare at the scar marks on my face. "You're not afraid of anything?"

"Aye," I lie again, shrugging her attention off me and walking to another painting further down the corridor.

Rosa quickens her steps to keep up with my wide strides, her high heels click-clacking loudly on the floor.

"You're lying to me. If we're going to be friends, we shouldn't lie to each other, Col."

Damnú.

How can I tell this woman that the only thing that puts fear into my heart is her and how she makes me feel? That since she let me in, both into her heart and into her body, I've been consumed with thoughts of only her? That there isn't a minute in my day where her sweet face doesn't cross my mind, and that the ache of not being by her side at all times physically pains me?

"Colin?" she insists, carefully placing her hand on my forearm, scorching me with her innocent touch.

"What are *you* scared of?" I ask, flipping the script on her.

She pulls her hand away and lowers her eyes from me to stare at the painting in front of us. This one is of an old windmill up on a hill, red poppies all around it.

"Everything. Everything scares me here," she explains, followed by a desolate sigh.

"Only here? Not back home in Mexico?"

She nods.

"How come?"

"I knew my place back home. My father made sure of that. Here I feel like I'm floating adrift in a vast unknown ocean, never knowing where to swim to for safety. Or even to whom."

Swim to me, sweet rose, swim to me.

The words burn on the tip of my tongue, but instead of confessing such forbidden and foolish thoughts, I find myself answering her previous question instead.

"The only thing that scares me is not being a good, loyal soldier to my boss. That somehow I might break his trust in me."

Like I have been doing since Rosa came into our lives.

"I didn't know you cared for Tiernan's opinion so much," she replies, disillusioned.

"Why wouldn't I? I'm a soldier. Soldiers should strive to gain their general's good opinion of them."

"You talk as if we're at war. The Mafia Wars are over, Colin. Didn't you get the memo? If they weren't, I wouldn't be here to begin with."

"The Mafia Wars might be over, but there are always battles to be fought."

"That's disheartening." She frowns. "If that's true, then when can we stop and just live our lives without the fear that death is just around the corner?"

"We can't. Death is a certainty. Either by the blade or from old age, it will come for us."

"Then I prefer the latter." She smiles sweetly, a twinkle in her eyes that pierces me right in the gut, deeper than any knife could.

"As do I." I can't help but give her a small smile of my own, making her grin stretch as far as the eye can see.

When Rosa stares into my eyes, only to drift back to the marks on my face, my miniscule smile falls dead onto the floor. It's the second time she's done that today, making my skin itch and my throat clog. I turn my back to her and walk further down the hall until I reach a dead end.

Fuck.

"I'm sorry," she says behind me, placing her hand on my shoulder blade. "I didn't mean to make you uncomfortable."

"You didn't."

Another lie.

But the truth would only make *her* feel uncomfortable, and I quite enjoy Rosa being at ease with me. Not many people are.

"Can I ask you a question?"

My shoulders tense up and my back straightens, already mentally preparing myself for what I know she will ask next.

I can't fault her inquisitiveness.

Most people have a morbid curiosity to know every detail of how I got so disfigured on the left side of my face and neck. But not many know the truth. All they know is that I got caught in a fire back when I was still living in Ireland. The specifics of said fire, however, I leave out. I'm not sure I can be so withholding with Rosa's intense gaze on me, though.

"Just ask," I grunt.

"Did we…" she begins to stammer. "I mean… did my family do that to you?"

I'm suddenly taken aback by the guilty sorrow in her voice.

"Is that really what you want to know?"

"Yes. I want to know how deep your hatred of me is."

I turn to her and snake my hand behind the nape of her neck, bringing her face closer to mine.

"I could never hate you, Rosa. Don't ever say or even think such things."

Again, her gaze softens, and this time when she glances up at my scars, I don't shy away from her. This gives her the courage to press her hand on my cheek, gently caressing the hideous part of my face.

"Does it hurt?"

I shake my head.

"The skin feels rough, ragged even."

"Aye. Scars tend to harden over time."

"Even the ones people can't see?"

"Especially those, sweet rose."

Her gaze begins to water in sadness, provoked both by the endearment and by the harsh truth of my words.

"Don't shed tears for me, lass. These scars no longer hurt me as much as they used to. They only serve as a reminder."

"A reminder of what?"

"That monsters exist."

And that all you can do is hope you become an even bigger monster to scare the others away.

She pulls away by taking a step back, a stern expression overtaking her delicate facial features.

"Just tell me. Was it my family? My father? My brother? Did one of them do this to you?"

I shake my head, to which she immediately lets out a sigh of relief, her stiff stance instantly relaxing with the knowledge her family had no part in hurting me. I don't have the heart to tell her that even though her family wasn't responsible for my scars, they had a hand in creating Tiernan's.

I pick up her hand and place a tender kiss to her open palm before letting it drop again to her side. I then turn to the painting, this one, oddly enough, of a forest deprived of sunlight. Its darkness calls out to me and pulls me back to a night where the sky was pitch black, and only my childhood home burning up in flames illuminated it.

"I was sixteen when it happened," I begin to explain, my gaze fixed on the painting, almost as if I'm being transported to that fateful night. "It started off as just another ordinary summer night in Ireland. Nothing gave me the inkling that after that night, I would never sleep in my bed again. I had spent most of my day with my Da and Patrick in town running some errands for my Ma. It was blissfully normal. Maybe if it wasn't, I would have been able to predict what was about to happen."

"Patrick was with you? As in Tiernan and Shay's brother, Patrick?"

"Aye. My uncle Niall had been worried about Patrick's mental wellbeing and constant melancholy. He thought sending him to spend the summer with us would improve his sullen disposition. Boston was in a full-fledged war at the time, with too many deaths to count. My cousin had always been softer compared to his brothers and sister. His bleeding heart just couldn't withstand attending another funeral, so my *uncail* thought sending him off to stay with us for a few months would lift his spirits. Maybe all my cousin needed was a change of scenery to get him out of the depressive state he had been in."

I frown, thinking how wrong that assumption was. Maybe if Patrick had stayed back in Boston, he'd still be alive somehow. I know for a fact that if he had, my family would be.

"Anyway, I was just happy to have someone my own age around. Most boys our age were already sworn into the war, fighting the good fight, but both Da and my Uncle Niall were reluctant to have us play a role in it. *Uncail* had his obvious reasons for keeping Patrick out of the war, and as for my Da... well... he had plenty of his own, too." I shrug despondently. "I was his only son, you see? Aside from me, my parents only had daughters. Three of them, to be precise. Aoife, Riona, and my baby sister of just eight months, Ciara. They were little rugrats, the lot of them, and though I loved them dearly, a part of me also resented them for not being boys. If they were, then maybe my father wouldn't have kept me from fighting in fear of losing his only heir."

I kick the air at my feet, hating how bloody ignorant and headstrong I had been that summer—always giving my Da a hard time for not letting me fight and complaining about it twenty-four-seven. My resentment had grown worse over the past couple of years after news broke out that Tiernan joined in the war. Since my *uncail* had three sons, he had no reservation in having Tiernan pick up a gun and fight for his family. There was no need for him to be cautious with his eldest when there were two more sons in line to take his throne if the worst was to happen. But if my uncle ever had an ounce of fear that he'd made a mistake, then Tiernan exceeding all expectations only solidified that he had made the right decision. Everywhere I went, people talked about how my cousin was making the Kelly name proud. Even from across the pond, news of my cousin's exploits in the war sounded more like tales of legends. You couldn't go into a pub and not hear Tiernan's name. All of Ireland was in utter awe of his bravery and calculating mind, and I desperately wanted to be at his side and have people sing my praises, too.

How fucking vain I was then.

I don't even recognize that boy anymore.

Not that it's surprising.

That Colin Kelly died that night, too.

"Anyway," I continue on with my shameful rant. "Safe to say that at the time, I didn't know any better and resented my father for restricting me and ordering me to stay put with my sisters. Now I realize he just wanted to protect me. Keep me safe as long as he could. Give me a childhood when most boys my age had been deprived of one."

"Sounds to me like your father loved you very much."

"Aye, that he did. I just wish I had told him how much I loved him while I had the chance instead of acting like a brat."

"I would have never used that word to describe you," she says, a trace of a smile playing on her lips.

"Aye, but that's what I was back then. Blame it on the Kelly gene. We're all cocky assholes when we're young. Some of us never outgrow it."

"Are you saying that you were like Shay?" She laughs.

"Ah, lass, I wasn't that bad. Just headstrong, that's all. At sixteen, I thought I was a man. It took that night happening for me to figure out I wasn't," I chastise myself.

"You don't have to tell me more if you don't want to, Colin. It's okay if you don't."

I shake my head.

"I want you to know," I tell her, entwining my fingers with hers.

It dawns on me how true those words are. I want Rosa to know everything about me, just as much as I want to know everything about her. It should trouble me how much I need to tell her every little secret I have. And it should trouble me even more that I want to share such intimate information with a woman who doesn't belong to me. With a woman who is married to a man I vowed to follow and obey until the end of my days. The word betrayal flashes in my mind, making the acrid taste of my treacherous feelings tough to swallow down.

"Okay," she replies, giving my hand a comforting squeeze, bringing me back to the conversation at hand and away from my duplicitous thoughts. "Tell me. I want to know."

"Aye." I take a deep inhale before continuing on. "That night, I had another row with my Da. It got so bad that he kicked me out of dinner and sent me to my room like I was a five-year-old in need of discipline. And like the unruly *shite* I'd become, I locked myself in my bedroom, cursing him and everyone else around me that had a hand at keeping me from the war. Little did I know that the war was going to come to me."

I clear my throat as if I can still smell the smoke all around me.

I close my eyes, comforted only by Rosa's tender hand in mine, silently urging that I continue.

"Sometime during the night, I must have dozed off in my tantrum, only to wake up startled by the heat in my room. When I opened my eyes and saw my room up in flames, I panicked. I forgot all the lessons my father taught me about dropping to the floor and crawling my way out to safety. Instead, I ran towards the flames, screaming my parents' and my sisters' names as loud as I could while trying to make my way up the stairs towards their bedrooms. It was only when a burning joist fell on top of me, pinning me to the floor, that I honestly believed we were all going to die that night. The fire on the wooden beam kissed my skin, and blistering heat began to claw its way through all my facial bones, muscles, and tendons, leaving its permanent mark and damaging every nerve ending. Whether it was the smoke inhalation or the pain of my third-degree burn, I must have passed out. It was only when I felt someone covering my face with a wet blanket and pushing the beam away from my chest that I came to." I swallow dryly.

I got you, Col.

I got you.

"It was Patrick who pulled me out of the fire that night. And once he made sure I was safely outside, he willingly went back into that hell. I just sat there on the lawn watching my home burn down as my cousin ran back into the burning inferno, in the hopes he could save someone else. I was so petrified with fear and pain that I couldn't move. I tried to tell my legs to get up, to save my family, but they wouldn't budge. It must have been only a few minutes until Patrick made it out of the house again, but to me it felt like hours. As he drew in closer to me, I could see he had my baby sister cradled in his arms, wrapped in a blanket."

My body trembles so hard at the memory, Rosa has to wrap her arms around me just to keep me steady.

"She didn't make it, did she?"

The sob that escapes me is all the answer she needs.

"Patrick, is that Ciara? Where is Da and Ma? Where is Aoife and Riona?!" I cry out, my tears stinging my raw flesh.

The smell of burnt skin churns my stomach, but as I try to move closer to my cousin the awful stench heightens. Patrick shakes his head, pain and misery coating his light blue eyes as he steps away from me.

"Give her to me! Give Ciara to me!"

"I'm sorry, Col. I'm so sorry," he cries, hugging my sister's small body to his chest.

"I said give her here," I yell. "Ciara!"

"I tried. I tried," he repeats, gripping the blanket.

"Give her to me, Pat. Please. Give me Ciara."

My arms shake as I stretch my arms out to him so that he can hand over my baby sister. Reluctantly, he places her in my arms as delicately as one would a sleeping newborn. He does it with such tenderness that my heart flicks with a speck of hope that she's alright. It's only when I lift the blanket off Ciara's sweet face that I have confirmation that she's not sleeping at all. All that's left of her is a mangled burnt corpse.

The scream that ripped through me afterwards must have been heard all throughout Ireland, coast to coast, and still it didn't reflect the pain I was experiencing. Nothing could.

"I lost my whole world that night. These scars can't even begin to truly depict the horror of watching everyone I ever loved go up in flames and turn to ash right in front of my eyes. I'd suffer a million scars like these ones if it meant that they wouldn't have had to."

"Who? Who did it?" Rosa asks between sobs.

"Who knows." I shrug defeatedly. "After *uncail* brought Patrick and me stateside, he put out feelers to find out who could have sent the order to kill his brother and his family. Soon word came back that both the Bratva and The Firm learned of a rumor that Uncle Niall's son was spending his summer in Ireland. It seems they were under the impression it had been Tiernan with us instead of Patrick. Killing the heir apparent to the Kelly dynasty would have been a great achievement for any of our enemies. We never really knew for sure if it had been Vadim Volkov or Trevor Butcher who gave the green light on the attack. Not that it ever mattered. By then, we Kellys had as much blood of the innocent on our hands as any of our enemies did. The names of my parents and sisters were just added to the long list of casualties of a war I had been thirsting to be a part of. Safe to say my first taste of it was less than bittersweet."

I wipe Rosa's tears away with my thumbs as I watch her heart break for me.

"It's all in the past, sweet rose. Your tears cannot bring back what I lost any more than mine can."

"Our world is so ugly, Colin. So ugly. How can we even look at ourselves in the mirror after all the depravities and monstrosities our families have committed in the name of preserving our way of life?"

"Aye. It's not an easy thing to do, but as you reminded me not a few minutes ago, those days are long over. Thanks to you, and women like you, there won't be another child or innocent soul taken before their time. And as the decades pass, and peace reigns, any recollection of the years we suffered during the Mafia Wars will be forgotten. As will the names of my parents and sisters. As will ours, sweet rose." Another stray tear falls down her cheek, and this time I kiss it away. "Best spend our time appreciating the beauty this world still holds, then waste it reminiscing on sad events we can't change."

"Is there still beauty in such a world?"

"Aye. I'm looking right at it."

She raises her head, her eyes colliding with mine.

"You're beautiful, too. I see you, Colin. And you're just as beautiful as any painting hanging on these walls. Both inside and out."

My heart squeezes in my chest at her words.

"No one has ever called me that," I croak out, emotion taking its toll on me.

"Then everyone is a fool. I see you. The real you. And you are beautiful."

Damnú.

I push her against the wall and grip her chin, turning her my way.

"You have to stop saying things like that to me, sweet rose.

You don't know how starved I am to hear them come out of your mouth."

"Then I'll keep saying them. I'll keep saying them until you believe me."

I scan her beautiful face in search of the lie I expect to see and find none. All that exists is sweet adoration, and fuck me, if it doesn't look a lot like love, too.

I spin her around, gaining a small shriek from her when I raise her skirt up to her waist and press her face against the wall.

"Colin, what are you doing?"

"Putting a fucking baby in you, that's what I'm doing," I growl, pushing her panties to the side.

"Someone might catch us," she says, her voice already thick with lust.

"Let them."

I couldn't give two fucks right now. As long as my cock is deep inside her pussy, stretching it out until she cums around it, I couldn't care less who sees.

Tiernan included.

"No. Wait, wait," she insists, earning a low grunt of disapproval from me.

"Why? Isn't this what you want?"

She shakes her head and slowly pulls herself off the wall, until we are yet again facing each other.

"I want to see you make love to me more. I want to see your face, Colin. Please."

My brows pinch together as she runs the pad of her finger over my scars.

"Every time we're together, you always take me from behind. I want to see you, Colin. Memorize your face as you cum inside me. Can you give me that?"

Can I give her that?

I don't think there is anything I wouldn't give this woman if she asked.

And that's the problem.

I stand still, my whole body quivering with need yet waiting for her instructions.

"Kiss me," she commands on bated breath.

I bend down and offer her my kiss, which she takes with greedy abandon. She tastes like the sweetest wine that ever touched my lips, and all too soon I am submitting to her tongue's every command. My fingers go to her core, her wet slit proof of her desire for me. Her body has always been welcoming, but a part of me was convinced that her invitation had only been extended to me because Shay had coaxed it out of her. Or worse, because her husband demanded so. It's only at this very moment that I realize my feelings aren't unrequited. My hold on her is just as strong as the one Rosa has on me.

"I need you, Colin. Please," she moans out in between kisses.

Not one for delaying gratification, I pull her legs up to cradle around my waist, unleashing my cock from my jeans and then thrusting it deep inside her in one brutal push.

"ARGH!" she shouts, making me clasp my hand over her mouth.

My eyes are on hers as I pound into her pussy like a man gone mad.

And God help me, I think I might have.

"This. I can never have enough of this. You've ruined me, sweet rose. All I dream about now is having this pussy clench around my cock," I groan in her ear, her muffled moans getting louder. "And then you go and tell a fucking monster like me how beautiful I am? Don't you know what you do to me? Can't you see how much you're under my skin?"

Her hooded gaze grows wild with heat as she claws at my shoulders, needing me to pound my love inside her until she can't walk without feeling me in between her thighs. I capture her lips in mine again as my hand travels in between us to play with her clit. I know Rosa well enough that a few well-placed strokes to it, as my cock impales her pussy, is enough to push her over the edge. It only takes a few moments after that for her to cry her release, making me cum right after her. My heart is still jackhammering in my ribcage when Rosa starts blinking fresh new tears from her eyes.

"What have we done?" she mumbles to herself more than to me, as I place her feet back on solid ground.

With those bleak words hanging in the air between us, I realize the repercussions my actions might have if Tiernan ever finds out.

My boss might take offense to me fucking Rosa raw without his say so.

In fact, I know he will.

Because if the roles were reversed, I'd kill him for it.

And that is a whole problem all on its own.

CHAPTER 18
Tiernan

MY NIGHTS HAVE BECOME ALMOST as unbearable as my days.

As inconceivable as it may seem, I used to be like those fortunate people who, no matter how many sins I had committed during the day, the minute my head hit the pillow, sleep would take me under, and the sweet darkness of slumber would welcome me with open arms.

That doesn't happen anymore.

If I sleep a full two hours straight, it's a miracle.

Most of my nights consist of me twisting and turning in bed, or staring at the ceiling above me, until daylight shines through my window curtains, its glowing rays taunting me that my torment is only going to get worse as the day unfolds.

For the past month, every day has been the same.

I get up and take a shower, always going to great pains not to look at my reflection in the mirror. I don't need the visual aid to know there are dark circles under my eyes and that those same eyes hold little life to them anymore.

I then rush towards Donavan's gym to get a workout in, praying that some cocky soldier of mine has mustered the nerve to bait me into a fight and is brave enough to face me in the ring. I relish in the pain of every jab and punch they punish my body with, needing the physical agony to overshadow the blistering ache living and breathing inside my tormented soul. A silent war is taking place in the confinements of my black heart, and every wound I suffer screams to be acknowledged. It demands that something or someone pull the misery out into existence and let the outside world bear witness to how mangled and bruised I truly am on the inside.

So, I stand in the center of the ring and let my men do their worst. If they've done a proper job of it, I even let them win the fight.

For them, it's a morale boost.

For me, it's a show of my gratitude.

Because it's in this small window of my day that I'm no longer a lie.

My broken, abused body is now a perfect reflection of my blackened marred soul.

Unfortunately for me, that's the highlight of my day.

After that moment of truth, everything goes to shit.

I go into the office, take my second shower of the day, and put on a suit that I despise. Once I'm wearing the lie the world expects of me, my autopilot kicks in, and I waste the morning growing the empire my father left me. But even as I'm on the phone with the Deputy Commissioner requesting a little extra every month so his boys in blue can turn a blind eye to my other business ventures, I zone him out. All because I can physically feel the seconds pass by through every limb, the infernal ring of a ticking clock in my ear telling me that soon it will be noon.

And once the clock strikes twelve, my hell begins.

My town car waits to take me back to The Avalon, only instead of going home when I arrive, I get out on the ninth floor and walk the small distance to the empty apartment where my brother, cousin, and wife are waiting for me.

What happens next is pure torture.

It always starts the same.

After I've taken off my suit jacket, I sit on my throne and order Rosa to come out of her hiding spot. Without delay, she emerges from the bathroom, always looking like a goddess, ready to seduce the soul of any mortal who dares even look at her.

Long dark hair that almost comes down to an ass that begs to be fucked.

Legs that stretch out for days on end and know how to trap a man in between them.

Small waist and wide hips perfect for grabbing and leaving fingermarks on.

And two natural fucking breasts that would put most porn stars' bought ones to shame.

The woman is a vision.

Yet, for all her flawless glory, she's always hesitant at first, walking into the room on featherlight feet as if she's afraid something will pop out of the corner of the room and eat her alive. But despite her nerves, my fierce wife always makes sure to look me dead in the eye before she walks over to her two lovers.

It's almost as if her gaze is telling me that I hold the power to stop what's about to go down.

All I have to do is open my mouth and say no.

But I don't.

I never do.

And since I don't utter a word, she walks over to Shay first, offering him a smile that she's never once gifted me with. I fist my hand every time I see her do it. Hating that my brother gets this sweet side of her when all I get is her animosity. But what's even more troubling is how Shay's eyes soften at the mere sight of her. Like she's the most precious thing there is.

I hate him for it.

I hate her even more.

Once Shay lifts her arms to cradle over his shoulders, Colin springs into action. He stands behind her, gripping her waist and grinding her ass against his already hard cock. Like clockwork, Rosa always looks over her shoulder and bats her long eyelashes at him.

"Hi," she says sweetly, her sultry voice better than any blue pill on the market to get a man hard.

Colin growls in response and kisses her like her mouth is his to own and conquer. After he's made sure she's left breathless from just one kiss, he turns her head to face Shay, who in turn, kisses my wife like she's a fragile flower.

After that, the rest of the hour spent in the room becomes my own personal purgatory.

Colin fucks my wife with brutish force, while Shay makes love to her.

Rosa screams incoherently, both in English and in her native tongue, as they coax out of her body orgasm after orgasm. Shay whispers sweet little praises in her ear, telling her how beautiful she is, how good she feels around his cock. Colin grunts and brands her body with his hands, his nonverbal way of mimicking Shay's words in the only way he knows how. Her body glistens with sweat, her lips part open to let out her sighs and moans of desire, all of which only serve to have me squirming in my seat.

Because it's in this moment I witness my wife come alive in between them.

Her whole being bursts into a bright light, ensuring she blinds me completely when she cums.

And once Shay and Colin are done, they kiss her temple and lips, honored for the privilege of having her.

And they do have her.

Heart, body, and soul.

I see it in her eyes every time they walk out of the room and leave.

Her gaze filled with sadness that she can't walk out the door with them.

That she has to stay in this room with me.

If I blinked, I probably would have missed it.

But I don't blink.

Not once do I take my eyes off her.

My heart only restarts with the sound of the door closing.

And that's when I take vengeance on what she's done to me.

I make her crawl on hands and knees, naked and still smelling of them, over to me. I pull her to my lap and remind her that her fate is in my hands, and that if I so wished, I could crush it into a pulp with my fists, just as she has obliterated my very sanity. I pull an orgasm out of her body that was always mine from the start, punishing her for thinking otherwise. I then push her brutishly to her knees, making her work for her second climax as she milks my cock dry of all the cum she wished she could fill her womb with.

After I've made sure to leave her a wanton mess, cursing to herself how she can loathe me and still want me, I get up and walk away as if nothing even transpired between us. It's a performance worthy of an Oscar, but I play my part to perfection.

It's only when I leave the apartment and am safely tucked in the backseat of my town car that I shatter. I punch the leather seat with all my might, cursing the fates for ever bringing Rosa into my life.

The woman has ruined me.

And to my bitter resentment, I gave her all the tools to do me in.

I underestimated her right from the start.

She called my bluff and raised me one. I thought I held all the cards in the deck, shuffled them in a way she could never win, and yet she beat me at my own game. She beat my full house with a four-of-a-kind of her own and fucking smiled at her victory over me.

When all of this started, I was sure that once I had her all alone in a room with my brother and cousin she would backpedal and wave the white flag of defeat. But I miscalculated her stubbornness as well as her deep wish to become a mother.

Fuck.

A baby.

She had to ask me for a damn child.

I could have given her the world, but she asked for the one thing I couldn't give her.

All the saints must have laughed at my pain when she demanded the treaty be fulfilled to the letter. I never once considered she wanted anything from me except space. And I gave that to her in spades. Apparently, it wasn't enough, and now I'm left to play this game of chicken with her, wondering who will cave first.

Not me.

And it's becoming evident, it won't be her either.

For the next hour or two I tell my driver to drive through my city's streets, for I have no desire to lock myself in my tower and pretend my world is as intact as it was before she came into my life. It's only when we get to Beacon Hill that I tell him to stop.

I bought her a house.

Nix that.

I bought her a fucking mansion.

Eight bedrooms.

Two living rooms.

Library.

Office.

And more bathrooms than she will ever know what to do with.

But even though I was the one to foot the bill, I'll never set one foot inside.

Why would I?

Why would she even want me to?

After all is said and done, I'm positive Shay and Colin will have an open invitation into her home, but never me. Once the deed is done, she'll ice me out, turning me persona non grata. Forcing me to wonder what kind of life she is living without me every time I drive down her street to visit my parents.

Why do I care, though?

Why does the thought of her living her life, pursuing her happiness without me, make me feel like I'm slowly losing my mind? As if she owes me for every ounce of joy she's about to have without me, and I want to punish her for not paying her dues to me.

It's irrational.

Nonsensical.

And yet I want her to pay me every last cent with her body and soul until I'm fully satisfied the debt has been paid in full.

Once I can't bear the sight of the home she will make without me, I order my driver to take me as far away as he can from this horrid place. But today, due to some work being done on the street ahead, he's forced to take a new route, ironically enough passing by the church that bound me to Rosa forever.

"Stop," I command, getting out of the car before I make sense of my actions.

I walk up the long flight of stairs, thankful that there are only a handful of parishioners praying to a God that is too busy causing natural disasters to pay them any mind.

"It comforts me," she told me once when I asked her why she wanted to go to church.

A part of me was skeptical in taking Rosa at her word, but now that I've become familiar with the kind of woman I'm married to, I know she was telling me the truth. I haven't gone to mass since that first time I took her, but every Sunday morning, I feel her absence in my apartment, knowing that's where she is.

And the fact that I'm jealous of the time she devotes to her faith instead of me only shows how much she's ruined me.

It comforts me.

Fuck.

Right now, comfort of any kind would be a blessing.

I walk through the large oak doors and pass the holy water, knowing that even if I bathed in it, it would never cleanse or absolve me of my sins. Two parishioners balk at the very sight of me, grabbing their crucifixes as if some beads could protect them from the devil walking in their midst. I pay them no heed and take a seat in a back pew, wondering if I have in fact lost my mind for being so desperate that I've decided to turn to God for aid. I stare at the figure hanging from the cross in front of me and wonder, if given the choice, would I willingly replace the shine of my gold crown for his thorned one?

It takes me a minute for me to realize that I already have.

I gave my life for the salvation of others by ending the Mafia Wars when I married Rosa.

And with that sacrifice, I'm now left to suffer a different kind of hell.

"Tiernan Kelly," I hear someone call out my name. "The Lord

must have heard my prayers to have you coming to church twice in as many months."

"Do you make it a habit of praying for murderers, Father?" I ask, not sparing Father Doyle a glance, keeping my gaze fixed on the cross on the altar.

"I make it a point to pray for all lost souls, my son."

"Hmm."

"But I won't pretend I'm not surprised to see you come into the house of God to worship of your own free will."

"Who says I'm here to worship him? Maybe I'm just here to ask him to explain himself."

"God can give you many things, justifications for his actions aren't among them, though. Those should remain a mystery."

"Why?" I snap my head his way. "Why should he hide behind his actions and not offer an explanation for them? Other men worth their salt do."

"God's decisions in our lives should never be questioned. He has a plan for all of us, Tiernan. Even for you."

I scoff at that.

"You don't believe me?"

"I believe only in what I can see and touch."

"Ah, I see. But it doesn't matter. He believes in you, even if you doubt him." Father Doyle then goes silent and follows my gaze to the front of the altar.

"You're conflicted. Burdened by the tribulations forced upon you. That's why you came here today. To look for answers to questions you do not have the insight yet to ask."

"I have all the answers I need."

"Do you?" He arches a skeptical brow. "Remember that God gives no burden he thinks we cannot handle. Take comfort in that. Soon light will shine down the path that has been laid in front of you. Then it won't seem so arduous as it does now."

I get up from my seat and look down at the priest.

"You speak as if God gives a damn about me. Your God has forsaken me and my family long before today. Only fools look to an imaginary entity for help. And I'm sorry to disappoint you, but I've never been a fool."

"Women make fools of even the strongest level-headed men."

I grind my teeth and offer him a sinister grin.

"If that's true, then your God really can't help me. Only the devil can."

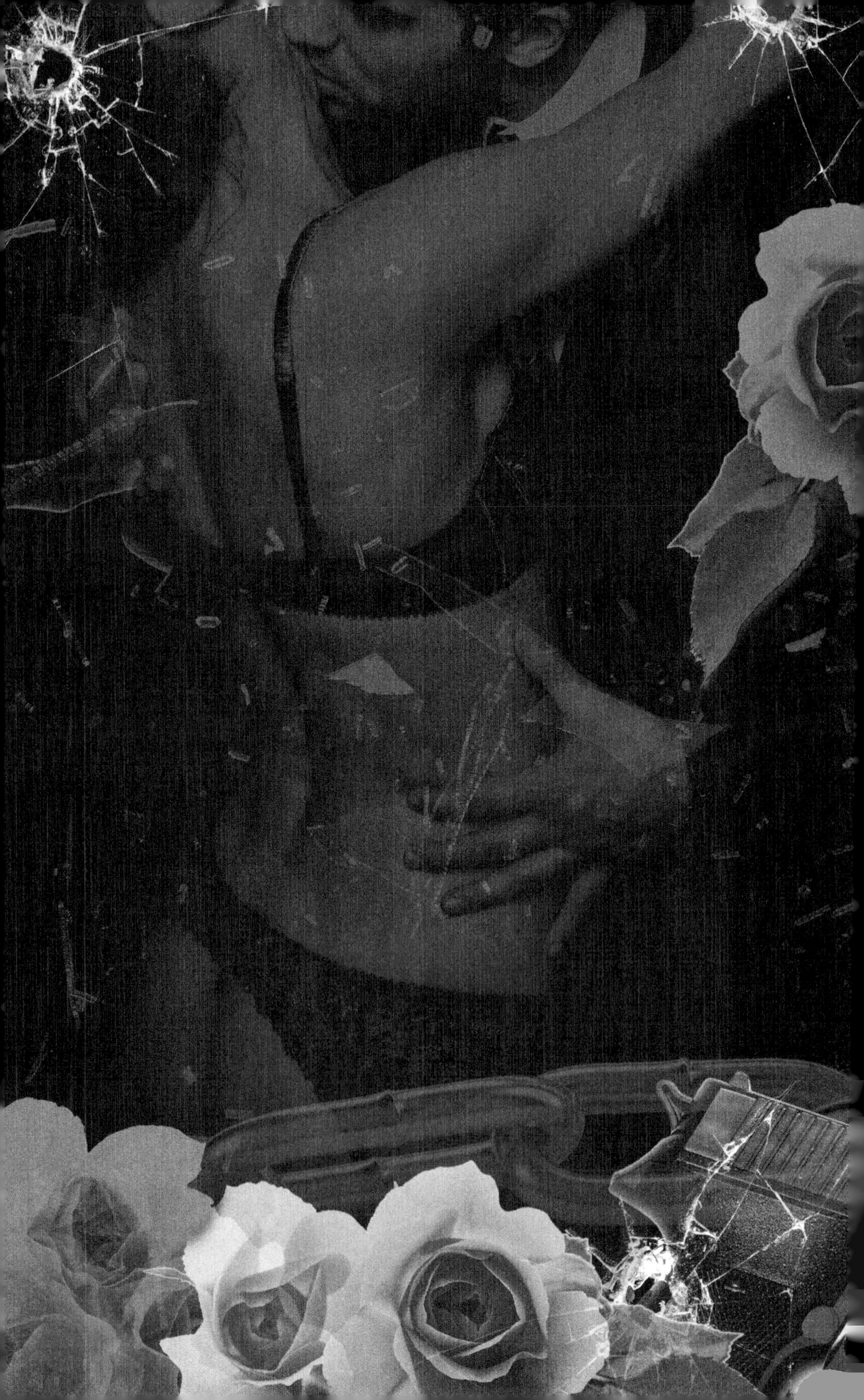

CHAPTER 19
Rosa

SOMETHING IS WRONG.

Tiernan isn't his usual eat-up-the-air-in-the-whole-room self. I felt it the moment he walked through the door.

No.

That's a lie.

I've been feeling his sullen and pensive mood get worse with each passing day. If we had a normal husband and wife relationship, I would have badgered him until he told me what ails him so. But since we made sure to create a division between us, using bricks of resentment and hate to stack up our invisible wall, I don't say a word and pretend I don't see his misery.

He picks at his dinner in silence as if his thoughts will swallow him whole. I usually take advantage of our dinner dates to pull him into conversation, so I can learn more about the man I'm married to, but tonight I'm hesitant to do that. I fear if I do, he might say something that will hurt me, and Tiernan does enough of that without my help.

Unfortunately, my concern only multiplies when he pushes his barely touched plate to the side, preferring to open another bottle of red wine so he can drown his sorrows. Against my better judgment to let this night end without uttering one word to each other, I'm the one who ends up breaking the heavy silence.

"You always wear black," I announce evenly, running a finger over the rim of my wine glass. "It's been two months since we got married, and I have yet to see you wear another color."

"If there is a question in there somewhere, I don't hear it," he replies dryly.

I brush his coldness away and continue on with my rhetoric.

"I'm just curious. Is there any other color in your closet, or are you committed to just the one?"

"Black suits me just fine. Unlike you, I could never pull off virgin white."

My cheeks flame crimson.

"Are you insinuating that I only wear white? I can guarantee you that I don't."

"No. You like to mix it up with eggshell, ivory, and sometimes a light cream. Still looks pretty damn white to me."

I can't help the laugh that tumbles out of me.

"What's so funny?" He cocks a brow.

"Sorry. It just seems out of this world hearing you, of all people, say words like eggshell. I would have never guessed you had such vast knowledge of color palettes."

When there is the smallest of tugs to his upper lip, my chest warms. I almost got him to smile. Needing to see just how far I can push him, I place my elbows on the edge of the table and lock my hands under my chin, purposely batting my eyelashes at him.

"How about I make you a deal? Wear some other color that isn't black just once, and I'll wear any color you'd like."

"Any color?" he asks, amused, actually considering my proposal.

"Any color. The sky's the limit."

"Very well. I'll indulge you in this little game of yours. What color does my wife want to see me in?"

I don't even hesitate.

"Midnight blue. Like the color your eyes darken to sometimes. Or at least like one of them does."

"Hmm. I'm surprised you even noticed such things about me."

I notice everything about you, husband.

I just wish I didn't.

"How could I not? It's not every day you meet someone with a non-matching set."

"But you prefer my blue to my green, otherwise you would have asked me to wear that color."

"Your Irish blood is green enough for me. It's the indigo blue that intrigues me."

"So, I intrigue you?" he muses, catching my slip of the tongue.

"Yes. Very much so," I confess, unsure if I should be this candid with him.

His blue eye goes pitch black as it always does when an unnamed emotion hits him.

"You intrigue me too, *acushla*. More than you know."

I bite my lower lip and bow my head, unable to keep eye contact when he's looking at me like that. Like I would be a better meal than anything I could have prepared for him tonight.

"You really can't help it, can you?" he announces, gaining my attention back on him.

"Can't help what?"

"Fucking with my head."

My forehead wrinkles at that statement, but I don't dare touch it with a stick.

"Red," he finally says after a long pregnant pause. "I want to see you in red. Do you think you can accommodate your husband's request on this?"

"Yes," I breathe out.

We both stare into each other's eyes, and for a split second the world disappears, and all there is is him and me. But just as I'm starting to enjoy this unexpected moment of truce, I feel something isn't right.

"No… No. No!" I shout, pushing my chair back and running to the ensuite in my bedroom.

I slip off my pants and sit on the toilet, grabbing toilet paper to wipe myself with. When I bring it back up and see droplets of blood on it, hot tears begin to blur my vision. It's only when I catch movement in my peripheral, that I see Tiernan is standing at my bathroom's door, watching me.

"You got your red, husband. Happy?"

He frowns.

I let my tears fall as I slump onto the bathroom tile floor, uncaring that I'm letting him see me like this.

Logical thought tells me that not getting pregnant the first month that I'm actively trying to is to be expected. That sometimes it can even take years for a woman to conceive and that I should just brush this off and not take it as my own personal failure. But even as I try to gain some perspective that this is normal, and that I should expect such disappointment in the future, my heart still weeps for the love that is just outside my grasp.

I'm so consumed with my suffering that I don't even pay attention to Tiernan's actions until he's kneeled down right beside me, brushing away the strands of my hair that are glued to my cheeks from my tears.

"Shh, *acushla*. Shh," he whispers, placing gentle kisses to my wet cheeks and eyelids.

My shoulders tremble with each sob that comes out, unable to control the wave of sadness gutting me. I don't even complain when Tiernan begins to undress me, peeling off my shirt, pants, and the stained panties that mock me for my failings. He then picks me off the floor and walks me over to the bathtub. Sometime during my grief, he must have managed to fill the tub with warm water. He gently lays me in it, and once I'm fully submerged, he kneels down beside me, folding his sleeves just above his elbow. He then picks up a bottle of liquid soap, fills his palms with it, and begins to wash my trembling form.

Misery has made me too exhausted to fight him off, and a part of me actually yearns for his soft caress, as if it could solve all my problems. I blink my tears away, biting my bottom lip to control the sobs that refuse to stop, as he ever so gently lavishes my every limb and soft curve with the floral-smelling soap.

We don't say anything as Tiernan thoroughly lavishes my body with white suds and then rinses me off. With the same care and attention, he washes my breasts and in between my legs without uttering a salacious or mean word. None of this is sexual, which not only surprises me, but also has my heart shattering that my husband is even capable of such selfless care. Once he's satisfied that my body is clean, he then begins to wash my hair with the same devoted attention.

My tears subside with the feel of his strong fingers washing each strand. He then rinses the shampoo out of my hair, shielding my eyes with his hand as he goes about it. Every action has my heart beating a song I never thought it could. A song that only Tiernan could ever coax from me. I let him pull me out of the water and wrap me in a towel to dry me off. He then picks me up and sits me on the sink, making my throat dry in anticipation of what he'll do or say next. I'm afraid to utter a word, thinking that my voice will somehow break this spell he's under.

As unlikely as it seems for a man like him, Tiernan is being kind.

More than that.

He's taking care of me. Loving me—in his own way.

And after all the bruises and cuts that he's inflicted on my heart, I soak in his kindness like a flower soaks up the sun to prevent it from withering away in the shadows.

Tiernan then picks up my hairbrush and begins to disentangle my wet hair. I can't remember a time anyone has ever done this for me, or even anyone who made such an effort to ensure I'm well taken care of. Once my hair is properly brushed to his standards, he goes back into my room and brings in my pajamas. When I understand that his intention is to dress me in them, I gently grab his wrist and shake my head.

"I can take it from here," I whisper.

His disappointed frown is immediate, but he relents and walks out of the bathroom to give me some privacy. I can't help my own displeasure resurfacing when he leaves the room, ending the rare moment of tenderness, but it had to be done. The next thing I'll have to do, I'd rather do in private without his intense eyes on me. Once he's closed the door behind him, I carefully jump off the sink's counter and put in a tampon before I get dressed. I blow dry my hair just enough for it not to be wet when I go to bed. I'm too exhausted for anything other than sleeping my grief away.

It's only when I open the door to my bedroom and see Tiernan sitting at the edge of the bed that I realize he never strayed far, even when I told him to go.

"You stayed."

"Aye."

"Why?"

"Does it matter?"

I shake my head and walk towards the bed. I slide under its covers, watching my husband slowly take off his clothes until he's left only in boxers. My gaze never trails down his beautiful body, no matter how much it craves to see him in all his glory. I keep my eyes on his face at all times and don't move an inch when he climbs in next to me. It's only when he wraps his arm around me so I can lie cradled against his warmth that I let out a sob at how perfect he's being.

"Sleep, *acushla*. Sleep."

I nestle my head on his chest and close my eyes, loving the feel of his hand stroking my back ever so lightly. And it's with the sound of Tiernan's heartbeat that I'm lullabied to sleep, to dream of a world where the only version that existed of my husband was this one.

The next morning when I wake up, I immediately feel his absence in my bed.

Tiernan must have left early in the morning to go to work or wherever else he goes when he's not home during the day. But even though the left side of my bed is cold without him, the memories of waking up throughout the night and him being right at my side, hugging me to him and whispering sweet nothings in my ear in Gaelic, remain. He didn't leave my side once, for which I'm grateful.

I turn to the clock on my nightstand and see that it is well past ten in the morning. I must have overslept. Not that there's anything for me to do today. With me being on my period, there is no reason to meet up with Colin and Shay today. And they were the only two reasons I would ever set foot out of this house anyway.

I get out of bed, my cramps already killing me, to use the bathroom and brush my teeth. Once that's done, I make my way into the kitchen, hoping a hot cup of coffee will warm my cold bones. I stop halfway when I see Tiernan sitting on the couch in the living room with his laptop open on the coffee table.

"You're here," I blurt out.

"That's the second time you seem surprised to see me in my

own home, *acushla*." He hides a small smile, looking straight at his computer screen.

"I just assumed you would have left for work already."

"I decided to work from home today. Unless you prefer that I leave, that is?" he replies automatically, still focused on whatever he's reading instead of making eye contact.

I shake my head, even though he can't see me, and walk into the kitchen to grab my morning coffee. When I see that the dishes from our dinner last night have been washed and put away, I crinkle my nose in confusion.

"Was Elsa here this morning? I thought she was only going to come in tomorrow."

"She is. Why?" Tiernan retorts, still engrossed in his work.

"I just assumed she came in today since the kitchen is spotless."

"I can put dishes into the dishwasher, *acushla*. It doesn't make me any less of a man to tidy up after myself and my wife."

"No. I guess not."

I bite the corner of my lip, filling my coffee mug, when a small white bag on the kitchen counter grabs my attention.

"What's this?" I ask, taking a peek inside.

"I asked Darren to go to the pharmacy and pick you up some things. I wasn't sure what you needed, so I told him to buy you some candy and chocolate, those artsy magazines you leave lying around the house, and some other things Iris used to bug me to get when she was on her period. I'm not sure any of it will help, but hopefully the meds will ease up some of the pain."

Who are you, and what have you done with my husband?

The words are right at the tip of my tongue, but I don't dare speak them out loud.

I walk over to the couch and take a seat, wrapping myself under a blanket, with my coffee mug in one hand and a magazine in the other. After I've drank my fill and read all the articles that interest me most, I'm a little unsure of what to do next. It's not like Tiernan and I have ever lived together. I mean, we have lived in the same apartment for the past two months, but that's still a far stretch from living as man and wife. Aside from me blackmailing him into having dinner with me every night, our interaction under this roof has been scarce and far between.

"You can turn the T.V. on if you want," he says as if reading my thoughts.

"Are you sure?" I ask, eyeing his laptop.

"A little noise won't disturb me from doing my job." He chuckles under his breath.

"Okay."

I turn on the T.V. and scour it for something to watch. Since I'm not in the best of moods, I pick a stand-up comedy, hoping some light humor will shift my disposition. As it goes on, Tiernan begins to laugh at a certain joke, closing his laptop and settling into the couch. I place my now empty mug on the coffee table and lean back into the cushion. I stay like that for a minute or so, before Tiernan's arm reaches over my shoulders and tugs me into his side.

He's still laughing away at the jokes being told, but his grip on me only tightens until I'm fully relaxed at his side. I take advantage, looking at him when his attention is diverted to the T.V. screen.

"You wore blue," I state, staring at his jeans and navy long sleeve.

"Aye. It's not the midnight blue you wanted, but it's all I could have come up with on such short notice."

I'm not sure why Tiernan indulging me by wearing a different color than his usual black has my heart pitter-pattering in my chest, but it does. I snuggle in closer to him, nestling my head on his shoulder, praying to *Virgen de Guadalupe* that this isn't some mean trick he's pulling on me. That this man who is being so thoughtful and kind lingers on, and that the man who only takes pleasure in seeing me crawl on my knees for him disappears once and for all.

And as if she heard my prayers, for the rest of the week, Tiernan works from home, taking long intervals just to be with me. It's as close to happiness as I've ever been with him since he put a ring on my finger. The only thing that dims its shine is the realization that I might be falling in love with him.

Or worse.

That I already have.

"Pizza's here," Tiernan shouts from the elevator, carrying a large box of sizzling pepperoni goodness in his hands.

"Oh, good. I'm starving." I jump off of the couch to help him bring our dinner in.

"It's hot, *acushla*," he warns when I try to take the box out of his hands. "Go and grab us some napkins and a couple of beers, and I'll set this up in the living room," he says before placing a chaste kiss to my cheek.

I don't even find it odd anymore that Tiernan has been so affectionate with me lately. For the past week or so, we've spent most of our time together. He's even slept in my room, holding me in his arms throughout the night. He hasn't tried to seduce me in any way, for which I was grateful in the beginning. Now I'm just frustrated.

I want him to kiss me.

Say all those naughty words that set my skin on fire.

To take me like a man who needs to own every part of his wife would.

I just need him.

And that need both irritates me and consumes me.

I take two bottles of Guinness out of the fridge, grab two plates and napkins, and walk over to the living room, taking my seat at his side.

"Have you picked something for us to watch tonight?"

"I have," I smile wickedly.

"Should I be concerned?" He laughs when he sees the mischief in my grin, placing a slice on a plate and handing it over to me.

"No. I don't think so. I think you'll actually enjoy this movie."

"Is that so?" He continues to chuckle.

"Aye," I retort, using his preferred dialect to drive the point home.

"Hmm. I'm intrigued. What's it about?"

"Mobsters."

He lets his head fall back and laughs a good-natured laugh, one that I seldomly hear from him and lap up like it's pure sunshine.

"If it's Goodfellas, The Untouchables, or The Godfather, I've already seen it. Besides those movies are more centered on La Cosa Nostra and The Outfit. Not really my cup of tea. I'm more of a Boondock Saints man myself."

"Of course, you are." I giggle. "And my baby brother Francesco prefers to binge Narcos."

"Have you talked to him recently?" he questions absentmindedly, taking a big bite out of his pizza while I pick out the movie on Netflix that I want him to watch.

"I have. I called him this morning. Thank you again for giving me a phone. Talking to him makes me feel less homesick."

"It was long overdue. I was just being a prick not giving you one sooner."

"Wow. Honesty," I tease.

"I've always been honest with you. You just never liked hearing my truth."

"I like hearing it now."

He snaps his head my way, his gaze falling to my lips for the smallest of moments and then back to my eyes.

"Put the fucking movie on, *acushla*," he mumbles, ripping another bite out of his pizza before he decides to take a bite out of me.

"Okay. You asked for it," I taunt, pressing play on the movie.

We both eat our dinner in silence as the story about a mafioso kidnapping a woman in the hopes she will eventually fall in love with him unfolds on the screen. Tiernan huffs and mumbles at the incredibility of a few scenes that depict our world, but for the most part, he's attentive. Interested in the outcome even. It's only when the sex scenes start that he goes rigidly quiet.

I, on the other hand, am very aware of every shift and move he makes, the moans on the screen only heating my already feverish skin. Every time the anti-hero grabs his love by the neck and kisses her, I swallow dryly, remembering the feel of Tiernan's fingers wrapped around my throat.

When my thighs push together to ease the ache in between them, I feel Tiernan's gaze fall to my lap.

"I forgot," he mumbles, running his thumb over his lower lip.

"Forgot what?" I breathe out, my traitorous voice hinting at the pain I'm currently in.

"I forgot that you know how to play dirty when it suits you."

"How am I playing dirty, husband? It's only a movie."

"Is it? Or is this your not-so-subtle way to tell me you want to get fucked?" he arches a brow, his tongue licking his lips.

"I have no idea what you're going on about." I feign ignorance.

"Right. Because you're *that* innocent."

"Neither one of us is innocent, husband. You most of all should know that."

"You're right. I do. There are a lot of things that I know. Like how your pussy is drenched right now, aching for me to make my move and fill it up with my cock."

I don't even try to hide my blush away and instead just stare him dead in the eye.

"You don't know everything, husband."

"That's true, too. I don't know everything," he whispers, tugging at the end of a strand of my hair. "But I know you."

The scoff that comes out of me is just as unconvincing as the woman's moans on the screen.

"Are you saying that if I put my hands on you right now, I wouldn't find you wet and wanting?"

"I'm saying that you have a bigger ego than you have sense." I smile sweetly at him.

"That's not the only thing that's big right now. Should I show you what I mean, *acushla*? All you have to do is ask."

My heart beats in my throat as I watch him stroke the large bulge in his pants.

"Show me," I whisper, my gaze glued to his large hand adding pressure to his sheathed cock.

"I thought you'd never ask," he grunts. "But I'll do you one better."

Before I realize his intentions, his hands are on my waist, pulling me up from my seat and straddling me on his lap. I moan when his hard cock rubs against my sensitive clit.

"Now, isn't this better?" He cocks a smile, his hands on my hips forcing me to rub up against him.

"Better for you, maybe. I'm not so easily impressed."

"You always did like to make me work for it." He chuckles, amused.

"Your memory is faulty, too. As I recall, I always did most of the work."

"Then why break from tradition?" he coos, his rich ale breath tickling my neck as he leans into my ear. "If you want to get fucked, then I suggest you work for it."

His words should embarrass me, but they don't. In fact, they spur me on, making me rub myself against him without his added persuasion. I ride his cock, our clothes starting to bother me, wanting him inside me already. But if I'm to be left hurting, then by God, so will he. It doesn't take long for both of us to be panting, my nipples hard as jewels each time they chafe against my shirt, while his hands cup my ass cheeks to keep our rhythm going. When I feel he's starting to lose all decorum, I lean in and bite his scruffy jaw, using my tongue to lick up his cheek.

"Fuck," he murmurs, dry humping me to the edge of oblivion. "Stop playing games, *acushla*."

"Who says I'm playing anything?" I taunt, my teeth sinking into his earlobe.

"Goddamn it," he growls, hurriedly pulling the hem of my t-shirt over my head.

Inwardly I stand on the podium to receive my award for making him break first, but the image soon vanishes away when his mouth begins to suck at my tender breasts.

"Argh!" I arch my back, seeking out his forbidden kiss.

"Hold still, wife. Fuck," he growls, pulling his mouth from one nipple to go to the next.

"Tiernan," I sigh in utter desperation, tugging at his hair.

"Just say it. Tell me what you want."

"Please," I beg.

My nipple pops out of his mouth as his fingers wrap themselves around my neck. I almost cum from just this.

"Tell me," he orders, his haughty gaze pouring gasoline on a large open flame burning inside me.

"I need you," I relent, hoping my confession is enough for him to show me some mercy.

"No. You don't. Tell me what you really need, and it's yours. Say it."

Virgen.

I swallow my pride and utter the words he yearns to hear.

"I need you to fuck me, husband. Please."

The words have barely touched the air between us, but it's all Tiernan needs to tip him over. His hands work double time to pull his cock out from his jeans and boxers, while I simultaneously pull down my pajamas and panties. It's messy and hectic and deranged, but it's only when I slide down his cock that true bliss occurs.

"Fuck. I missed this," he groans, his eyes snapping closed for a moment as if it's all too much for him.

"Tiernan," I plead, so desperate for him to move that I'm sure I'll lose my mind if he doesn't.

"Ride me, wife. Ride my cock like it's yours. Because it is, my sweet *acushla*. It is," he mumbles incoherently, his hands back on my hips ready to guide me home.

Our gazes lock on where we are joined as I pull myself up and sink back to the base of his cock. Bringing air into my lungs becomes a useless necessity compared to this. This is all I need to keep breathing. To feel alive. Just this. Tiernan owning every part of me, claiming me body and soul, is all I need in this precise moment to feel free.

"Tiernan," I whisper between gasps of pleasure, my hands holding on to his shoulders for balance.

I push myself up and down his shaft, my legs trembling with each ruthless thrust he impales me with.

"Look at me. Look at me," he commands on a strained breath.

I do as he says, still overwhelmed with all the sensations traveling through my body. His hooded gaze pierces mine, and even though I didn't ask him to, he leans in and kisses me. Tears start to sting my eyes at the knowledge of how much I missed his lips on mine. It's like he's breathing life into my broken, bruised heart and mending all its shattered pieces with his love.

But for that to be possible, Tiernan would have to love me.

And he doesn't.

I'm just his plaything.

Something he can entertain himself with and then push away once he's grown bored of it.

So why does this kiss feel like that's a lie?

Why does it make me believe in the impossible? That deep inside my cold-hearted husband lies a heart that beats to the tune of my name?

"Be here with me, *acushla*. Be here with me," he whispers in between breaths, kissing me like his lips are the window to his soul's desire.

I push all deprecating thoughts away and do as he commands. I commit myself to this one moment and let myself believe the beautiful lie his lips imprint on mine. I feel my core clench around him, needing to trap him inside so that he can fill all the hollow places that dwell in my soul from the lack of his love.

"Tiernan," I whisper again, only this time it feels like an admission of my love for him.

He looks into my eyes, his green one softening so much I almost believe that this is real. And as I lap that lie up and nurture it in my heart, hoping one day it will blossom into the truth, I cum hard on his impaling cock, shuddering profusely as the orgasm wrecks my body.

"FUCK!" Tiernan shouts, pushing me inches away from his lap so that he can cum on my stomach.

Sadness, more than bitter disappointment, cuts through the moment of bliss I just experienced, tearing it up into tiny pieces of confetti. I pull off his lap and cover myself with the sofa's blanket, trying everything in my power not to come undone and cry in front of him. His forehead wrinkles in confusion as he stares at me while tucking himself back into his jeans.

"Why?" I utter, my voice thick with despair.

"Why what?" he counters, reaching his arm to pull me closer, but I just inch further away from him.

"Why is the idea of having a baby with me so repulsive to you?"

His features instantly harden to stone, his demeanor closing off to me.

"This is what you want to talk about? Now?"

"Why not? You never gave me a reason."

"That's because I don't need to."

I shake my head.

"No. I will not let you bully me into submission. I've earned the right to know. Tell me."

"You've earned nothing," he growls, getting up from his seat to walk away.

"Don't you dare walk out on me, Tiernan Kelly!" I shout, getting up to my feet, the blanket pooling on the ground.

His gaze scans my naked body, focusing on the cum on my belly and the bruises his digits left on my hips.

"I don't want to talk about this now."

"You don't want to talk about this ever!" I yell in outrage. "But I deserve to know. I deserve to know why you would rather have me bear another man's child than your own. Tell me."

His lips curl into a snarl that sends a cold chill down my spine, making me very aware of how vulnerable I am in front of him.

"I could never father a child I knew from the start I would hate. Does that satisfy your curiosity? The mere idea of you pregnant with my child in your belly disgusts me. I would rather have my cock torn right off than ever let that happen."

His callous, cruel words take the air out of my sails, making my legs crumble from underneath me and having me fall to the floor.

"You can't mean that." I shake my head, trying to push his words out by force.

"I mean every word. I'll indulge you in this fantasy of being the mother to the next Kelly line, but that is as far as my participation in it goes. Your tears will never change my mind or how I feel. I'm sorry if I ever gave you any inclination you could change my mind on that front. It wasn't purposely meant."

"You're sorry? You're sorry?!"

"Believe me that apologizing for anything, especially something I feel so strongly against, isn't done lightly. If ever. Take that as your win, wife, and be content in the small victory."

"Only you would see this as a victory," I seethe as hot tears run down my cheeks.

"It's the only one I can give you." He frowns, his hands fisting and releasing at his sides. "I'll call Shay and Colin in the morning. You'll have the life you want. I just won't be a part of it."

And with those words carving my chest and making me bleed onto his Persian rug, he turns his back on me and walks away.

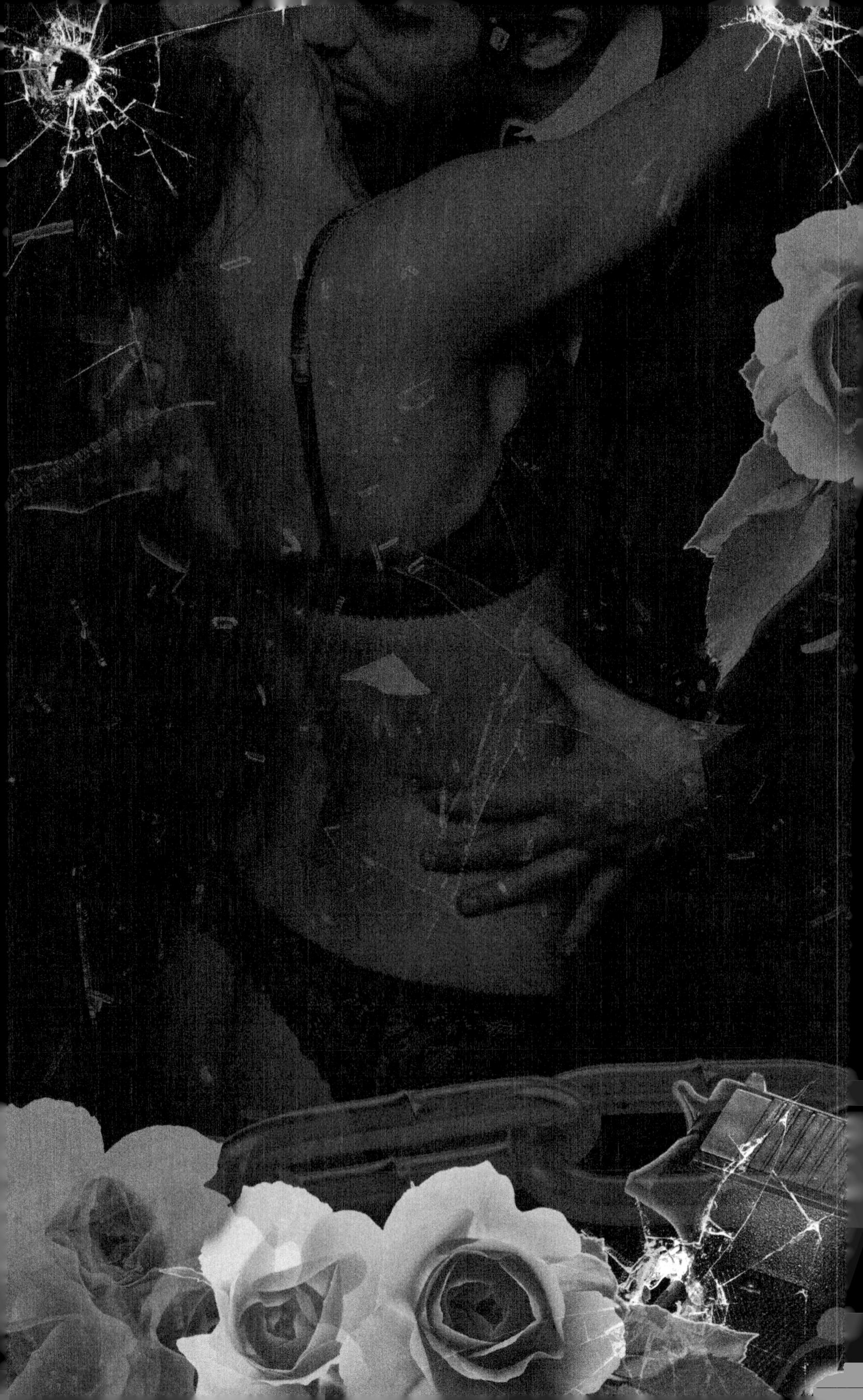

CHAPTER 20
Shay

WHEN COLIN and I arrive at The Avalon, it's hard to keep our feelings in check. My brother has kept Rosa from us going on a fortnight now, and time spent without her gracing my days has been utter torture. The way Colin is standing stiff beside me, staring daggers at each elevator button lighting up that isn't our floor, tells me he's just as antsy as I am.

"Best take that scowl off your face, or you'll scare our girl away."

"Rosa isn't scared of me," he retorts, cracking his neck to the side to relieve the tension built up there.

"Aye. She isn't, is she? How she can love that ugly mug of yours is anyone's guess," I tease him, hoping it will ease his anxiety somewhat. "But I'll tell you one thing. If you keep that deep-rooted scowl on any longer it's going to be permanently tattooed to your face. It doesn't make you look any prettier if that's what you're going for."

Instead of him shrugging off my taunt, I watch my cousin's brows pull together while he just stares at his feet.

"I don't know how she feels about me," he mumbles despondently, to which I pull 'a Colin' and slap him across the head.

Before he has time to growl at me, I slap him again for good measure.

"Don't be a daft fool, Col. You fucking well know how she feels about you. About us. Even if she hasn't said it yet."

"Stop saying *shite* like that, Shay. Don't go giving a desperate man room to hope when there isn't any to have. She's Tiernan's. Not ours."

"Fuck Tiernan," I rebuke, eliciting the growl I expected to hear from my cousin. "And fuck you if you think being loyal to him will make a difference when he finds out you fell in love with his wife."

"He already knows."

"Nah. You think he does. If he knew for sure, I doubt he would have called us in today."

"Now who's acting like a daft fool?" Colin scoffs. "What's a greater test of loyalty than to taunt us with the one thing that we want and can never have while requiring us to do as he commands?"

When the elevator doors swing open, I step out and turn to my cousin.

"I don't want to talk to you anymore. Not when you're talking sense. I like living in my delusional bubble, thank you very much. You should try it sometime. It hurts less."

I flip him the bird and walk in the direction of where the woman who has captured my heart and soul is currently confined. Colin takes my words to heart and shuts his trap as he follows me into the apartment and down the hall to the bedroom. When we reach inside, I know things are about to go to shit.

"Off work already?" I ask my brother, who is currently sitting in his chair, whiskey in hand. "You don't usually show up this early."

"I didn't know my punctuality would be so inconvenient for you."

"Not inconvenient. Just surprising."

"Hmm."

"Where's petal?"

"If by petal you mean my wife, she'll be with us shortly. Just getting ready." He tilts his chin to the locked bathroom door.

I sit on the bed in front of him, while Colin prefers to give us a wide berth, standing by the door.

"It's been so long since you called us, I was starting to think you were going to put an end to our little clandestine meetings. Haven't heard a peep out of you in weeks. No one has seen you around, either. You haven't even come to Sunday lunches up at Ma and Da's place."

"Are you upset that you didn't see me for so long or that I kept *her* from you?" he says, going to the root cause of my frustration.

"What do you think?" I throw him my toothy grin.

"I think not fucking my wife has made you irritable. And frankly, I don't care for it."

"Like I give a shit."

"Careful there, Shay. Remember who you're talking to. I have no qualms in cutting you down a peg if you need a reminder of who holds your strings."

"I'm no man's puppet," I seethe.

"Maybe just a woman's then."

I get up to my feet, ready to punch his smug grin off his face, when Rosa opens the door to the bathroom and steps into the room. Usually, Tiernan is the one to give her the green light to come out, but today she's taken matters into her own hands. My hackles rise further when instead of her making an appearance in her preferred discreet white teddy, she comes out in a hot little number that leaves very little to the imagination.

"You wore red," Tiernan gasps, slinking further down into his seat, white-knuckling his tumbler.

"I promised I would," she replies, her cold voice pinching a nerve inside me.

What the fuck is going on?

From Tiernan being here early, drinking before noon no less, to Rosa making her presence known in fuck-me red lingerie, something is definitely not right here.

"What's going on?" I ask outright.

"I have no idea what you mean," Tiernan retorts, drinking his whiskey in one pull, only to refill his glass for seconds. He slams the half-drunk bottle back to the side table and then proceeds to blankly stare at his wife.

"It's your show, *acushla*. Have at it."

I watch her hide the flinch his insensitive words provoke and begin to walk over to us. Like me, Colin must sense that something is amiss, because he's right at my side, taking inventory of our woman.

"Petal?" I whisper, running my hand through her hair to caress her cheek. Her eyes are bloodshot, proof that she must have spent her night crying. But it's the dull emptiness in her gaze that really sets my teeth on edge. "The fuck did you do to her?!"

"Nothing," Tiernan grumbles under his breath, taking another shot of whiskey.

"The fuck do you mean nothing? You broke her!"

"I didn't break anything. Stop being overdramatic," he slurs, his half-drunken voice taking me aback.

I've never once heard Tiernan slur a day in his life. Even before he was crowned king, he always kept his wits about him. I've seen him pour bottles and bottles of alcohol down his throat, and not once did he even look like he was intoxicated.

But that's not the case today.

The fucker is two sheets to the wind.

It seems while Rosa cried herself to sleep, my brother drank his body weight in booze.

The fuck happened between them?

I turn to my girl again, this time palming her face in my hands so I can have a clear view of her pain.

"Talk to me, petal. What's wrong?"

Her dim-lit gaze meets mine, and in her eyes, I see a woman who is near the brink of succumbing to her misery. This isn't her.

My Rosa is a fighter. He did this. He fucking did this to her. I'm about to call the fucker out when Colin halts me in place, putting himself between Rosa and me and my brother.

"Leave," I hear Colin command. "Now."

If I wasn't so pissed off, hearing Colin talk that way to Tiernan would have dropped me on my ass with shock. Even more so, when my brother's gaze falls behind Colin's broad build to look at his wife one last time before he gets up from his seat and leaves just as our cousin ordered him to.

"The fuck?" I mumble, still in a daze that shit went down.

But all too soon am I pulled to the here and now when Rosa begins trembling so hard, I have to sit her on the bed so her legs don't give in.

"Petal, oh fuck, petal. Please don't cry," I beg, her tears making me feel like my heart is being sliced open by a million papercuts.

Colin brushes her hair away from her face and rubs her back, trying his best to soothe her pain away. I kiss her cheeks, squeezing her cold hands in mine, hoping some warmth will trickle down to her soul.

"Talk to us. Let us make it all better."

"He hates me," she whispers, pained. "He really hates me."

"And you're not okay with that?"

She shakes her head, tears still pouring down her face.

"I've tried to play by his rules. Tried to understand him. But every time I think I'm getting close, he shuts the door on me. Reminds me that all he could ever feel for me is hate."

"Why, petal? Why does that bother you so? Tiernan has always been upfront with you about this marriage. You knew it could never be real. So why, after all these months, does it bother you what my dick of a brother thinks or feels about you?"

She doesn't answer me, pulling her hands away from my grip to clean her tears away. She then leans into Colin, cradling her head in the crook of his neck to hide her face from me. It's unsettling, to say the least. A quick glance at my cousin's face tells me he feels just as unbalanced. All because there is a truth in the air we can't ignore any longer.

I expected a lot of things coming here today.

To be with the woman I love.

To tell her how much living these past two weeks without her suffocated the very air out of my lungs.

But never did I expect this.

"You love him," I finally acknowledge the big fucking elephant in the room. "You fucking fell in love with him." I get up off the bed, pulling at the strands of my hair in such a way some come out by their roots. "Shit, petal. I knew you had a big motherfucking heart of gold to care for Col and me, but this is just too much."

"Shay?" She hiccups between sobs, pulling away from Colin to wrap her trembling arms around my waist.

"Tell me I'm wrong. Tell me that you didn't fall in love with your husband after he's been a total asshole to you."

"The heart wants what it wants. Even if it's a killer. Even if he's the last man I should ever want."

"Jesus!" I yell, turning around and gripping her arms. "So, it's true? You have fallen for him?"

She nods, as if the admission of her love is the death sentence she's been trying to avoid all along.

"Where does that leave me and Col, huh? What about us? What happens to us when you both decide to play house without us?"

She shakes her head vehemently, a fresh batch of tears coating her eyes.

"It changes nothing. Not for me." She entwines her fingers in mine and reaches out for Colin to take her other hand. My mute cousin gets off the bed and immediately takes it, as if it's the lifeline he needs to keep from drowning in his despair. "It's true. Somehow without my say so, I fell in love with Tiernan, but that changes nothing for what I feel for you. I gave you both my heart long before I ever gave him a piece of it. You are my family. The ones I see myself growing old with. Please don't take that away from me just because I committed the sin of falling in love with a man that can never love me back."

Her words burn as much as they calm my errant heart.

"Are you sure, sweet rose?" Colin asks, pulling her hand to his mouth to pepper tender kisses on her knuckles.

"It's the only truth I know for sure, and I don't take it for granted. I love you, Colin. With all my heart, I love you."

When the big guy sniffles and pretends he's not seconds away from bawling, all the tightness I was feeling begins to subside. She leans into him, never taking her hand out of mine, and presses the sweetest kiss on his lips.

"I'm yours as long as you'll have me. That I promise you. I'll be yours until my final days."

"I love you, sweet rose. I fucking love you, too."

Suddenly the air in the room shifts, each vow uttered sounding more sacred and profound than its predecessor. When Rosa turns to me, her eyes filled with newfound hope, I swallow the mountain-sized boulder lodged in my throat.

"Shay, please don't hate me. But if you promise me that you can love me just a sliver of how much I love you, then I'll be the happiest woman this world has ever known. I love everything about you, but most of all, I love how you make me feel. How at peace and safe I am in your arms. Please don't shun me, love me instead. Love me, as I love you."

Jesus, Mary, and Joseph

How the hell can I say no to that?

I bridge the small gap in between us and hold her to me, making sure her connection with Colin stays intact.

"I'm yours, petal. I think since the first day I saw you, I've been yours. *Te amo.*"

"*Te amo.*"

I kiss her until my words of love and devotion fill her bloodstream, only pulling back once I've made sure I've left her boneless and content.

Her hooded gaze tells me she's ready for Colin and me to drag her to bed and have our way with her, but that's going to have to wait.

"I'd love nothing more than to consummate our vows to one another, but I have a better idea in mind."

"You do, do you?" She giggles shyly, the sweet melody making my heart want to leap out of my chest.

"Aye, I do. Get dressed, petal. We're going shopping."

"Shopping?" She says the word like it's a curse, and by the way my cousin groans I can tell he has a million different ideas on how to fill up our afternoon. Most of them involve being inches deep inside our woman.

But again, that is going to have to be placed on the back-burner. For a day at least.

Right now, I want to fill the home she bought with all the furniture we need to start our lives together. We may be a family, but the faster we start acting and living like one, the better. We need to get her knocked-up as quickly as possible and moved into our home and away from my brother's influence. Permanently.

Rosa won't bat an eye at my suggestion, especially because she thinks Tiernan hates her.

But I know my brother.

And even if I didn't, I saw it in his eyes just minutes ago.

There wasn't an ounce of hate in them.

Only love.

And that will be a problem.

CHAPTER 21
Tiernan

I WAKE up drenched in sweat, my heart beating unnaturally fast, like a runaway freight train about to come off its rails. Most bosses and dons have nightmares about the blood they've shed in the war. They're haunted by crushed skulls and cries for mercy they never gave.

I, however, have had the same consistent nightmare for the past five years.

No matter how it starts, it always ends the same way—me opening Patrick's bedroom door and finding him hung by a rope slung around the ceiling fan. Every time the nightmare comes, so do the cold sweats it provokes and the rancid taste of bile clawing at my throat.

I run to the bathroom and throw up all my stomach's contents, heaving so loudly it is sure to wake up the dead. Once there is nothing left to purge, I get up off my knees, brush my teeth, and jump in the shower just so I can feel human again.

The memory of my brother giving in to his suffering never gets any easier with time.

People are fond of saying that time heals all wounds.

That's a lie.

Some wounds just fester until they rot your soul and blacken your heart.

After Patrick died, this family has never been the same.

I haven't been the same.

I was his older brother, the one he came to when he had nightmares of his own and needed a protector to cast them away. But somewhere between childhood and adolescence, he no longer turned to me for help. Instead, he shrunk into his melancholic cocoon until all that was left of him was a shell of the sweet, sensitive brother I used to hold in my arms to help him sleep.

Of course, I had to find someone to blame for his death.

I couldn't stomach the thought of blaming him for being so weak.

For being so cruel to leave us like that.

No.

There was another party that deserved my wrath, and their name was Hernandez.

If it wasn't for their drugs, Patrick would have never summoned the courage to kill himself. I can still see the needle and smack on top of his dresser. He knew that his suicide would cause the ultimate suffering to his family. And because he couldn't handle that, he needed to get high to be able to take the easy way out.

But life for Patrick was never easy.

He never understood the life of *made men*.

Never agreed with our actions nor how we earned our living.

He attended too many of his friends' and kins' funerals, sang too many Danny Boys, for it not to have made a deep impact on his soul. He was too good. Too kind. Too damn empathetic to the world's pain, and he suffered even more for the part our family had in such destruction. And so, he did the only thing he could do to stop his misery. He killed himself just so he could finally find the peace that had eluded him all his life.

My brother was the least selfish person I have ever met.

And yet, it was his last and only selfish act that permanently scarred me.

"I miss you, brother. But I still can't forgive you," I whisper, letting the water fall down my face, pretending my tears aren't mixed in with it.

After there are no more tears to be shed, I get out of the shower and walk into my bedroom to put on some sweatpants. A quick glance at my phone tells me it's not yet four in the morning. Too early to start the day and too late to go back to sleep. I decide to answer some emails from my office, but when I pass Rosa's room and hear her small cries coming from inside, panic sets in. I stand by the door, hearing her weep, knowing I'm the cause of such anguish. The way I treated her last night and again today still shames me. I couldn't even handle the damage I had done to her sober, needing to drink myself into a stupor just to gain my nerve to do what had to be done.

I shouldn't be surprised that lately my nights are filled with nightmares of Patrick.

My guilty conscience has always had a way of manifesting at the most inopportune times.

And after all I've done to my wife, the devil himself should come to me in my sleep and have his way with me.

I know I should leave Rosa to her grief, but as each of her pained wails get louder, so does my resolve to stay away from her evaporate. I creak the door open and see her twist and turn in the bed, tears similar to the ones I just shed streaming down her face.

The devil is even crueler than I gave him credit for.

Instead of continuously tormenting me in my sleep, he decided my wife was fair game.

I quickly run inside, slide in next to her on the bed, and wrap my arms around her.

"Shh, *acushla*. It's only a bad dream," I coo softly in her ear.

She nestles into me, hiding her face in the crook of my neck, her tears scorching my skin.

"Shh, love. You're safe. Shh. All is well. Shh," I try to comfort her, rubbing her back so her tears can subside. But each one that falls is another cut to my already slashed-up heart.

"Tiernan," she croaks, her voice still sounding half asleep and in pain.

"I'm here, *acushla*. I'm here. You're safe, love. You're safe," I repeat on a loop, hoping my voice will coax her fully awake and away from the demons that plague her.

I run a hand down her spine while craning her head back just enough so I can look at her properly. I brush her wet locks away from her face and kiss her temple. Then her cheek. Then the other cheek. Then the tip of her nose.

"Tiernan," she whispers again, her palm going to the nape of my neck, while her other hand presses up against my pec where my family crest is tattooed.

"You had a bad dream, *acushla*. All is well now."

"No." She shakes her head adamantly, tears still freefalling. "It wasn't a dream. It was real. It was real, Tiernan."

My palms cup her face so she can look me in the eye.

"Just a dream, wife. No other demon here aside from your husband."

She sobs on a hiccup at my failed attempt at humor. Shay has always been the funny one in the family. I lack the capacity.

"I can't have children, Tiernan. I can't," she cries, making a large lump clog my throat at the desperation in her eyes. "God is punishing me. For what I've done. For what my family has done. I'll never have children because of it. I don't deserve such a blessing when all my life I've lived at the expense of other people's suffering."

"Stop." My tone is so severe that her sob actually stops midway. "You are not being punished. God has a long list of assholes who deserve his wrath way before you ever make the list. You are good, *acushla*. So fucking good, my soul weeps sometimes at how good your heart is."

She tries to shake her head, but I force her to keep still.

"God does not punish the kind-hearted. He does not punish

those who still see beauty in this world. He does not punish the frail and delicate. If that is the kind of God you believe in, then fuck him. He doesn't deserve your kind soul. In fact, I don't think there is anyone who does. I sure as fuck don't."

Her lashes beat a mile a minute, as if stunned with all the things that I'm saying.

"You don't think you deserve me?" she asks, apparently the only thing she got out of my rant.

"I know I don't, *acushla*. Not after everything I've put you through," I confess mournfully.

Not after last night when I purposely hurt you with my lies just so you wouldn't see my fear.

Her eyelashes continue to flutter, but at least there are no more tears.

"Why are you here, Tiernan?" she asks outright, pushing herself out of my grip. My arms feel naked without her in them, but I don't make a move to pull her to me.

"Because I heard you hurting," I admit, hoping she hears the truth in my words.

"Why did that bother you? You've done worse than just hear my pain and done nothing to stop it. You've even gone as far as to provoke it," she accuses, but her tone is so soft that it pains me further that there is no malice behind her words.

"I know."

Shit.

Fuck.

How can I start making amends when I can't even find the right words to explain myself?

I turn onto my back and stare up at the ceiling, feeling her gaze on me the entire time.

"I lied to you."

"When did you lie?"

"Last night when I told you that I didn't want to have a child with you because I would hate it. It was a lie."

She doesn't so much as breathe, waiting for me to explain.

"I'm sure by now someone must have told you about my brother Patrick. My mother, perhaps? Shay or Colin?"

Again, she stays silent.

"Whatever they told you about him, it's true. He had the purest of hearts. So pure that it was easy to wound and hurt. When we were children, Ma used to say we were each other's shadows. Where I went, Patrick was never far behind. Maybe it was because Patrick and I already had a strong brotherly connection before Shay and Iris were born, or maybe it was due to the fact that we were closer in age than we were with our other brother and sister. Whatever the reason, we were more than just brothers. He was my best friend. Where I was cocky and hard, he was humble and kind. Opposites in every way, yet we never fought. Never said one mean thing to the other."

Rosa's breathing begins to slow down so as to not miss a single word, completely enthralled by my story.

"But once we became teenagers, we started to drift apart. I was so hungry to do my part in the Mafia Wars, help *Athair* fight the enemies that wanted to see us buried ten feet under, that I badgered my father until he relented and let me fight. I made my first kill just days shy of my fifteenth birthday. It was one of the proudest moments of my life, but Patrick didn't speak to me for a full month when he found out what I had done. He couldn't understand how I could condone taking a life in any capacity. He said there was no honor to be found if my actions spilled even one drop of innocent blood. That someone needed to be brave enough to put old feuds aside. That was the only way we could ever guarantee our family's survival. And for me to pick up a gun and knife and intentionally steal any life was a sin in his book. My brother spoke passionately of peace, while my heart burned only for vengeance."

I let out a long exhale, thinking about how many times I called him naïve. That this feud between the families would never cease until one family ruled them all. And I was determined that it'd be us.

"As the years passed by and I got more involved in protecting our family, making a name for myself on the streets, my brother became more withdrawn from me. From all of us. The war at that time was taking lives, left and right. Each name in the obituary section was either an acquaintance, friend, or loved one. Not a week went by that there wasn't a funeral to attend, and Patrick made sure he went to each one to pay his respects. I could see my brother's soul slowly being ripped out of his chest with each eulogy he heard, each pint of Guinness he drank in honor of the fallen. He began walking around the house like he was a ghost, not making a sound, too afraid we would tell him another one of his friends had perished in the war. It got so bad that *Athair* sent him away to Ireland, hoping that fresh air and countryside living would bring back the good-natured son he loved so much."

"But... the fire," Rosa gasps, her eyes wide in alarm.

"Aye. The fire," I repeat sullenly, thankful Colin gave her the details of how his family died that night and spared me going into them now.

Guilt twists my heart and gives it an infernal tug at the memory of picking up Colin and Patrick at the airport. My cousin was eager to stand at my side and burn all our enemies to the ground for what they took from him. But my brother? He was more lost to us than he had been when he left on his trip.

"I was the one they'd wanted. It was because of me and my fucking pride in wanting to rise up the ranks of my father's kingdom and let the world know not to fuck with us Kellys that Colin's family paid the price for my ambition. Though my cousin never once put the blame on my doorstep, Patrick wasn't as forgiving."

When Rosa places a comforting hand over my heart, I cover it with mine, locking our fingers together, hoping her silent strength will give me the courage to continue.

"After that, I couldn't get through to him. He didn't want anything to do with me or our family. And in doing so, he felt more alone than he had ever been before. Too afraid to reach out to anyone for help, fearing that sooner or later the war would take them away from him, too. So he searched for an escape, any relief that could ease his suffering, and the one he found sealed his fate."

As if reading my thoughts and what I'm about to say next, Rosa tries to pull her hand away from mine, but I keep my hold on her, not wanting to let her go. Not again. Not ever.

"I have no idea who sold him his first eight-ball or how Patrick even knew where to get it. If I did, then I would have taken my time in killing them. I would make sure to inflict the same pain on them as we suffered watching my beloved brother become a soulless zombie right in front of our eyes. *Athair* sent him to every rehab in the state, but those never worked. Patrick would stay clean for a month or two there, but all it took was him coming home for him to start using again."

"It was my family's poison that killed him in the end, wasn't it?" she whispers in anguish.

"My brother's veins had been polluted with my hate and cold venom long before your family's drugs played a role in his life. At the time I didn't see that, but now I know we are as much to blame for what happened to him as the heroin that he used to ease his misery. The worst part in all of this, was that he was right. Patrick saw the writing on the wall before any of us did. Even as a child, he knew that peace was the only way to prevent our extinction. Maybe if one of us had taken the time to hear him out, we would have come to the same conclusion and saved us all a mountain of regret."

I turn to my love and see her eyes water, suffering the same pain I went through all those years ago. Like Patrick, Rosa feels everything. Every nasty word. Every horrible cut. But where I failed my brother, I refuse to fail my wife.

Ironic how life brought the means of a ceasefire to us and handed me a second chance to do right by the person I loved. Maybe there is a God out there after all. It's the only explanation I can come up with for the treaty to have been fulfilled after years of struggle and hardship. It's also the only way I can explain Rosa coming into my life. It's almost as if the universe knew the aching need inside me to make right the mistakes of the past. What isn't surprising is how long it took me to realize the gift I'd been given.

Better late than never, I suppose.

I just hope my love is of the same mindset.

I wouldn't hold it against her if she isn't.

"There was a moment that I did dare to hope, though. When *Athair* told me that the families were willing to unite and discuss our chances for peace, I was certain that was the thing that would bring my brother back to us. That somehow the treaty would erase years of his suffering, and Patrick would snap out of his depression once and for all. Unfortunately, I miscalculated how deep his scars ran. Even after *Athair* and I came back from the negotiation table with the other bosses and dons, the news never mended Patrick's heart as I thought it would. In fact, he reprimanded us for the plan put in place. Chastising us that in our attempts to stop the war, we couldn't find a better way but to sacrifice innocent lives once again. Iris being one of them. Then five years ago, the pain must have been too much for him to withstand. He just couldn't go on in a world where death and grief were all around him. So, he took his life."

I wipe away the silent tears my wife sheds for a man she never met, but somehow found it in her heart to care for in the space of time it took me to tell his story.

"After his death, my father stepped down as boss. He couldn't function. Couldn't see past his pain, much less ensure that the other families' demands were set in place before the ten-year deadline arrived. I stepped up, took the burden onto my shoulders, and became the cold, heartless man you're married to today. I had to become this lie you see, *acushla*. Because if anyone saw how raw and broken I was on the inside, they would have taken everything my family had worked so hard to keep. All those lives lost, including my brother's, would have been in vain."

"But that's not why I'm telling you this. I want you to know why I lied to you last night. Why I said all those awful things to push you away. When Patrick died, it almost killed my parents. It almost killed all of us. But the sorrow and heartache I went through paled in comparison to my parents' despair. I was scared, *acushla*. I *am* scared. Losing a brother that I loved was painful enough, but after witnessing my parents' strife, I don't think I would ever survive the kind of loss they went through. I know I wouldn't."

"What are you saying?" She blinks her tears away.

"I'm saying that even with the treaty in place, I will always have enemies. Enemies that will do everything in their power to break me and steal what I have. If I had a son… a daughter… there would be no greater weapon they could use to destroy me."

She closes her eyelids as if I just eviscerated all her hopes and dreams.

"Look at me, love." Hesitantly she lifts her gaze to me. I turn on my side, grip both of her hands in mine, and place a chaste kiss on them. "My fear is real and debilitating, but so is the thought of losing you. You will be a mother, *acushla*. If that is your desire, then you will be a mother. Either by my blood or not, you shall have children. I give you my word, wife. From here on out, I will make you happy and give you all your heart's desires."

"Are you saying you would love any child I gave you?"

"I'm saying I already do. Whether it'd be mine or not, love. I will protect and love it with all my heart, just as much as I love its mother."

There is a small smile that tugs at her lower lip, making my eyes land on her gorgeous mouth. As if reading my inner thoughts and turmoil, she softly presses her lips to mine, ending my agony with one simple kiss.

And for the first time in a long time, I dare myself to hope.

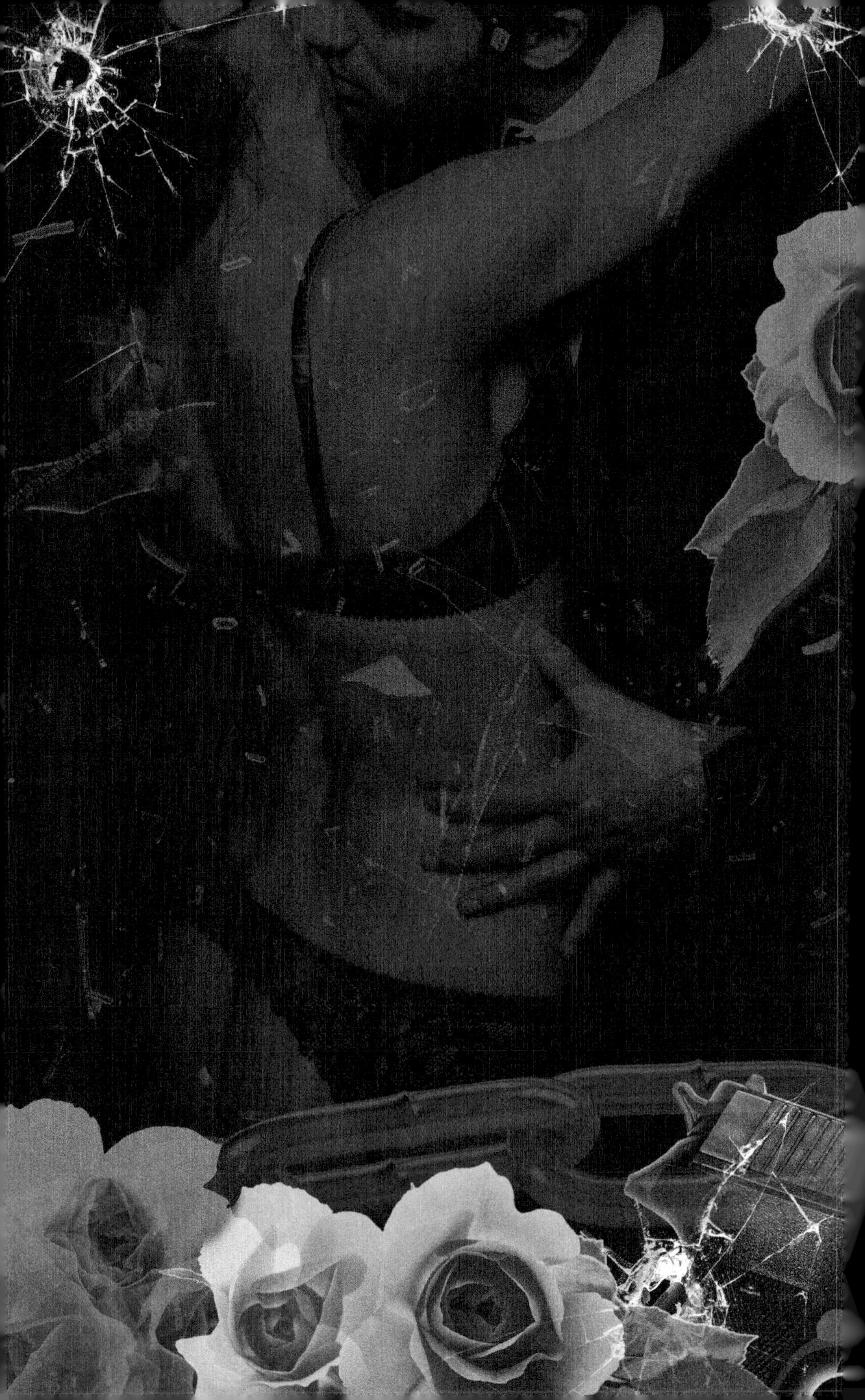

CHAPTER 22
Rosa

"HOW BADLY DO YOU HATE ME?" Tiernan asks once we break our kiss.

"On a scale of one to ten?"

He nods.

"Zero," I confess, to which his brows pull together skeptically. "It's true. I wanted to be angry at you. Hate you even. Sometimes I convinced myself that I did. But there was a part of me, right here," I place his hand over my heart, "that refused to hate you. Even when you gave me plenty of reasons that I should."

My hand goes to his chest, pressing on the beating organ underneath while I keep his on mine.

"You're a fool, *acushla*. With no self-preservation to speak of."

"That might be true. But this foolish heart still fell in love with you."

His eyes slant shut as if my admission of love hurts him as

much as it heals. He leans his temple to kiss mine and breathes me in, his heart thumping madly under my hand.

"I'm not a good man, love. I can never promise you that I'll become one. I've seen too much. I've done too much to be given absolution. But if your words are true, if you do love me, then I promise I'll be good to you. I'm tired of fighting this, *acushla*. So fucking tired. But I'm ready now. If you'll have me, I'm ready for you and the life you want to build. All you have to do is let me."

I let his loving words wash over me, unable to hide the joy they give me.

"All I ever wanted was love, Tiernan. True and unconditional love. Give me that, and I'm yours. Forever."

"Fuck," he grunts before grabbing the nape of my neck and crashing his lips on mine.

His kiss is possessive, stealing the air from my lungs and claiming it as his own. He pushes me down onto the mattress and covers my body with his. I sigh into his mouth, loving the way his tongue wrestles with mine, dominating it completely. I don't even put up a fight, needing him to own every little part of me. When he pulls away, I almost cry in desperation, needing his lips on me at all times.

"Tiernan," I beg, my nails digging into his broad shoulders to keep him still.

"Shh, *acushla*. Let me love you. Just let me love you."

I nod, aching for him to do what he promised.

Tiernan smiles at me, making my heart squeeze inside my chest at how beautiful he is. He crawls down my body, pulls my pajama top over my head, and then relieves me of my pants and panties.

On his knees he looks down at me, naked and wanting. He runs his hand down my neck to the inside of my breasts, never stopping until he reaches my core. I moan when his hand brushes up against my bundle of nerves.

"I've barely touched you, and already you're soaked," he croaks, caressing my pussy until it's aching for him. "So fucking responsive. So fucking needy."

"For you, husband," I wail on a loud moan, arching my back as he slides two digits inside me. He pulls them out and sucks on them, grunting as he licks his fingers clean.

"So goddamn sweet, it should be illegal," he growls, making my back lift off the bed again when he plunges his fingers into me with brute force.

"Oh my God!" I cry as he fucks me with his digits, grabbing one of my breasts with his free hand and giving it a hard squeeze.

"Cry for me, *acushla*. Say my name as loud as you can. I want to hear you scream it as you cum riding my hand."

I white-knuckle the bedsheets as he pounds into my pussy without mercy or restraint, watching my body cave into his ruthless touch. The sound of my juices and smell of my desire invades all my senses, and before I know it, I'm giving him exactly what he wants, coming undone on his expert fingers.

"TIERNAN!" I wail as I shatter underneath him, the orgasm making every limb spasm.

I've barely gotten my wits about me when he crouches down in between my thighs and licks my slit clean of my release. His tongue is just as merciless as his fingers, his teeth grazing my clit until I'm shouting in both pain and pleasure. My hands grip his hair, my nails digging into his scalp to keep me from losing my mind and falling off the edge of the earth like he's intent on causing.

"I want it all, *acushla*. Every last drop. And you're going to give it to me," he warns, licking and biting my drenched core until his chin and mouth are covered in my want for him.

It's all too much.

His kiss.

His words.

His hands on my naked flesh.

When another shudder runs down my spine, my pussy clenching at the hollowness I'm desperate for him to fill, my vision begins to blur, white spots of light making it impossible to see. Hot tears start falling down my cheeks as I'm hit with a tidal wave of pleasure, wreaking havoc on my body. I combust yet again, fearing that I'll be forever ruined if he ever decides to take this away from me.

As if sensing my pain, he slinks up my body, pressing his chest against mine while cupping my face in his palms.

"Did I hurt you, love?" he asks, his voice uncharacteristically gentle.

I shake my head.

"Are you afraid?"

"Yes," I admit, hating that my tears are still falling.

"I am, too, *acushla*."

"You are?"

"Petrified," he chuckles half-heartedly. "But this is real. It's real, wife. Let me prove it to you."

I nod, biting my lower lip as his thumb cleans my tears away. He pulls his sweatpants down his legs and settles in between my thighs. I instantly wrap my legs around his waist, trapping him to me. He lets out another small chuckle, amused by my knee-jerk reaction.

"Do you want it slow, or do you want me to rip off the band-aid in one go?" he asks the same question he did on the night he took my virginity.

"Rip it off," I answer, similar to my reply from that night.

When his crown meets my center, I hold on to his shoulders for support, my gaze fixed on his. My jaw slackens, and my eyelids shut when he thrusts inside me in one go.

"Jesus, fuck!" he growls. "This pussy will be the death of me."

I don't ask him to explain, mostly because I couldn't even string one sentence together right now if I tried. Not when he's filling up all the empty spaces in my soul. He continues to pound into me, his cock deliciously hitting every wall inside me, while his lips take mine hostage once again. Our love-making isn't sweet or tender, but neither is our love. It's messy and complicated, with too many battle wounds to count. But with each thrust and passionate kiss, we start to heal. Every whispered moan, every soft sigh, glues the broken pieces of our hearts and binds them together until we are just one beating organ, unified in our love.

"*Acushla*," he moans, his gaze half-mast and hungry to give in and surrender to this feeling bubbling up inside us.

"Let go, Tiernan. Be mine as I am yours."

His gaze softens for a split second, and then he bites into my bottom lip, his teeth piercing my tender flesh.

"Argh!" I scream when his cock finds that delicious pressure point inside me.

My soul is momentarily ripped out of my body and spread across the room, illuminating it with vivid color and casting out the shadows once and for all. Tiernan pounds even more furiously into me, making me ride this celestial wave until he comes undone and fills me with his essence. Breathing hard, he falls onto my chest, holding me close as his cum begins to streak down my thighs.

I pull the strands of his hair so he has no choice but to lift his gaze to mine.

"I love you, husband."

"Not as much as I love you, wife. Not nearly as fucking much." He smiles before he leans in to kiss me.

Once he's had his fill, he falls to his back beside me and pulls me close so that I can't stray far. His possessiveness is almost as endearing as the look of utter joy that is softening his hard features right now.

"You're happy," I muse, nestling my head on top of his chest.

"I am."

"I don't think I've ever seen you happy. It looks good on you. You look softer somehow."

"Aye. The love of a good woman can do that to a man. Didn't you know, wife?" he teases, giving my ass a little slap.

"Does that mean I should look forward to a future without my husband having the incessant need to spank me?" I taunt, feeling relaxed and filled with utter contentment.

"Hmm. I wouldn't say that, *acushla*. I think you'd quite enjoy a little light spanking from time to time. If I recall, you ruined a perfectly good pair of pants cumming on my lap with my hand slapping your ass," he jokes, giving my ass cheek another love tap. "Give me five minutes and I'll show you just how much you enjoy it."

My heart flips over of its own accord, my pussy clenching its approval.

"I'll take your word for it." I giggle, placing a gentle kiss on his chest.

He chuckles under his breath, running his hand up and down my spine.

But it's in this tranquil moment, that my two other loves come into the forefront of my mind.

"Tiernan?" I whisper, running circles with the tip of my finger over his chest.

"Yes, love?"

"What happens now? I mean, how will this work with Shay and Colin?"

"It doesn't. Their services will no longer be needed, obviously." He shrugs.

"What do you mean?" I ask, baffled, perching my chin on his chest so I can look at him.

He runs the pad of his finger along the seam of my bottom lip, his gaze fixed on the movement.

"It means that I'm your husband and you're my wife. I shouldn't have gotten them involved in the first place. I take full responsibility in regards to my actions, but now I want us to start fresh. Start building the family you always envisioned."

"But they are my family."

"*Acushla—*"

"No, Tiernan. They are my family. I refuse to build anything with you without them."

"You don't mean that," he retorts, his forehead wrinkled.

"But I do. Tiernan, I love you with all my heart. I promise you that I do. But I love them just as much."

"Stop, Rosa. If you still feel the need to hurt me after all I have done to you, then do it. I deserve it for what I've put you through. I'll take every jab and punch that you want. But don't lie and tell me you love someone else that isn't me. That's too cruel. Even for me."

I lift off the bed and kneel beside him, staring him in the eye.

"It's not a lie, nor is it a way to take vengeance on you. I'm not that heartless. But what did you expect to happen, Tiernan? That I would spend time with Shay and Colin, get to know them intimately, both physically and mentally, and that it wouldn't spark up feelings of love for the both of them? If you thought that was possible, then you were fooling yourself. I love them, Tiernan. And my life will have no meaning if they aren't in it."

"Enough," he growls, getting up from the bed to run away from the truth he's unwilling to face.

"No! You don't get to tell me when it's enough. Not when you refuse to listen to me."

He fists his hands at his sides while I jump off the bed and breach the distance between us.

"If you love me like you say you do, bury your pride and ego, and let me live the life I want—with you and them. If you force me to do otherwise, you'll only have a sliver of my heart. I'll never be fully yours if you keep them from me."

He turns around and grips my chin with a familiar brutish force.

"You're wrong, *acushla*. I'm all that you need," he spits out, making my shoulders slump in disappointment.

"That might have been true in the beginning. Not anymore. Actions have consequences, husband. It's time you faced yours."

I snap my chin out of his grip and then turn around to lie back in bed, turning my back towards him. I can feel the waves of uncertainty flow from him. Unsure if this is just another one of our games, or if I truly mean my threat.

I mean every word.

After a few minutes, he slides in next to me, his hands gripping my waist, his breath in my ear.

"You're mine, *acushla*. You're just confused. You don't know what you're saying."

I slant my neck just enough to face him.

"No, Tiernan. You're the one who's confused. If you fight me on this, you'll lose me. Is that what you want?"

"I won't," he seethes with gritted teeth. "I meant what I said when I told you that I will make you happy and give you all that your heart desires."

"My heart desires Shay and Colin. Until you give them to me, then there is no happiness to be had. For either of us."

"You're wrong. And I'll prove it to you," he threatens, biting on my earlobe and then sinking his teeth into my bare shoulder.

He lifts my leg just a tad, enough to sink his cock inside me.

One hand snakes around my throat, choking me, while his other hand begins to play with my clit. His hands are showing me no mercy while his cock fucks me ever so slowly, building up a crescendo my body is powerless to fight off. He knows every secret it's ever had and forces it to dance to the tune of his own making. When he wrings another orgasm from me, he cums inside me once more, thinking he's proven his point.

I press my palm to his cheek and stare at him, sweat covering his brow.

"All you'll get is this, husband. You can have my body, but as long as you deprive me of what I want, you'll never have my heart. The choice is yours."

CHAPTER 23
Tiernan

I'VE BECOME my wife's warden yet again.

For the past month I have kept her hidden away in our apartment, unwilling to let her step one foot outside it. Fear of losing her has driven me mad, but as each day passes, I feel my obsession is slowly driving her out of my reach.

In war, I have always known what to do, what is expected of me. But binding Rosa to me is a battle I'm not sure I'm equipped to win. I'd lay my empire to ruin, burn it all down, if I thought it would be the key to unlocking her heart. I had a taste of its sweetness once, but nothing I do seems to grant me access to it again.

As promised, she has let me into her body, but never into her heart, and it's driving me insane. I fuck the insubordination out of her at every turn. Fucking her seven or eight times a day if needed. I've even resorted to waking her up in the middle of the night just so she can ride my cock until the glimmer of the woman that professed her love for me shines through. I fucking live for those few seconds when she truly is mine, but once it disappears and evaporates into thin air, my grief multiplies tenfold.

Her flawless petals are withering right before my very eyes, and my love is the cold winter that is slowly killing her.

If all of this wasn't doing me in, then my brother coming into my office every day, hassling me and demanding to see my wife, isn't doing me any favors, either. The only one that hasn't come out and made his demands of me is Colin. No. He's done far worse. After the first few weeks when I ceased all access to her, Colin requested to leave Boston and return to Ireland. Unlike my hot-tempered brother, he understood why I no longer wanted them near her. That I wanted my rose only for myself and refused to share her. After I declined his request to leave, every time he looks at me now, I can see the growing resentment starting to build up inside him. Soon he'll forget we're kin, forget his allegiance to me, and become my enemy—all in the name of love.

And fuck, he does loves her.

Even my whoremonger of a brother has fallen under her spell.

The woman has bewitched us all.

The question is, do I love her like they do—unconditionally and unselfishly?

A part of me screams to submit and give her whatever she wants, but the possessive part of me, the one where my obsession for her completely corrupts me, selfishly wants her only to myself. I feel my resolve waning with each day that passes and then reprimand myself for being so weak.

"Any mail for me, Jermaine?" I ask the doorman when I pass

through The Avalon's front doors after a day of ruling over an empire that no longer excites me as it once did.

When I was part of the grime and dirt of the streets, using my gun and blade to put fear into the hearts of men, it had its appeal. Now that I'm forced to reign over Boston from up high in my tower, where my days are full of board meetings, sleazy politicians, and dirty cops, it lacks its luster.

A part of me used to envy Colin and Shay for being able to fight down in the ditches.

Now my envy has only increased with the knowledge that not only do they have the life I wish I could have back, but they also have my wife's heart.

"Here it is," Jermaine says, handing me my mail.

"Thank you."

I walk into the elevator, flipping through the envelopes, one by one, until a postcard with the Vegas strip grabs my attention.

Iris.

Hurriedly, I flip it over and smile at what she's written.

I'm still alive and kicking.

Giving the Volkovs a run for their money.

Someone should have told them lady luck was a woman.

And Irish.

Xoxo

Iris.

I let out a relieved exhale, knowing that my sister still has her humor. She's either found a way to coexist with them, or she has them eating out of the palm of her hand. Whatever she's up to, I can breathe easy knowing that the Volkovs haven't broken her yet.

You mean like you're breaking Rosa?

Fuck.

Guilt immediately replaces the good feeling Iris' postcard gave me, and once again I'm burdened with my conscience as well as my heavy heart. Once the elevator doors swing open to my apartment, my guilt strangles me further when I see my wife sitting on the hardwood floor, spinning something in front of her with her finger.

When she lifts her head up, I can tell she must have spent most of her day crying. I take off my suit jacket and loosen my tie.

"The only time I like seeing you on your knees is when you're sucking my cock, *acushla*. Otherwise, the floor is off-limits to you. A queen should never be found kneeling in any circumstance."

"Is that what I am? Your queen?" she scoffs.

I kneel down beside her and lovingly caress her cheek with my knuckles.

"You are my heart, wife. Far more precious to me than the crown on your head."

"I wish that was true," she mumbles, gripping in her hand whatever toy she was playing with when I walked in.

"What can I do to make you believe me?" I plea softly.

"Give me what I want, and I will."

I pull my hand away from her and sit on my legs in front of her.

"I can't do that."

"Then you don't love me."

I run my fingers through my hair and pull on its strands. It's obvious that my wife will only be satisfied once she has successfully turned me into a raging lunatic. I breathe in and count to ten just so I don't hurt her with my frustration and words I don't actually mean. I've been hurting her enough as it is.

"Let me help you off the floor, love. I'll give you a bath and order some food for us. How does that sound?"

When she doesn't move, and I verify that her face is awfully pale, my hackles rise with new concern.

"What's wrong? Are you hurt?"

She snaps her eyes at me like I should know better than to ask that question.

"I meant physically, wife. If you're hurt or sick, I need to know so I can call a doctor."

"If that's your only concern, then yes. I'll be sick for the foreseeable future. At least I think I will."

I pull out my phone and immediately start dialing our family doctor. I pay him a small ransom to always be on call in case one of my men needs tending to. When he picks up, I don't even greet him.

"Come to The Avalon now. My wife needs to be looked at. You have ten minutes."

"Tiernan," she whispers, latching her hand over my wrist once I've hung up. "You didn't have to do that. I already know why I feel sick."

"I'll feel a whole lot better once a professional has a look at you."

I slide my hands under my love and lift her up off the floor. Her arms lace around my neck while I walk her over to the kitchen island and set her down.

"I've tried to be patient with you, love, but if you're sick you need to tell me," I beg, scanning her body up and down to see if I can figure out what ails her.

"It's just morning sickness, Tiernan. Women don't die from it. It just sucks throwing up all the time."

"Morning sickness?" I repeat, puzzled, not fully understanding what she's saying, but as I do, she picks up my hand, places a kiss to its center, and then places the white gadget she had been fiddling with earlier in my grip.

"What's this?"

"It's a pregnancy test, Tiernan. You're going to be a daddy."

"Are you serious?" I exclaim in utter glee and excitement, completely taken aback by how this news just brought with it new hope.

"I am, husband."

I grab her face and look into her big brown eyes, sadness as well as joy all mixed in together.

"I thought this was what you wanted," I utter in confusion.

"It was. *It is.*" She shakes her head. "Starting a family with you is a dream come true, but I can't pretend that there isn't something missing."

"Fuck, *acushla*! Not this shit again!" I shout and then hate myself when she flinches away from me. "I'm sorry. I'm sorry. It's just I thought when this day came, we would be happy. *You* would be happy."

"And I am," she says softly. "But I feel like I've been cheated out of the happiness that I could have felt today. And that's because of you. Your pride and ego are killing us. Are killing the life we could have had. This baby could have been surrounded by pure love, and now all he'll know is resentment."

"You resent me?" I ask, hurt like she's just slapped me across the face.

"Not yet. But I will." She lowers her head in sadness.

"I can't live in a world where you resent me, *acushla*. I'd die first before I'd let that happen."

"Then change. Submit to me, my king. Show me that you can kneel at my feet as I have done for you since the moment we met. Give me what I want, the future that should be ours, and I promise you won't regret your decision. My future," she exclaims, pressing my palm to her belly, "*our* future happiness is in your hands. All you have to do is take it."

I stare into her watery abyss, witnessing the solemn truth embedded in her eyes, and realizing for the first time that submission is the only way I can keep her—keep them both.

It's true what I told her. I'd rather die than have her hate me, resent me in any way. It's also true that I've given her more than one reason to treat me with such animosity. But she never once showed signs that there was even a chance that she had given up on me. It was only when I refused to give her Colin and Shay that her heart started to turn to stone. If there is any chance that I can save our marriage, save us, then there is only one road I can take. I will not let my child be born into a loveless home. I refuse to steal its happiness. I know all too well what the repercussions of a sad, hopeless life can do to a person. I will not be the reason why the people I love most suffer.

With new resolve, I keep my hand on her belly and kneel down, bowing my head in surrender.

"Tá mo chroí istigh ioná," I confess in a whisper. "I know I've lost my way, love, but I promise you from here on out, I will make it my mission to uphold our marriage vows and love you like you deserve. If sharing you is how you'll bloom and open your heart to me, then that's what I'll do. My heart lives in you, *acushla*, and it always will."

She slowly slides off the kitchen island and lifts my chin to look at her.

"Stand up, my love. My king. My Hades," she sings softly, her eyes shining with love. "The only time I take pleasure in seeing you on your knees is when your head is in between my thighs. Stand up, Tiernan."

I kiss her belly and get up to my feet, cupping her face in my hands.

"I love you, wife. You know that, don't you?"

She kisses the inside of my wrist and then melts into my caress.

"I do now. I love you, Tiernan. With all my heart."

I press my temple to hers and inhale her scent.

"I can't believe we're going to be parents."

"Believe it, my love. It's the first of many."

"Is that so?" I tease, kissing the corner of her lips. "Then I guess it's a good thing I'll have Shay and Col to help me then."

The genuine smile that crests her lips and the utter devotion that twinkles in her eyes fill my cold heart with bursting light, warming me from the inside out. If all I had was a sliver of her love, then this shows me what a fool I'd be to not be content with it.

"Tell you what? After the doctor has made sure that you and the baby are okay and gives you something to ease your nausea, how about we go over to my parents and tell them the good news? Shay will be thrilled with the groveling I'm about to do, and I suspect Colin will, too."

"I sure don't mind seeing you sweat for a while, husband," she teases, rubbing her nose against mine.

"Aye, I guess you wouldn't. But make a note of this day, wife. I doubt I'll grovel like I'm about to ever again."

"We'll see about that. Don't think you're off the hook for the hell you put us through this month, husband. I expect a lot of groveling in the near future."

"If that's what I need to do, then so be it. As long as you forgive me."

"You're already forgiven. Doesn't mean I won't make you work for it."

"I wouldn't expect anything less from you, *acushla*."

When Rosa steps inside my parents' house, Shay rushes towards us, wrapping his arms around my wife, afraid that she's some false mirage sprung from his heartache. He breathes her in, coming close to tears at how much he's missed her and how happy he is that they are now reunited. Colin leans against the door frame, biding his time until Shay lets go and he can have his turn.

Guilt rears its ugly head again at how cruel I was to keep her from the both of them. If the roles had been reversed, I don't know how I would have handled it.

Fuck.

If I wasn't their boss and blood, I'm sure the fuckers would have killed me just to get to her.

That's what I would have done.

Shame like I've never felt before pollutes my bloodstream with the realization that my selfishness was causing pain for not only my wife, but also for my baby brother and beloved cousin.

"I'm sorry," I say in the way of an apology, but it feels too unworthy of a word to make amends for what I've done.

"What are you sorry about?" I hear Ma ask as she comes out of the dining room, *Athair* and Father Doyle right at her heel. "If you're apologizing for not showing your mug here for over a month, and keeping my daughter-in law-away from the rest of us, then aye, apologize all you want, but I'm still cross at ye." My mother slants her eyes at me and then pulls Colin's arms off my wife to give her a hug of her own. "Let me look at you, child. I was almost certain my wicked son had you tied up to his bedpost just to keep ye from straying. Kelly men have always had an obsessive streak about 'em. After I married my Niall, my own mother didn't set eyes on me for almost half a year. Man damn near killed me trying to put Tiernan in my belly."

"Geez, woman. Don't go telling our boys our business. Father Doyle also doesn't want to know such things.

"Our boys have been sniffing up skirts since their balls dropped. I doubt them knowing they take after their Da in the bedroom is news to them. And Father Doyle, I mean no offense, but you've baptized enough babies to know where they come from."

She laughs, pretending to give the evil eye to my pink-cheeked father, and then turns her attention to my rose once more.

"Now let me look at ye," she coos, staring at my wife and scanning her every facial feature.

"Well, I guess my Tiernan one-upped his Da. It took six months for my Niall to get me pregnant, whereas Tiernan only took three.

One, but who's counting.

"You're pregnant?" Shay asks in utter shock.

"Aye, she is," I confirm.

"So, it's yours?" he rebukes, pissed.

"What kind of question is that?" my mother interrupts, confused. "Of course, it's Tiernan's. Whose did you think it was? Another miraculous conception?"

We all stare at each other, my brother's resentment and my cousin's sadness making the air in the room so thick you could cut it with a knife.

"Saoirse, do you mind if Tiernan and I talk to Shay and Colin in private? There's some things we need to discuss."

My mother looks reluctant to leave us alone, but it's *Athair* that comes to our rescue.

"How about you kids go upstairs and talk it out? Come, Saoirse. Our dinner is getting cold, and we're being rude to our guest."

He wraps an arm around her waist and physically pulls my

mother away, Father Doyle taking the lead back to the dining room.

"Come on," I order, walking up the stairs, not wanting anyone to eavesdrop on our conversation. Rosa follows my lead, Shay and Colin right behind her. I walk over to my old bedroom and close the door once everyone is inside.

"Let me guess," my brother is quick to shout, already bursting with rage. "This is the bit where you tell us that Col and I are no longer needed, isn't it, you fucking prick?"

"No, it's not," I tell him, shrugging off his insults while taking off my suit jacket and throwing it to the floor. I look at the piece of discarded clothing and cringe. "Did you know I fucking hate this suit? That this tie I put on every morning feels like a noose around my neck? I hate it so much I sometimes fantasize about using a blowtorch to set my whole wardrobe on fire."

"So don't wear it," Shay mutters, confused. "No one is putting a gun to your head, forcing you to wear that shit."

"You're right. From here on out, I won't."

"Are you drunk right now, Tiernan, because you aren't making any sense? What does that have to do with anything? What does it have to do with us? With petal?"

"Everything," I let out an exaggerated exhale, slumping my shoulders. "After Patrick died and I had to take over for *Athair*, I lost myself in my grief and in the role of Boss. And somewhere along the line, I also lost who I was. This suit, the big corner office, all of it isn't me. But I put it on and did a job I hate, just because the world expected it of me. I'm tired of living a lie, brother. I want to live a life that's full. Truly full. And it took me marrying the daughter of my enemy to realize that."

Rosa beams her big bright smile at me, standing at my side and entwining her hand in mine. I lift her chin to me and kiss her lips.

"I didn't realize how dead I was before you breathed life into me. I can never truly express how grateful I am for you, but I will try and show you every day what an honor it is to have you as my wife."

"I love you," she mouths, squeezing my hand in hers.

"The fuck?! Is this why you wanted to talk to us? To rub it in our faces that you two are now together?" Shay exclaims, pulling out strands of his hair.

"I don't think that's why they are here," Colin answers for me, hope making his green jeweled eyes glimmer.

"You always were a quick read, Col. My brother here isn't as fast at catching on to things."

"Will someone please tell me what the fuck is going on here?!"

Rosa unlocks her hand from mine, walks over to my brother, and presses her flat palms on Shay's chest until he is forced to sit on the bed. She then sits on his lap, shocking him silent when she plants a kiss to his lips. Of course, the greedy fucker deepens it, jamming his tongue down my wife's throat so all of us can see. When they pull apart, my wife is wearing the cutest little blush on her cheeks, and Shay is no longer the belligerent fool he was acting like a few minutes ago.

"He'll behave now," she singsongs, nestling her head on his shoulder. "Continue, husband."

"Thank you, wife. I'll remember to use that little trick in the future when Shay is acting like an ass."

"Bite me, fucker," he retorts, but there's no heat in his words. Only adoration as he entertains himself by brushing his petal's long hair off her shoulder and down her back.

When I feel Colin's gaze on me, silently asking for permission to draw closer to his woman, I give him a nod. In three long strides he sits beside Shay, pulling Rosa's long legs to also fall on his lap, his hand carefully cupping her cheek.

"Hi," she coos, batting her eyelashes.

"Hi," he chokes out as if in pain.

"Missed me that much, have you?" she taunts when he takes off her shoes and begins rubbing the soles of her feet.

"Yes," he groans, keeping his answers short and to the point.

"He missed you so much that he wanted my blessing to move across the pond and back to the old country," I explain, thankful I didn't submit to his demand.

"You were going to leave me?" she asks, hurt.

"I thought it was for the best. I'm sorry."

"Oh, Col." She shakes her head sorrowfully, stretching her arm out so he can hold her hand.

"There is no need for you to apologize, Colin. I'm the one at fault here," I interject, needing to relieve myself of this guilt for keeping them apart.

"That's true, asshole, but so far we're liking where this conversation is heading." Shay smirks. "Don't we, big guy?"

Colin grunts his approval.

"Then you'll like the next part even more." I smile. "My wife has given me an ultimatum, one where I would be a fool not to do as she bids. She loves you. Both of you. But as inconceivable as it may seem, she also loves me. Now I'm going to give you both the same choice my love has given me. We can have her heart, bask in her love, fully knowing that to have it, we must share her. If that is something that you are unable to do, say it now. I will not have my wife suffering just because one of you prefers her all to himself. I've been down that path, and I can tell you from experience that it is filled with thorns."

Rosa goes rigid still, fear and apprehension making her swallow dryly. Thankfully, Shay quickly ends her agony before it's able to lay any roots.

"Col and I were all in before you pulled your head out of your ass. We love her through and through. And she's a bloody saint in my book for taking you on."

"That she is." I grin, my heavy heart suddenly light from all its burdens.

We all take turns staring at each other, smiling like lunatics as if the air is breathable again.

"Now that that's settled, I guess there is only one thing left to do." I grin mischievously, grabbing my desk chair and straddling it in front of the three of them.

"Colin, relieve my wife of her clothes. She's been in them long enough."

Colin is quick to get up on his feet and do as instructed, as Rosa's eyes become hooded and Shay smacks his lips, ready to sink his teeth in her.

"Fuck! Now that's what I'm talking about!" Shay exclaims like an eager kid ready for his dessert.

My love stands just inches away from me as Colin pulls her cream-colored dress off her in one smooth move. She holds her hand out to me, needing the connection while my cousin snaps off her bra and pulls down her lace panties. The goddess stands straight with her head held high as if knowing the power she has over us. And she does. She has wielded it like a sword since day one, and I was the fool who thought I could resist her charms, her flawless beauty, and her kind-natured heart without getting cut. Now I vow only to preserve its grace instead of trying to dim its light.

"On your knees, Col. I want to hear my wife scream as she cums on your tongue.

Colin doesn't even hesitate, going to the floor and placing his head at her apex. All it takes is one stroke of his tongue to have her moaning.

"Does that feel good, wife? His tongue lapping at your pussy?"

"Yes," she moans, squeezing my hand to a pulp while her other latches onto Colin's hair.

"Brother, I think our woman needs some more attention. Get up off your ass and give it to her."

"Aye, aye, captain." He salutes, making Rosa laugh and coaxing me to release a snicker of my own.

But that all comes to a halting stop when my brother's teeth and tongue begin to play with one of her nipples. Then our little game becomes all that more intense and exquisite. My cock hardens at the small sounds she's making while giving in to all the sensations they are ringing out of her body.

"How does she taste, Shay?"

"Like sweet cherries," he hums, making her nipples pucker into hard diamonds.

"And you, Colin? Is my wife ready for us?"

"Yes," he grunts in between laps, his fingers digging into her hips.

"Hmm. I'm not convinced. Make her cum, Col, just to be sure."

When my beautiful wife's legs begin to shake, threatening to give in, I count to five on my fingers until a wail of ecstasy rips from her throat.

"Much better," I coo, stroking my cock to relieve the ache. "Now, wife, I think it's your turn to return the favor. Don't you think?"

Her eyelids are so heavy it's hard to see the gold flecks in her chestnut gaze. Shay and Colin quickly get undressed while my perfect wife goes to her knees in between them. She cranes her head back to look at their faces before she turns her attention to their quivering members. Hesitantly she sticks her tongue out to lick Shay's shaft from base to crown.

"Jesus, Mary, and Joseph. That feels good."

She grabs his cock at the base, giving it a tight squeeze as she turns her head and licks Colin's cock next.

He grunts his approval, entwining his fingers into her hair so she can swallow him whole.

"Fuck," he grunts in sweet agony.

Rosa's cheeks hollow more, deep-throating him as far as she can in tandem with her stroking Shay's cock in her hand. She then pops Colin's cock out of her hot mouth and switches her attention to Shay. Consumed with lust from this little show she's giving, I kick the chair away, take off my clothes, and kneel behind her, my hand diving in between her folds. I insert two fingers and then three, four, and fuck her pussy as she sucks them off.

"Such a pretty little slut, aren't you, wife? Just fucking perfect," I coo in her ear, a delicious shudder running down her spine at my words. "You always did like the nickname, didn't you, *acushla*? You like being our perfect little whore, knowing that in a few minutes, this drenched cunt is going to be filled with more cocks than she could ever dream of."

Drool begins to drip down the corner of her mouth, and I lap it up with my tongue.

Her eyes widen for a split second and then become thin slits of want yet again.

"Tiernan," Shay begs, close to coming undone.

"Don't even think of cumming, brother. Not until our woman is properly fucked. You hear me?" I threaten, pumping my hand in her pussy while my thumb begins to play with her clit.

"Get her off, for fuck's sake, 'cause this is too much," he begs on a whine.

"Amateur," Colin taunts and then groans, sounding awfully close to the brink himself.

"You hear that, *acushla*? You've got them so riled up with your mouth they can't stand it. Now be a good little girl and cum for us."

I add pressure to her clit, and like a keg of dynamite, she explodes. I pull us both to our feet and kiss her madly, stealing the remaining air from her lungs. She melts into my chest and lets me have my fill, surrendering fully to the burning need inside us.

"I fucking love you, *acushla*. You're doing so well, my love," I praise, gaining a shy, triumphant smile from her.

All of her is glistening with sweat, completely boneless and sated, yet I know she still has much more to give. And I fully intend to drink it all in and consume every last drop of love she has to offer. I want it all—body, heart, and soul.

"Shay, sit on the bed."

My brother doesn't even give me any lip, too out of it to even argue, and follows my order to a T.

"Now you're going to straddle Shay's cock facing me, *acushla*. Nod if you understand."

She nods as Colin and I help her towards the bed, ever so trusting that we will always take care of her. And fuck, if it isn't true. We will protect her with our lives if we have to since she has entrusted us with her heart.

Ever so slowly she sinks her soaked pussy up and down Shay's shaft, both of them moaning as she does it. Since I know my brother is close to his limit, I have to hurry up and guide them to what I want to happen next.

"You're up, Colin."

He snaps his head my way in hesitation.

"She can take it, Col. Trust me."

When Shay realizes what my intentions are, he curses under his breath and slows down his thrusts.

"This is going to feel good, sweet rose. Trust us," Colin explains, his thumb running circles on her clit as he guides his cock into her center where Shay currently resides.

My gaze fixes on Colin, as he carefully makes room for himself in her cunt. Once he's fully seated inside, the cry that she lets out is both agony and ecstasy. I rush to her side, plucking her chin in my hand while I fiddle with her pert nipple.

"Tiernan," she cries as she rides them both. "It's too much. I can't… I can't…" she half moans, half pleads.

"You're doing so well, *acushla*. I'm so fucking proud of you," I commend as Shay and Colin start speeding up their thrusts in complete syntony.

"OH MY GOD!" she yells, her eyes rolling into the back of her head as they fuck her soul out of her body to meet its maker.

"Fuck! Fuck! Fuck!" Shay blubbers, cumming inside my wife in two more thrusts.

Colin pounds into Rosa's pussy, making sure she rides the wave of pleasure to its highest peak. Only when he's made sure that she's returned from her out-of-body experience does he cum and pull out.

My beautiful wife's forehead is drenched, sweat pouring down her neck and in the valley between her breasts. She looks so peaceful that a better man would leave her be and let her sleep off the pounding she just took.

But I'm not a better man.

Nor do I pretend to be.

She knows this.

So when I pull her off of Shay and lie her face down on the bed, with me on top of her, she doesn't even blink.

"Did you enjoy that, wife? Being fucked by two cocks at the same time?"

She turns her head to the side and throws me a mischievous wink.

A siren if I ever saw one.

I slap her ass, to which she sighs in contentment.

"My turn, wife. If you wanted three lovers, you should have come prepared to satisfy all of us."

"You talk too much, husband," she sings, rubbing her ass on my cock. "What's taking so long for you to claim what's yours?"

Fuck!

The woman really knows how to set my blood on fire.

I lift her ass off the bed until she's fully kneeling beneath me. With her hair nicely bound to my wrist, I pull her head back, my lips to her ear.

"All of you is mine, *acushla*. Every last hole, every last morsel of love. You won't deny me access to your heart ever again. You're mine, just as I am fucking yours. Always and forever."

Her lust-filled eyes take a softer hue, true love piercing through my heart.

"Take me, Tiernan. My body and my heart are yours. Always and forever."

I soak my cock in her juices, making sure it's well lubricated, and center my crown on her puckered, forbidden hole. On bated breath, she waits patiently for me to corrupt all of her, inch by inch.

I watch her hands clench the sheets as I sheathe into her most secret of places. Like our love, pain and pleasure collide, singing its tune that our souls are well familiar with. She moans out my name, telling me how full she feels with me inside her as I ride her ass like it's mine to tame. In one breath she begs God to rescue her from such rapture, while on another, she pleads for me to fuck her harder, faster, more. I give her all that and then some, slapping her pussy and ass cheeks when she's close to falling off the ledge without me. It's only when her calves begin to shake and she starts talking in her mother tongue that I show her mercy. I fuck her pussy with my fingers while pounding into her tight passage, and when her climax finally hits her, I let go and follow her lead into paradise, knowing that when I return, she'll be here in my arms. I then fall to her side, kissing her bare shoulder and broadcasting the first genuine, elated smile to ever see the light of day on my lips. I brush her hair out of her face and place another chaste kiss to her lips.

"Heaven, *acushla*. You've given a devil like me heaven."

"That's how life will be for the four of us now, my king. Pure. Utter. Bliss." She smiles, turning her soft peaceful gaze to Shay and Colin.

They both instantly draw closer, as if her eyes alone were enough of a command to call them to her. We cradle our woman in our embrace as she gives in to her exhaustion and falls asleep, knowing that heaven will be here waiting for her when she wakes up.

However, the next morning when I wake up, it isn't to my wife's gentle kiss but to Shay's light snoring in my ear.

Hmm.

As much as I enjoyed myself last night—and I did thoroughly enjoy myself many times over during the night, fucking my wife raw after Shay and Colin had their way with her—waking up to my brother's snoring is not how I envision my mornings in the future. We'll have to make arrangements and rules about how our peculiar relationship will work to ensure its success. But those are just small details we can easily resolve. The hard part was seeing if we had a chance at the life my wife wanted, and after last night, I know we do.

When I see that neither Rosa nor Colin are in bed, I walk over to my old dresser, pick out some torn jeans and a t-shirt—blue since I know how much Rosa likes the color—and go downstairs in search of the both of them. When I reach the kitchen and see only *Athair* and Colin there, my brows pinch together.

"Where's Rosa?"

"At Holy Cross Cathedral. Your *máthair* and her left early this morning to pray and light a candle for the wee babe's safe arrival. Although if you ask me, your wife should probably say a few Hail Marys too after what we all heard last night over dinner. Jesus, lad. This house isn't soundproof you know. Damn near gave Father Doyle a stroke hearing you four go at it like rabbits." My father shakes his head in disapproval. Colin hides his smile with his coffee mug while I take a seat at the kitchen table.

"We have to talk, *Athair*."

He raises his hand up and stops me before I get a word in.

"If you are going to tell me that you've decided to take the Bratva route and share your wife with your brother and cousin, I'd rather you spare me the details. Rumor has it that the Volkovs aren't the only ones who decided that the families' daughters be shared amongst their men. To each their own, I say. Just keep me out of it. As far as I'm concerned, the Hernandez girl has performed her duty in marrying you and getting pregnant with the next Kelly. Everything that comes after that is none of my business."

Colin's scowl is rooted on Da's face as he takes a seat beside me. And frankly, so is mine.

"Rosa is not the Hernandez girl, as you put it. She's my wife and is more than just the woman to bear the next Kelly line. She is going to be the mother of your grandchildren, *Athair*, and deserves your respect."

My father frowns, staring at his tea mug instead of looking me in the eye.

"Her family took too much from us, Tiernan. You can't expect me to welcome her with open arms and let bygones be bygones."

"She's not responsible for Patrick's death, *Athair*. Her family might have had a hand in it, but in a way, so did we. Not Rosa. In fact, she's done the very opposite. Her sacrifice in the treaty made it so she fulfilled his one true desire. Because of her, there is peace. How can you hate a woman that gave Patrick the very thing he always wanted most in his life?"

My father's expression reveals sadness at the memory of his lost son.

"I miss him, too. Every fucking day. But I refuse to not be happy with Rosa just because you still hold a grudge. It isn't fair to her, and it isn't fair to us that want to move on and have a life worth living. I love her, *Athair*. Shay and Colin do, too. I will not feel ashamed or guilted into not loving the one woman who has finally given me a reason to wake up in the morning. She's my heart, *Athair*. And the sooner you realize that she's family, the sooner you can be a part of mine."

I get up from my seat, Colin right at my side, when my phone decides to blow up and ruin my dramatic exit. When I see my mother's name on the screen, I answer it immediately.

"Ma?"

"Tiernan! Thank Saint Brigid you answered."

"What's wrong," I ask hurriedly, the hairs on the back of my neck rising with the sound of panic in her voice.

"It's Rosa! She's gone."

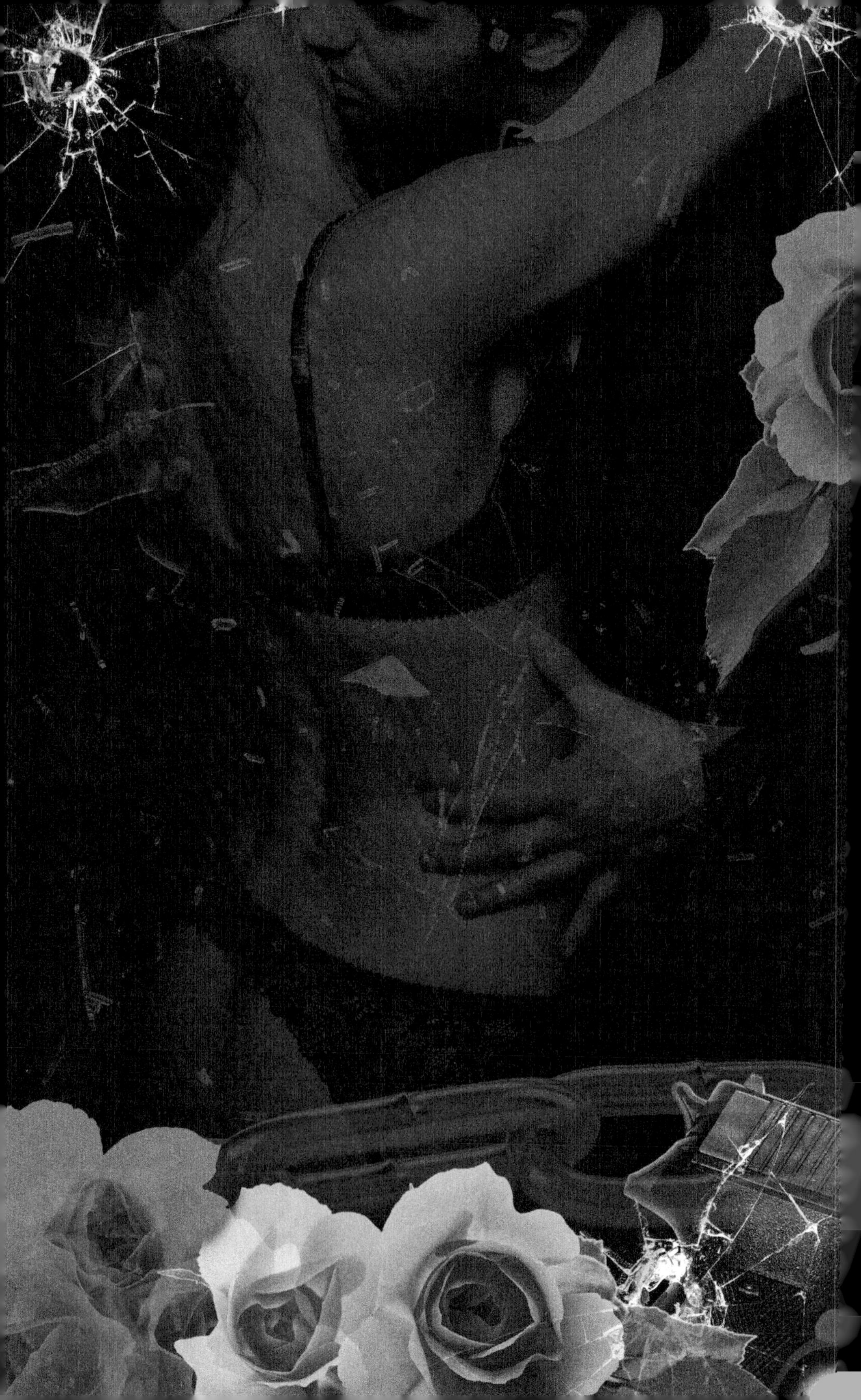

CHAPTER 24
Rosa

I FIDGET in my seat as my mother-in-law keeps throwing not-so-subtle glances at me on the ride over to the Holy Cross Cathedral. As much as I would have preferred to go to the church I've been attending on Baker Street for the past few months, I couldn't refuse accompanying the matriarch of the Kelly family to her preferred place of worship when she announced this morning she wanted to pray for the health of my unborn child and its quick delivery. However, I didn't think I'd have to suffer being placed under a microscope the whole ride through. I try to feign nonchalance at her constant staring, but when she starts to giggle like a schoolgirl, that's when my poised composure starts to crack.

"Please, Saoirse. If you have something to say, just come out and say it."

"Now girl, call me Ma like I told ye." She nudges her shoulder playfully against mine. "I didn't mean to make you uncomfortable.

It's that it only just occurred to me why my Shay wasn't sure if the *babaí* in your belly was Tiernan's or not."

"It is," I state evenly, hoping my stern tone is enough to dissuade her from asking any further questions.

I don't want to sound rude, but I'm at a loss as to what to say if she does ask me what Shay meant by that remark last night. It's not like we four have had much time to talk about the logistics of our relationship and what we're going to tell people.

I mean, how would that conversation even start?

I'm in love with not only my husband but also his brother and cousin. And we've decided that we're all going to be one big happy family together.

Not exactly a statement people will accept, no matter how open-minded they are.

"Aye, this one maybe," Saoirse muses, pulling me out of my reverie and bringing my attention back to her. "But I doubt you'll be too sure of the next younglings that might come along after. Am I wrong?" She hikes up her brow suggestively.

Virgen.

I guess *this* is how the conversation starts.

"Maybe not," I admit, chewing my lower lip nervously. "Will you think any less of me if that happens?"

"Why would I?" She dismisses my apprehension with a smile. "From what I saw and heard last night, you've got all my boys tied around your finger, and they couldn't be happier about it. Those three are head over heels for ye, and if the broad smile my Colin was wearing when he came downstairs this morning is any inkling, then I'm sure you are making all three extremely happy. And that's all a mother like me would want for her children. For them to be happy. You'll see that soon enough when your own little one is born."

Relief relaxes my tense posture, making my head fall back onto the leather seat.

"I was so afraid you wouldn't feel that way. I know your husband doesn't like me very much, but hearing you say those words lifts a huge weight off my shoulders. I doubt many people will be as understanding."

"Ah, don't pay my Niall any mind. He has a good heart underneath his stubbornness. He'll come around. You just wait and see."

"I hope so."

"I know so." She pats my knee lovingly. "As for the rest of them? Who cares? We Kellys have never cared much for popular opinion. We've always danced to the beat of our own drum." She throws me another comforting grin. "However, next time you four decide to sleep under my roof, give an old woman some notice. At least long enough for me to run to the store and buy some good earplugs. I think most of Beacon Hill heard you four go at it last night. If I was a betting woman, I'd put money down on how a lot of babies were made on account of listening to you lot."

"Oh my God!" I cover my face in embarrassment.

"Yep. I heard that one, too. Always knew you were religious, I just never assumed that much." She winks.

"I've never wished for the floor to open up and swallow me whole more than I do at this very minute."

"Relax, child. I'm only messing with ye. You're a Kelly now. Through and through. You're going to need tougher skin than that.

Teasing and making fun of each other is how we show we love one another."

She entwines her hand in mine and gives it a little squeeze, my heart swelling with gratitude at her words. My mother died a little while after Francesco was born, so to have Saoirse's motherly affection feels like a gift all on its own.

When I first arrived in Boston, I thought this city would be a prison for me—grey, dull, and stifling. I was sure that I'd never find peace here, much less love. But in just three months, my predictions were all proven false. Just as my opinion for this great city has shifted, so has my life turned on its axis, giving me room to hope and live a love well beyond anything I could have ever dreamed of. Now as I stare at the passing scenery, with my mother-in-law at my side, I see all the vibrant colors I missed before—the blue sky above and the smiling pedestrians buying their fresh flowers, fruits, and vegetables from street vendors and market places. How the new skyscrapers blend with the old architecture that gives this city its warmth and appeal.

This is my home.

And it is magical.

When our driver pulls up at the church, any apprehension I had about coming here vanishes. I no longer look at it as a symbol of my impending doom, but as the place where I took my first steps toward leading the life I have now. Humility, as well as gratitude, fill me up with joy as I walk alongside Saoirse into the large cathedral, wishing I could tell the old me not to be afraid. That marrying my enemy would be the greatest thing that could have ever happened to me.

We walk down the aisle and find a pew in the front to say our prayers. I take out my rosary and begin to thank the Virgin Mother for all her blessings and pray that the child growing inside me knows only love and joy in its future. After I've said my prayers, I get off my knees and give Saoirse a little tap on the shoulder.

"I'm just going to light a candle for the baby and some other ones for my brothers."

"Aye, don't forget to light some for my boys, too." She grins widely.

"They're the first ones on my list." I smile.

I walk over to the other side of the church where the candles are and begin my ritual of praying for the men in my life. I'm so consumed in my task that I don't hear someone walk up behind me until it's too late. Strong hands cover my mouth to prevent me from screaming, and before I can lift my head to see who it is, my attacker strikes a blow to my head that knocks me out cold.

The next time I open my eyes, I'm tied to a large pillar with my arms behind my back. My heart thumps madly in my chest as I see a small altar in front of me, Father Doyle pacing back and forth, mumbling to himself.

"Father Doyle?" I ask, confused, tugging at my binds.

He snaps his head to me, his gaze looking completely unhinged.

"What... what am I doing here? What is this place? Where am I?" I swallow dryly, looking around the dimly lit room, trying to gather any detail that might tell me where I am.

The detailed religious imagery on the windows and the small altar in front of the room tell me that I'm still somewhere inside the church. Probably somewhere underneath it. This room must be a private chamber where priests come to pray. However, something tells me that Father Doyle is going to use it for nefarious reasons—reasons that have my heart shriveling up inside my chest.

"I'm not sure what your intentions are, Father, but I can tell you now, this will not end well for you."

He marches over to me and grabs my throat, almost crushing my windpipe as he does it.

"I don't want to hear a word from you, jezebel. Don't try to seduce me with your wicked tongue, you she-devil. Your kind have no effect on me," he snarls before releasing me from his grip.

I gasp for air, my lungs burning from being deprived for so long. He begins to pace back and forth again, mumbling incoherent babble. It's hard to make out what he's saying, but the few words I'm able to comprehend only heighten my fear.

"The devil must be cast out…"

"Weak men pulled from their righteous path…"

"Adulteress whore…"

"Devil child…"

He's lost his ever-loving mind.

Ayúdame, Virgen de Guadalupe.

Por favor, te lo ruego.

For el niño.

I look around the room, scouring it to see if I can find a way out of here. My purse, which contains my phone, is stashed away on the altar, too far away for me to grab it and call for help.

But then it hits me.

Unlike the men I love, the priest isn't used to doing this type of thing, which made him sloppy in his first kidnapping attempt. If he lived in our world, then he would have known that my phone and belongings should have been the first thing he had gotten rid of. Colin is too overprotective of me to not have put a tracker on my phone. Which thankfully is a good thing right now for more than one reason. My husband is a possessive beast which means he'd burn the whole city down to find me. If Colin has a tracker on it, then Boston can breathe easy from Tiernan's wrath. I can't say the same thing for Father Doyle, though. Once Shay is through flaying him with his knives, I doubt there will be anything left of his body that's even recognizable. All I have to do is buy them some time to get here and rescue me.

I'm not entirely comfortable playing this role of damsel in distress, but to my bitter resentment, it's the card this lunatic of a priest has dealt me. I look over to the small stained-glass windows one more time and see that the sun's shadow on the grass has moved from its position. I must have been out for at least an hour. I'm sure by now Saoirse has noticed my absence and has called my men to warn them. They know I would never leave them of my own accord. Which means I've been kidnapped. Unfortunately, by the deranged look on the priest's face, there will be no ransom asked for sparing my life. That realization chills me to the bone, but I square my shoulders and keep my head held high, determined to not let fear rule over me.

Both my child and my men need me to be strong right now.

And by God, I will not disappoint them.

"Just how do you think this is going to play out, priest?" I smile sinisterly at him, summoning the worst parts of my family behaviors. "You've made a grave mistake taking me. Now you will pay with your life."

"Shut up you worthless whore! I will not let your serpent tongue break my resolve. God is with me. This is what needs to be done." He rushes at me and slaps me across the face so hard that his rings slice my lip and cheek.

"God has left you, priest," I spit out the blood in my mouth to continue. "He turned his back on you the minute you tied me up to this pillar. Let me go, and maybe you can still save your soul, if not your life."

Because that was forfeited the minute you put your hands on me.

"I said shut up! You will not deter me from my calling."

"And just exactly what is that? What do you think you will accomplish today?"

"I will send you back to the hell that you should have never left. I know the kind of woman you are. The things you let men do to you so they stray away from God's grace. I heard it with my own ears last night. You let them all into your body and corrupted their souls."

"Don't talk to me about corruption, priest. Not when your church has benefited from both pain and misery. I know the Kellys are this church's main benefactors. You don't bat an eye at their monetary contributions, knowing full well the blood that was spilled to obtain it."

"That is different," he blanches.

"Right, because greed, violence, and murder are a more acceptable sin than sex is." I sneer sarcastically. "Than love."

This time the slap that he deals me has my teeth rattling. He steps away from me, walking backwards to his altar as if afraid to turn his back on me, even though I'm the one tied up.

"I know what you're doing," he says maniacally. "I've heard the stories about what you heathens do in Mexico. Slaughter and sacrifice the innocent to pay homage to the devil. Your spells and sorcery will not work on me, witch! I am a man of God, and I have vowed to purge the devil from the souls of men."

When he finally turns his back on me to face the altar, I frantically rub the rope around my wrists on the edge of the pillar in hopes of being set free.

"When I learned that you were coming, that your arrival would mean there would be a ceasefire amongst the mafia families, I tried to keep an open mind. This city has seen too much destruction and death as it is. I should know since I gave the last rites and carried out more funerals than most in my position. But the minute I laid eyes on you, jezebel, I knew in my heart you were not the answer to our problems or my prayers for peace. No. You would be the thing that would finally destroy us all. I can't sit on the sidelines any longer and watch you corrupt our sons and lead their souls into hell. You are an abomination, and that child inside you is the spawn of Satan himself."

My heart stops when he turns around with a dagger in his hand.

"I'll cut the sin out of you and clean the earth of the threat you want to bestow on it."

"You're insane!" I shout, thrashing around to break free from my bindings.

"No, whore. I'm one of the last remaining few that see you for what you are. Do not think I'll be the only one against these unions. I'm sure more God-fearing men like me will see through this façade and take matters into their own hands. The treaty be damned if it compromises the salvation of our souls. You'll see. You all will."

When he starts walking in my direction, my back goes ramrod straight, flush against the pillar.

"You'll see hell long before my men or I ever will, priest. On my life and The Virgin Mother's, I guarantee you that." I spit in his face and growl like a woman possessed.

This time he doesn't slap me but purposely punches me in the gut, pain and fear for my unborn child wrecking my senses. He rips my shirt open, buttons flying across the small room until I'm bare-chested in front of him, my lace bra the only garment left intact. My chest heaves up and down as he places the blade to my neck and then lowers it down to my belly.

"No. Please," I cry out, true fear clawing away at me.

"Your fake tears hold no sway over me, harlot! Jezebel! Witch!" he shouts. "Watch as I cut the devil's spawn from inside you." He grins menacingly, making him sound even more mad.

When the tip of the blade pierces through my skin, I scream.

I scream so loudly that it breaks his concentration, and he falls back on his heels.

I only stop when the door to the room flings open, Colin kicking it down. Tears of relief fall down my cheeks, as Colin pushes the priest away from me, his hand wrapped around his neck. Shay runs to my side, agitatedly asking me if I'm okay while untying my binds. Tiernan, however, barely walks into the room, preferring to remain close to its door. My husband looks like Hades himself, ready to raise hell. His rage is so pronounced that I'm actually thankful he doesn't try to come closer to me right now, for I fear his fury would swallow me whole.

"Petal?" Shay questions again softly after he's successfully untied me. "Fuck, say something. Tell me you're alright!"

"I'm okay. I'm okay," I repeat on a loop, trying to pull my shirt closed as he helps me up to my feet.

"No, you're not," he growls, running a soft finger over my swollen cheek and the blood smeared on my lips.

He then looks down at my stomach and sees the small flesh wound the priest was able to make. Shay then turns to his brother, his expression morphing into something one would only expect to find in a nightmare. "He's hurt her. Made her bleed."

"Has he, now?" Tiernan states dryly, but I hear the bubbling fury underneath it. "Then I guess it's his turn to bleed. Bring him upstairs."

Tiernan then turns his back on us and disappears. My gaze falls on Father Doyle, who is dangerously close to being strangled to death by the way Colin's gripping him.

"Don't kill him yet, Col. I'll be fucking pissed if he dies so easily," Shay orders, pulling me to his side and wrapping a protective arm around me.

Colin growls, loosening his grip as he pulls the priest by his throat out of the room. Colin only stops long enough in front of me to see for himself the damage Father Doyle has inflicted. I reach a hand out to caress his cheek, gently giving it a stroke so he knows I'm not broken. Relief flashes across his eyes, but then it's replaced with hatred when the priest starts whimpering and begging for his life.

"Shut him up, Col, or I will," Shay warns through gritted teeth, pulling me away from the madman who is currently pissing himself with fear.

Colin tightens his hold on the priest's neck, enough to end his pleas for mercy but not enough to kill him, and pushes him out the door. Shay and I follow him down a long dark corridor and then up a flight of stairs. When we step through another door, my suspicions that I never left the Holy Cross Cathedral are confirmed. However, now the church isn't as empty as it was when Saoirse and I walked through its doors earlier this morning. Most of the pews are full of familiar faces I recognize from my wedding ceremony. My confusion multiplies when the two wide entrance oak doors are currently being guarded by police officers, standing shoulder to shoulder with Irish *made men*, preventing anyone else from passing through.

I'm about to ask Shay what's going on when Saoirse rushes in my direction, pulling me away from her son and hugging me ever so fiercely.

"I thought I lost you, child," she weeps, tightening her embrace.

Niall Kelly looks just as distraught standing behind her.

"Can you sit with her, *Athair*, while we deal with this shit?" Shay asks, pulling me away from his mother just to place a gentle kiss on my lips.

"Aye, Shay. Your woman is safe with me."

I'm at a loss for words as Niall and Saoirse both lead me away from Shay just so we can sit in the first pew of the church. But as I stare at the altar where the jeweled cross I had once admired on my wedding day stood proudly, my forehead creases now that I see it laid flat on the altar's surface. Only now does it dawn on me that I —alongside everyone else sitting here—am about to witness Father Doyle's torturous execution. My father and mother-in-law both hold on to my hands, either to comfort, or to keep me from stopping this madness.

If it's the latter, then their concerns are unjustified.

The man in front of me awaiting his trial deserves my men's wrath.

He tried to kill our family before it had a chance to bloom.

I don't pity him.

Nor will I lose sleep over what's about to go down.

My gaze falls on my husband as he cracks his neck from left to right and orders his men to place the priest on the laid-out cross and hold him down. Shay fans out his razor-sharp blades on the altar and begins to twirl his favorite one in his hand. He then grins as he stands just above the priest's head while Colin stands opposite him at Father Doyle's feet.

Tiernan throws the evil man another searing look and then turns his back on him to address his audience.

"You all know why you are here. This man... this pitiful excuse for a human being, tried to kill the woman I married in this church not so long ago. You were all here that day as he pronounced us husband and wife and said those who God has joined together, let no man put asunder. Apparently, he was under the misguided assumption that excluded him." Tiernan scoffs, his nostrils flaring. "Worst of all, he tried to kill my child inside her."

The few women in attendance gasp at the statement, but mostly everyone else just remains silent, impatiently waiting on their Irish king to start wreaking vengeance.

Tiernan's eyes then land on me, giving me a glance at the anguish and fear he must have felt when he thought my life was in danger.

"He deserves what's coming to him, *acushla*. But if you tell me this is not what you want, I'll follow your command. Reluctantly, but I'll do it. For you."

Mercy.

That's what he's willing to show the monster.

For me.

He's willing to go against his very nature and give the priest a quick death just to spare me from witnessing what kind of men I've fallen in love with and the horrific things they are capable of.

But I already know who I gave my heart to, and even if I didn't, I'm a Kelly now.

And long before that, I was a Hernandez, my father's blood coursing through my veins, whispering that I must set an example for anyone else who wishes to do me and my family any harm. On steady legs, I get up from my seat and bridge the gap between us.

His blue eye is almost as black as his heart, compared to the softness of his green.

Two men live inside my husband.

One is capable of kindness and mercy, while the other hungers to swim in his enemy's blood.

I give in to the one whose bloodthirst will only be satisfied with the screeching howls of pain from my kidnapper and would-be murderer.

"Those who God has joined together, let no man put asunder, husband. Show him what happens to men who are foolish enough to try."

Tiernan grabs me by the nape of my neck, and crashes his mouth to mine, sealing the priest's fate with a kiss.

And for the next few hours, I sit back in my seat with my in-laws and watch Shay nail the priest's hands and feet to the cross with his blades, pulling out each fingernail and then cutting off his fingers and toes as he goes about it. Tiernan takes his time beating Father Doyle's face into a bloody mess with his knuckles, while Colin does the same with the rest of his body. Once they tire of that, Tiernan grabs hold of Shay's dagger and starts cutting into the priest's body, making sure he feels every wound and waking him up every time the pain is too much for him to remain conscious. After Tiernan guts his belly from navel to neck, pulling his insides out while the priest watches in horror, my husband's men pull the cross back up to its rightful standing position. That's when Colin brings his blowtorch into play. He lights the priest on fire, his tormented screams sure to give most people in attendance nightmares for years to come.

But not me.

I watch in utter fascination, as the blood of my enemy streaks down my men's faces, surprised that his burning flesh doesn't churn my stomach as I thought it would.

I'm suddenly reminded of Alejandro's words to me as he

described the family I was about to become a part of. My brother said that the Kellys were nothing but animals. Filthy, unscrupulous, vicious animals, he made sure to add.

But that's not what I see here today.

I see men who would do everything in their power to protect those they love.

I see a hand of just retribution for those who decide to take it upon themselves to hurt us.

But most of all, I see love and what they would do to anyone who dared take it away from them.

If this is what my brother meant when he called them savages, then I guess I am one, too.

A vicious savage who couldn't be prouder to call herself a Kelly.

Come hell or high water, that's who I intend to be for the rest of my days.

CHAPTER 25

Rosa

NINE MONTHS later

"MOVE!" Colin shouts, pushing people out of our way, left and right.

I'm too focused on doing my Lamaze breathing to reprimand him for being rude. Tiernan wheels me down the corridor, cursing in Gaelic while Shay stares at his watch, counting the seconds down to my next contraction.

And here comes another.

"ARGH!!!" I wince, clawing at Shay's arm as the pain physically rips me in two.

"Fuck!" he grunts, pained, more from seeing me in so much agony than at the damage I'm causing him with my nails.

I try to breathe through it while praying to the *Virgen de Guadalupe* to give me the strength I need to deliver this baby. I have no doubt I want to have more children, but right now, I'd sell my soul to the devil himself for an epidural. Once the worst of the contraction has passed, I let go of Shay's arm and entwine my hand in his instead.

"It's okay. I'm okay."

"You fucking don't look it, petal," he chokes, looking awfully pale himself.

"I'll be fine. Just find me our doctor and get me in a room. This baby wants to come out now. He's just as headstrong as his father, calling the shots before he's even born."

I crane my neck back and look up and smile at my husband. He throws me a conspiring wink, but I can tell he's just as anxious and nervous as the rest of them.

When a nurse at the end of the hall waves her hand, calling us into a room, Tiernan speeds up.

"Mrs. Kelly, seems like your boy is in a hurry to come into the world," Doctor McNamara greets with a warm, kind smile as he ushers us into my private room.

"Less talking, more moving, Doc. Rosa is in a world of pain, and I can't guarantee if she screams again that my cousin won't break a wall in," Shay tries to joke, but it falls flat on the floor with the worried expression on his face.

Colin picks me up from the wheelchair and lies me on the bed like I'm made of crystal. I press my hand to his cheek to ease his worry.

"I'm okay, Col. This is normal. Millions of women do this every day."

"None of those women belong to us. You do," he whispers, kissing my sweaty temple.

I'm about to say something to console him, but then another contraction blows any chance of that happening.

"OHHHH GOD!" I scream, biting down on my bottom lip so hard, I pierce the flesh.

Tiernan grabs my face in his hands while Colin and Shay take one of my hands on opposite sides of me.

"No more of that, *acushla*. I won't have you in any more pain than you necessarily have to be in," he coos, releasing my lip from my teeth's grip. "Can you give her something to ease the pain?" he asks the doctor, who is currently under my blue hospital dressing gown, head deep in between my legs.

His head pops up and then gives it a saddened shake.

"Unfortunately, Rosa's labor has progressed too far already. The bad news is that we can't risk giving her an epidural now."

"*Virgen*. And what's the good news?" I pant.

"The good news is that your boy will be in your arms sooner than you think. Now Rosa, when the next contraction starts and I say push, I need you to give me all that you've got. Can you do that for me?"

"She can do it. She's a fighter," Shay proclaims proudly, giving my hand a light squeeze.

"I don't doubt that." Dr. McNamara grins, his head going back to monitor my progress.

"Doctor, should we start clearing the room? There seems to be a lot of unnecessary people here," one of the nurses says, giving my men the evil eye.

"You. Out," Tiernan orders, pointing at her. "The only unnecessary person in this room is you. Don't show your face again. My wife does not need your toxicity around her."

The nurse pales and looks to Dr. McNamara for support, but since he's elbow deep in helping me give birth, her fragile ego takes the hint that he won't come to her rescue. When Colin looks like he's going to forcefully pull her out of the room by her hair if he has to, she quickly hurries out and disappears from my sight.

Maybe in another life I would have been patient with her closed mindedness and tried to make her understand that my relationship with my men is as natural and solid as any other. But after the Father Doyle incident, I found I have little tolerance for those who look down on me or try to shame me and my men and the love we share.

Just because it's unconventional and on the fringe of society's rules on what they deem is an acceptable relationship, doesn't make what I feel for my men any less real. We are a family. One that loves, cherishes, and takes care of each other. If the world had more love in it like what I feel on a daily basis, then a wondrous place it would be.

"Here it comes," I shout when another contraction hits me.

"Push, Rosa. Push!" the doctor orders, and I do as he says.

My eyes squint shut, and I push as hard as I can. When the contraction stops, I let out a relieved exhale that I've survived it.

"Good job, Rosa. We're almost there," the doctor praises.

I keep breathing in and out, happy that at least there is one person in this room that doesn't look like they are about to keel over.

"What are you doing?" I ask Shay in alarm when he moves

away from me to catch a peek of what's happening under my dressing gown.

"I just want to have a quick look." He shrugs mischievously.

"Shay Liam Kelly, you come back here right this second! I don't want you to see any of... that." I point to whatever is happening down there.

"Ah, petal. Don't be a buzzkill. Just a little peek," he teases with a wink.

I'm about to order him to move his ass, but then another contraction decides my energy is best served in dealing with the real matter at hand.

"That's it, Rosa. Push! Push!" Doctor McNamara shouts.

As I try to push with all my might, I catch a glimpse of Shay's expression turning from curious to green. He then starts moving as fast as he can away from where Doctor McNamara has his hands. I would laugh if I wasn't in so much pain.

"What? What's wrong? Is the baby okay?" Colin asks with concern when Shay returns with a sickly, ashen expression on his face.

When Colin tries to let go of my hand to see for himself, Shay shakes his head to stop him.

"I wouldn't do that if I was you. Some things are better off left unseen." He then tilts his head over to Tiernan and points a menacing finger at his brother.

"If your baby ruins my favorite place in the whole wide world, I'll spank your behind raw."

"He's not just my baby, he's ours. Now shut your trap and hold our woman's hand. She needs you," Tiernan rebukes.

Shay's facial features soften as he takes my hand in his and kisses the inside of my wrist.

"Sorry, petal. But you know how much I love my secret playground. It's killing me seeing it in so much pain and suffering."

"Remind me when this is over for Colin to slap you across the head." I laugh.

"Will do," Colin states, not missing a beat.

Later, I'll set Shay's concerns at ease and explain that his favorite playground will be good as new in no time. I knew from the start that my body was bound to change when I got pregnant, a fact that my men all loved during these later stages of pregnancy. They couldn't get enough of my swollen belly, tender large breasts, and my insatiable appetite of wanting them in my bed twenty-four-seven. And I have to admit, I was starting to enjoy it immensely, too.

But now I'm eager to start this new adventure in my life, stretch marks and all.

"I can see the head now, Rosa. Give us one last push," my doctor shouts in excitement.

"You're doing so well, *acushla*. I'm so proud of you. We're so damn proud of you," my husband coos, wiping the sweat off my brow.

My gaze softens as I throw my three loves one more glance before my fourth love breathes his first breath, and is welcomed into the world. I push with all my might, my nails sinking into my men's hands, summoning up all their strength.

When a small cry rings out in the room, and Doctor McNamara holds up my son, tears blur my vision at the miracle I've been blessed with. After the nurse has cleaned him off, making sure there isn't any residue in his mouth, she swaddles my baby in a blanket and places him on my chest.

One green eye.

One blue.

The eyes of my loves all combined in this perfect little miracle.

"*Te amo, hijo.* With all my heart," I whisper to him, overwhelmed with the immense gratitude at receiving such a gift.

My men all circle around us, tears in their eyes, joyous laughter on their lips, and wide-open smiles on their faces.

A few minutes later, Doctor McNamara lets my in-laws into the room.

Saoirse smiles at me with the motherly pride I've been deprived of for most of my life.

"What's the wee babe's name?" Niall asks, looking completely besotted as my son grabs hold of his pinkie with his little hand.

"Patrick," Tiernan chokes out proudly, his own emotions getting the best of him.

"Patrick?" Niall whispers, his eyes beginning to water.

"Yes. I know nothing will replace the son you lost," I begin to say, "but I hope that maybe you can find it in your heart to love my son just the same."

"Oh, lass. I'd love him even if you'd given him any other name. He is as much my family as you are, daughter. I'm sorry if I ever made you feel differently."

My heart swells tenfold, and for a second, I actually consider asking someone to pinch me.

This all seems like a dream.

"It's real, *acushla*," Tiernan whispers in my ear as if he has a direct link to all the thoughts in my head. "All of this is real. I love you."

"I love you, too," I cry happily. I then turn to Shay and Colin, squeezing their hands in mine, so they can feel my love. "I love you all so much. My life wouldn't be the same without either one of you in it."

"We know, petal," Shay croaks emotionally.

"Aye," Colin adds, wiping the tears away from his eyes.

I stare at my family and then look at my son, overwhelmed by the love in the room.

"You are so lucky, Patrick. So very blessed. You have a family who would die to protect you as well as love you with all their hearts. I prayed for you, *hijo*. But God, in his graceful mercy, gave me more than I could ever have dreamed of. He gave me this family. And now it's yours, too. Welcome to the Kelly clan, *pequeño. Tá mo chroí istigh ionat.*"

Epilogue
TIERNAN

TEN YEARS later

I lie back on the lounge chair on my patio roof and just appreciate the view. Everyone that I care about is here to celebrate St. Patrick's Day with me and my family. The heaters I have spaced out all along the rooftop enable everyone to enjoy themselves without fearing they'll catch pneumonia. It's been a harsh winter this year, but the chill has never once infiltrated my home.

All you'll find living under my roof is warmth, cheerful laughter, and love.

But then again, it's always like that, no matter the season.

"Da! Da!" Patrick shouts, running towards me with his cousins at his heels. "When are the fireworks going to start?"

A quick glance at my wristwatch tells me the light show I contracted for tonight should start in the next twenty minutes or so. I tell my eldest son as much.

"How about you all grab some hotdogs or burgers while you wait? It won't be too long now."

He jumps for joy and races over to where Javier and Shay are shooting the shit, drinking their beers, and tending to the grill.

"He's grown," Alejandro muses beside me, drinking a glass of whiskey.

"They all have." I smile proudly, pulling my eyes off of Patrick in search of his two other brothers.

Like I expected, Conor and Cian have their heads bowed down in front of their iPad, watching some YouTuber play a game I'm sure one of us has already bought for them. My nephews are also glued to the screen beside them, laughing away at whatever idiocy is happening in the video. I then pull away from my boys and scan the perimeter for my little rose. I grin when I catch Roisin on top of Colin's lap, placing her toy tiara on his head, so he's appropriately dressed for the tea party she wants to have with him and her dolls and teddy bears.

Ten years ago, I might have told you that the chances of seeing my big, brooding cousin pretend to have tea with inanimate objects while wearing a tiara on his head was as likely as seeing pigs fly over the Charles River. But as the years have passed, stranger and more miraculous things have happened. Enjoying St. Paddy's Day with a sworn enemy by my side, for one.

Alejandro takes another pull of his drink, looking as relaxed in my home as he would feel in his.

And why wouldn't he be?

The treaty did much more than guarantee a ceasefire between

us and declare peace. It broadened our horizons and entangled all of us in such a way that the outcome of it could only have been one. Where before we saw a foe, now we cherish as kin.

If that isn't a fucking miracle, then I don't know what is.

When a sweet melodic laugh rings out in the night, my eyes go right to its source and find my wife laughing at something her beloved brother, Francesco, must have said. Wearing my preferred red, while everyone else wears green, she stands out from the rest.

Like a moth to a flame, my penetrating gaze calls her to me, and in an instant, she excuses herself from her brother and sashays those fucking gorgeous hips of hers my way. When she's close enough, I grab her wrist and pull her down to lie on top of me. I silence her shriek of surprise with a kiss, and all too soon she melts into my embrace.

"I'll leave you to it, Kelly. It's about time I tend to my own flower," Alejandro states with mirth in his voice as he goes in search of his wife.

"I think you made my brother uncomfortable," she teases, giving me a little love tap on my chest.

"Nothing he hasn't seen before." I shrug, nonchalant.

"True. But even you have to admit that seeing his younger sister getting groped and fondled isn't anything a brother wishes to witness up close and personal. Speaking of which, where is Iris by the way? You said the fireworks were going to start at eight on the dot, and I haven't laid eyes on her in hours. She'll miss the show."

When I scan my rooftop and see that it's also three Bratva men short, I relax.

"My sister is smarter than any one of us. She knows the real fireworks that are worth their weight in gold happen behind closed doors."

"Is that so?" She arches a flirtatious brow.

"Aye, wife. It is. If our kids weren't here, I'd show you."

"We're not exactly behind closed doors now, are we?" She giggles, rubbing her ass cheek against my already hard cock.

"Keep doing that, and I'll call this party off just to fuck you on my roof so all our neighbors can watch."

"I think our neighbors have seen enough throughout the time we've lived here. I doubt you could shock them anymore."

"Hmm," I hum, skating my thumb over her full bottom lip. "I hear a challenge, wife. And you know how much I like those."

Her breathing quickens, her eyes becoming so hooded they hide the small golden flecks in them. It's when my siren of a wife licks her lips and then not-so-discreetly sucks on my thumb that I know she's game for whatever I'm thinking.

I'm seconds away from lifting up her dress and pulling my cock out when the fireworks commence and stop me in my tracks. As luck would have it, someone turns the patio lights off so we can fully enjoy the thirty-minute fireworks display, and by my count, that gives me plenty of time to demonstrate to my wife that our nosy neighbors are yet again in for one hell of a show. She should know me well enough by now that I never back down from a challenge.

With everyone's eyes on the sky, backs turned to us, my hands begin to trail up her skirt.

"Tiernan, what are you doing?" she half-pants, half-pleads.

"Shh, *acushla*," I whisper in her ear while I make sure our kids are on the other side of the roof, too enraptured by the sounds and vibrant colors being launched into the sky.

I can't help the smirk that comes out when my fingers find her pussy bare and wanting. My wife gave up on wearing panties years ago. Before she made that wise decision, not a day went by that one of us didn't end up ripping them to shreds, getting them off her.

She lets out the softest of moans when my cock sheathes itself inside her. As if her wanton cries of pleasure were a beacon to them, Colin and Shay look over their shoulders and catch me in the act. Shay cackles his approval while putting an arm around Javier and walking him further to where my boys and nephews are. Colin swings Roisin off his lap, firmly placing her on his broad shoulders and walking over to where Shay is, making sure I have all the privacy I need from our guests and kids, so I can fuck our woman properly and without restraint.

"*Cristo*," my wife breathes out as my thrusts start to speed up, hitting every nerve ending inside her.

My beautiful Rosa's gentle wails begin to grow louder as glorious light illuminates the sky above us, its thunderous noise camouflaging the ones she's making riding my cock.

This.

This is as close as a devil like me will ever get to heaven.

And I'll never be cast out of paradise again.

I'll make sure of it.

I'll burn everything to ashes before anyone dares to even think they can come for me and mine.

If the world trembled in fear of the Mafia Wars, then they should shudder in utter terror at what Colin, Shay, and I could do if anyone tries to steal our rose.

May God have mercy on whoever tries.

Because I'll never give them any.

The End

Thank you so much
FOR READING BINDING ROSE.

If you enjoyed this book baby of mine, please consider leaving an honest, spoiler-free review.

I hope you fell in love with The Mafia Wars world and that you check out how the rest of the girls traded amongst the families will fare with their *made men*.

Gunmetal Lily
Ruining Dahlia
Wilted Orchid
Forget-Me-Not Bombshell
Blade of Iris

I'd also love it if you would check out my website and invite you to join my Facebook Reader's Group, **Ivy's Sassy Foxes**.

THANK YOU SO MUCH

Much Love,

                Ivy
              XOXO

If you need help
DON'T STRUGGLE ALONE

If you or someone you know is struggling and are having suicidal thoughts, please know you are not alone and help is available.

Please contact any one of the following organizations.

United States
National Suicide Prevention Lifeline
800 273 8255 (Available 24 hours in English and Spanish.)
https://suicidepreventionlifeline.org/

United Kingdom
National Suicide Prevention Helpline UK
0800 689 5652 (In a life-threatening emergency, always dial 999 first)
https://www.spbristol.org/NSPHUK

IF YOU NEED HELP

Australia

Lifeline

Call: 13 11 14

https://www.lifeline.org.au/

Ivy Fox Novels

The Society

See No Evil

Hear No Evil

Fear No Evil

Speak No Evil

Do No Evil

The Privileged of Pembroke High

Heartless

Soulless

Faithless

Ruthless

Fearless

Restless

Rotten Love Duet

Rotten Girl

Rotten Men

Bad Influence Series

Her Secret

Archangels MC

Room for Three

After Hours Series

The King

Co-Write with C.R. Jane

Breathe Me

Breathe You

Mafia Wars

Binding Rose

Acknowledgments

I wrote The End to Binding Rose as the year 2021 was coming to its end.

And I, for one, was so ready to kick that year to the curb, wave it goodbye and sing it good riddance. "Don't you ever come back; you hear?"

If you know me, either personally or on social media, you know that I'm the kind of person that prefers to look on the bright side of life and maintain a positive approach to everything.

But 2021 kicked me hard in the ass and made me reevaluate everything in my life.

I can honestly say that the middle to the end of the year, I have never experienced such crippling grief and fear—both as a mother and as an author. Certain events occurred—which I won't go into detail since it has to do with my own private family life—that shocked me to my core and gave me a wake-up call that I never saw coming.

And because of it, I struggled putting pen to paper for months.

When I finally found some balance and my family obtained the help we so desperately needed, Rosa's story just came at me like a tidal wave. I could either swim or drown in its waters, but one way or another, I would write her story.

And thank God, I did.

This story was unique and invigorating, breathing new life to me... and it dared me to hope again.

Now that's a term I had lost sight of.

Hope.

That word may be small, but damn does it deliver a hell of a punch.

Hope is a powerful thing, and if you have that and love, well... there is no mountain that you can't climb and no battle you can't fight.

Thankfully, I have warriors standing beside me, that never let me lose focus of what's truly important.

First, I would like to thank the lovely ladies that worked on this incredible world with me. Mafia Wars might be our brainchild but it is also the thing that brought us altogether so we could form an amazing friendship. To CR Jane, Katie Knight, Rebecca Royce, Loxley Savage, Susanne Valenti, and Caroline Peckham, thank you all for welcoming me with open arms and let me geek out when talking about all things mafia related. I adore you ladies!

A huge, and I mean HUGE hug, goes out to my incredible PA, Courtney Dunham. This book baby could not have been completed without you. Thank you for always checking up on me, my dear friend. I so appreciate you and or friendship.

Another shout out goes to Laura Bakis, Becca Steele and Jennifer Mirabelli, who tried their best to also be my support system, even when I tried not to bother them with all my woes. I'm not the easiest friend to have, since I usually stay in my corner and be silent, or worse—put on a smile and pretend that everything is okay. Thank you for your support and offering me your shoulders to cry on. I could not ask for better friends.

And now to my fearless beta readers.

Tell me honestly, what would I ever do without you?

Nothing.

Richelle Zirkle, Heather Lunt, Emma Brooks and Jesse Adler Wheeler, you all are QUEENS in my book. I have no idea what I did to be so blessed to have you all in my life, but I'm so happy that I do. I love you all.

To all the bloggers and instagrammers who have shared their love for Binding Rose and The Mafia Wars series—thank you all so much. I'm so thankful to have your support.

Another extra special huge hug goes to my readers and my ride-or-die tribe—my Sassy Foxes. You beautiful women make even my darkest of days shine bright. Thank you for the love.

And lastly, to the men in my life.

To my wonderful husband and, especially, to my beautiful son.

I love you more than words.

My life holds no meaning without you in it.

You are my happily ever after.

Never forget that.

With lots of love and gratitude,

Ivy
XOXO

About the Author

Lover of books, coffee, and chocolate ice cream!

Writer of angsty new adult, contemporary romance, some of them with an unconventional twist, Ivy lives a blessed life, surrounded by her two most important men—her husband and son.

She also doesn't mind living with the fictional characters in her head that can't seem to shut up and keep her awake at night.

Books and romance are her passion.
    A strong believer in happy endings and that love will always prevail in the end, both in life and in fiction.

Printed in Great Britain
by Amazon